GREAT WHITE
SHARK
ADVENTURE

FABIEN COUSTEAU
EXPEDITIONS

GREAT WHITE SHARK ADVENTURE

WRITTEN BY
JAMES O. FRAIOLI

ILLUSTRATED BY
JOE ST.PIERRE

MARGARET K. MCELDERRY BOOKS

NEW YORK   LONDON   TORONTO   SYDNEY   NEW DELHI

AUTHORS' NOTE

Great White Shark Adventure is a work of fiction
based on actual expeditions and accepted ideas
about the ocean and its inhabitants.

MARGARET K. McELDERRY BOOKS
An imprint of Simon & Schuster Children's Publishing Division
1230 Avenue of the Americas, New York, New York 10020
Text copyright © 2019 by James O. Fraioli and Fabien Cousteau
Illustrations copyright © 2019 by Joseph St.Pierre
MARGARET K. McELDERRY BOOKS is a trademark of Simon & Schuster, Inc.
For information about special discounts for bulk purchases, please contact Simon & Schuster
Special Sales at 1-866-506-1949 or business@simonandschuster.com.
The Simon & Schuster Speakers Bureau can bring authors to your live event.
For more information or to book an event, contact the Simon & Schuster Speakers
Bureau at 1-866-248-3049 or visit our website at www.simonspeakers.com.
Book design by Sonia Chaghatzbanian
The text for this book was set in Chaparral Pro.
The illustrations for this book were rendered digitally.
Manufactured in China
1218 SCP
First Margaret K. McElderry Books paper-over-board edition March 2019
10 9 8 7 6 5 4 3 2 1
Library of Congress Cataloging-in-Publication Data
Names: Fraioli, James O. (Cookbook author), author. | St.Pierre, Joe, illustrator. |
Cousteau, Fabien.
Title: Great white shark adventure/ written by James Fraioli ; illustrated by Joe St.Pierre.
Description: First edition. | New York : Margaret K. McElderry Books, [2019] |
Series: Fabien Cousteau expeditions ; 1 | Summary: Bella, twelve, and Marcus, thirteen,
join Fabien Cousteau's research team off the coast of South Africa as they try to find and
tag an extraordinarily large great white shark. Inserts include facts about sharks and other
marine animals, equipment used by researchers studying sharks, and more.
Identifiers: LCCN 2017049313 (print) | ISBN 9781534420878 (paper-over-board) |
ISBN 9781534420885 (hardcover) | ISBN 9781534420892 (eBook)
Subjects: | CYAC: White shark—Fiction. | Sharks—Fiction. | Wildlife conservation—
Fiction. | Cousteau, Fabien, Fiction. | Scientists—Fiction. | Marine animals—Fiction.
Classification: LCC PZ7.1.F715 Gre 2019 (print) | DDC [Fic]—dc23
LC record available at https://lccn.loc.gov/2017049313

GREAT WHITE
SHARK
ADVENTURE

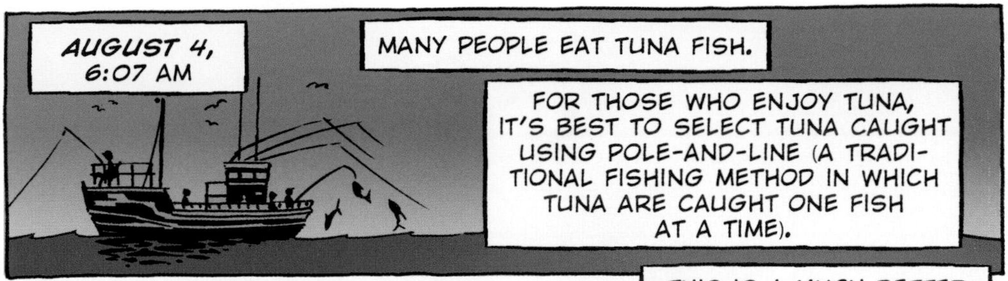
AUGUST 4, 6:07 AM
MANY PEOPLE EAT TUNA FISH.
FOR THOSE WHO ENJOY TUNA, IT'S BEST TO SELECT TUNA CAUGHT USING POLE-AND-LINE (A TRADITIONAL FISHING METHOD IN WHICH TUNA ARE CAUGHT ONE FISH AT A TIME).

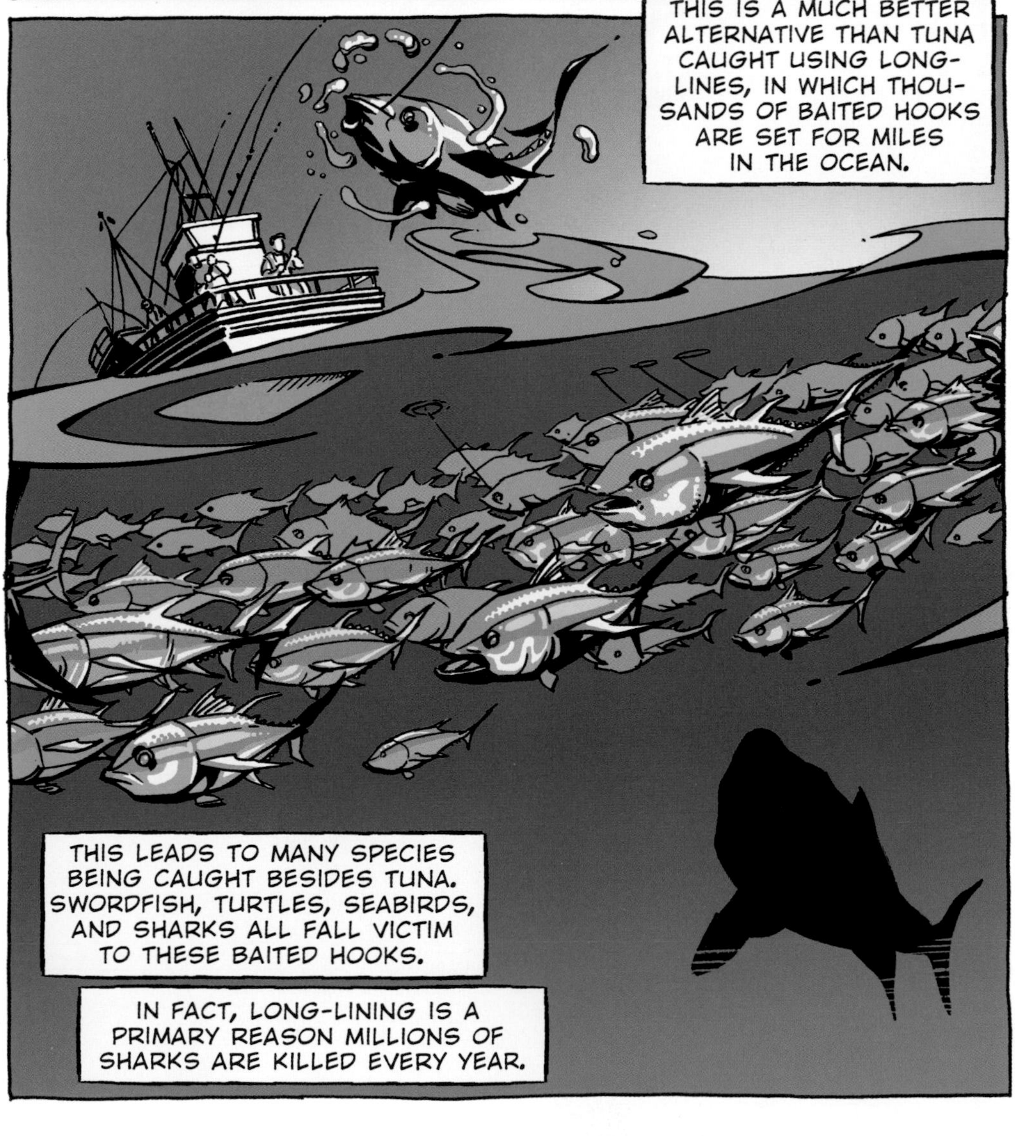
THIS IS A MUCH BETTER ALTERNATIVE THAN TUNA CAUGHT USING LONG-LINES, IN WHICH THOUSANDS OF BAITED HOOKS ARE SET FOR MILES IN THE OCEAN.
THIS LEADS TO MANY SPECIES BEING CAUGHT BESIDES TUNA. SWORDFISH, TURTLES, SEABIRDS, AND SHARKS ALL FALL VICTIM TO THESE BAITED HOOKS.
IN FACT, LONG-LINING IS A PRIMARY REASON MILLIONS OF SHARKS ARE KILLED EVERY YEAR.

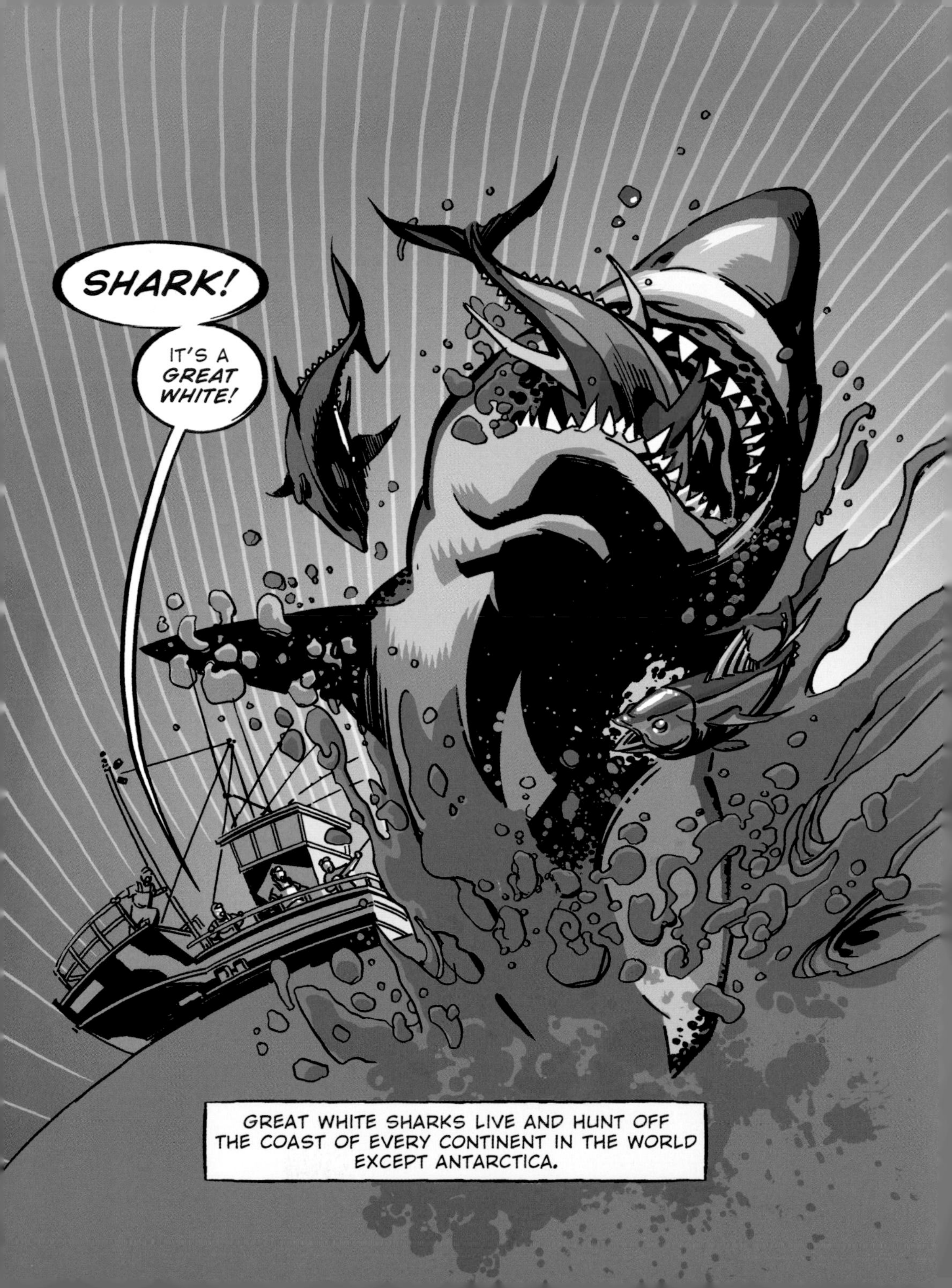
SHARK!
IT'S A GREAT WHITE!
GREAT WHITE SHARKS LIVE AND HUNT OFF THE COAST OF EVERY CONTINENT IN THE WORLD EXCEPT ANTARCTICA.

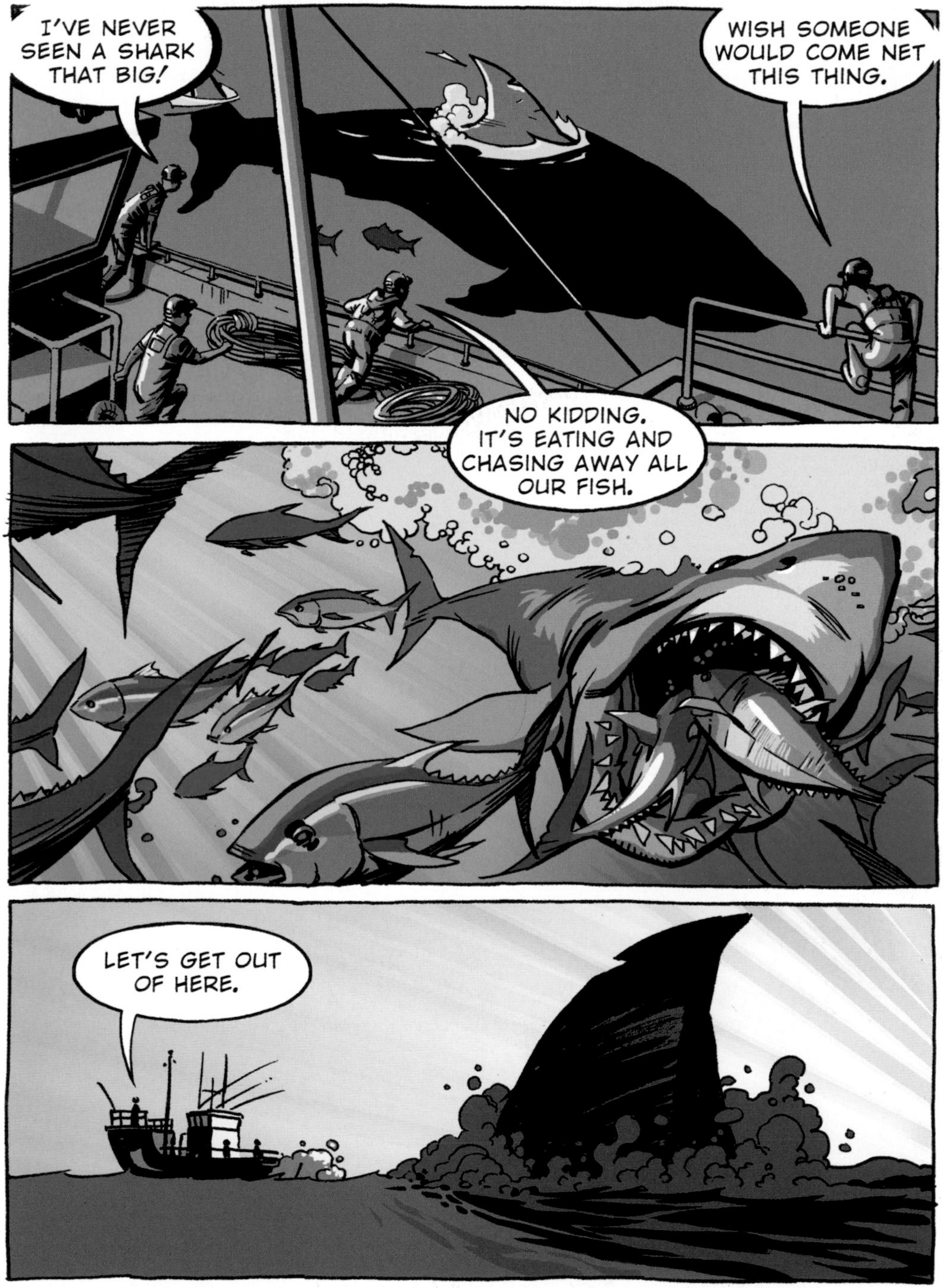
I'VE NEVER SEEN A SHARK THAT BIG!
WISH SOMEONE WOULD COME NET THIS THING.
NO KIDDING. IT'S EATING AND CHASING AWAY ALL OUR FISH.
LET'S GET OUT OF HERE.

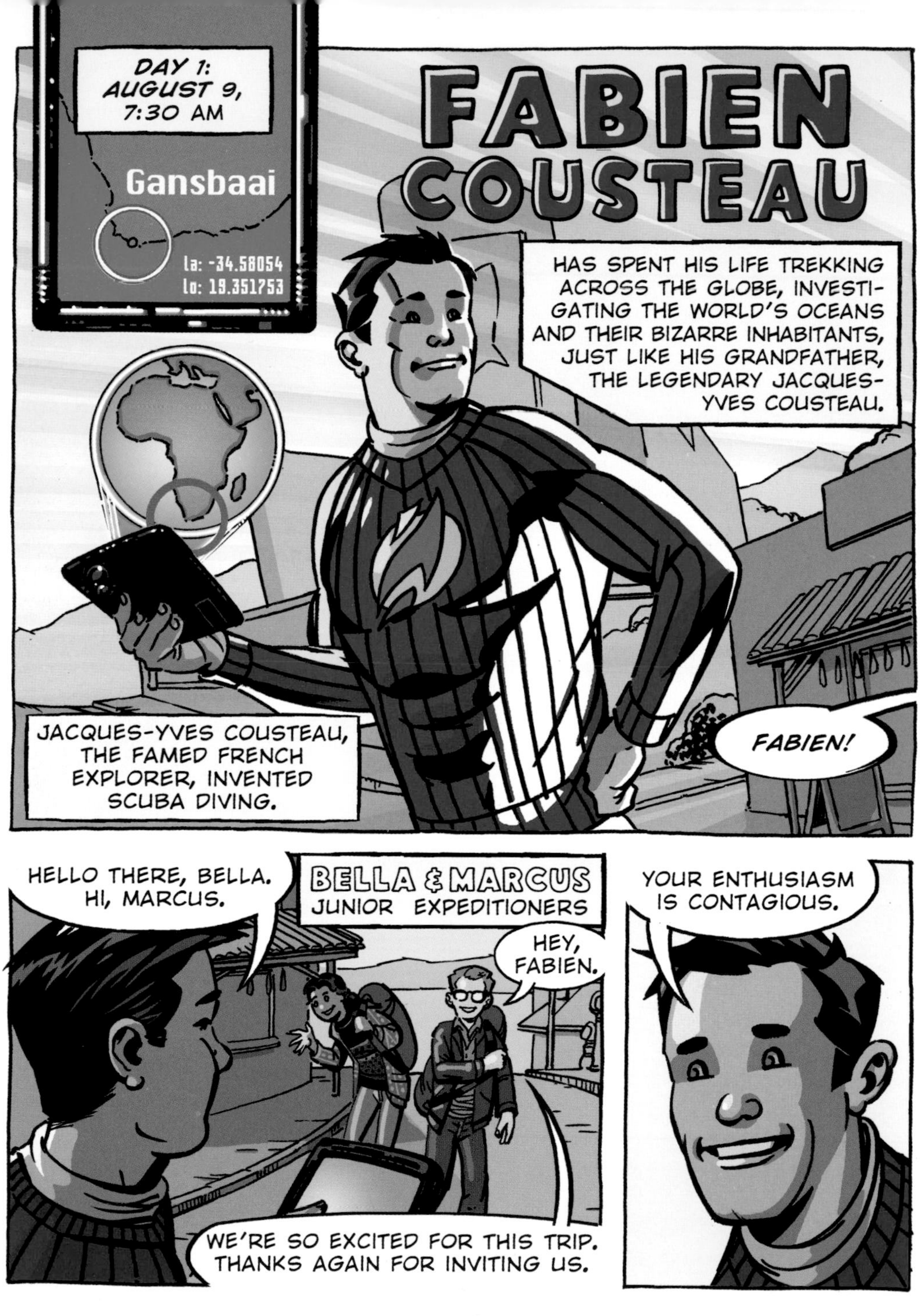

DAY 1: AUGUST 9, 7:30 AM
Gansbaai
la: -34.58054
lo: 19.351753
FABIEN COUSTEAU
HAS SPENT HIS LIFE TREKKING ACROSS THE GLOBE, INVESTI-GATING THE WORLD'S OCEANS AND THEIR BIZARRE INHABITANTS, JUST LIKE HIS GRANDFATHER, THE LEGENDARY JACQUES-YVES COUSTEAU.
JACQUES-YVES COUSTEAU, THE FAMED FRENCH EXPLORER, INVENTED SCUBA DIVING.
FABIEN!
HELLO THERE, BELLA. HI, MARCUS.
BELLA & MARCUS JUNIOR EXPEDITIONERS
HEY, FABIEN.
WE'RE SO EXCITED FOR THIS TRIP. THANKS AGAIN FOR INVITING US.
YOUR ENTHUSIASM IS CONTAGIOUS.

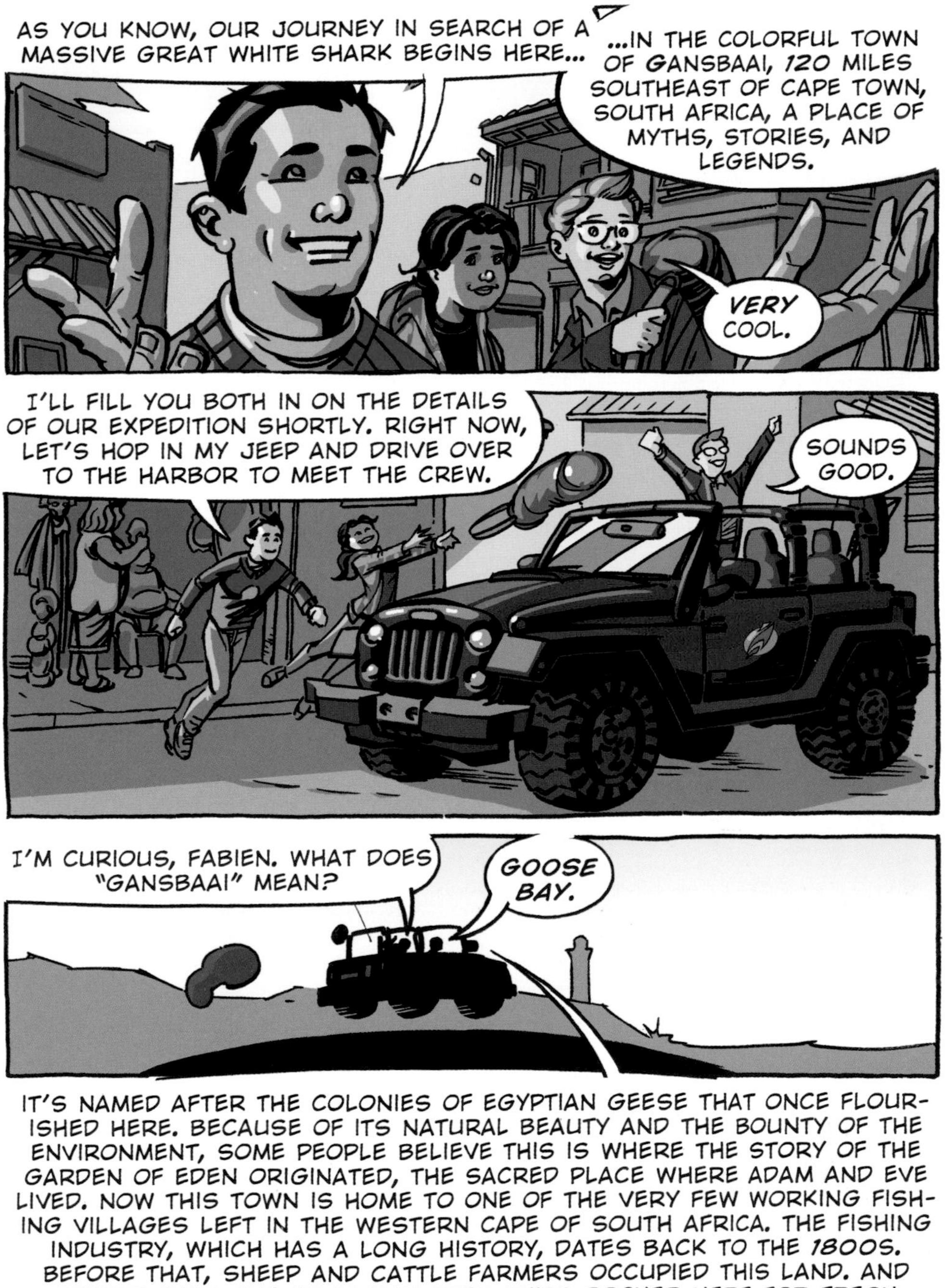
AS YOU KNOW, OUR JOURNEY IN SEARCH OF A MASSIVE GREAT WHITE SHARK BEGINS HERE...
...IN THE COLORFUL TOWN OF GANSBAAI, 120 MILES SOUTHEAST OF CAPE TOWN, SOUTH AFRICA, A PLACE OF MYTHS, STORIES, AND LEGENDS.
VERY COOL.
I'LL FILL YOU BOTH IN ON THE DETAILS OF OUR EXPEDITION SHORTLY. RIGHT NOW, LET'S HOP IN MY JEEP AND DRIVE OVER TO THE HARBOR TO MEET THE CREW.
SOUNDS GOOD.
I'M CURIOUS, FABIEN. WHAT DOES "GANSBAAI" MEAN?
GOOSE BAY.
IT'S NAMED AFTER THE COLONIES OF EGYPTIAN GEESE THAT ONCE FLOURISHED HERE. BECAUSE OF ITS NATURAL BEAUTY AND THE BOUNTY OF THE ENVIRONMENT, SOME PEOPLE BELIEVE THIS IS WHERE THE STORY OF THE GARDEN OF EDEN ORIGINATED, THE SACRED PLACE WHERE ADAM AND EVE LIVED. NOW THIS TOWN IS HOME TO ONE OF THE VERY FEW WORKING FISHING VILLAGES LEFT IN THE WESTERN CAPE OF SOUTH AFRICA. THE FISHING INDUSTRY, WHICH HAS A LONG HISTORY, DATES BACK TO THE 1800S. BEFORE THAT, SHEEP AND CATTLE FARMERS OCCUPIED THIS LAND. AND BEFORE THAT, THE FIRST EXPLORER SHIPS DOCKED HERE FOR FRESH FOOD AND WATER.

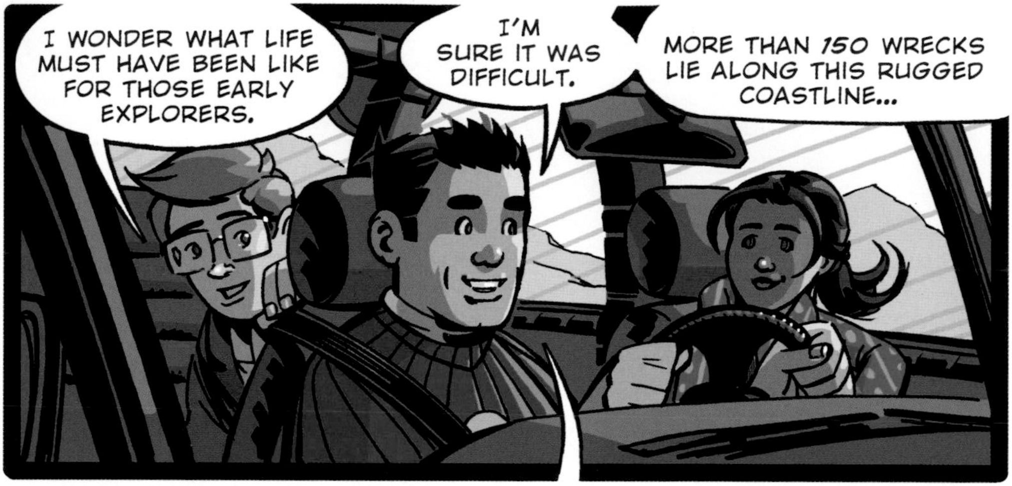
I WONDER WHAT LIFE MUST HAVE BEEN LIKE FOR THOSE EARLY EXPLORERS.
I'M SURE IT WAS DIFFICULT.
MORE THAN *150* WRECKS LIE ALONG THIS RUGGED COASTLINE...

...AT THE BOTTOM OF THE INDIAN OCEAN, A SILENT TESTIMONY TO THE PERILOUS SEA THOSE MARINERS ENCOUNTERED DURING THEIR VOYAGES AROUND SOUTH AFRICA. ONE SUCH SHIP IS THE HMS *BIRKENHEAD*, A FAMOUS TWO-MAST IRON-HULLED PADDLE-WHEEL SHIP BUILT FOR THE ROYAL NAVY. SHE WENT DOWN OFF GANSBAAI IN *1852*, SUPPOSEDLY WITH *3* TONS OF GOLD AND SILVER COINS...WHICH HAS NEVER BEEN FOUND.

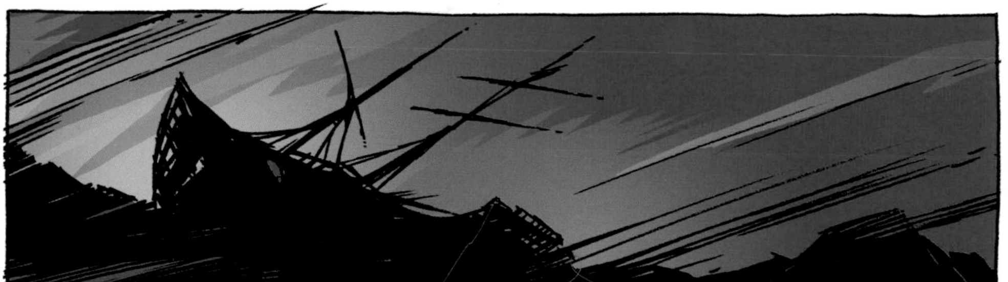

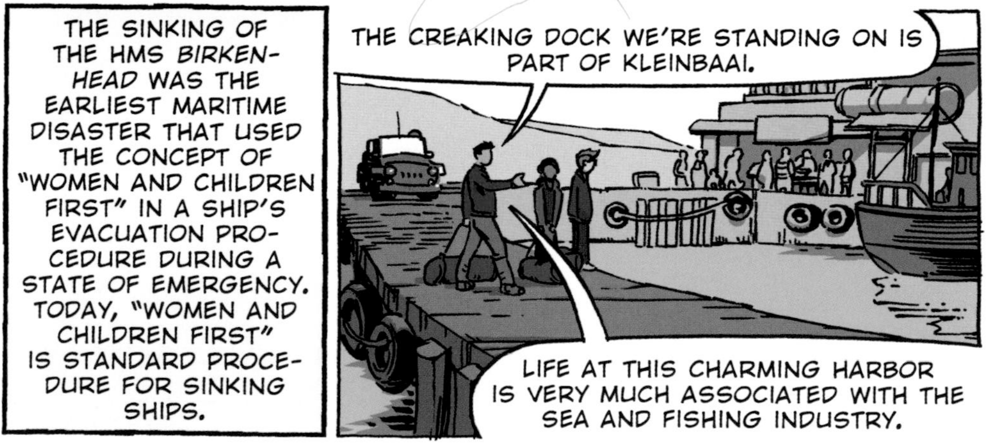
THE SINKING OF THE HMS *BIRKENHEAD* WAS THE EARLIEST MARITIME DISASTER THAT USED THE CONCEPT OF "WOMEN AND CHILDREN FIRST" IN A SHIP'S EVACUATION PROCEDURE DURING A STATE OF EMERGENCY. TODAY, "WOMEN AND CHILDREN FIRST" IS STANDARD PROCEDURE FOR SINKING SHIPS.
THE CREAKING DOCK WE'RE STANDING ON IS PART OF KLEINBAAI.
LIFE AT THIS CHARMING HARBOR IS VERY MUCH ASSOCIATED WITH THE SEA AND FISHING INDUSTRY.

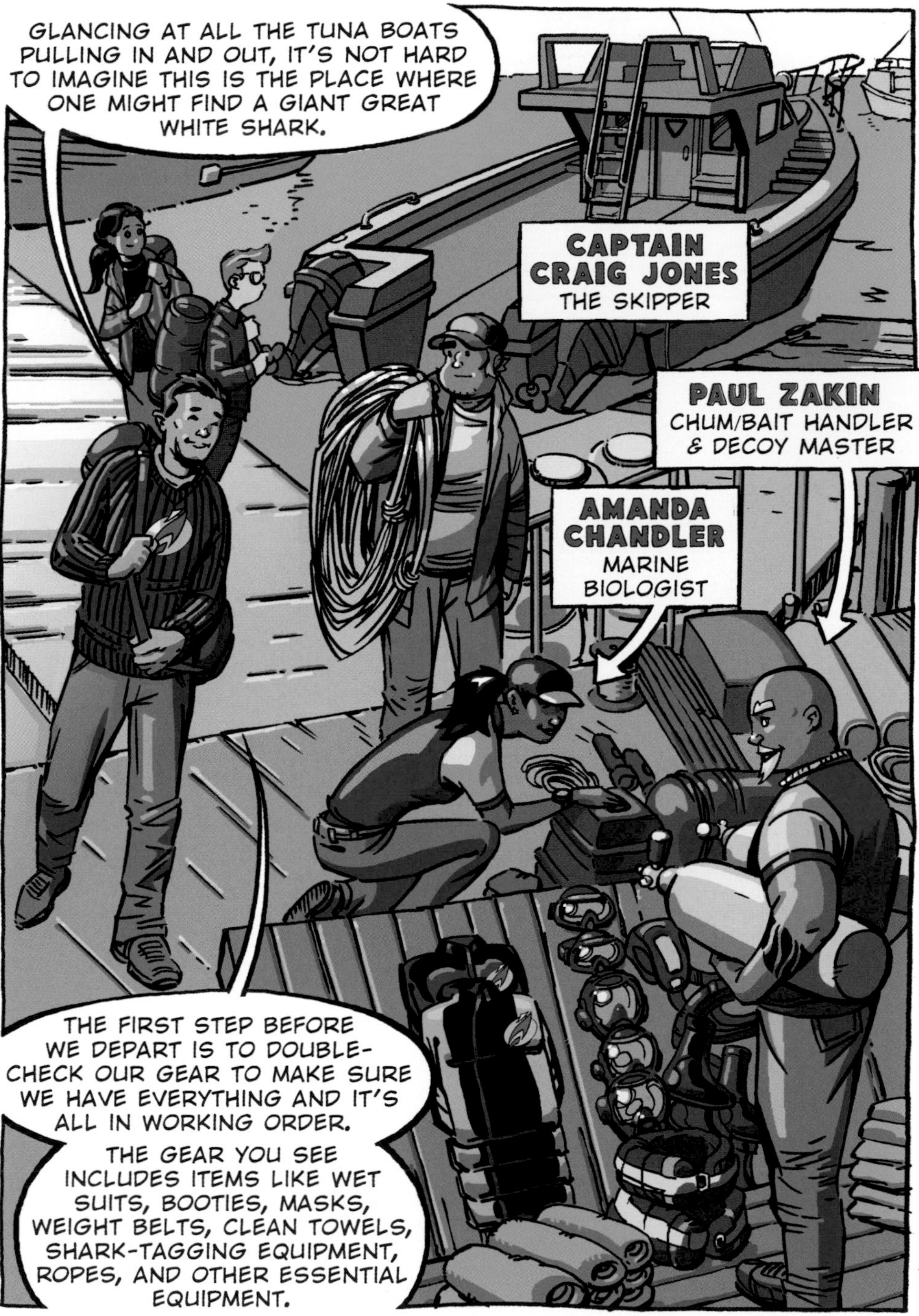
GLANCING AT ALL THE TUNA BOATS PULLING IN AND OUT, IT'S NOT HARD TO IMAGINE THIS IS THE PLACE WHERE ONE MIGHT FIND A GIANT GREAT WHITE SHARK.
CAPTAIN CRAIG JONES THE SKIPPER
PAUL ZAKIN CHUM/BAIT HANDLER & DECOY MASTER
AMANDA CHANDLER MARINE BIOLOGIST
THE FIRST STEP BEFORE WE DEPART IS TO DOUBLE-CHECK OUR GEAR TO MAKE SURE WE HAVE EVERYTHING AND IT'S ALL IN WORKING ORDER.
THE GEAR YOU SEE INCLUDES ITEMS LIKE WET SUITS, BOOTIES, MASKS, WEIGHT BELTS, CLEAN TOWELS, SHARK-TAGGING EQUIPMENT, ROPES, AND OTHER ESSENTIAL EQUIPMENT.

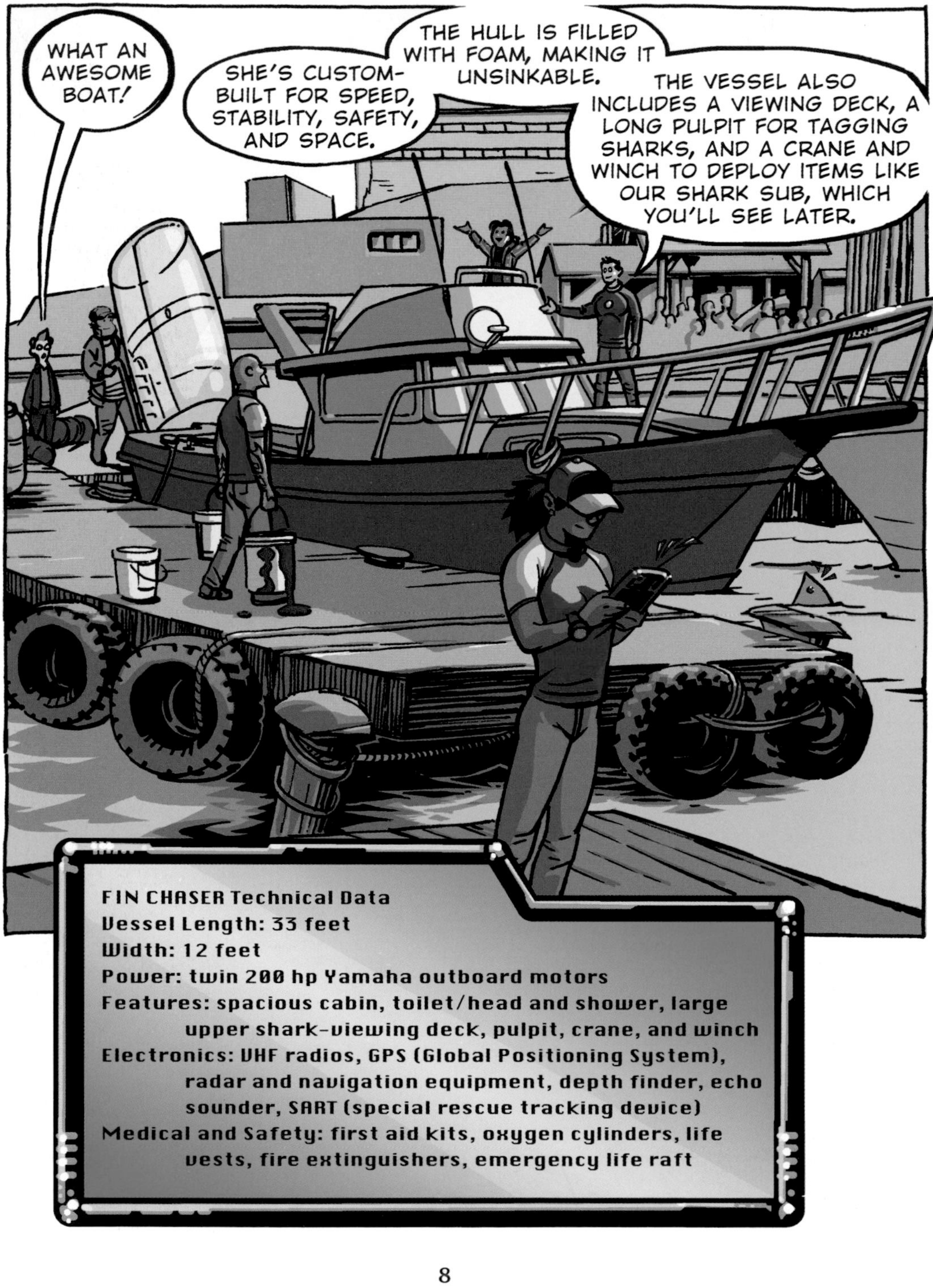
WHAT AN AWESOME BOAT!
SHE'S CUSTOM-BUILT FOR SPEED, STABILITY, SAFETY, AND SPACE.
THE HULL IS FILLED WITH FOAM, MAKING IT UNSINKABLE.
THE VESSEL ALSO INCLUDES A VIEWING DECK, A LONG PULPIT FOR TAGGING SHARKS, AND A CRANE AND WINCH TO DEPLOY ITEMS LIKE OUR SHARK SUB, WHICH YOU'LL SEE LATER.

FIN CHASER Technical Data

Vessel Length: 33 feet

Width: 12 feet

Power: twin 200 hp Yamaha outboard motors

Features: spacious cabin, toilet/head and shower, large upper shark-viewing deck, pulpit, crane, and winch

Electronics: VHF radios, GPS (Global Positioning System), radar and navigation equipment, depth finder, echo sounder, SART (special rescue tracking device)

Medical and Safety: first aid kits, oxygen cylinders, life vests, fire extinguishers, emergency life raft

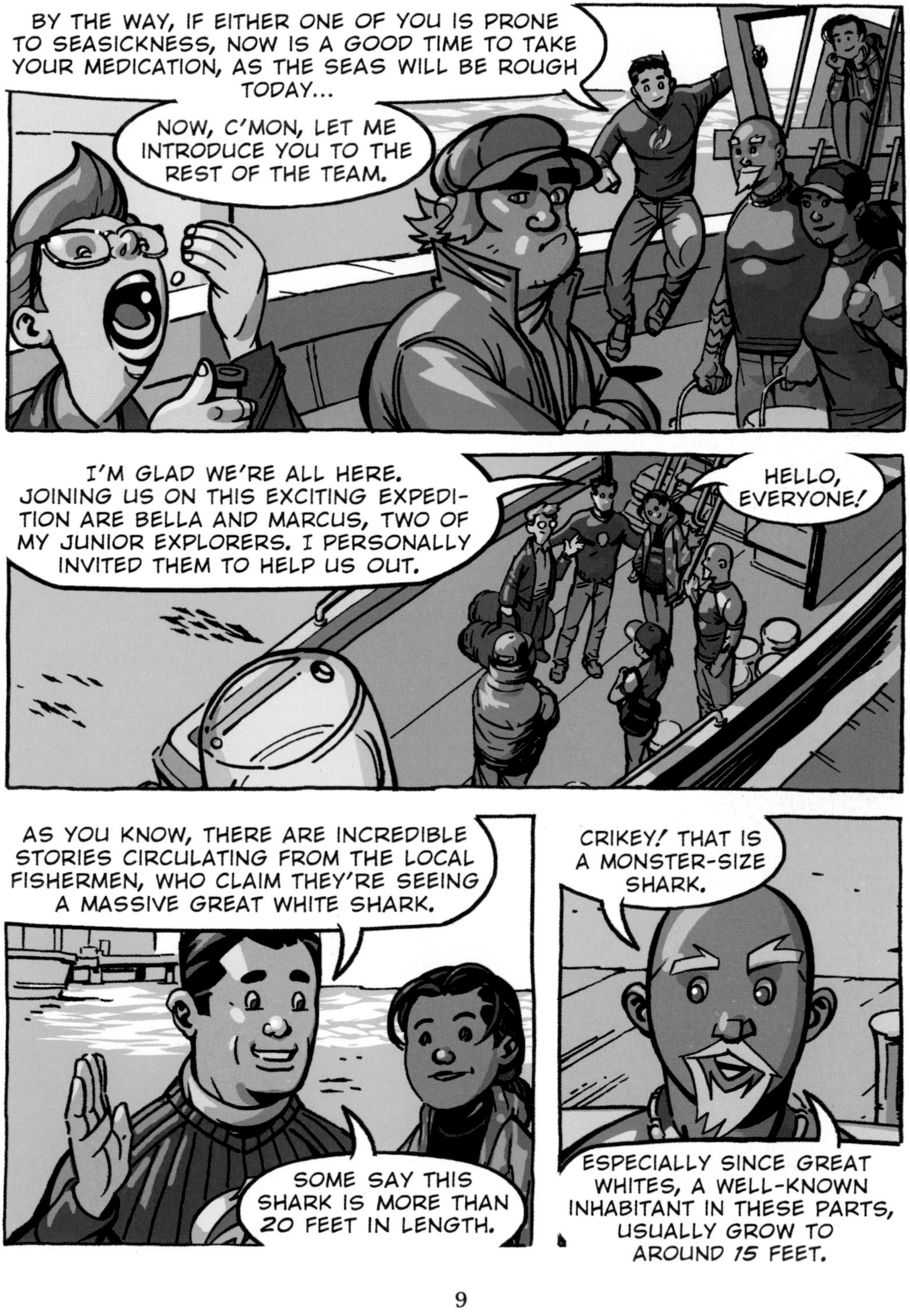
BY THE WAY, IF EITHER ONE OF YOU IS PRONE TO SEASICKNESS, NOW IS A GOOD TIME TO TAKE YOUR MEDICATION, AS THE SEAS WILL BE ROUGH TODAY...
NOW, C'MON, LET ME INTRODUCE YOU TO THE REST OF THE TEAM.
I'M GLAD WE'RE ALL HERE. JOINING US ON THIS EXCITING EXPEDITION ARE BELLA AND MARCUS, TWO OF MY JUNIOR EXPLORERS. I PERSONALLY INVITED THEM TO HELP US OUT.
HELLO, EVERYONE!
AS YOU KNOW, THERE ARE INCREDIBLE STORIES CIRCULATING FROM THE LOCAL FISHERMEN, WHO CLAIM THEY'RE SEEING A MASSIVE GREAT WHITE SHARK.
SOME SAY THIS SHARK IS MORE THAN 20 FEET IN LENGTH.
CRIKEY! THAT IS A MONSTER-SIZE SHARK.
ESPECIALLY SINCE GREAT WHITES, A WELL-KNOWN INHABITANT IN THESE PARTS, USUALLY GROW TO AROUND 15 FEET.

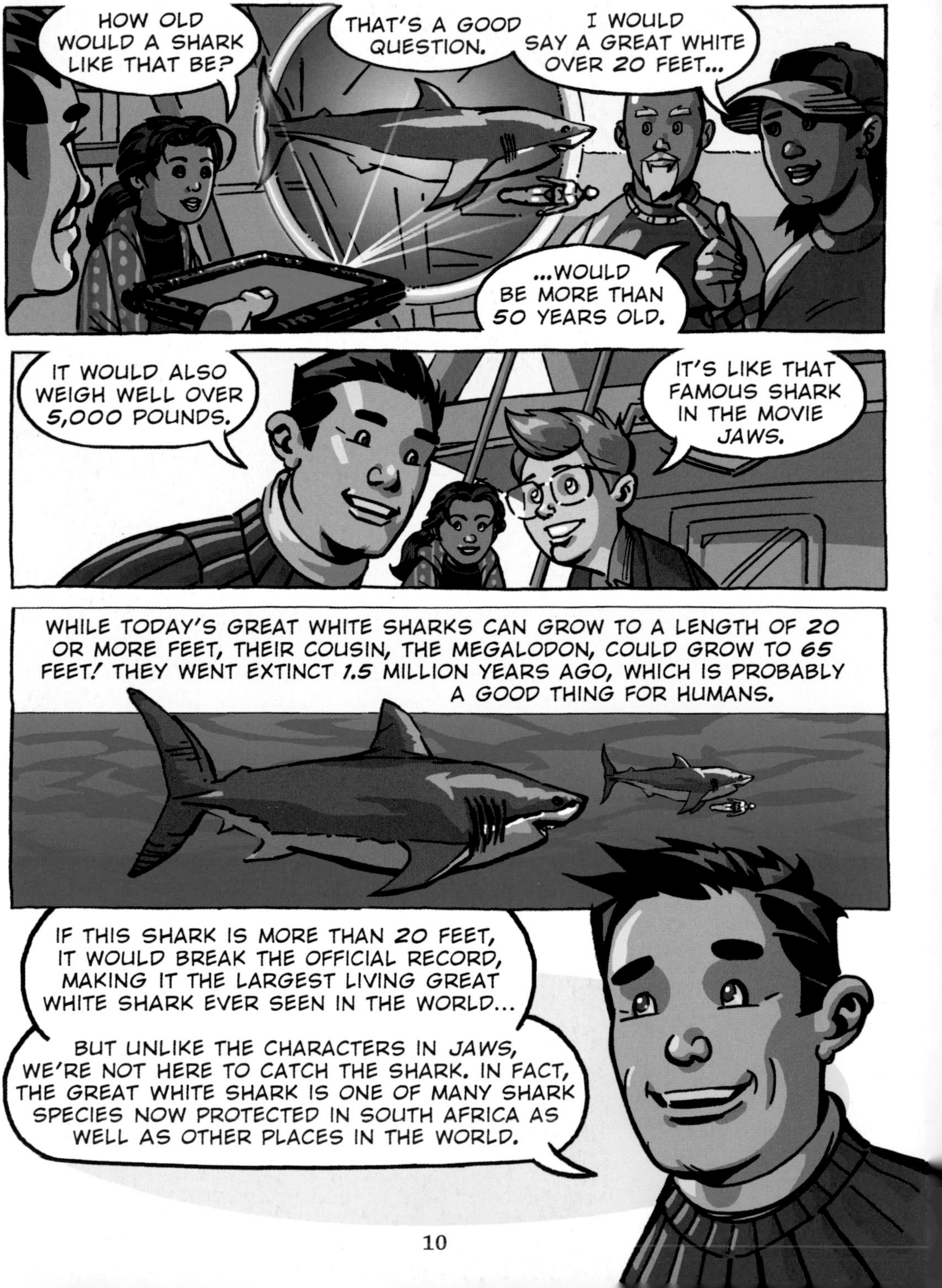
HOW OLD WOULD A SHARK LIKE THAT BE?
THAT'S A GOOD QUESTION.
I WOULD SAY A GREAT WHITE OVER 20 FEET...
...WOULD BE MORE THAN 50 YEARS OLD.
IT WOULD ALSO WEIGH WELL OVER 5,000 POUNDS.
IT'S LIKE THAT FAMOUS SHARK IN THE MOVIE *JAWS*.
WHILE TODAY'S GREAT WHITE SHARKS CAN GROW TO A LENGTH OF 20 OR MORE FEET, THEIR COUSIN, THE MEGALODON, COULD GROW TO 65 FEET! THEY WENT EXTINCT 1.5 MILLION YEARS AGO, WHICH IS PROBABLY A GOOD THING FOR HUMANS.
IF THIS SHARK IS MORE THAN 20 FEET, IT WOULD BREAK THE OFFICIAL RECORD, MAKING IT THE LARGEST LIVING GREAT WHITE SHARK EVER SEEN IN THE WORLD...
BUT UNLIKE THE CHARACTERS IN *JAWS*, WE'RE NOT HERE TO CATCH THE SHARK. IN FACT, THE GREAT WHITE SHARK IS ONE OF MANY SHARK SPECIES NOW PROTECTED IN SOUTH AFRICA AS WELL AS OTHER PLACES IN THE WORLD.

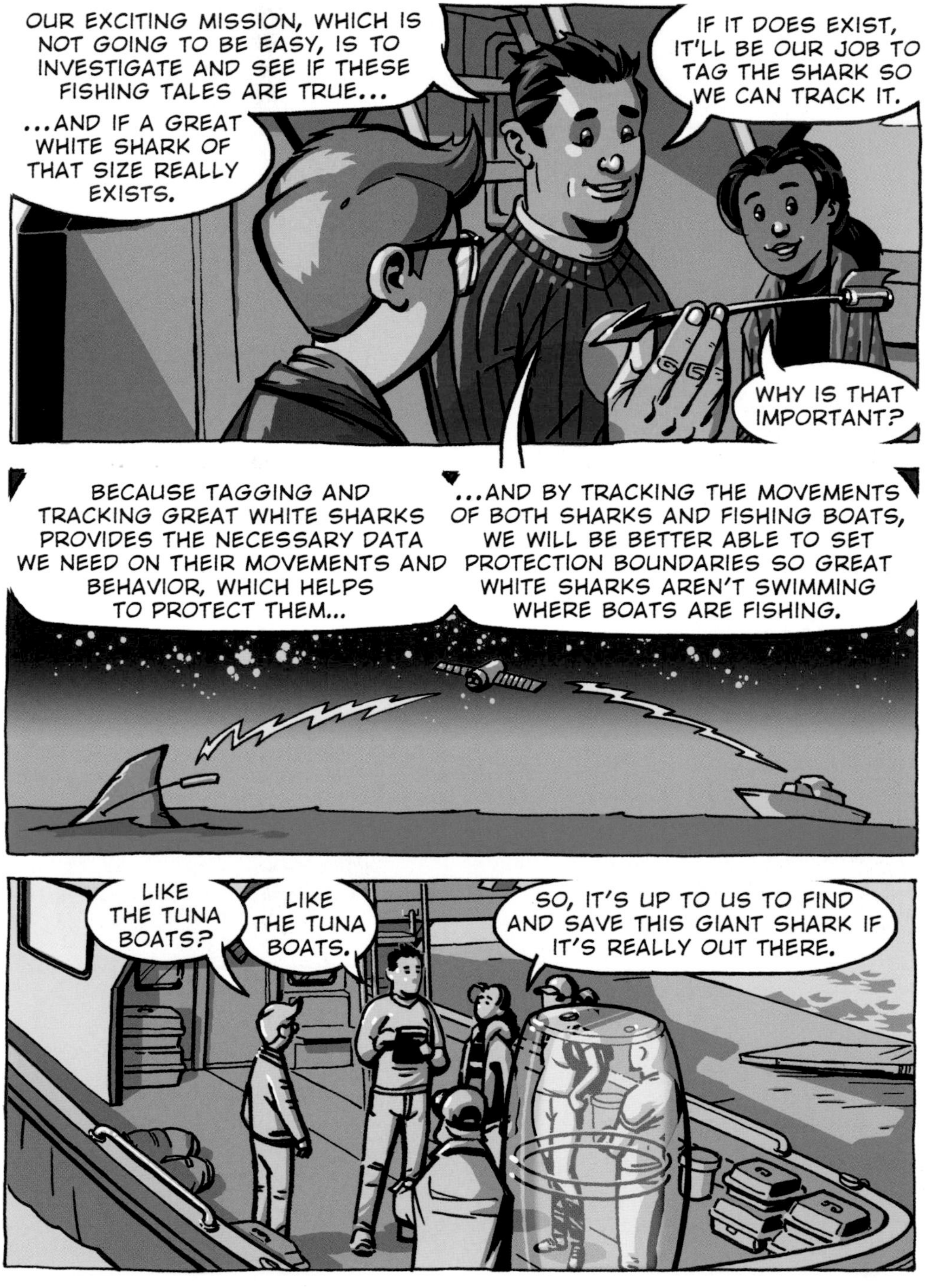
OUR EXCITING MISSION, WHICH IS NOT GOING TO BE EASY, IS TO INVESTIGATE AND SEE IF THESE FISHING TALES ARE TRUE...
...AND IF A GREAT WHITE SHARK OF THAT SIZE REALLY EXISTS.
IF IT DOES EXIST, IT'LL BE OUR JOB TO TAG THE SHARK SO WE CAN TRACK IT.
WHY IS THAT IMPORTANT?
BECAUSE TAGGING AND TRACKING GREAT WHITE SHARKS PROVIDES THE NECESSARY DATA WE NEED ON THEIR MOVEMENTS AND BEHAVIOR, WHICH HELPS TO PROTECT THEM...
...AND BY TRACKING THE MOVEMENTS OF BOTH SHARKS AND FISHING BOATS, WE WILL BE BETTER ABLE TO SET PROTECTION BOUNDARIES SO GREAT WHITE SHARKS AREN'T SWIMMING WHERE BOATS ARE FISHING.
LIKE THE TUNA BOATS?
LIKE THE TUNA BOATS.
SO, IT'S UP TO US TO FIND AND SAVE THIS GIANT SHARK IF IT'S REALLY OUT THERE.

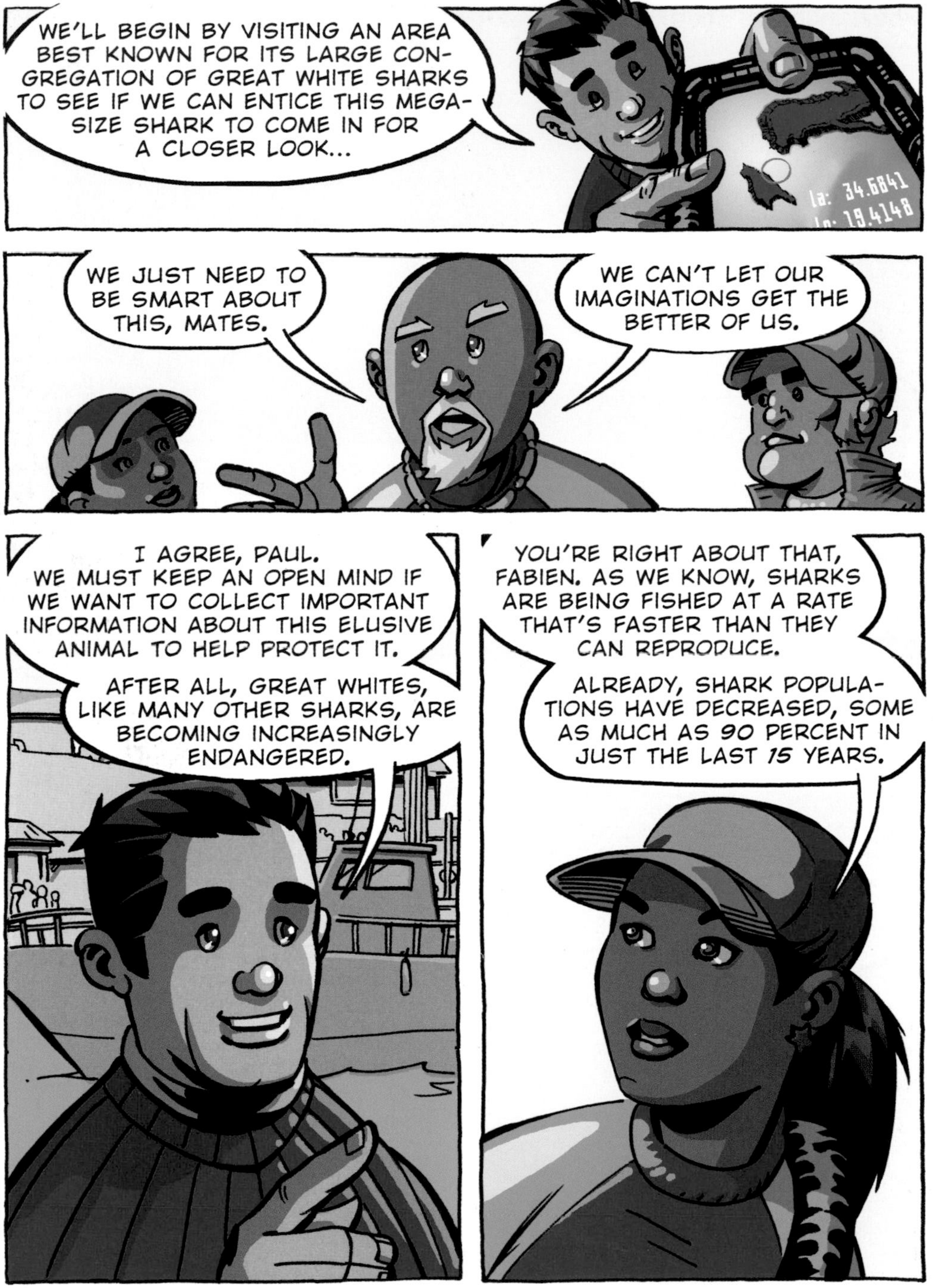
WE'LL BEGIN BY VISITING AN AREA BEST KNOWN FOR ITS LARGE CONGREGATION OF GREAT WHITE SHARKS TO SEE IF WE CAN ENTICE THIS MEGA-SIZE SHARK TO COME IN FOR A CLOSER LOOK...
la: 34.6841
lo: 19.4148
WE JUST NEED TO BE SMART ABOUT THIS, MATES.
WE CAN'T LET OUR IMAGINATIONS GET THE BETTER OF US.
I AGREE, PAUL. WE MUST KEEP AN OPEN MIND IF WE WANT TO COLLECT IMPORTANT INFORMATION ABOUT THIS ELUSIVE ANIMAL TO HELP PROTECT IT.
AFTER ALL, GREAT WHITES, LIKE MANY OTHER SHARKS, ARE BECOMING INCREASINGLY ENDANGERED.
YOU'RE RIGHT ABOUT THAT, FABIEN. AS WE KNOW, SHARKS ARE BEING FISHED AT A RATE THAT'S FASTER THAN THEY CAN REPRODUCE.
ALREADY, SHARK POPULATIONS HAVE DECREASED, SOME AS MUCH AS 90 PERCENT IN JUST THE LAST *15* YEARS.

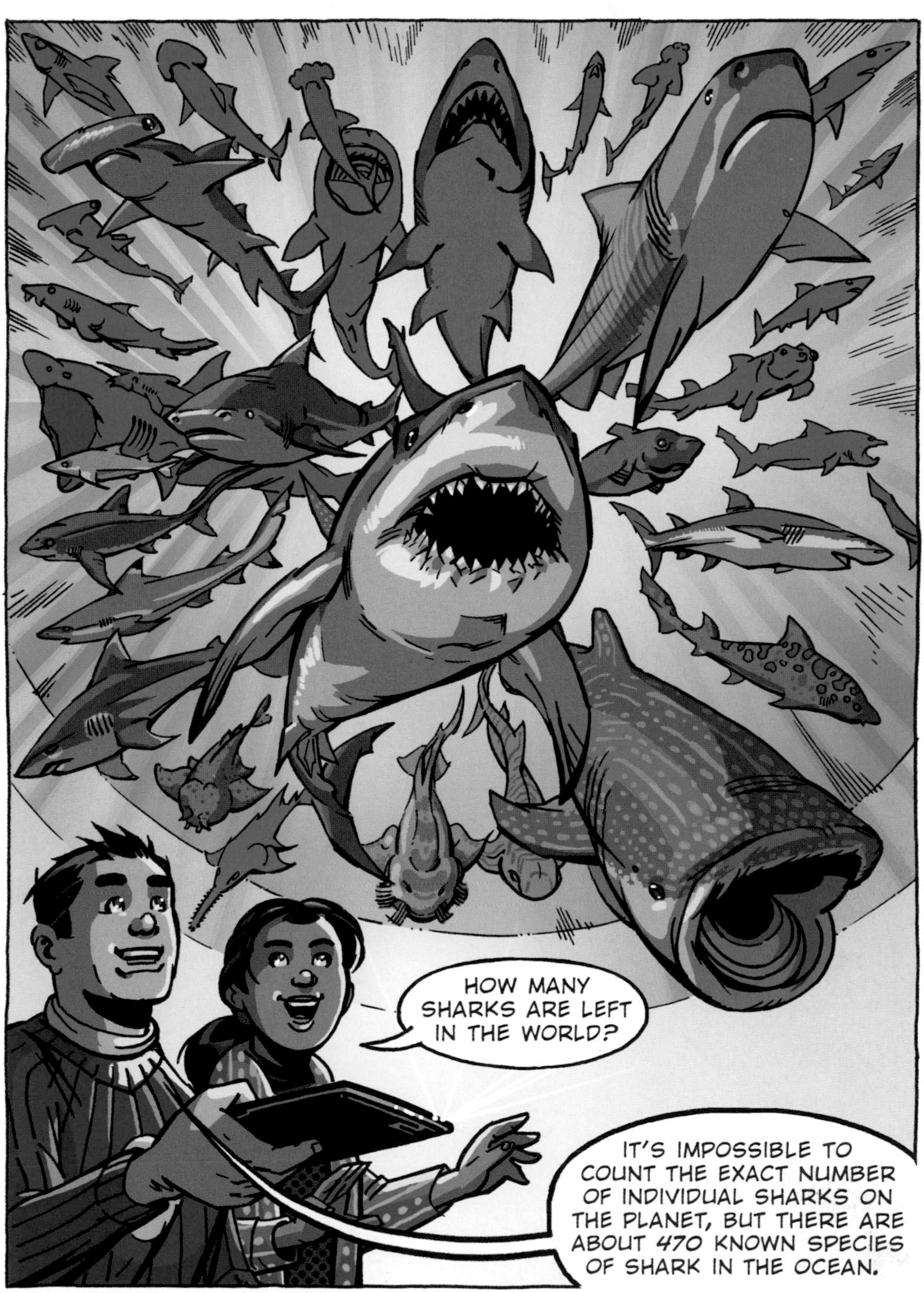
HOW MANY SHARKS ARE LEFT IN THE WORLD?
IT'S IMPOSSIBLE TO COUNT THE EXACT NUMBER OF INDIVIDUAL SHARKS ON THE PLANET, BUT THERE ARE ABOUT 470 KNOWN SPECIES OF SHARK IN THE OCEAN.

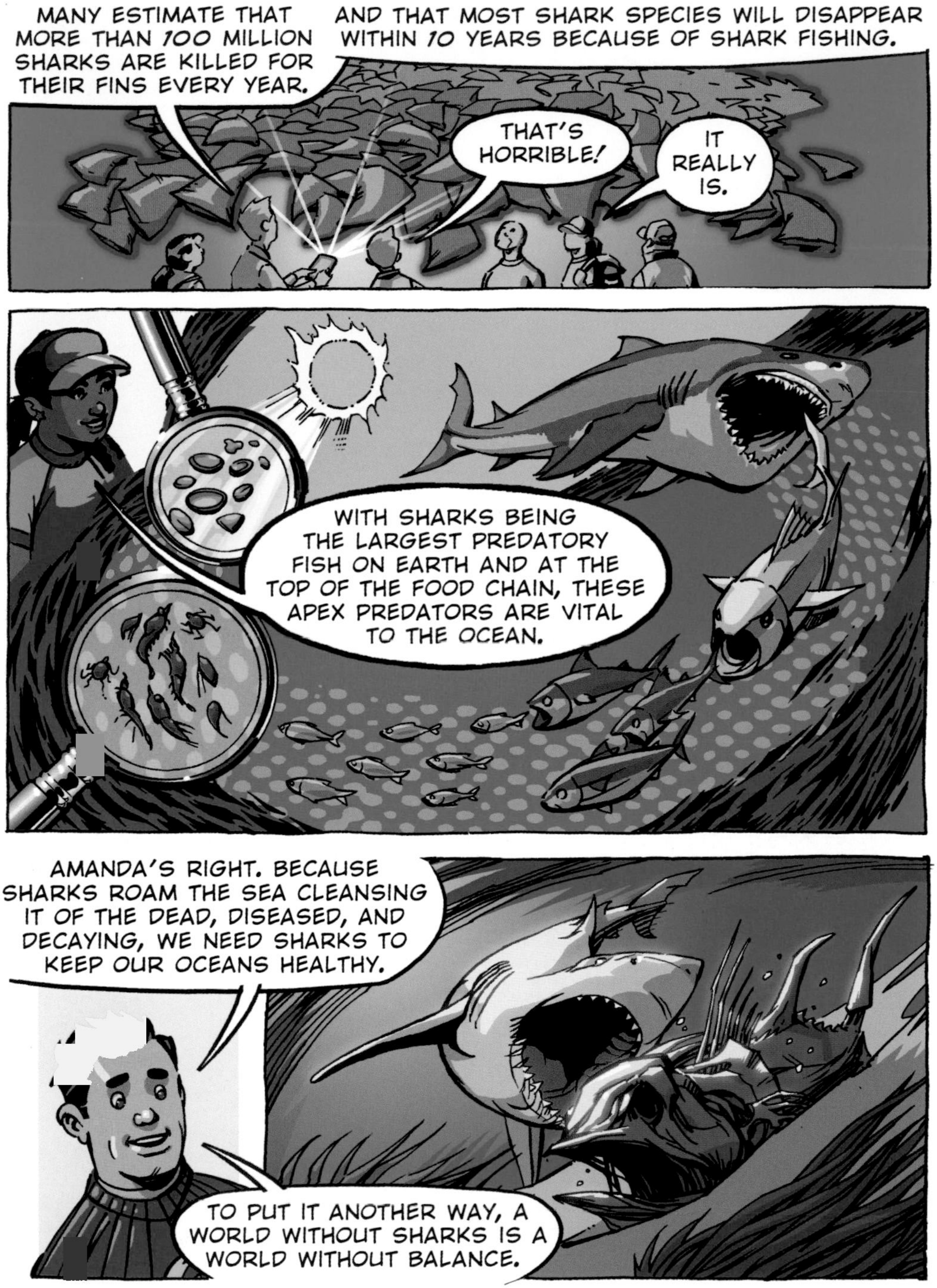
MANY ESTIMATE THAT MORE THAN 100 MILLION SHARKS ARE KILLED FOR THEIR FINS EVERY YEAR.
AND THAT MOST SHARK SPECIES WILL DISAPPEAR WITHIN 10 YEARS BECAUSE OF SHARK FISHING.
THAT'S HORRIBLE!
IT REALLY IS.
WITH SHARKS BEING THE LARGEST PREDATORY FISH ON EARTH AND AT THE TOP OF THE FOOD CHAIN, THESE APEX PREDATORS ARE VITAL TO THE OCEAN.
AMANDA'S RIGHT. BECAUSE SHARKS ROAM THE SEA CLEANSING IT OF THE DEAD, DISEASED, AND DECAYING, WE NEED SHARKS TO KEEP OUR OCEANS HEALTHY.
TO PUT IT ANOTHER WAY, A WORLD WITHOUT SHARKS IS A WORLD WITHOUT BALANCE.

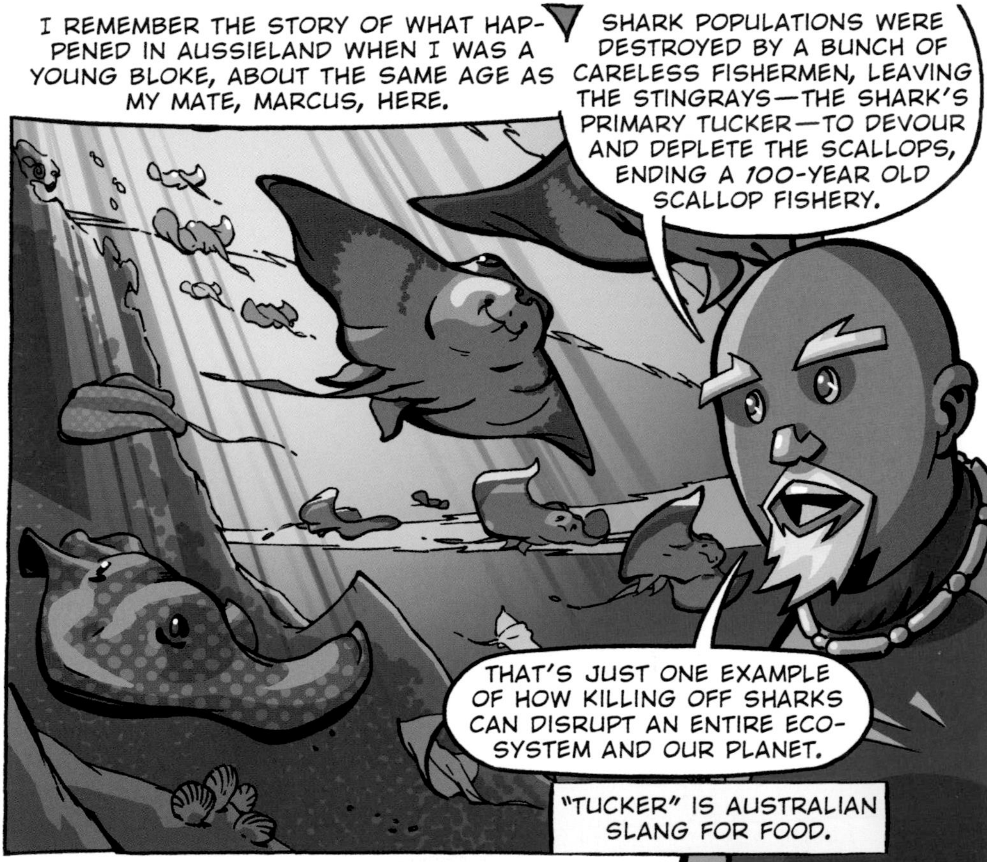
I REMEMBER THE STORY OF WHAT HAPPENED IN AUSSIELAND WHEN I WAS A YOUNG BLOKE, ABOUT THE SAME AGE AS MY MATE, MARCUS, HERE.
SHARK POPULATIONS WERE DESTROYED BY A BUNCH OF CARELESS FISHERMEN, LEAVING THE STINGRAYS—THE SHARK'S PRIMARY TUCKER—TO DEVOUR AND DEPLETE THE SCALLOPS, ENDING A 100-YEAR OLD SCALLOP FISHERY.
THAT'S JUST ONE EXAMPLE OF HOW KILLING OFF SHARKS CAN DISRUPT AN ENTIRE ECOSYSTEM AND OUR PLANET.
"TUCKER" IS AUSTRALIAN SLANG FOR FOOD.

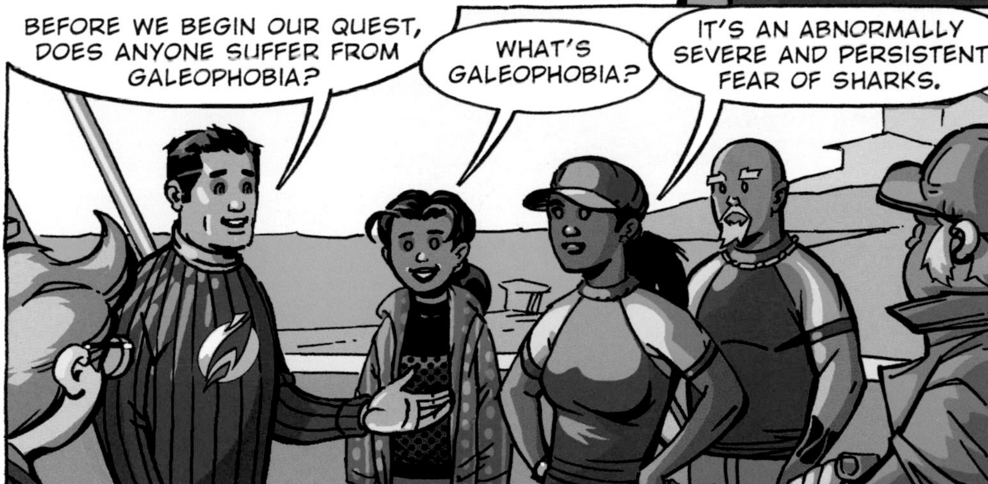
BEFORE WE BEGIN OUR QUEST, DOES ANYONE SUFFER FROM GALEOPHOBIA?
WHAT'S GALEOPHOBIA?
IT'S AN ABNORMALLY SEVERE AND PERSISTENT FEAR OF SHARKS.

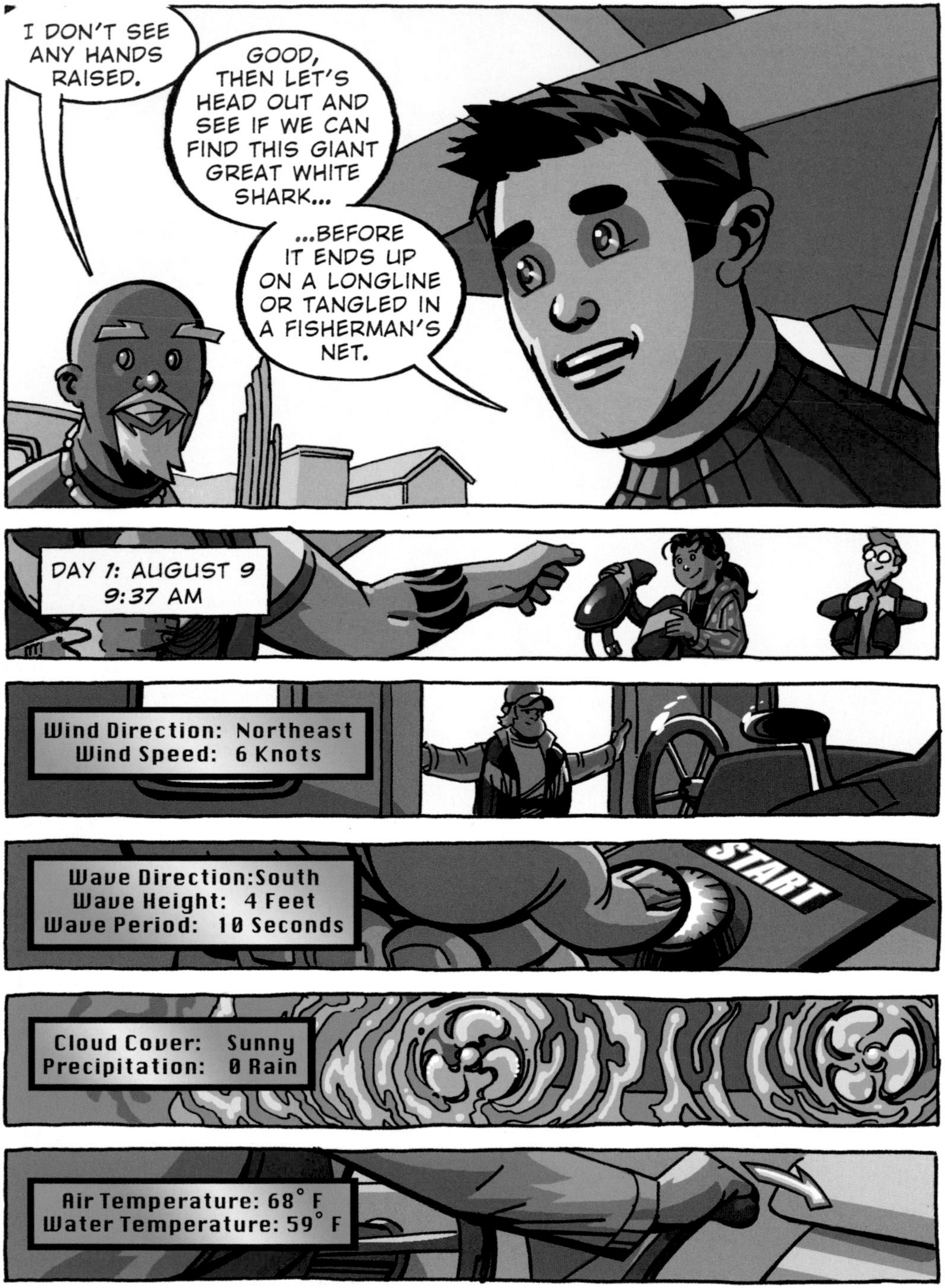
I DON'T SEE ANY HANDS RAISED.
GOOD, THEN LET'S HEAD OUT AND SEE IF WE CAN FIND THIS GIANT GREAT WHITE SHARK...
...BEFORE IT ENDS UP ON A LONGLINE OR TANGLED IN A FISHERMAN'S NET.
DAY 1: AUGUST 9
9:37 AM
Wind Direction: Northeast
Wind Speed: 6 Knots
START
Wave Direction:South
Wave Height: 4 Feet
Wave Period: 10 Seconds
Cloud Cover: Sunny
Precipitation: 0 Rain
Air Temperature: 68° F
Water Temperature: 59° F

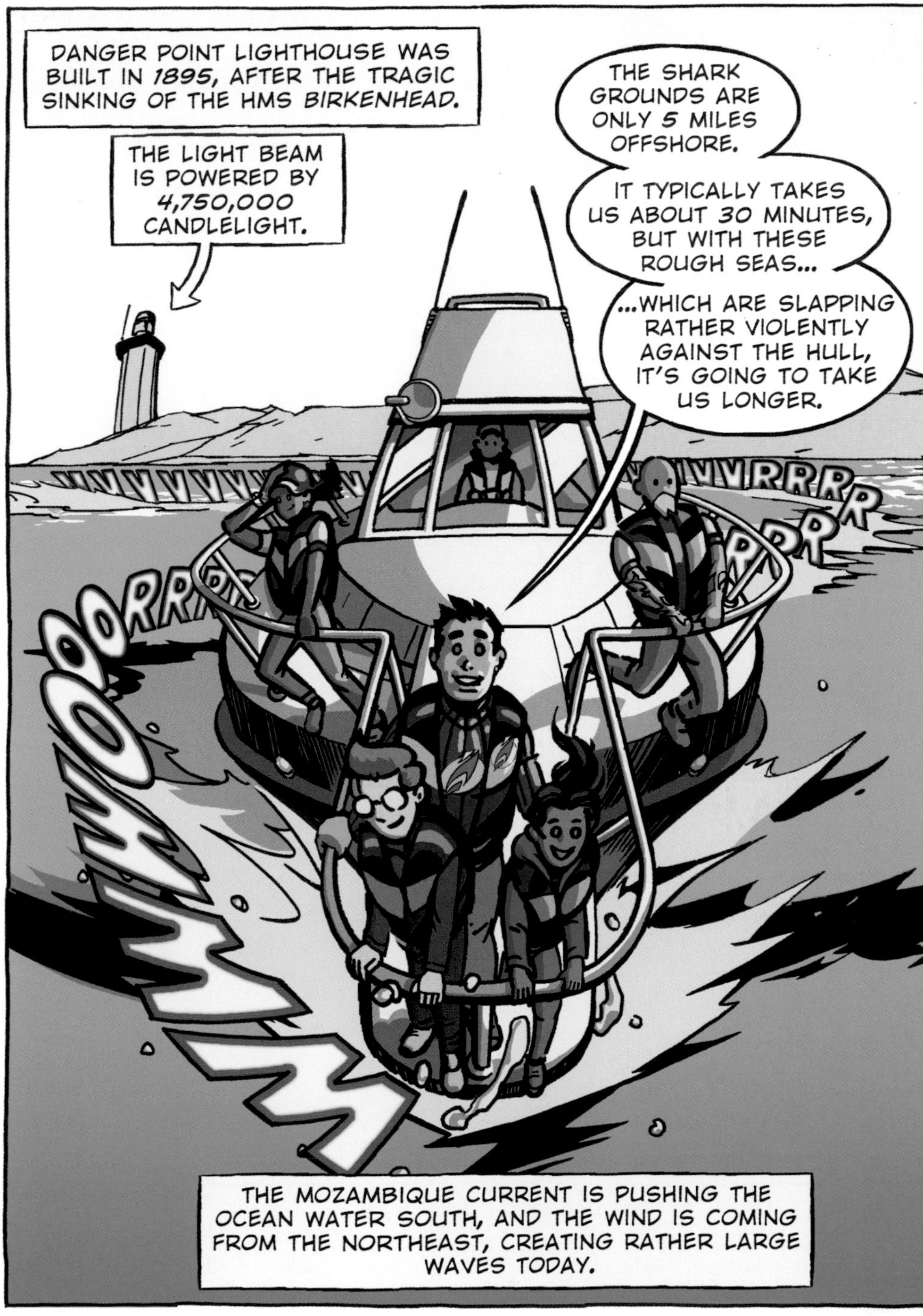
DANGER POINT LIGHTHOUSE WAS BUILT IN *1895*, AFTER THE TRAGIC SINKING OF THE HMS *BIRKENHEAD.*
THE LIGHT BEAM IS POWERED BY *4,750,000* CANDLELIGHT.
THE SHARK GROUNDS ARE ONLY *5* MILES OFFSHORE.
IT TYPICALLY TAKES US ABOUT *30* MINUTES, BUT WITH THESE ROUGH SEAS...
...WHICH ARE SLAPPING RATHER VIOLENTLY AGAINST THE HULL, IT'S GOING TO TAKE US LONGER.
VVVVVVVVVVVVVVVVVVVVRRRRRRR
OORRRR
WHOOOSH
THE MOZAMBIQUE CURRENT IS PUSHING THE OCEAN WATER SOUTH, AND THE WIND IS COMING FROM THE NORTHEAST, CREATING RATHER LARGE WAVES TODAY.

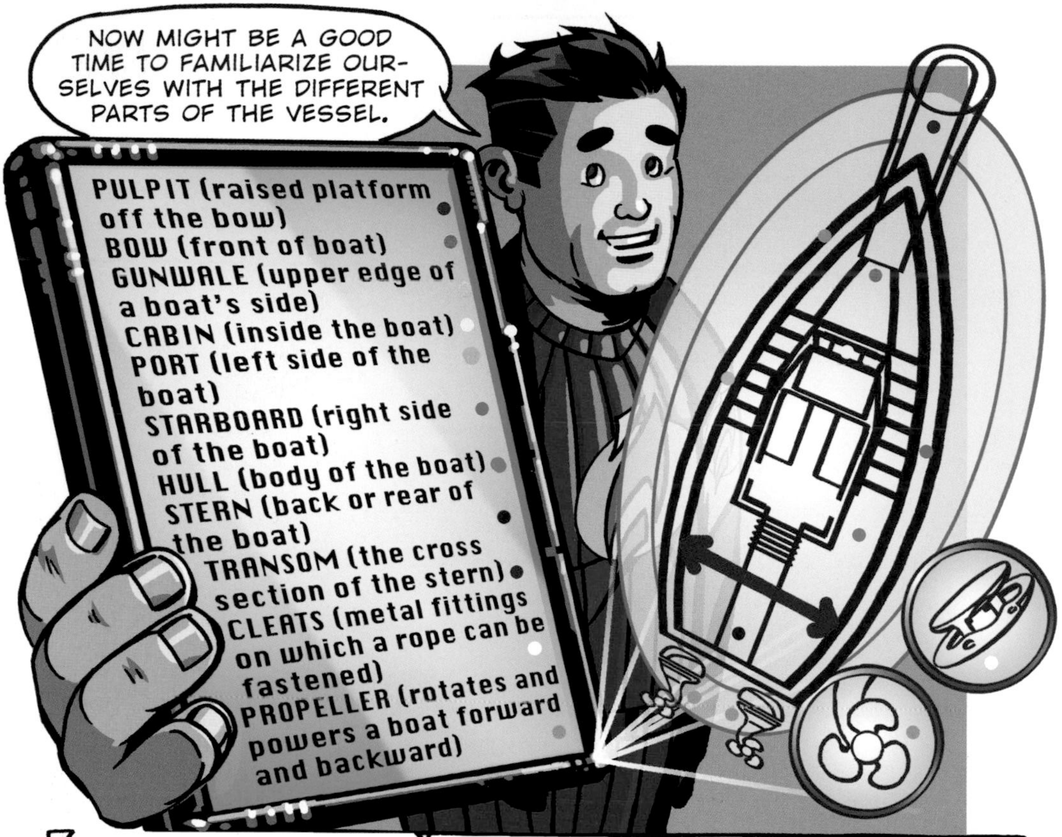
NOW MIGHT BE A GOOD TIME TO FAMILIARIZE OURSELVES WITH THE DIFFERENT PARTS OF THE VESSEL.
PULPIT (raised platform off the bow)
BOW (front of boat)
GUNWALE (upper edge of a boat's side)
CABIN (inside the boat)
PORT (left side of the boat)
STARBOARD (right side of the boat)
HULL (body of the boat)
STERN (back or rear of the boat)
TRANSOM (the cross section of the stern)
CLEATS (metal fittings on which a rope can be fastened)
PROPELLER (rotates and powers a boat forward and backward)

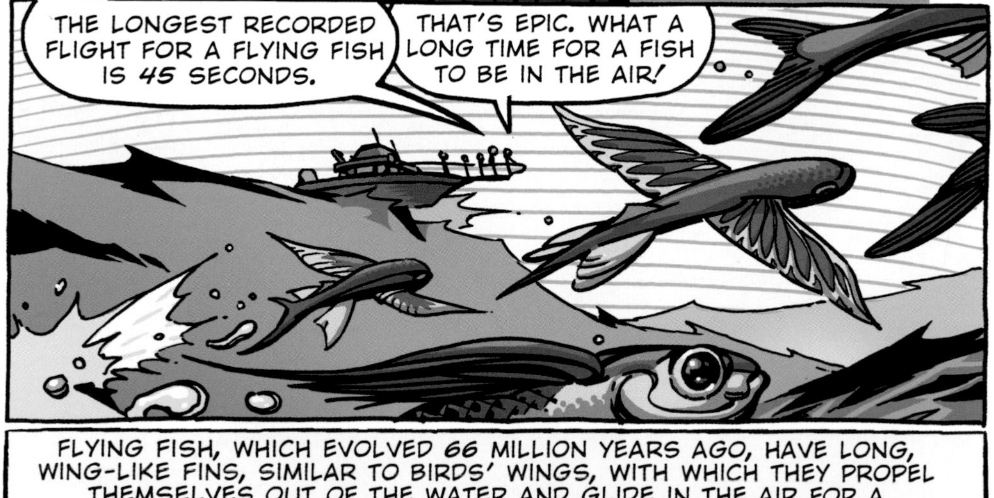
THE LONGEST RECORDED FLIGHT FOR A FLYING FISH IS 45 SECONDS.
THAT'S EPIC. WHAT A LONG TIME FOR A FISH TO BE IN THE AIR!

FLYING FISH, WHICH EVOLVED 66 MILLION YEARS AGO, HAVE LONG, WING-LIKE FINS, SIMILAR TO BIRDS' WINGS, WITH WHICH THEY PROPEL THEMSELVES OUT OF THE WATER AND GLIDE IN THE AIR FOR A CONSIDERABLE DISTANCE. THIS IS THEIR NATURAL DEFENSE TO ELUDE PREDATORS SUCH AS SHARKS.

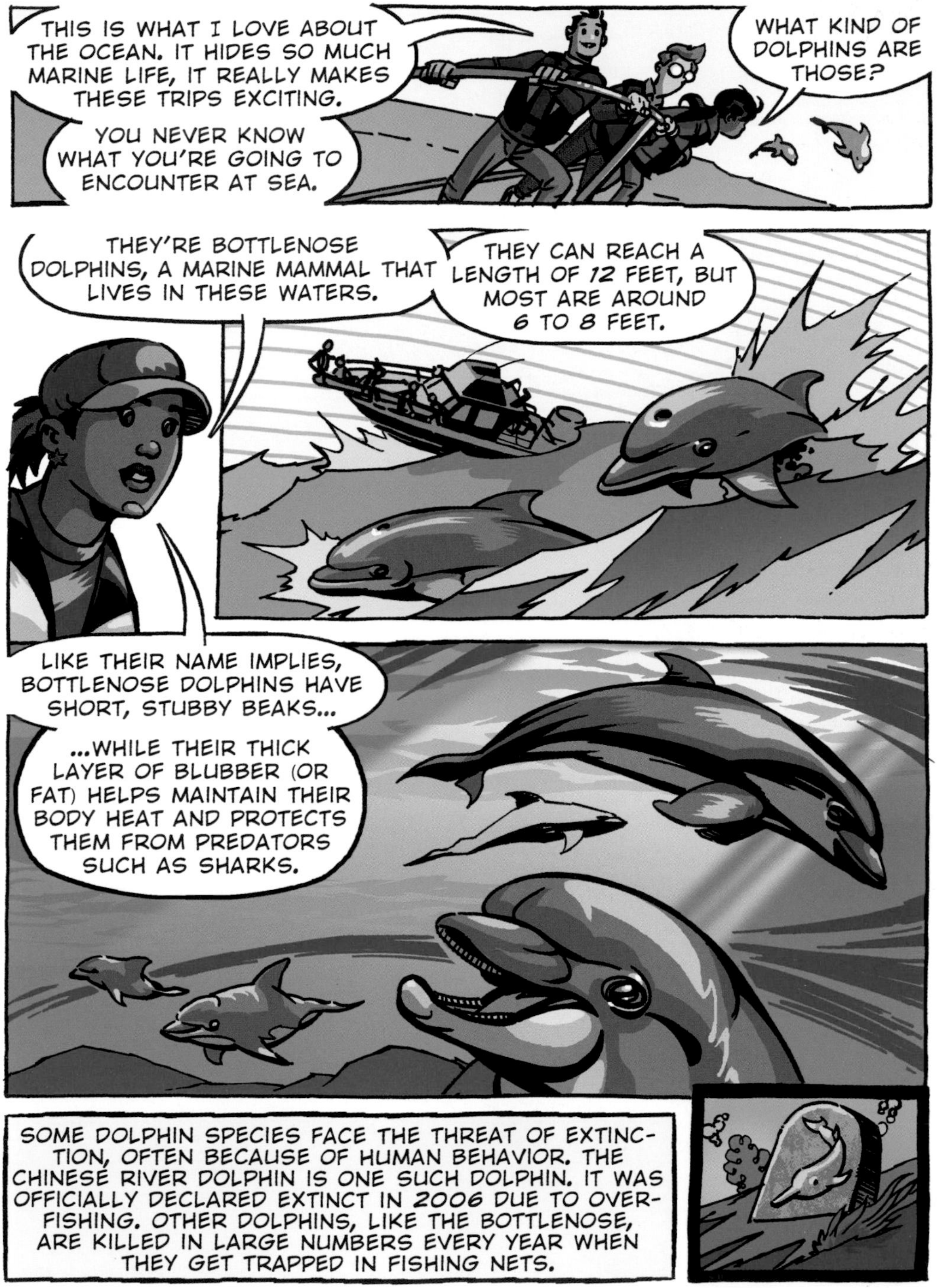
THIS IS WHAT I LOVE ABOUT THE OCEAN. IT HIDES SO MUCH MARINE LIFE, IT REALLY MAKES THESE TRIPS EXCITING.
YOU NEVER KNOW WHAT YOU'RE GOING TO ENCOUNTER AT SEA.
WHAT KIND OF DOLPHINS ARE THOSE?
THEY'RE BOTTLENOSE DOLPHINS, A MARINE MAMMAL THAT LIVES IN THESE WATERS.
THEY CAN REACH A LENGTH OF 12 FEET, BUT MOST ARE AROUND 6 TO 8 FEET.
LIKE THEIR NAME IMPLIES, BOTTLENOSE DOLPHINS HAVE SHORT, STUBBY BEAKS...
...WHILE THEIR THICK LAYER OF BLUBBER (OR FAT) HELPS MAINTAIN THEIR BODY HEAT AND PROTECTS THEM FROM PREDATORS SUCH AS SHARKS.
SOME DOLPHIN SPECIES FACE THE THREAT OF EXTINCTION, OFTEN BECAUSE OF HUMAN BEHAVIOR. THE CHINESE RIVER DOLPHIN IS ONE SUCH DOLPHIN. IT WAS OFFICIALLY DECLARED EXTINCT IN 2006 DUE TO OVERFISHING. OTHER DOLPHINS, LIKE THE BOTTLENOSE, ARE KILLED IN LARGE NUMBERS EVERY YEAR WHEN THEY GET TRAPPED IN FISHING NETS.

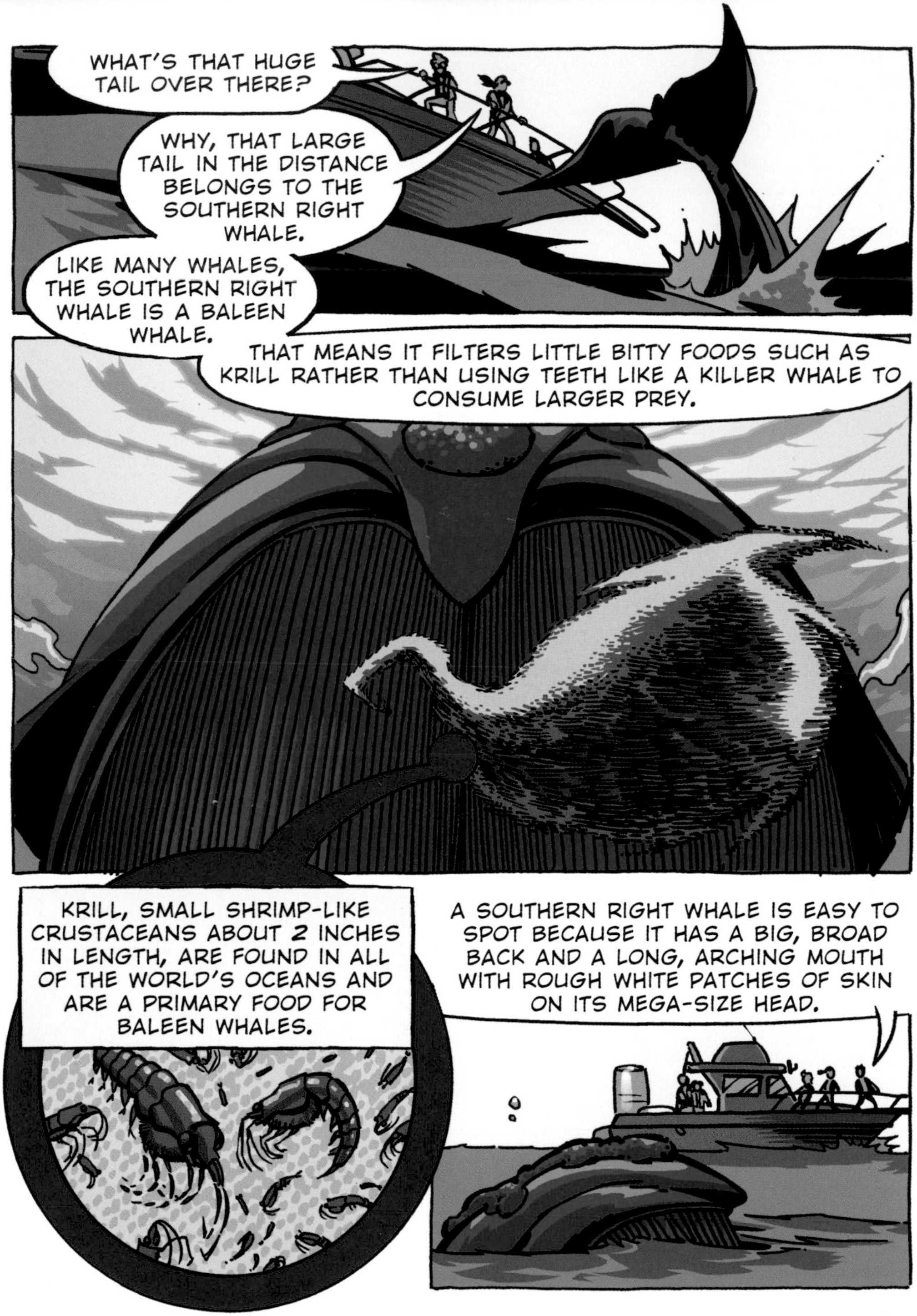

WHAT'S THAT HUGE TAIL OVER THERE?
WHY, THAT LARGE TAIL IN THE DISTANCE BELONGS TO THE SOUTHERN RIGHT WHALE.
LIKE MANY WHALES, THE SOUTHERN RIGHT WHALE IS A BALEEN WHALE.
THAT MEANS IT FILTERS LITTLE BITTY FOODS SUCH AS KRILL RATHER THAN USING TEETH LIKE A KILLER WHALE TO CONSUME LARGER PREY.
KRILL, SMALL SHRIMP-LIKE CRUSTACEANS ABOUT 2 INCHES IN LENGTH, ARE FOUND IN ALL OF THE WORLD'S OCEANS AND ARE A PRIMARY FOOD FOR BALEEN WHALES.
A SOUTHERN RIGHT WHALE IS EASY TO SPOT BECAUSE IT HAS A BIG, BROAD BACK AND A LONG, ARCHING MOUTH WITH ROUGH WHITE PATCHES OF SKIN ON ITS MEGA-SIZE HEAD.

THE SOUTHERN RIGHT WHALE GOT ITS NAME FROM AUSTRALIAN WHALERS IN THE *1800S*, WHO CLAIMED THESE WHALES WERE THE "RIGHT" WHALES TO CATCH BECAUSE OF THE LARGE AMOUNT OF WHALE OIL THAT COULD BE EXTRACTED FROM THEM AND USED TO ILLUMINATE LAMPS AND PROVIDE LUBRICATION FOR MACHINERY. WHALERS ALSO PREFERRED THE SOUTHERN RIGHT WHALE BECAUSE THEY WERE SLOW SWIMMERS, MAKING THEM AN EASY TARGET. FORTUNATELY, SOUTHERN RIGHT WHALES ARE NOW PROTECTED, WITH POPULATIONS ON THE RISE, MEANING MORE SIGHTINGS LIKE TODAY.

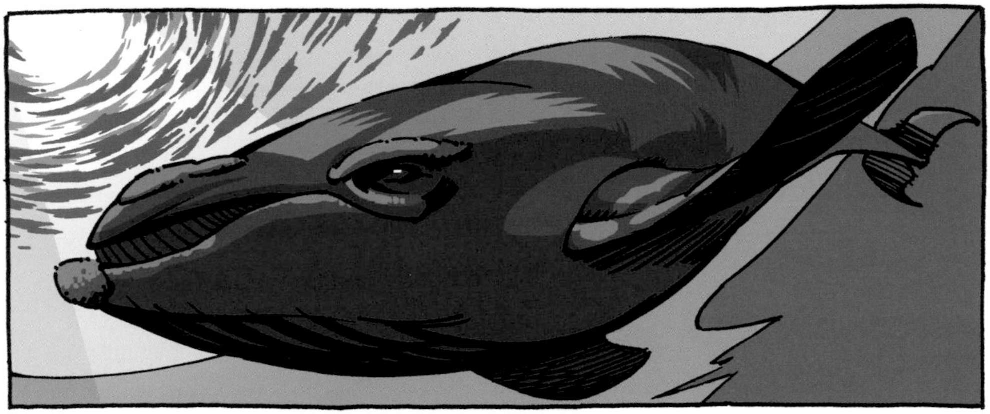

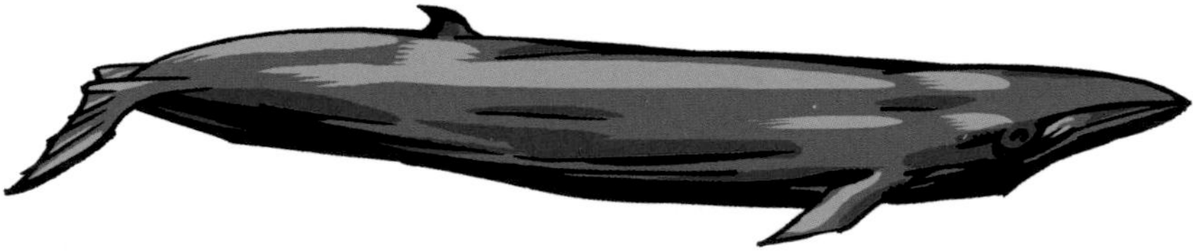

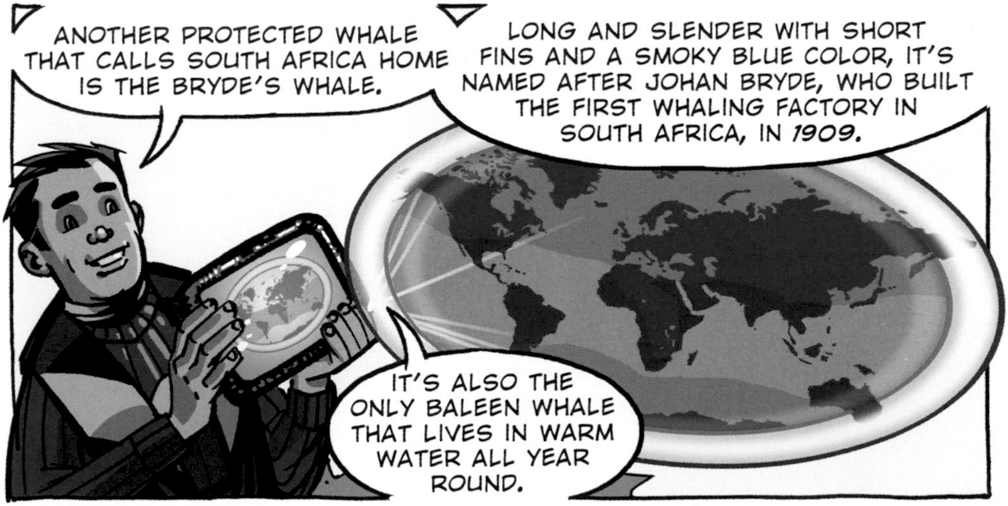
ANOTHER PROTECTED WHALE THAT CALLS SOUTH AFRICA HOME IS THE BRYDE'S WHALE.
LONG AND SLENDER WITH SHORT FINS AND A SMOKY BLUE COLOR, IT'S NAMED AFTER JOHAN BRYDE, WHO BUILT THE FIRST WHALING FACTORY IN SOUTH AFRICA, IN 1909.
IT'S ALSO THE ONLY BALEEN WHALE THAT LIVES IN WARM WATER ALL YEAR ROUND.

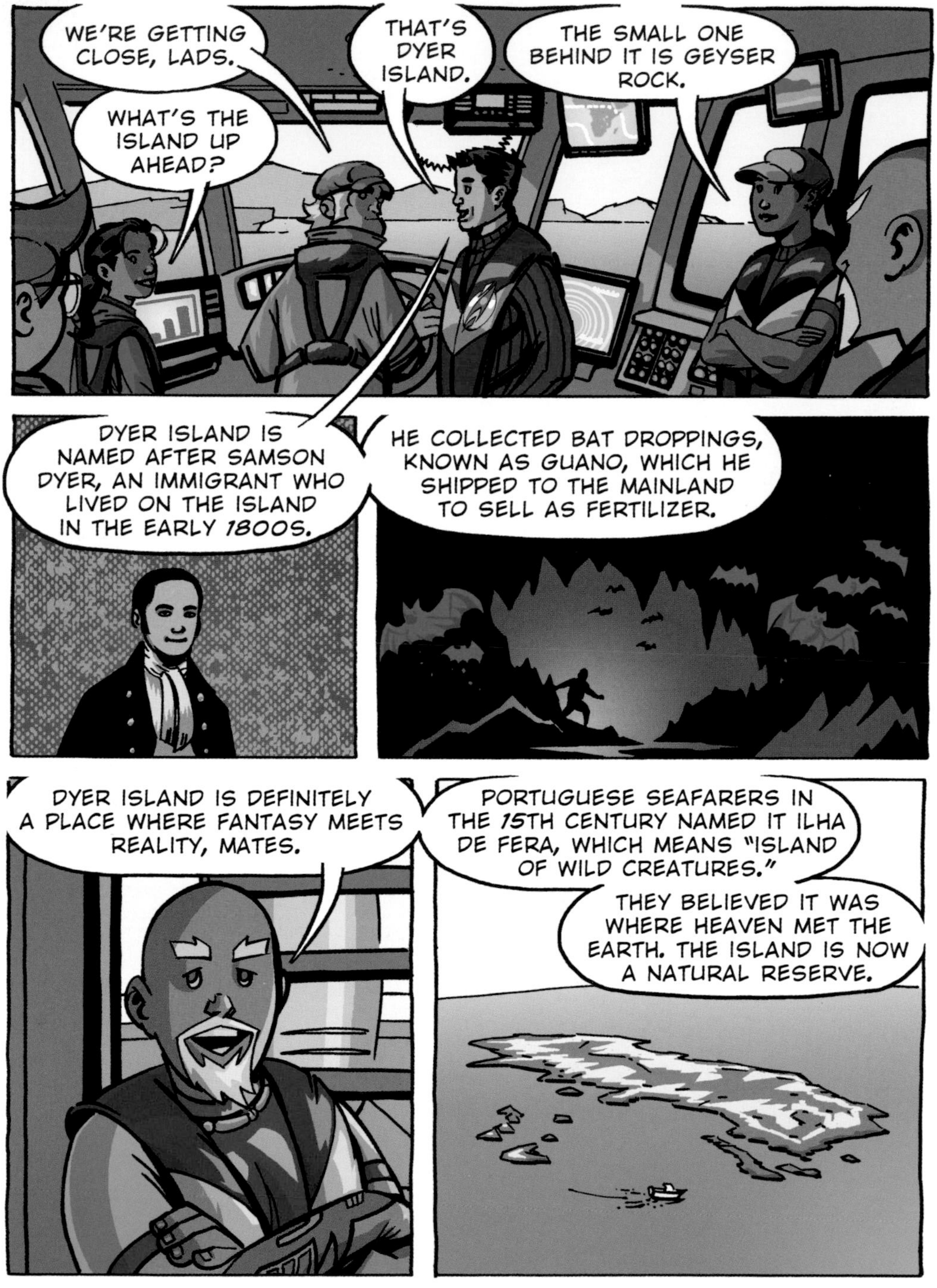
WE'RE GETTING CLOSE, LADS.
WHAT'S THE ISLAND UP AHEAD?
THAT'S DYER ISLAND.
THE SMALL ONE BEHIND IT IS GEYSER ROCK.
DYER ISLAND IS NAMED AFTER SAMSON DYER, AN IMMIGRANT WHO LIVED ON THE ISLAND IN THE EARLY 1800S.
HE COLLECTED BAT DROPPINGS, KNOWN AS GUANO, WHICH HE SHIPPED TO THE MAINLAND TO SELL AS FERTILIZER.
DYER ISLAND IS DEFINITELY A PLACE WHERE FANTASY MEETS REALITY, MATES.
PORTUGUESE SEAFARERS IN THE 15TH CENTURY NAMED IT ILHA DE FERA, WHICH MEANS "ISLAND OF WILD CREATURES."
THEY BELIEVED IT WAS WHERE HEAVEN MET THE EARTH. THE ISLAND IS NOW A NATURAL RESERVE.

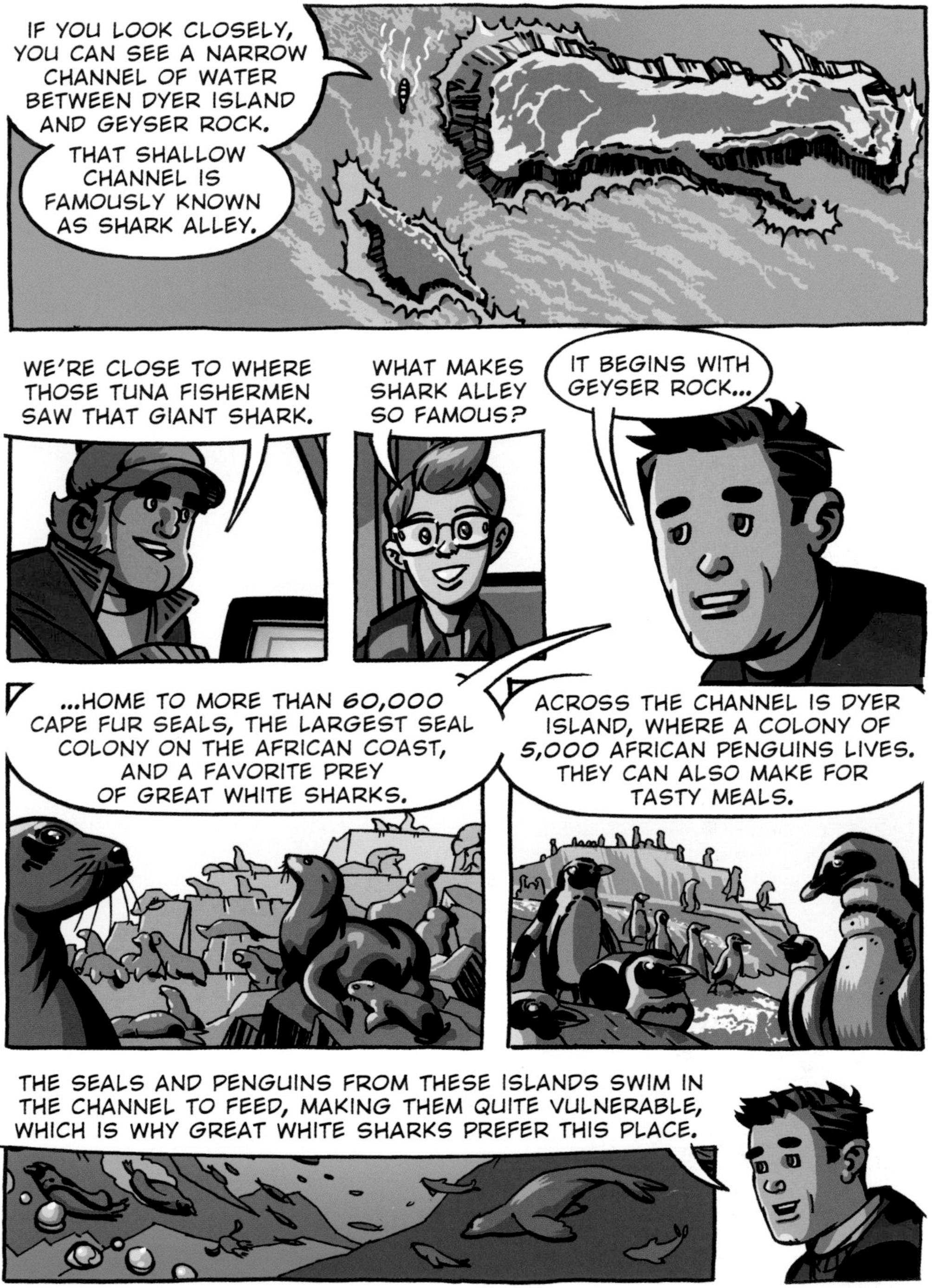
IF YOU LOOK CLOSELY, YOU CAN SEE A NARROW CHANNEL OF WATER BETWEEN DYER ISLAND AND GEYSER ROCK.
THAT SHALLOW CHANNEL IS FAMOUSLY KNOWN AS SHARK ALLEY.
WE'RE CLOSE TO WHERE THOSE TUNA FISHERMEN SAW THAT GIANT SHARK.
WHAT MAKES SHARK ALLEY SO FAMOUS?
IT BEGINS WITH GEYSER ROCK...
...HOME TO MORE THAN 60,000 CAPE FUR SEALS, THE LARGEST SEAL COLONY ON THE AFRICAN COAST, AND A FAVORITE PREY OF GREAT WHITE SHARKS.
ACROSS THE CHANNEL IS DYER ISLAND, WHERE A COLONY OF 5,000 AFRICAN PENGUINS LIVES. THEY CAN ALSO MAKE FOR TASTY MEALS.
THE SEALS AND PENGUINS FROM THESE ISLANDS SWIM IN THE CHANNEL TO FEED, MAKING THEM QUITE VULNERABLE, WHICH IS WHY GREAT WHITE SHARKS PREFER THIS PLACE.

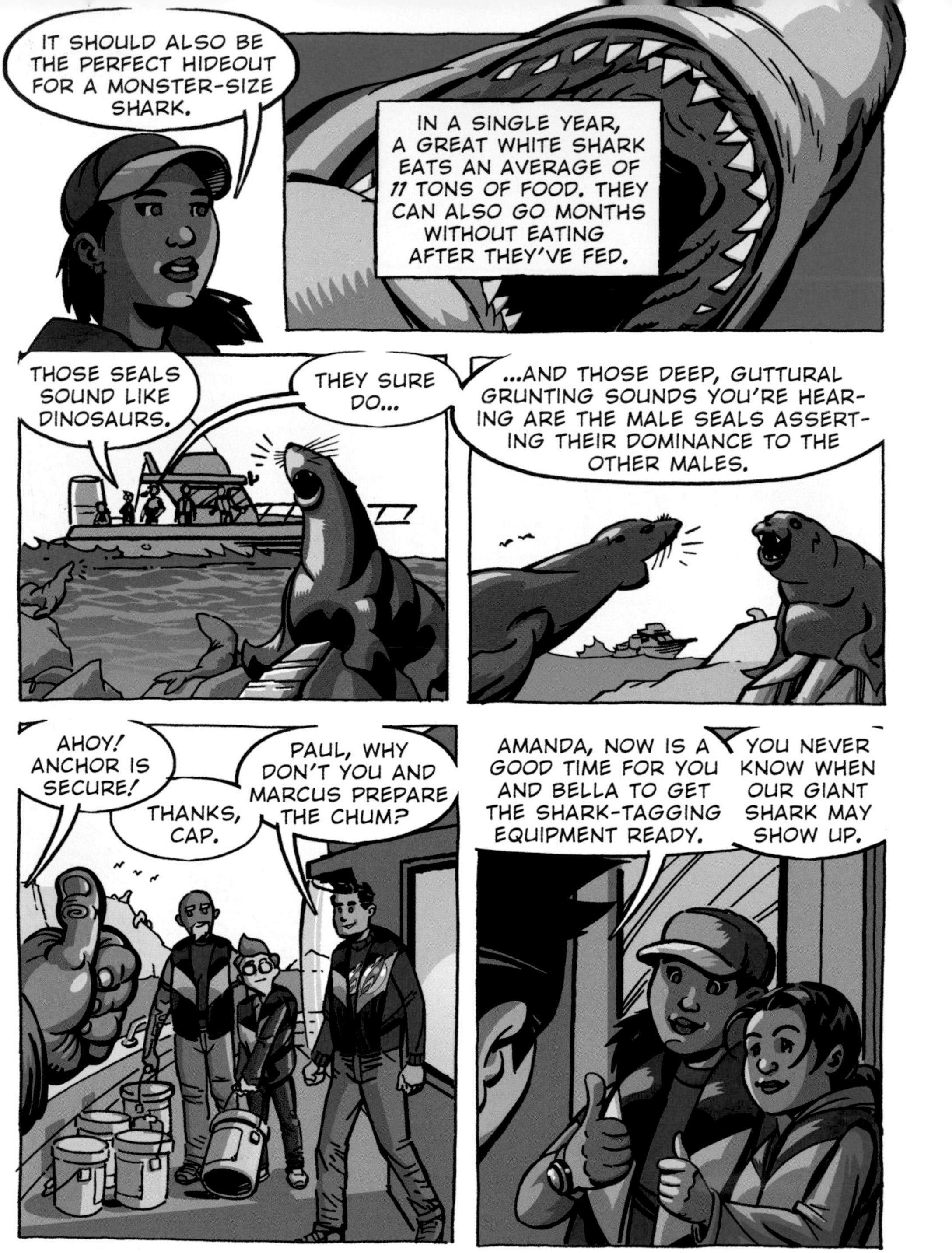
IT SHOULD ALSO BE THE PERFECT HIDEOUT FOR A MONSTER-SIZE SHARK.
IN A SINGLE YEAR, A GREAT WHITE SHARK EATS AN AVERAGE OF 11 TONS OF FOOD. THEY CAN ALSO GO MONTHS WITHOUT EATING AFTER THEY'VE FED.
THOSE SEALS SOUND LIKE DINOSAURS.
THEY SURE DO...
...AND THOSE DEEP, GUTTURAL GRUNTING SOUNDS YOU'RE HEARING ARE THE MALE SEALS ASSERTING THEIR DOMINANCE TO THE OTHER MALES.
AHOY! ANCHOR IS SECURE!
THANKS, CAP.
PAUL, WHY DON'T YOU AND MARCUS PREPARE THE CHUM?
AMANDA, NOW IS A GOOD TIME FOR YOU AND BELLA TO GET THE SHARK-TAGGING EQUIPMENT READY.
YOU NEVER KNOW WHEN OUR GIANT SHARK MAY SHOW UP.

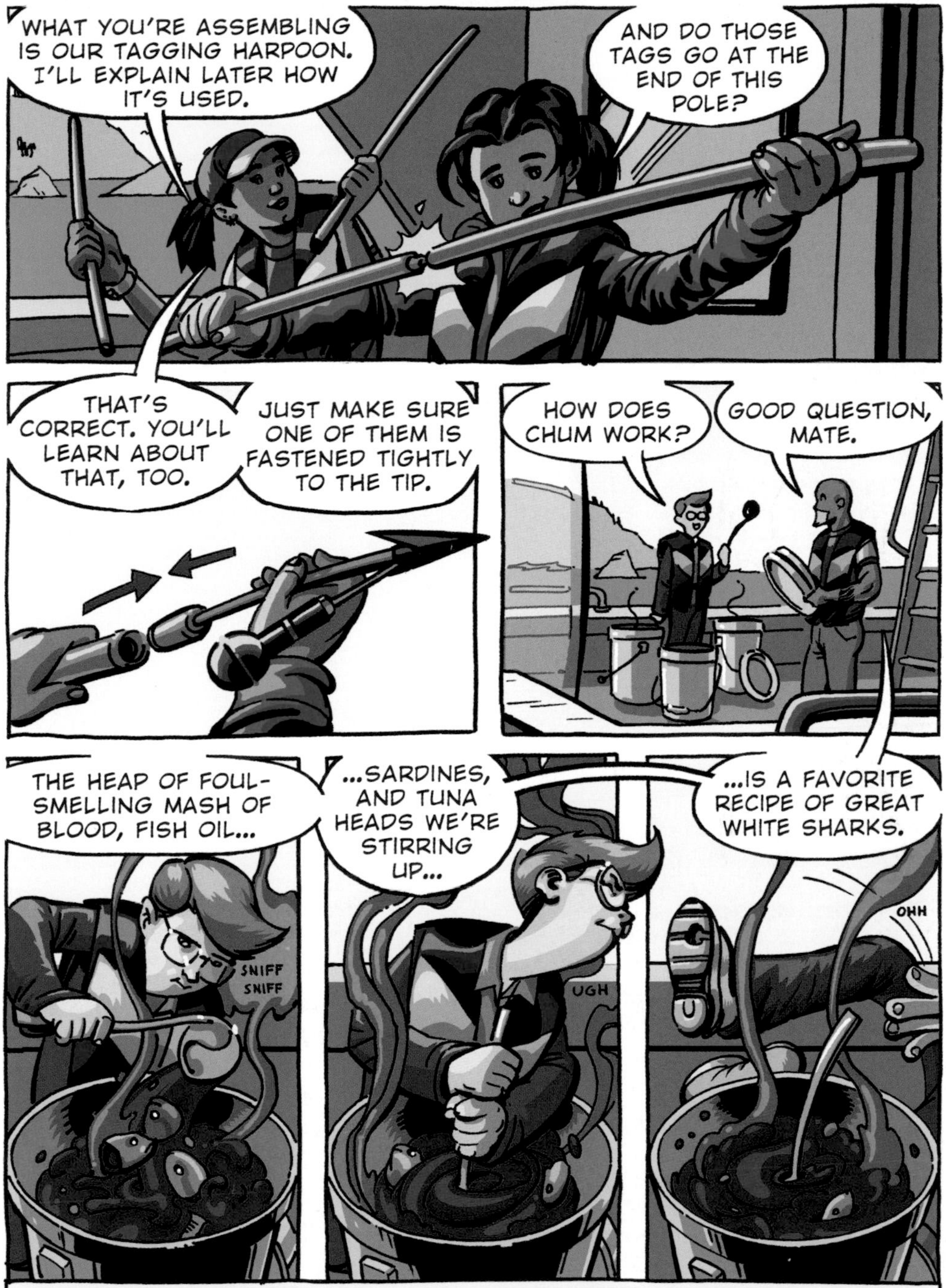
WHAT YOU'RE ASSEMBLING IS OUR TAGGING HARPOON. I'LL EXPLAIN LATER HOW IT'S USED.
AND DO THOSE TAGS GO AT THE END OF THIS POLE?
THAT'S CORRECT. YOU'LL LEARN ABOUT THAT, TOO.
JUST MAKE SURE ONE OF THEM IS FASTENED TIGHTLY TO THE TIP.
HOW DOES CHUM WORK?
GOOD QUESTION, MATE.
THE HEAP OF FOUL-SMELLING MASH OF BLOOD, FISH OIL...
SNIFF SNIFF
...SARDINES, AND TUNA HEADS WE'RE STIRRING UP...
UGH
...IS A FAVORITE RECIPE OF GREAT WHITE SHARKS.
OHH
CHUM IS A SOUP-LIKE CONCOCTION, OFTEN USED TO ATTRACT SHARKS.

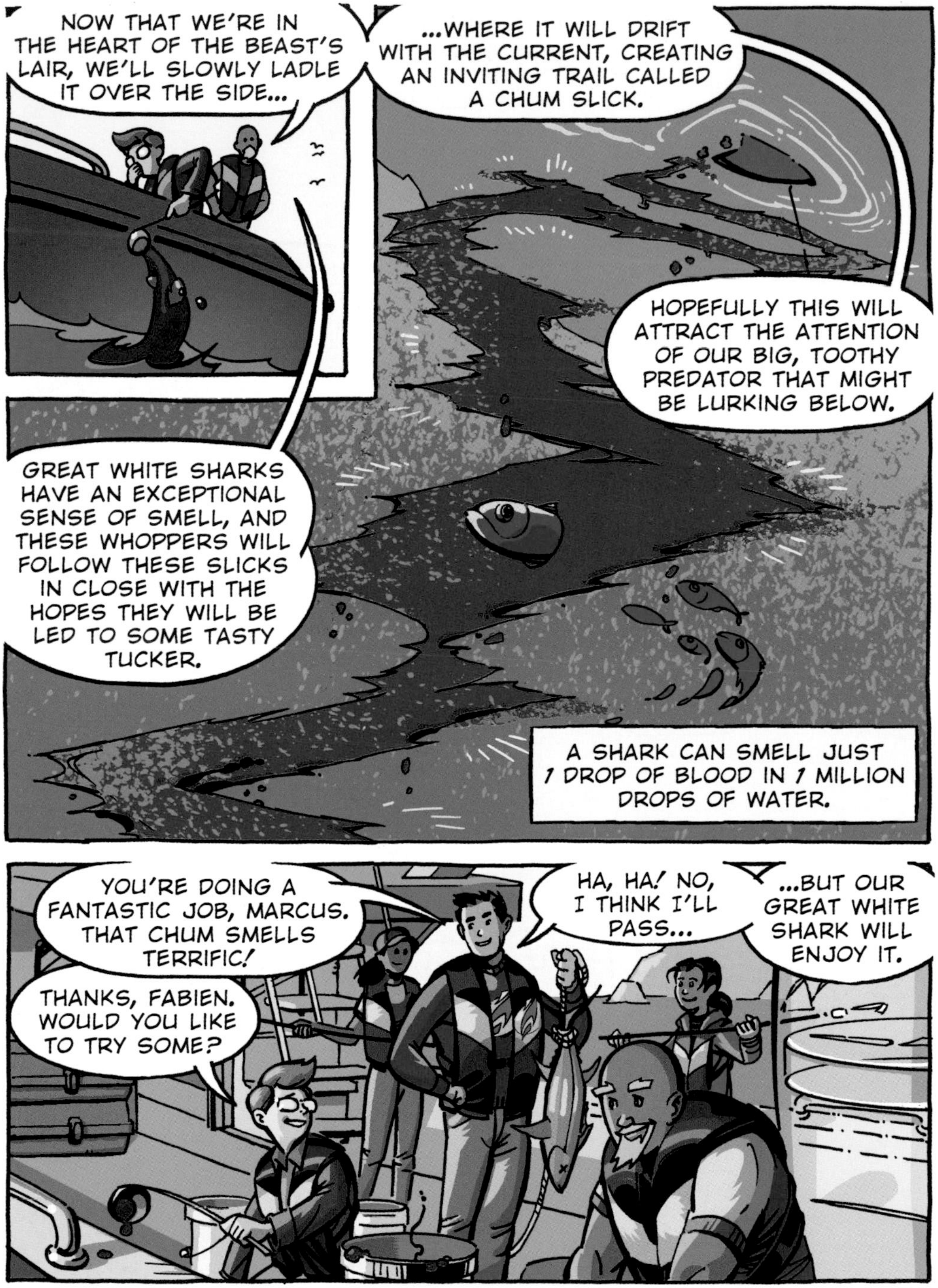
NOW THAT WE'RE IN THE HEART OF THE BEAST'S LAIR, WE'LL SLOWLY LADLE IT OVER THE SIDE...
...WHERE IT WILL DRIFT WITH THE CURRENT, CREATING AN INVITING TRAIL CALLED A CHUM SLICK.
HOPEFULLY THIS WILL ATTRACT THE ATTENTION OF OUR BIG, TOOTHY PREDATOR THAT MIGHT BE LURKING BELOW.
GREAT WHITE SHARKS HAVE AN EXCEPTIONAL SENSE OF SMELL, AND THESE WHOPPERS WILL FOLLOW THESE SLICKS IN CLOSE WITH THE HOPES THEY WILL BE LED TO SOME TASTY TUCKER.
A SHARK CAN SMELL JUST 1 DROP OF BLOOD IN 1 MILLION DROPS OF WATER.
YOU'RE DOING A FANTASTIC JOB, MARCUS. THAT CHUM SMELLS TERRIFIC!
THANKS, FABIEN. WOULD YOU LIKE TO TRY SOME?
HA, HA! NO, I THINK I'LL PASS...
...BUT OUR GREAT WHITE SHARK WILL ENJOY IT.

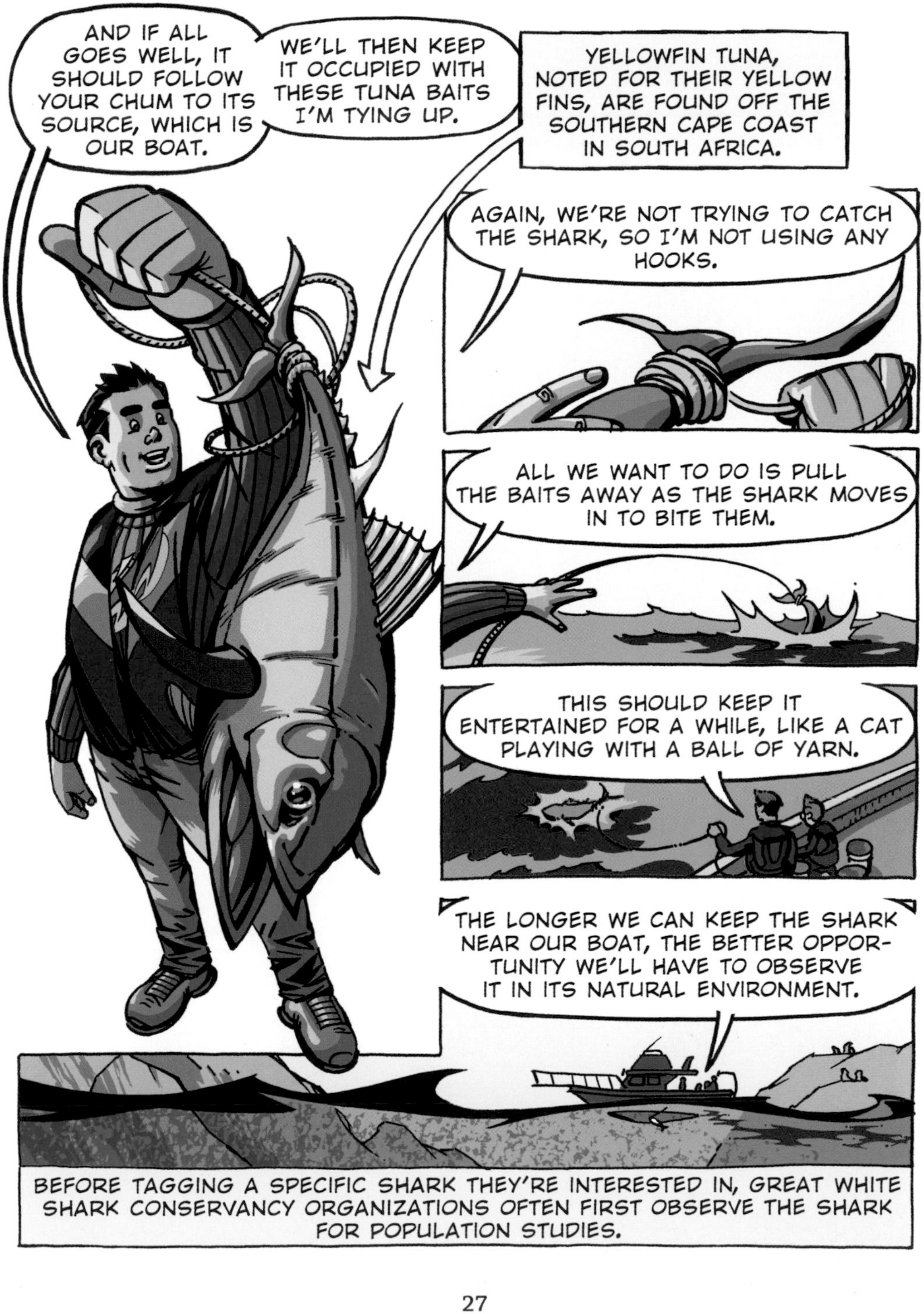
AND IF ALL GOES WELL, IT SHOULD FOLLOW YOUR CHUM TO ITS SOURCE, WHICH IS OUR BOAT.
WE'LL THEN KEEP IT OCCUPIED WITH THESE TUNA BAITS I'M TYING UP.
YELLOWFIN TUNA, NOTED FOR THEIR YELLOW FINS, ARE FOUND OFF THE SOUTHERN CAPE COAST IN SOUTH AFRICA.
AGAIN, WE'RE NOT TRYING TO CATCH THE SHARK, SO I'M NOT USING ANY HOOKS.
ALL WE WANT TO DO IS PULL THE BAITS AWAY AS THE SHARK MOVES IN TO BITE THEM.
THIS SHOULD KEEP IT ENTERTAINED FOR A WHILE, LIKE A CAT PLAYING WITH A BALL OF YARN.
THE LONGER WE CAN KEEP THE SHARK NEAR OUR BOAT, THE BETTER OPPORTUNITY WE'LL HAVE TO OBSERVE IT IN ITS NATURAL ENVIRONMENT.
BEFORE TAGGING A SPECIFIC SHARK THEY'RE INTERESTED IN, GREAT WHITE SHARK CONSERVANCY ORGANIZATIONS OFTEN FIRST OBSERVE THE SHARK FOR POPULATION STUDIES.

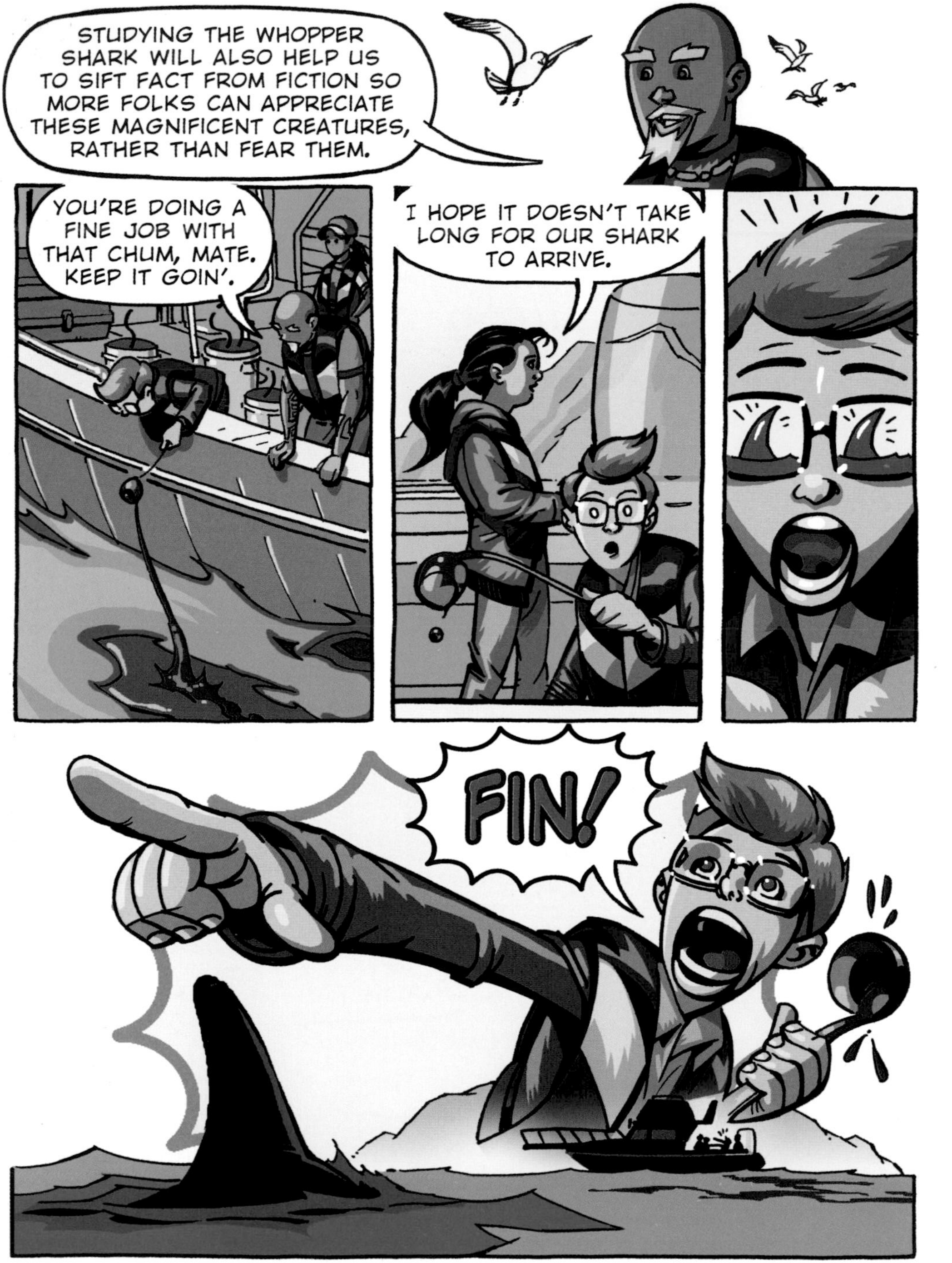
STUDYING THE WHOPPER SHARK WILL ALSO HELP US TO SIFT FACT FROM FICTION SO MORE FOLKS CAN APPRECIATE THESE MAGNIFICENT CREATURES, RATHER THAN FEAR THEM.
YOU'RE DOING A FINE JOB WITH THAT CHUM, MATE. KEEP IT GOIN'.
I HOPE IT DOESN'T TAKE LONG FOR OUR SHARK TO ARRIVE.
FIN!

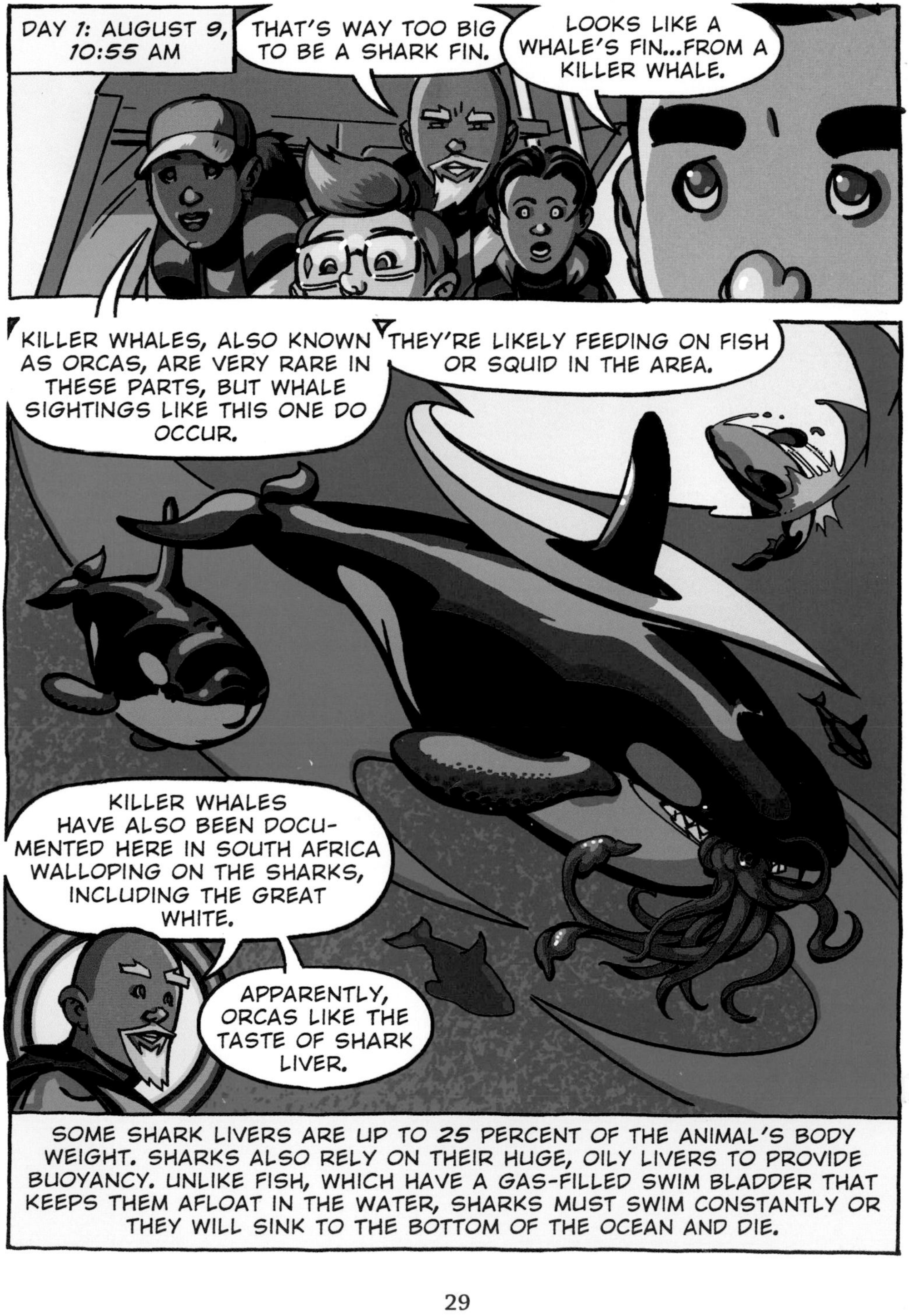
DAY 1: AUGUST 9, 10:55 AM
THAT'S WAY TOO BIG TO BE A SHARK FIN.
LOOKS LIKE A WHALE'S FIN...FROM A KILLER WHALE.
KILLER WHALES, ALSO KNOWN AS ORCAS, ARE VERY RARE IN THESE PARTS, BUT WHALE SIGHTINGS LIKE THIS ONE DO OCCUR.
THEY'RE LIKELY FEEDING ON FISH OR SQUID IN THE AREA.
KILLER WHALES HAVE ALSO BEEN DOCUMENTED HERE IN SOUTH AFRICA WALLOPING ON THE SHARKS, INCLUDING THE GREAT WHITE.
APPARENTLY, ORCAS LIKE THE TASTE OF SHARK LIVER.

SOME SHARK LIVERS ARE UP TO 25 PERCENT OF THE ANIMAL'S BODY WEIGHT. SHARKS ALSO RELY ON THEIR HUGE, OILY LIVERS TO PROVIDE BUOYANCY. UNLIKE FISH, WHICH HAVE A GAS-FILLED SWIM BLADDER THAT KEEPS THEM AFLOAT IN THE WATER, SHARKS MUST SWIM CONSTANTLY OR THEY WILL SINK TO THE BOTTOM OF THE OCEAN AND DIE.

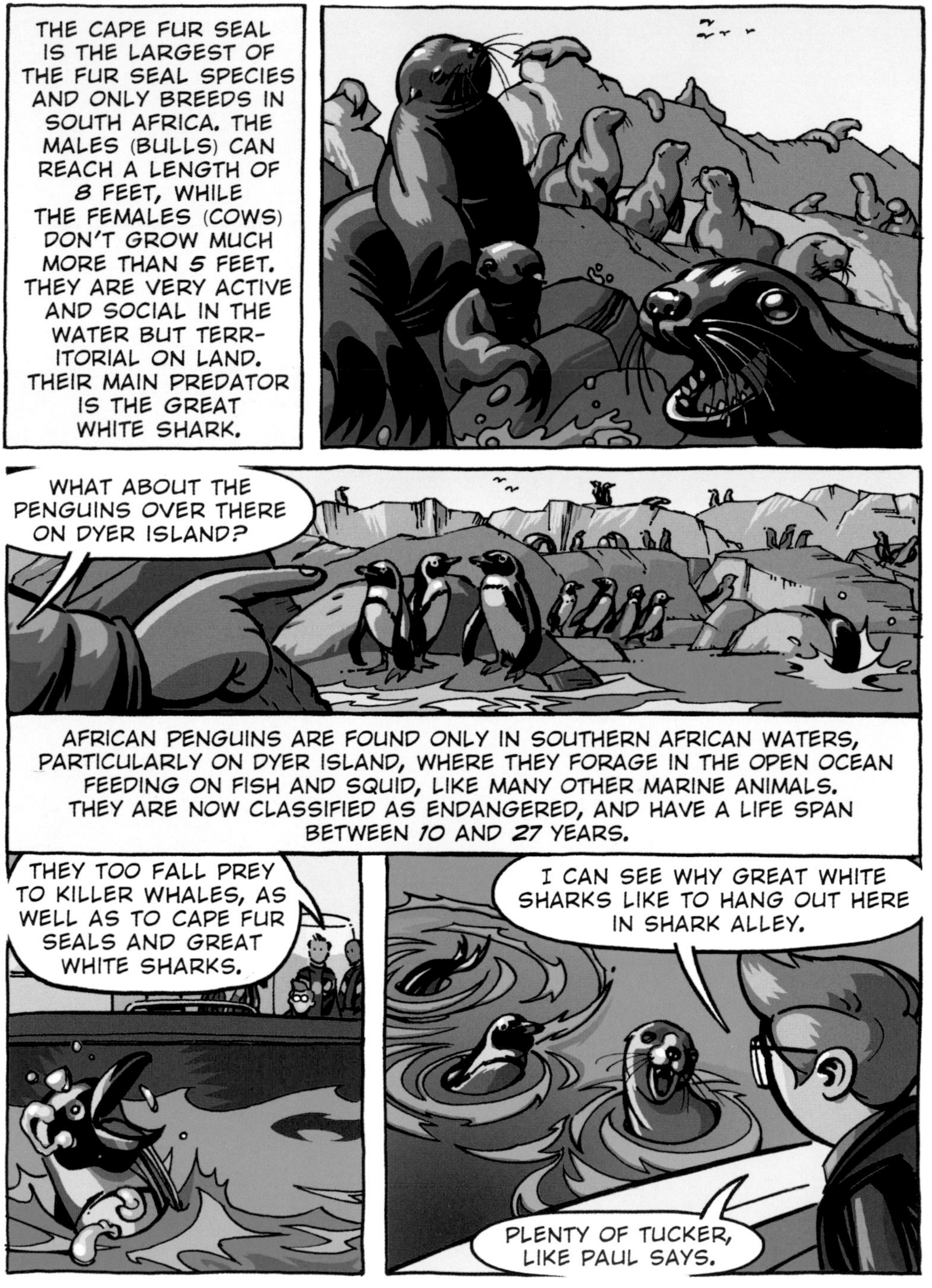
THE CAPE FUR SEAL IS THE LARGEST OF THE FUR SEAL SPECIES AND ONLY BREEDS IN SOUTH AFRICA. THE MALES (BULLS) CAN REACH A LENGTH OF 8 FEET, WHILE THE FEMALES (COWS) DON'T GROW MUCH MORE THAN 5 FEET. THEY ARE VERY ACTIVE AND SOCIAL IN THE WATER BUT TERRITORIAL ON LAND. THEIR MAIN PREDATOR IS THE GREAT WHITE SHARK.
WHAT ABOUT THE PENGUINS OVER THERE ON DYER ISLAND?
AFRICAN PENGUINS ARE FOUND ONLY IN SOUTHERN AFRICAN WATERS, PARTICULARLY ON DYER ISLAND, WHERE THEY FORAGE IN THE OPEN OCEAN FEEDING ON FISH AND SQUID, LIKE MANY OTHER MARINE ANIMALS. THEY ARE NOW CLASSIFIED AS ENDANGERED, AND HAVE A LIFE SPAN BETWEEN 10 AND 27 YEARS.
THEY TOO FALL PREY TO KILLER WHALES, AS WELL AS TO CAPE FUR SEALS AND GREAT WHITE SHARKS.
I CAN SEE WHY GREAT WHITE SHARKS LIKE TO HANG OUT HERE IN SHARK ALLEY.
PLENTY OF TUCKER, LIKE PAUL SAYS.

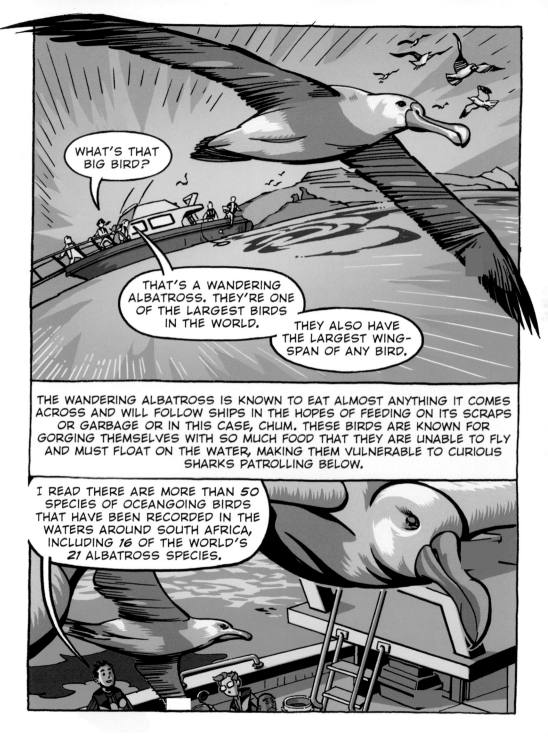

WHAT'S THAT BIG BIRD?

THAT'S A WANDERING ALBATROSS. THEY'RE ONE OF THE LARGEST BIRDS IN THE WORLD.

THEY ALSO HAVE THE LARGEST WING-SPAN OF ANY BIRD.

THE WANDERING ALBATROSS IS KNOWN TO EAT ALMOST ANYTHING IT COMES ACROSS AND WILL FOLLOW SHIPS IN THE HOPES OF FEEDING ON ITS SCRAPS OR GARBAGE OR IN THIS CASE, CHUM. THESE BIRDS ARE KNOWN FOR GORGING THEMSELVES WITH SO MUCH FOOD THAT THEY ARE UNABLE TO FLY AND MUST FLOAT ON THE WATER, MAKING THEM VULNERABLE TO CURIOUS SHARKS PATROLLING BELOW.

I READ THERE ARE MORE THAN 50 SPECIES OF OCEANGOING BIRDS THAT HAVE BEEN RECORDED IN THE WATERS AROUND SOUTH AFRICA, INCLUDING 16 OF THE WORLD'S 21 ALBATROSS SPECIES.

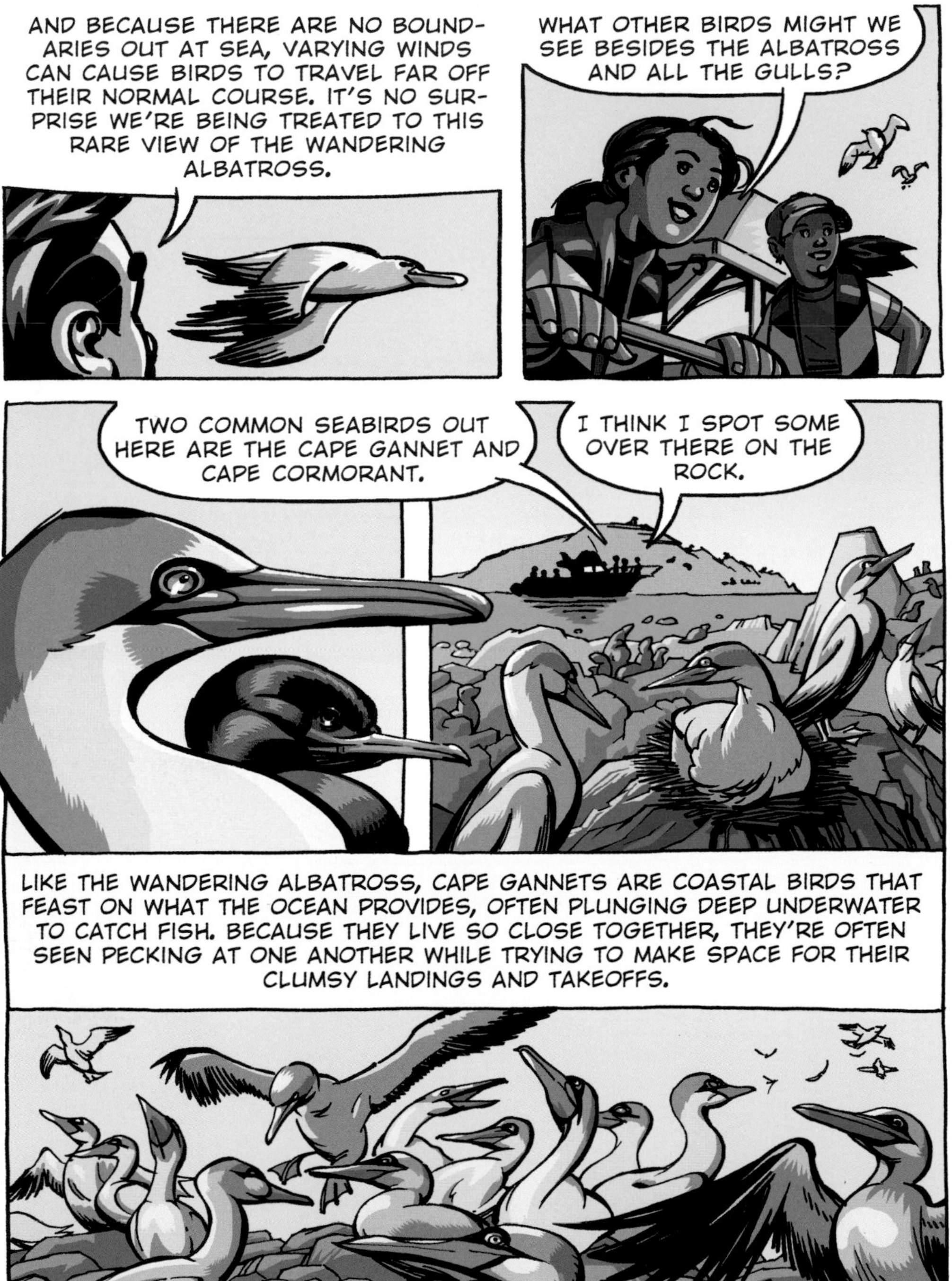
AND BECAUSE THERE ARE NO BOUNDARIES OUT AT SEA, VARYING WINDS CAN CAUSE BIRDS TO TRAVEL FAR OFF THEIR NORMAL COURSE. IT'S NO SURPRISE WE'RE BEING TREATED TO THIS RARE VIEW OF THE WANDERING ALBATROSS.
WHAT OTHER BIRDS MIGHT WE SEE BESIDES THE ALBATROSS AND ALL THE GULLS?
TWO COMMON SEABIRDS OUT HERE ARE THE CAPE GANNET AND CAPE CORMORANT.
I THINK I SPOT SOME OVER THERE ON THE ROCK.
LIKE THE WANDERING ALBATROSS, CAPE GANNETS ARE COASTAL BIRDS THAT FEAST ON WHAT THE OCEAN PROVIDES, OFTEN PLUNGING DEEP UNDERWATER TO CATCH FISH. BECAUSE THEY LIVE SO CLOSE TOGETHER, THEY'RE OFTEN SEEN PECKING AT ONE ANOTHER WHILE TRYING TO MAKE SPACE FOR THEIR CLUMSY LANDINGS AND TAKEOFFS.

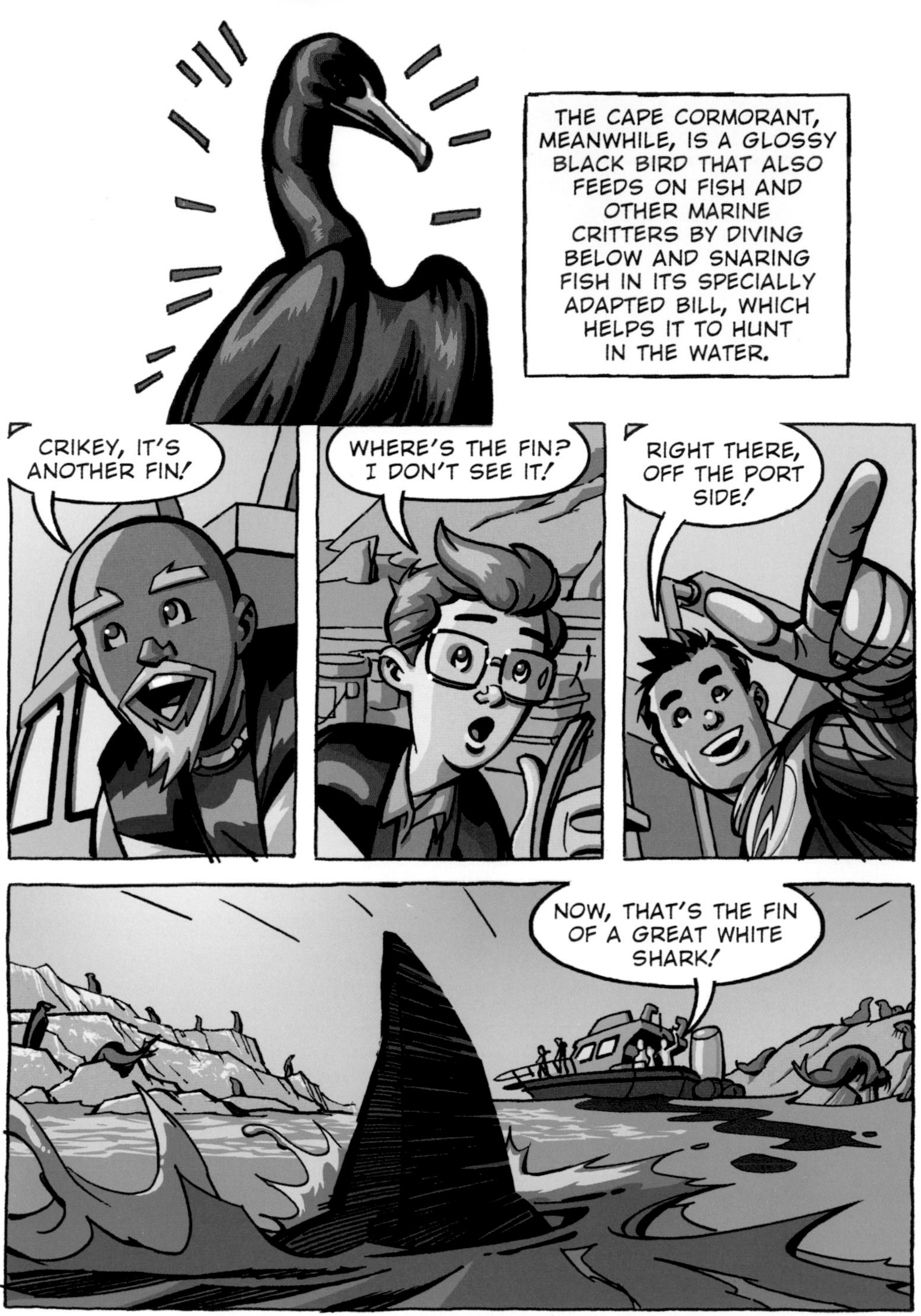
THE CAPE CORMORANT, MEANWHILE, IS A GLOSSY BLACK BIRD THAT ALSO FEEDS ON FISH AND OTHER MARINE CRITTERS BY DIVING BELOW AND SNARING FISH IN ITS SPECIALLY ADAPTED BILL, WHICH HELPS IT TO HUNT IN THE WATER.
CRIKEY, IT'S ANOTHER FIN!
WHERE'S THE FIN? I DON'T SEE IT!
RIGHT THERE, OFF THE PORT SIDE!
NOW, THAT'S THE FIN OF A GREAT WHITE SHARK!

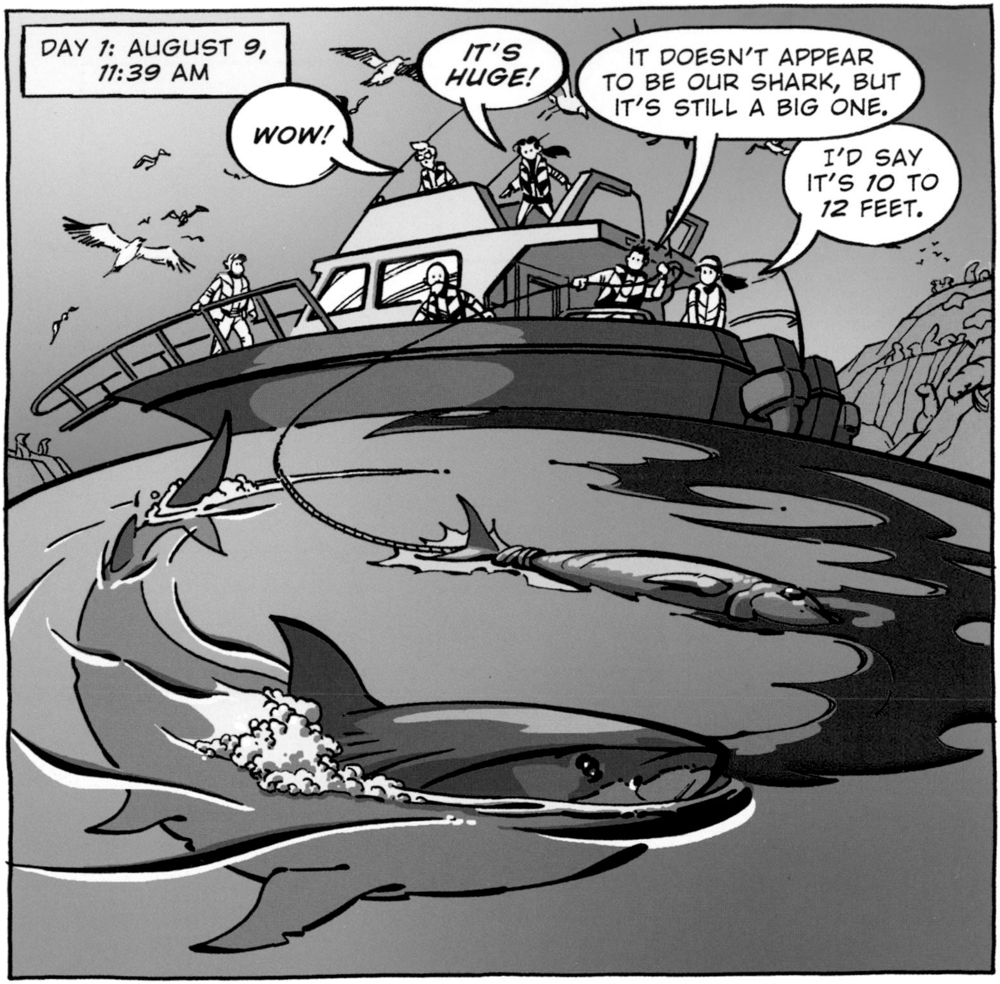
DAY 1: AUGUST 9, 11:39 AM
WOW!
IT'S HUGE!
IT DOESN'T APPEAR TO BE OUR SHARK, BUT IT'S STILL A BIG ONE.
I'D SAY IT'S 10 TO 12 FEET.

THERE ARE NO GREAT WHITE SHARKS THAT LIVE AROUND DYER ISLAND AND GEYSER ROCK YEAR ROUND. THE SHARKS THAT COME HERE FOR A FEW WEEKS TO A MAXIMUM OF SEVERAL MONTHS ARE TRANSIENT SHARKS, MEANING THEY MIGRATE TO DIFFERENT PLACES THROUGHOUT THE YEAR.

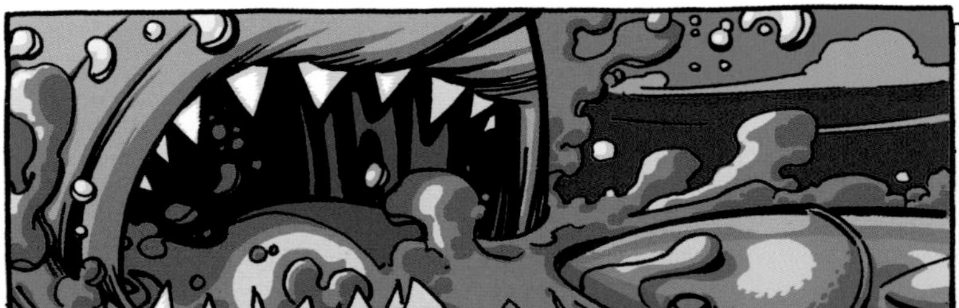

THE SCIENTIFIC NAME OF THE GREAT WHITE SHARK IS *CARCHARODON CARCHARIAS*, WHICH MEANS "RAGGED TOOTH."

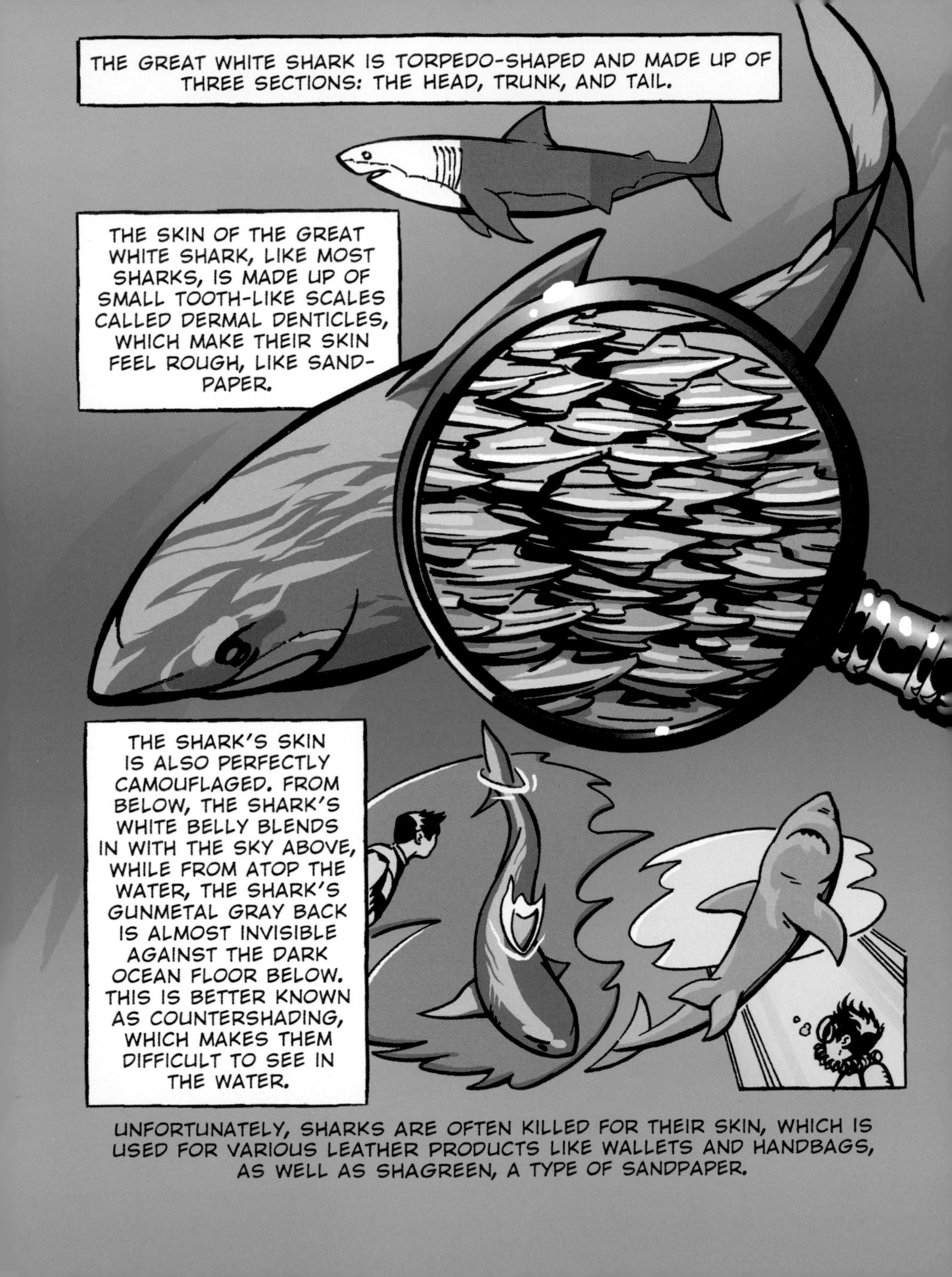
THE GREAT WHITE SHARK IS TORPEDO-SHAPED AND MADE UP OF THREE SECTIONS: THE HEAD, TRUNK, AND TAIL.
THE SKIN OF THE GREAT WHITE SHARK, LIKE MOST SHARKS, IS MADE UP OF SMALL TOOTH-LIKE SCALES CALLED DERMAL DENTICLES, WHICH MAKE THEIR SKIN FEEL ROUGH, LIKE SAND-PAPER.
THE SHARK'S SKIN IS ALSO PERFECTLY CAMOUFLAGED. FROM BELOW, THE SHARK'S WHITE BELLY BLENDS IN WITH THE SKY ABOVE, WHILE FROM ATOP THE WATER, THE SHARK'S GUNMETAL GRAY BACK IS ALMOST INVISIBLE AGAINST THE DARK OCEAN FLOOR BELOW. THIS IS BETTER KNOWN AS COUNTERSHADING, WHICH MAKES THEM DIFFICULT TO SEE IN THE WATER.
UNFORTUNATELY, SHARKS ARE OFTEN KILLED FOR THEIR SKIN, WHICH IS USED FOR VARIOUS LEATHER PRODUCTS LIKE WALLETS AND HANDBAGS, AS WELL AS SHAGREEN, A TYPE OF SANDPAPER.

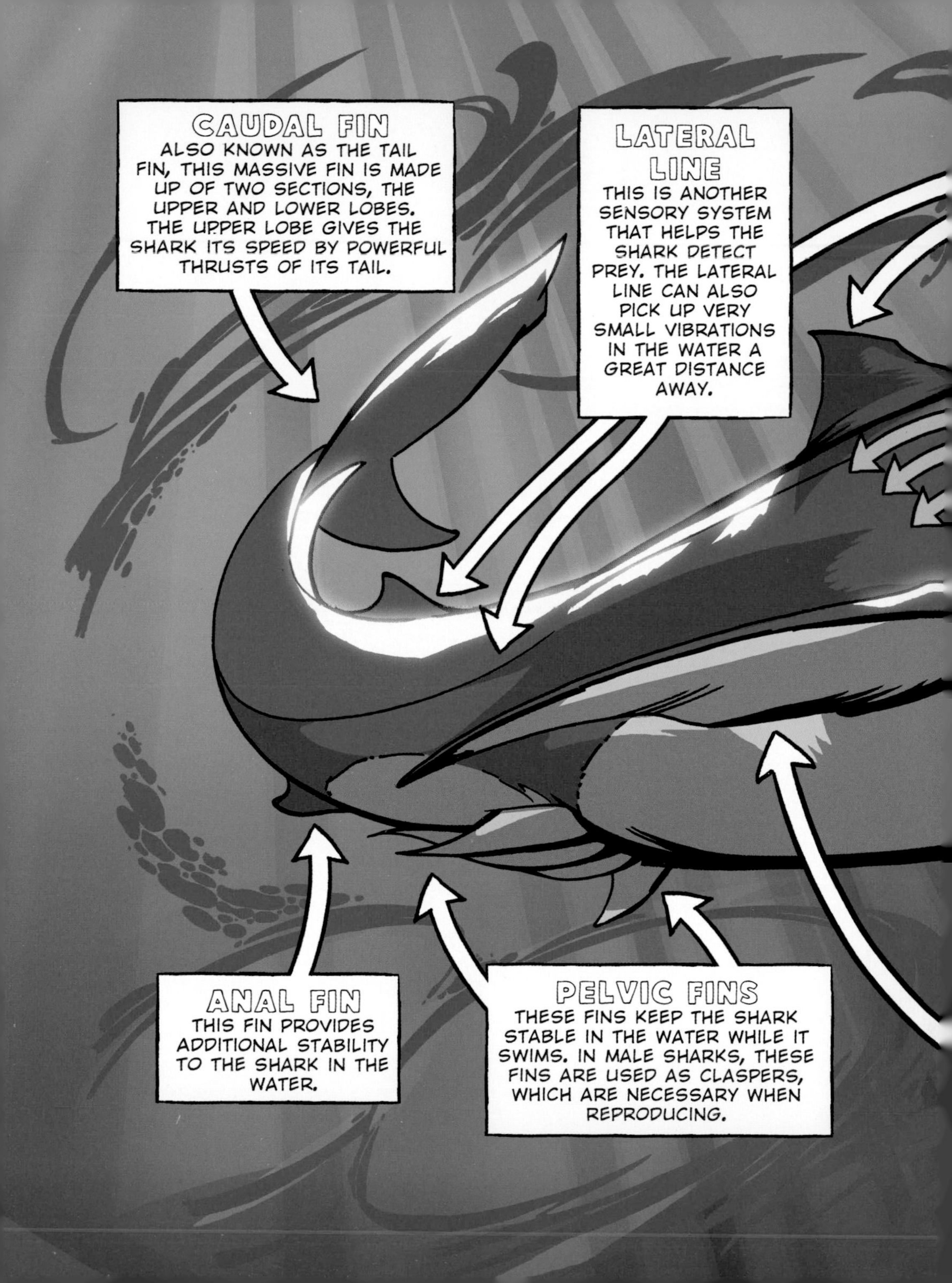
CAUDAL FIN
ALSO KNOWN AS THE TAIL FIN, THIS MASSIVE FIN IS MADE UP OF TWO SECTIONS, THE UPPER AND LOWER LOBES. THE UPPER LOBE GIVES THE SHARK ITS SPEED BY POWERFUL THRUSTS OF ITS TAIL.
LATERAL LINE
THIS IS ANOTHER SENSORY SYSTEM THAT HELPS THE SHARK DETECT PREY. THE LATERAL LINE CAN ALSO PICK UP VERY SMALL VIBRATIONS IN THE WATER A GREAT DISTANCE AWAY.
ANAL FIN
THIS FIN PROVIDES ADDITIONAL STABILITY TO THE SHARK IN THE WATER.
PELVIC FINS
THESE FINS KEEP THE SHARK STABLE IN THE WATER WHILE IT SWIMS. IN MALE SHARKS, THESE FINS ARE USED AS CLASPERS, WHICH ARE NECESSARY WHEN REPRODUCING.

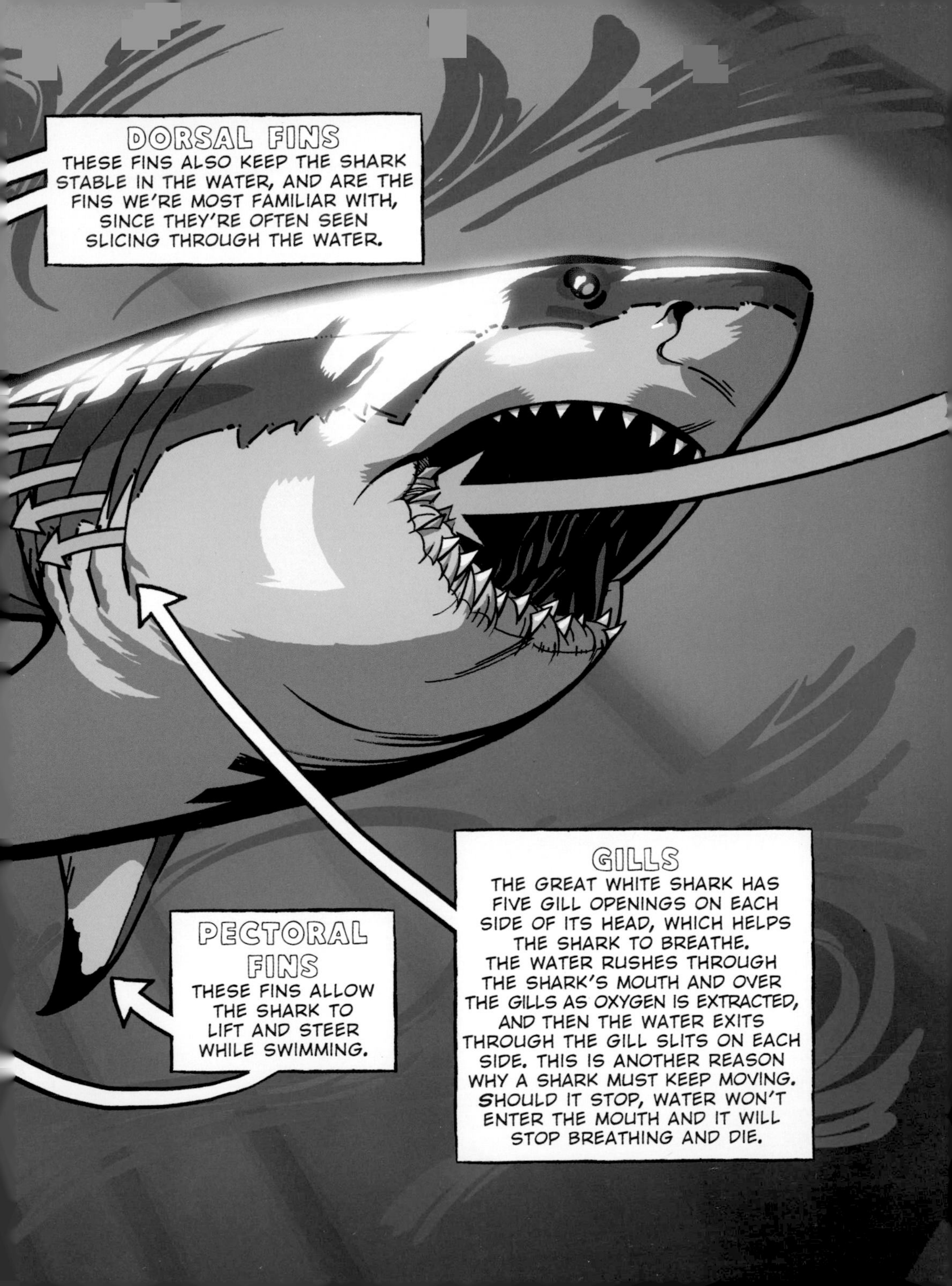
DORSAL FINS
THESE FINS ALSO KEEP THE SHARK STABLE IN THE WATER, AND ARE THE FINS WE'RE MOST FAMILIAR WITH, SINCE THEY'RE OFTEN SEEN SLICING THROUGH THE WATER.
GILLS
THE GREAT WHITE SHARK HAS FIVE GILL OPENINGS ON EACH SIDE OF ITS HEAD, WHICH HELPS THE SHARK TO BREATHE. THE WATER RUSHES THROUGH THE SHARK'S MOUTH AND OVER THE GILLS AS OXYGEN IS EXTRACTED, AND THEN THE WATER EXITS THROUGH THE GILL SLITS ON EACH SIDE. THIS IS ANOTHER REASON WHY A SHARK MUST KEEP MOVING. SHOULD IT STOP, WATER WON'T ENTER THE MOUTH AND IT WILL STOP BREATHING AND DIE.
PECTORAL FINS
THESE FINS ALLOW THE SHARK TO LIFT AND STEER WHILE SWIMMING.

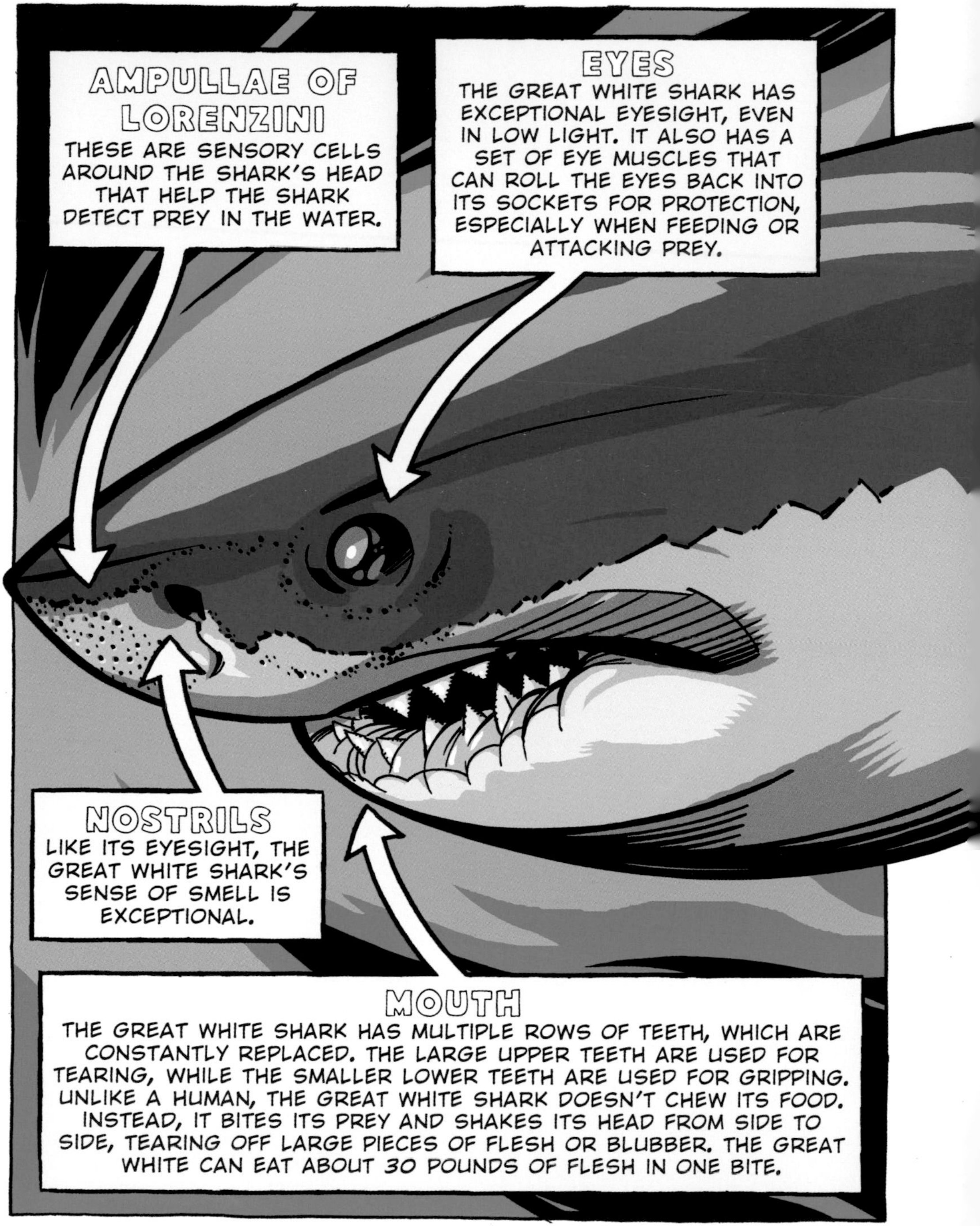
AMPULLAE OF LORENZINI
THESE ARE SENSORY CELLS AROUND THE SHARK'S HEAD THAT HELP THE SHARK DETECT PREY IN THE WATER.
EYES
THE GREAT WHITE SHARK HAS EXCEPTIONAL EYESIGHT, EVEN IN LOW LIGHT. IT ALSO HAS A SET OF EYE MUSCLES THAT CAN ROLL THE EYES BACK INTO ITS SOCKETS FOR PROTECTION, ESPECIALLY WHEN FEEDING OR ATTACKING PREY.
NOSTRILS
LIKE ITS EYESIGHT, THE GREAT WHITE SHARK'S SENSE OF SMELL IS EXCEPTIONAL.
MOUTH
THE GREAT WHITE SHARK HAS MULTIPLE ROWS OF TEETH, WHICH ARE CONSTANTLY REPLACED. THE LARGE UPPER TEETH ARE USED FOR TEARING, WHILE THE SMALLER LOWER TEETH ARE USED FOR GRIPPING. UNLIKE A HUMAN, THE GREAT WHITE SHARK DOESN'T CHEW ITS FOOD. INSTEAD, IT BITES ITS PREY AND SHAKES ITS HEAD FROM SIDE TO SIDE, TEARING OFF LARGE PIECES OF FLESH OR BLUBBER. THE GREAT WHITE CAN EAT ABOUT 30 POUNDS OF FLESH IN ONE BITE.

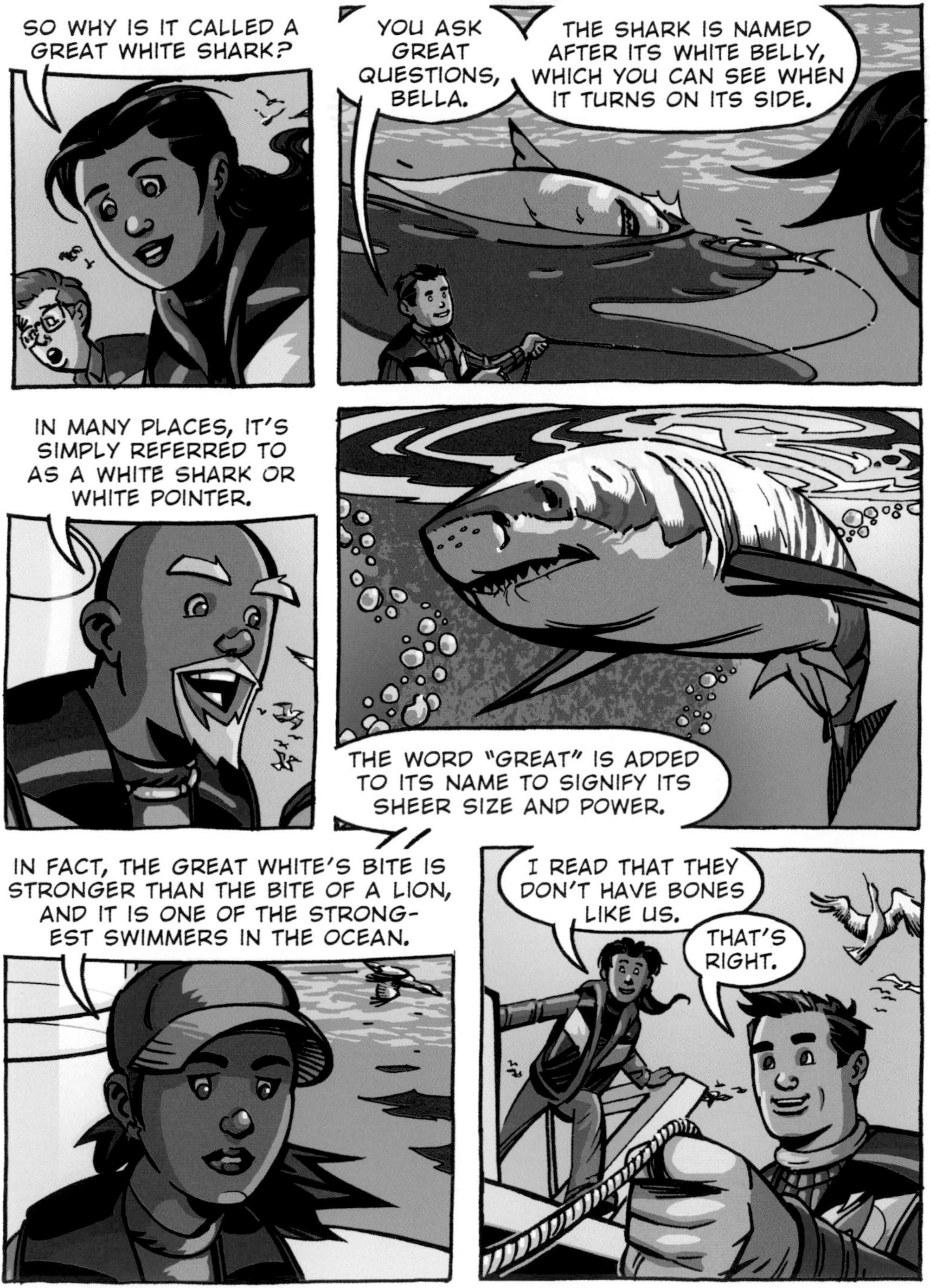

SO WHY IS IT CALLED A GREAT WHITE SHARK?
YOU ASK GREAT QUESTIONS, BELLA.
THE SHARK IS NAMED AFTER ITS WHITE BELLY, WHICH YOU CAN SEE WHEN IT TURNS ON ITS SIDE.
IN MANY PLACES, IT'S SIMPLY REFERRED TO AS A WHITE SHARK OR WHITE POINTER.
THE WORD "GREAT" IS ADDED TO ITS NAME TO SIGNIFY ITS SHEER SIZE AND POWER.
IN FACT, THE GREAT WHITE'S BITE IS STRONGER THAN THE BITE OF A LION, AND IT IS ONE OF THE STRONG-EST SWIMMERS IN THE OCEAN.
I READ THAT THEY DON'T HAVE BONES LIKE US.
THAT'S RIGHT.

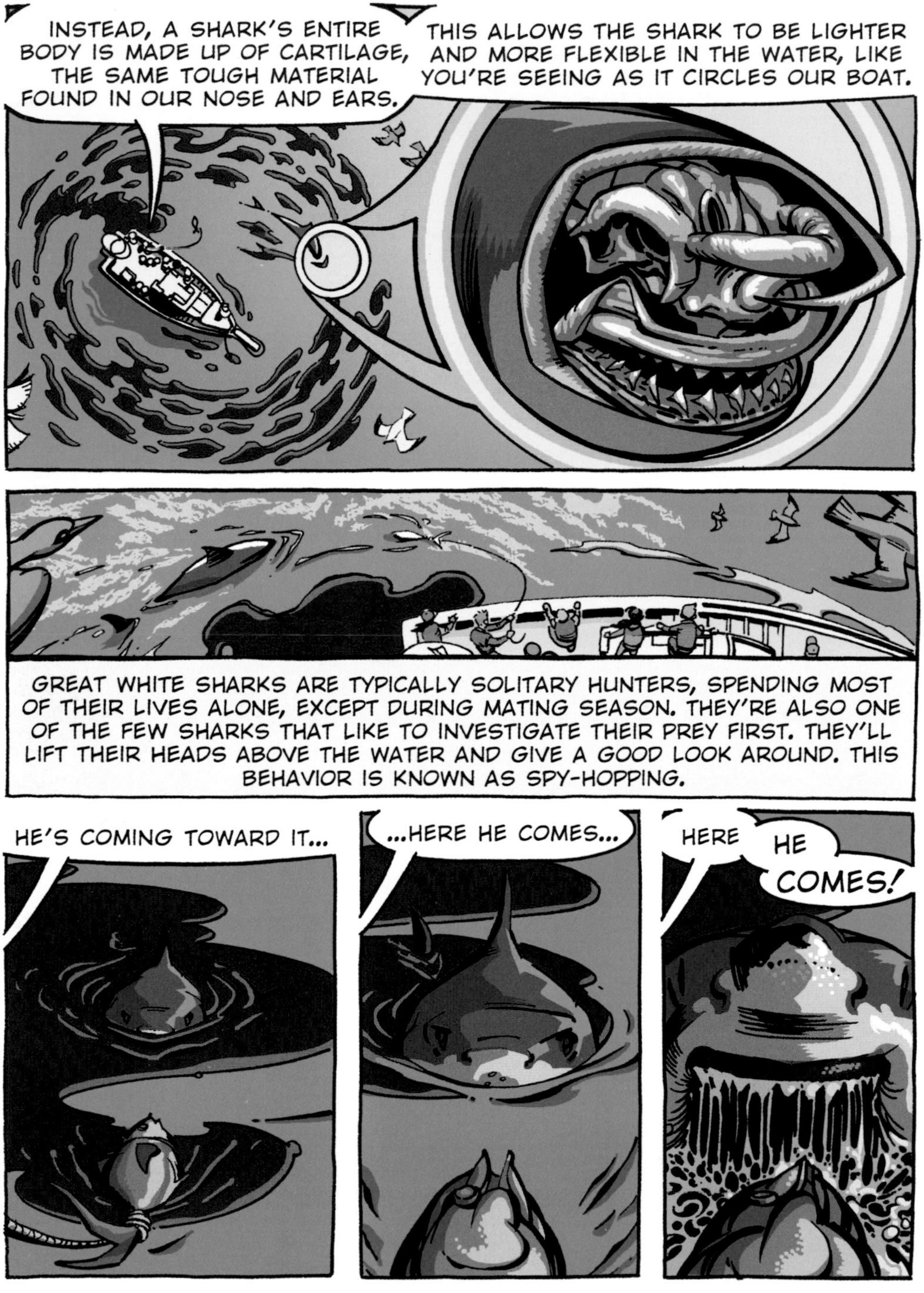
INSTEAD, A SHARK'S ENTIRE BODY IS MADE UP OF CARTILAGE, THE SAME TOUGH MATERIAL FOUND IN OUR NOSE AND EARS.
THIS ALLOWS THE SHARK TO BE LIGHTER AND MORE FLEXIBLE IN THE WATER, LIKE YOU'RE SEEING AS IT CIRCLES OUR BOAT.
GREAT WHITE SHARKS ARE TYPICALLY SOLITARY HUNTERS, SPENDING MOST OF THEIR LIVES ALONE, EXCEPT DURING MATING SEASON. THEY'RE ALSO ONE OF THE FEW SHARKS THAT LIKE TO INVESTIGATE THEIR PREY FIRST. THEY'LL LIFT THEIR HEADS ABOVE THE WATER AND GIVE A GOOD LOOK AROUND. THIS BEHAVIOR IS KNOWN AS SPY-HOPPING.
HE'S COMING TOWARD IT...
...HERE HE COMES...
HERE
HE COMES!

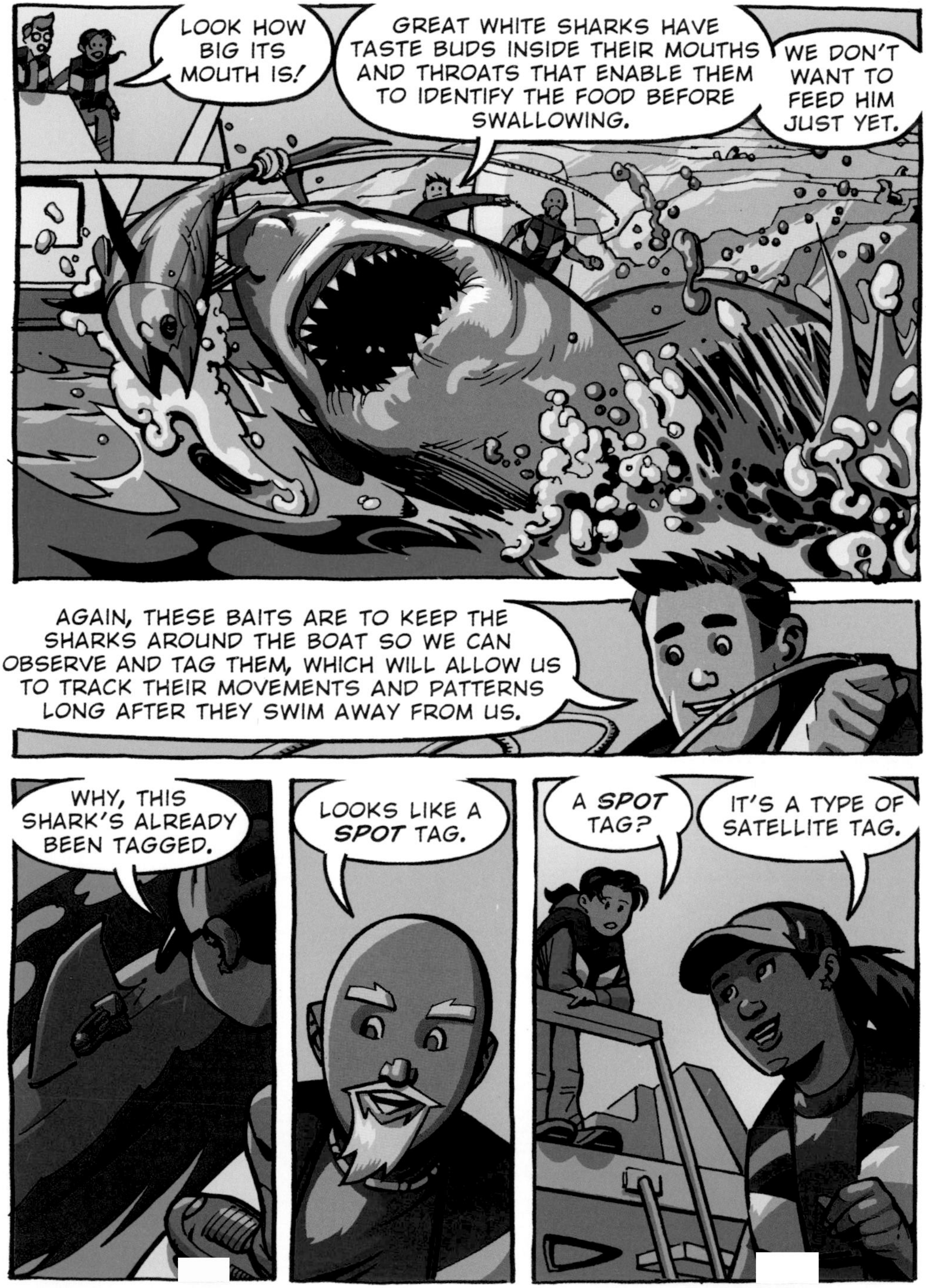
LOOK HOW BIG ITS MOUTH IS!
GREAT WHITE SHARKS HAVE TASTE BUDS INSIDE THEIR MOUTHS AND THROATS THAT ENABLE THEM TO IDENTIFY THE FOOD BEFORE SWALLOWING.
WE DON'T WANT TO FEED HIM JUST YET.
AGAIN, THESE BAITS ARE TO KEEP THE SHARKS AROUND THE BOAT SO WE CAN OBSERVE AND TAG THEM, WHICH WILL ALLOW US TO TRACK THEIR MOVEMENTS AND PATTERNS LONG AFTER THEY SWIM AWAY FROM US.
WHY, THIS SHARK'S ALREADY BEEN TAGGED.
LOOKS LIKE A *SPOT* TAG.
A *SPOT* TAG?
IT'S A TYPE OF SATELLITE TAG.

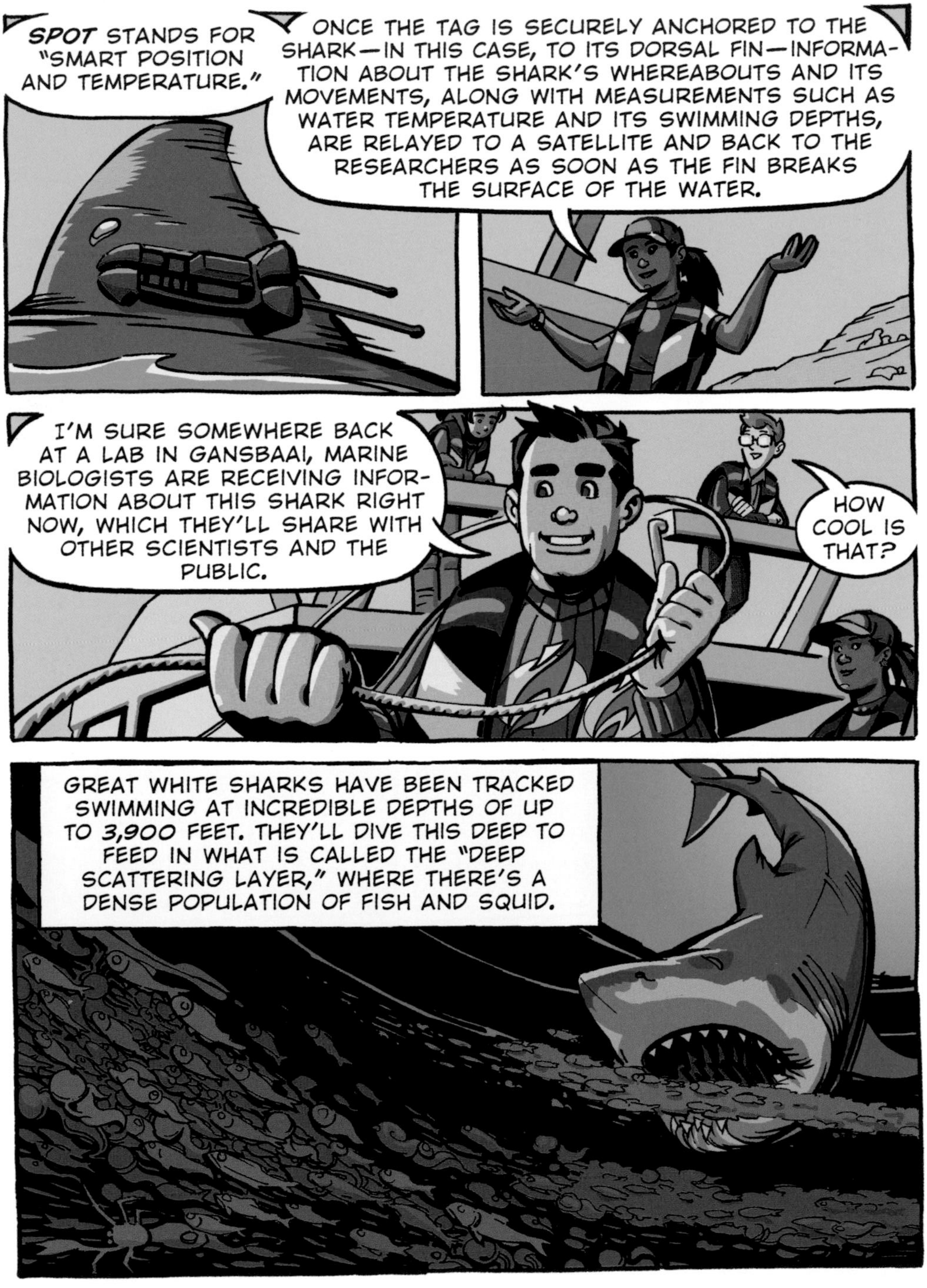
SPOT STANDS FOR "SMART POSITION AND TEMPERATURE."
ONCE THE TAG IS SECURELY ANCHORED TO THE SHARK—IN THIS CASE, TO ITS DORSAL FIN—INFORMATION ABOUT THE SHARK'S WHEREABOUTS AND ITS MOVEMENTS, ALONG WITH MEASUREMENTS SUCH AS WATER TEMPERATURE AND ITS SWIMMING DEPTHS, ARE RELAYED TO A SATELLITE AND BACK TO THE RESEARCHERS AS SOON AS THE FIN BREAKS THE SURFACE OF THE WATER.
I'M SURE SOMEWHERE BACK AT A LAB IN GANSBAAI, MARINE BIOLOGISTS ARE RECEIVING INFORMATION ABOUT THIS SHARK RIGHT NOW, WHICH THEY'LL SHARE WITH OTHER SCIENTISTS AND THE PUBLIC.
HOW COOL IS THAT?
GREAT WHITE SHARKS HAVE BEEN TRACKED SWIMMING AT INCREDIBLE DEPTHS OF UP TO 3,900 FEET. THEY'LL DIVE THIS DEEP TO FEED IN WHAT IS CALLED THE "DEEP SCATTERING LAYER," WHERE THERE'S A DENSE POPULATION OF FISH AND SQUID.

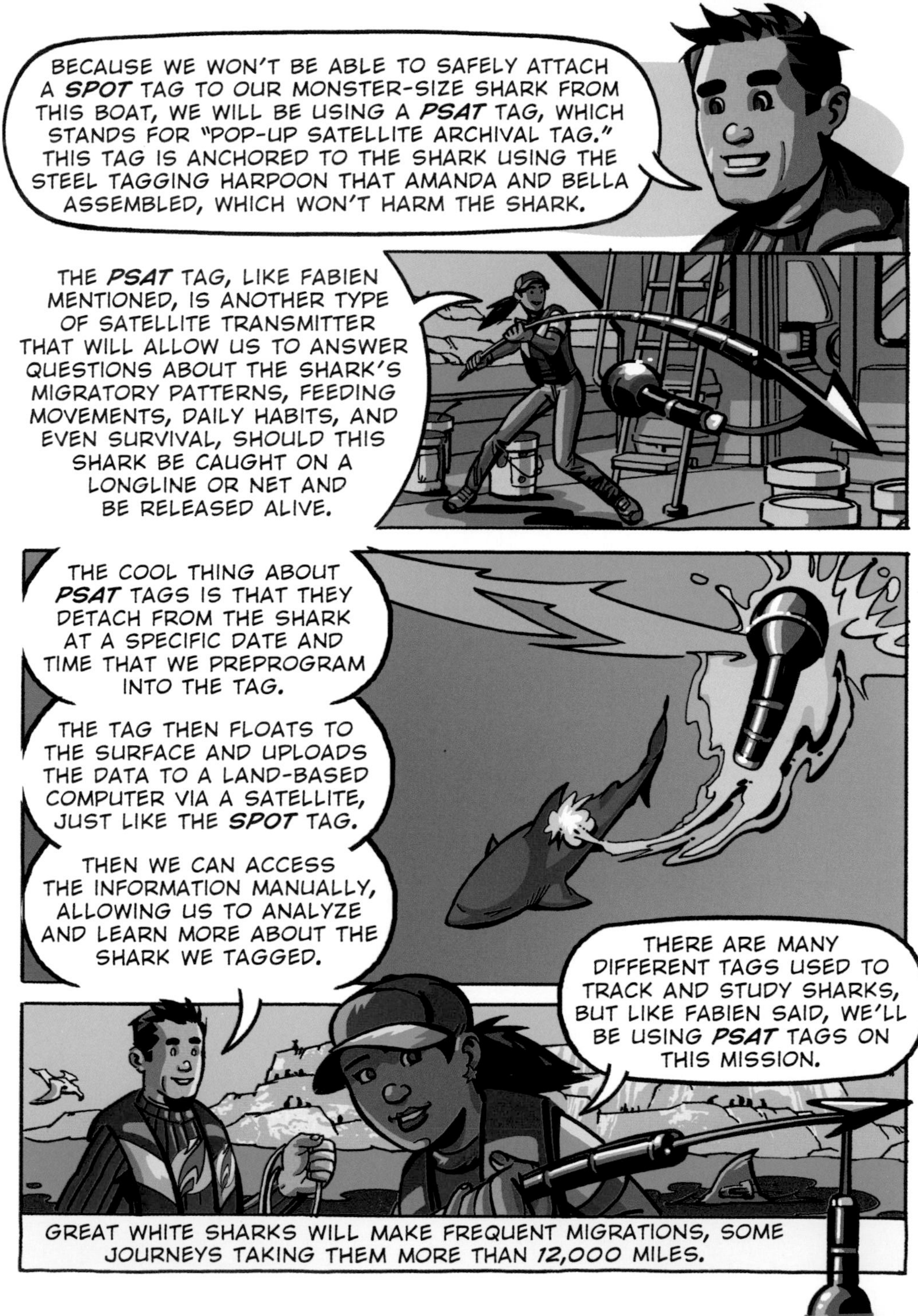
BECAUSE WE WON'T BE ABLE TO SAFELY ATTACH A *SPOT* TAG TO OUR MONSTER-SIZE SHARK FROM THIS BOAT, WE WILL BE USING A *PSAT* TAG, WHICH STANDS FOR "POP-UP SATELLITE ARCHIVAL TAG." THIS TAG IS ANCHORED TO THE SHARK USING THE STEEL TAGGING HARPOON THAT AMANDA AND BELLA ASSEMBLED, WHICH WON'T HARM THE SHARK.
THE *PSAT* TAG, LIKE FABIEN MENTIONED, IS ANOTHER TYPE OF SATELLITE TRANSMITTER THAT WILL ALLOW US TO ANSWER QUESTIONS ABOUT THE SHARK'S MIGRATORY PATTERNS, FEEDING MOVEMENTS, DAILY HABITS, AND EVEN SURVIVAL, SHOULD THIS SHARK BE CAUGHT ON A LONGLINE OR NET AND BE RELEASED ALIVE.
THE COOL THING ABOUT *PSAT* TAGS IS THAT THEY DETACH FROM THE SHARK AT A SPECIFIC DATE AND TIME THAT WE PREPROGRAM INTO THE TAG.
THE TAG THEN FLOATS TO THE SURFACE AND UPLOADS THE DATA TO A LAND-BASED COMPUTER VIA A SATELLITE, JUST LIKE THE *SPOT* TAG.
THEN WE CAN ACCESS THE INFORMATION MANUALLY, ALLOWING US TO ANALYZE AND LEARN MORE ABOUT THE SHARK WE TAGGED.
THERE ARE MANY DIFFERENT TAGS USED TO TRACK AND STUDY SHARKS, BUT LIKE FABIEN SAID, WE'LL BE USING *PSAT* TAGS ON THIS MISSION.
GREAT WHITE SHARKS WILL MAKE FREQUENT MIGRATIONS, SOME JOURNEYS TAKING THEM MORE THAN *12,000* MILES.

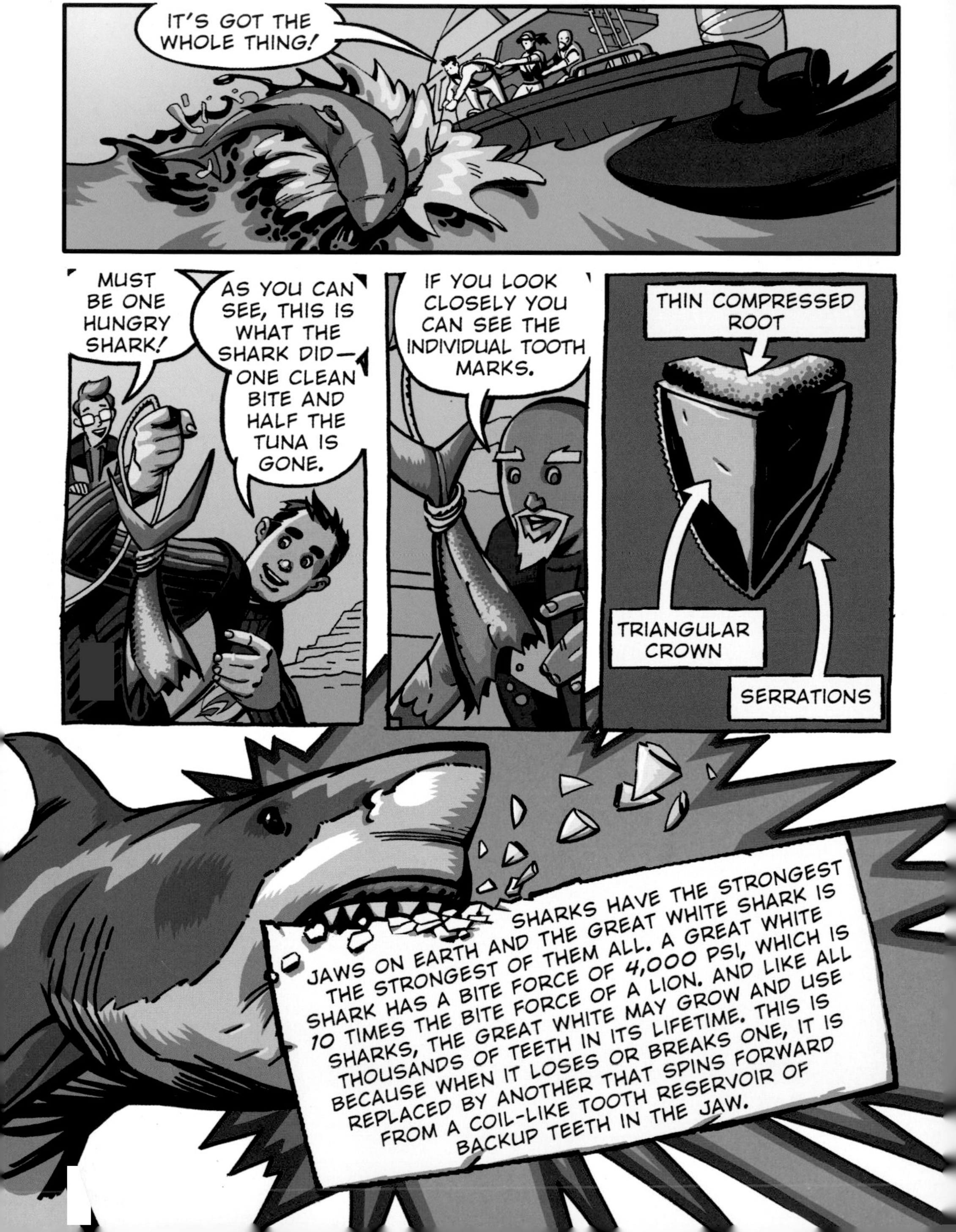
IT'S GOT THE WHOLE THING!
MUST BE ONE HUNGRY SHARK!
AS YOU CAN SEE, THIS IS WHAT THE SHARK DID—ONE CLEAN BITE AND HALF THE TUNA IS GONE.
IF YOU LOOK CLOSELY YOU CAN SEE THE INDIVIDUAL TOOTH MARKS.
THIN COMPRESSED ROOT
TRIANGULAR CROWN
SERRATIONS
SHARKS HAVE THE STRONGEST JAWS ON EARTH AND THE GREAT WHITE SHARK IS THE STRONGEST OF THEM ALL. A GREAT WHITE SHARK HAS A BITE FORCE OF 4,000 PSI, WHICH IS 10 TIMES THE BITE FORCE OF A LION. AND LIKE ALL SHARKS, THE GREAT WHITE MAY GROW AND USE THOUSANDS OF TEETH IN ITS LIFETIME. THIS IS BECAUSE WHEN IT LOSES OR BREAKS ONE, IT IS REPLACED BY ANOTHER THAT SPINS FORWARD FROM A COIL-LIKE TOOTH RESERVOIR OF BACKUP TEETH IN THE JAW.

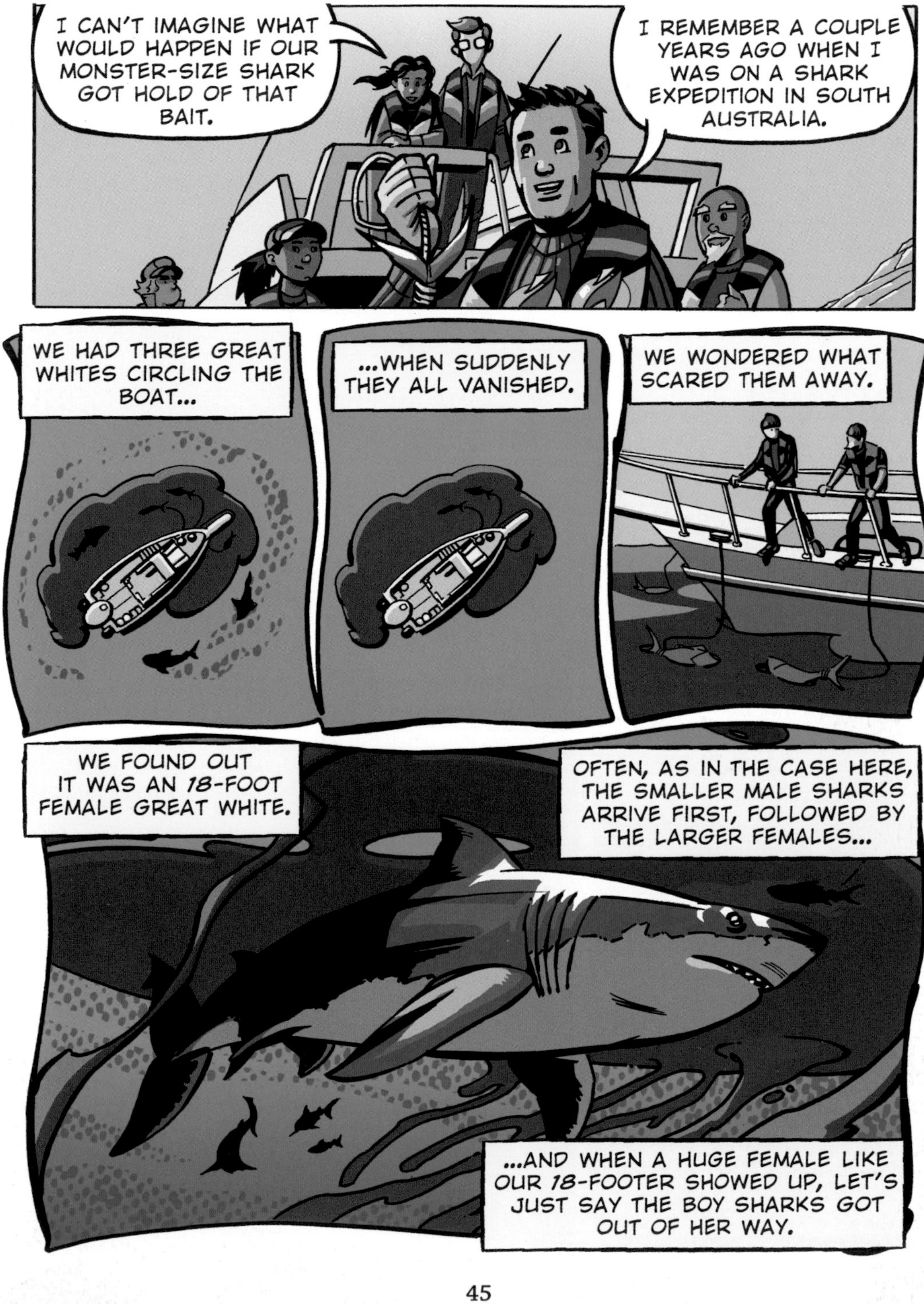
I CAN'T IMAGINE WHAT WOULD HAPPEN IF OUR MONSTER-SIZE SHARK GOT HOLD OF THAT BAIT.
I REMEMBER A COUPLE YEARS AGO WHEN I WAS ON A SHARK EXPEDITION IN SOUTH AUSTRALIA.
WE HAD THREE GREAT WHITES CIRCLING THE BOAT...
...WHEN SUDDENLY THEY ALL VANISHED.
WE WONDERED WHAT SCARED THEM AWAY.
WE FOUND OUT IT WAS AN *18*-FOOT FEMALE GREAT WHITE.
OFTEN, AS IN THE CASE HERE, THE SMALLER MALE SHARKS ARRIVE FIRST, FOLLOWED BY THE LARGER FEMALES...
...AND WHEN A HUGE FEMALE LIKE OUR *18*-FOOTER SHOWED UP, LET'S JUST SAY THE BOY SHARKS GOT OUT OF HER WAY.

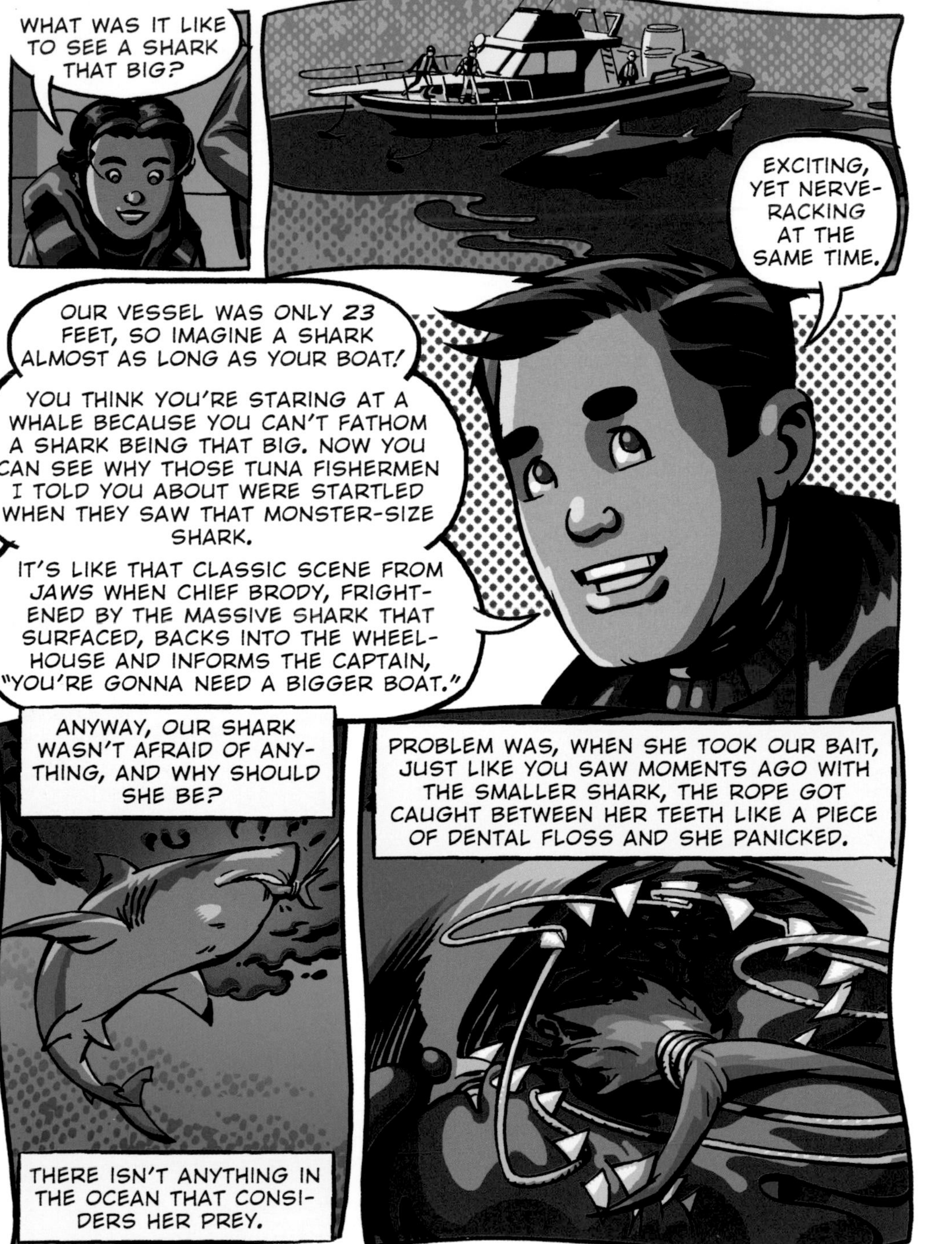
WHAT WAS IT LIKE TO SEE A SHARK THAT BIG?
EXCITING, YET NERVE-RACKING AT THE SAME TIME.
OUR VESSEL WAS ONLY 23 FEET, SO IMAGINE A SHARK ALMOST AS LONG AS YOUR BOAT!
YOU THINK YOU'RE STARING AT A WHALE BECAUSE YOU CAN'T FATHOM A SHARK BEING THAT BIG. NOW YOU CAN SEE WHY THOSE TUNA FISHERMEN I TOLD YOU ABOUT WERE STARTLED WHEN THEY SAW THAT MONSTER-SIZE SHARK.
IT'S LIKE THAT CLASSIC SCENE FROM JAWS WHEN CHIEF BRODY, FRIGHT-ENED BY THE MASSIVE SHARK THAT SURFACED, BACKS INTO THE WHEEL-HOUSE AND INFORMS THE CAPTAIN, "YOU'RE GONNA NEED A BIGGER BOAT."
ANYWAY, OUR SHARK WASN'T AFRAID OF ANY-THING, AND WHY SHOULD SHE BE?
THERE ISN'T ANYTHING IN THE OCEAN THAT CONSI-DERS HER PREY.
PROBLEM WAS, WHEN SHE TOOK OUR BAIT, JUST LIKE YOU SAW MOMENTS AGO WITH THE SMALLER SHARK, THE ROPE GOT CAUGHT BETWEEN HER TEETH LIKE A PIECE OF DENTAL FLOSS AND SHE PANICKED.

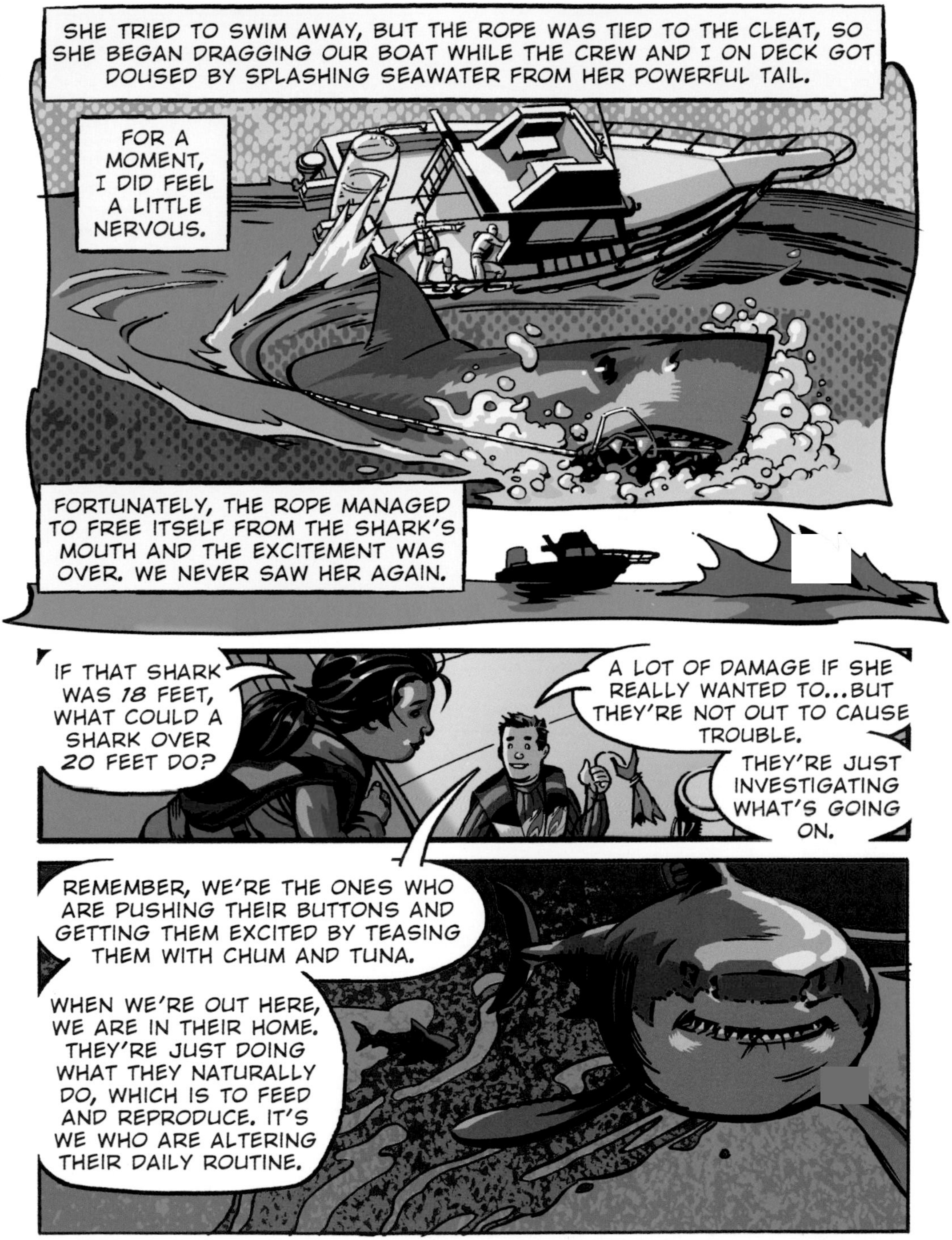
SHE TRIED TO SWIM AWAY, BUT THE ROPE WAS TIED TO THE CLEAT, SO SHE BEGAN DRAGGING OUR BOAT WHILE THE CREW AND I ON DECK GOT DOUSED BY SPLASHING SEAWATER FROM HER POWERFUL TAIL.
FOR A MOMENT, I DID FEEL A LITTLE NERVOUS.
FORTUNATELY, THE ROPE MANAGED TO FREE ITSELF FROM THE SHARK'S MOUTH AND THE EXCITEMENT WAS OVER. WE NEVER SAW HER AGAIN.
IF THAT SHARK WAS 18 FEET, WHAT COULD A SHARK OVER 20 FEET DO?
A LOT OF DAMAGE IF SHE REALLY WANTED TO...BUT THEY'RE NOT OUT TO CAUSE TROUBLE.
THEY'RE JUST INVESTIGATING WHAT'S GOING ON.
REMEMBER, WE'RE THE ONES WHO ARE PUSHING THEIR BUTTONS AND GETTING THEM EXCITED BY TEASING THEM WITH CHUM AND TUNA.
WHEN WE'RE OUT HERE, WE ARE IN THEIR HOME. THEY'RE JUST DOING WHAT THEY NATURALLY DO, WHICH IS TO FEED AND REPRODUCE. IT'S WE WHO ARE ALTERING THEIR DAILY ROUTINE.

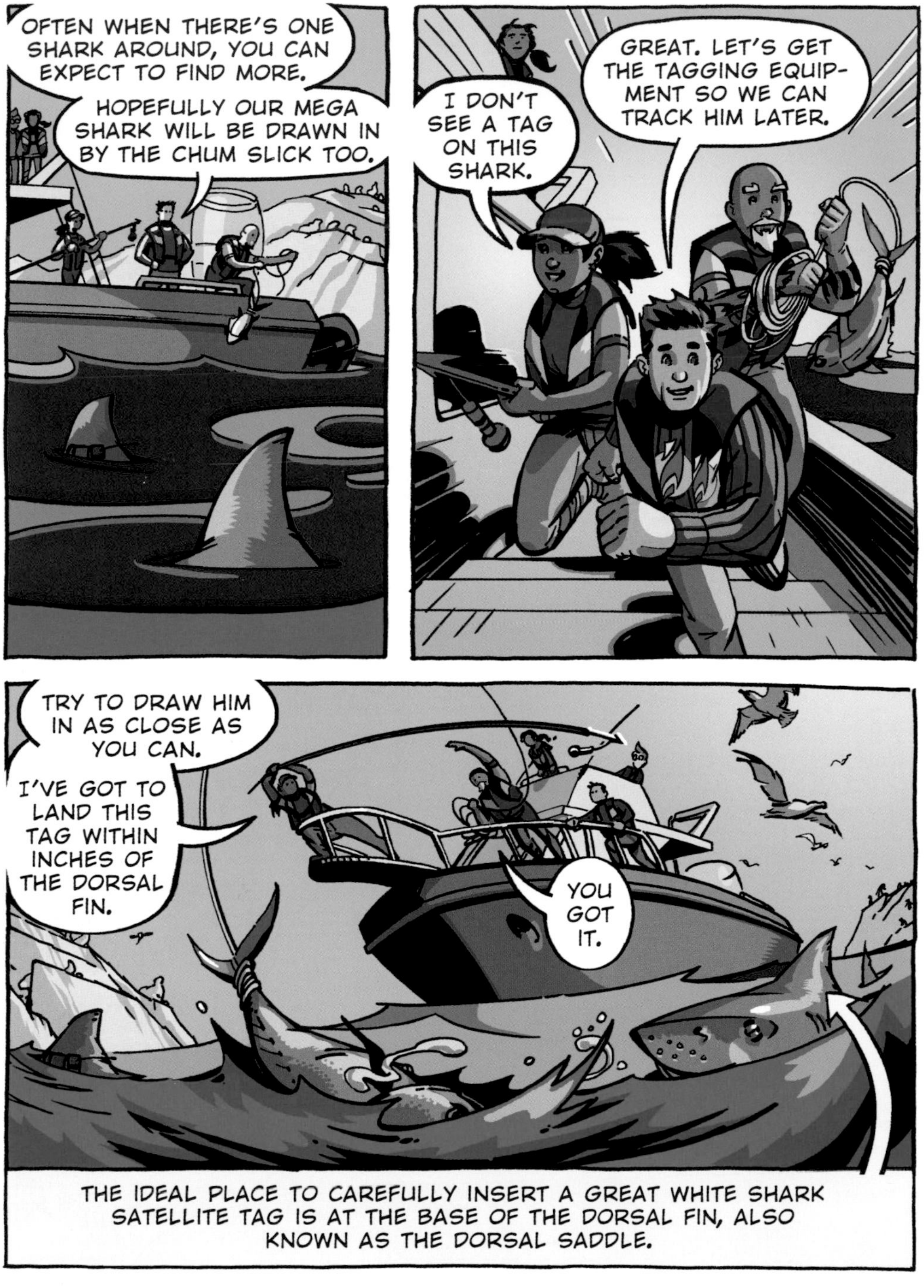
OFTEN WHEN THERE'S ONE SHARK AROUND, YOU CAN EXPECT TO FIND MORE.
HOPEFULLY OUR MEGA SHARK WILL BE DRAWN IN BY THE CHUM SLICK TOO.
I DON'T SEE A TAG ON THIS SHARK.
GREAT. LET'S GET THE TAGGING EQUIPMENT SO WE CAN TRACK HIM LATER.
TRY TO DRAW HIM IN AS CLOSE AS YOU CAN.
I'VE GOT TO LAND THIS TAG WITHIN INCHES OF THE DORSAL FIN.
YOU GOT IT.
THE IDEAL PLACE TO CAREFULLY INSERT A GREAT WHITE SHARK SATELLITE TAG IS AT THE BASE OF THE DORSAL FIN, ALSO KNOWN AS THE DORSAL SADDLE.

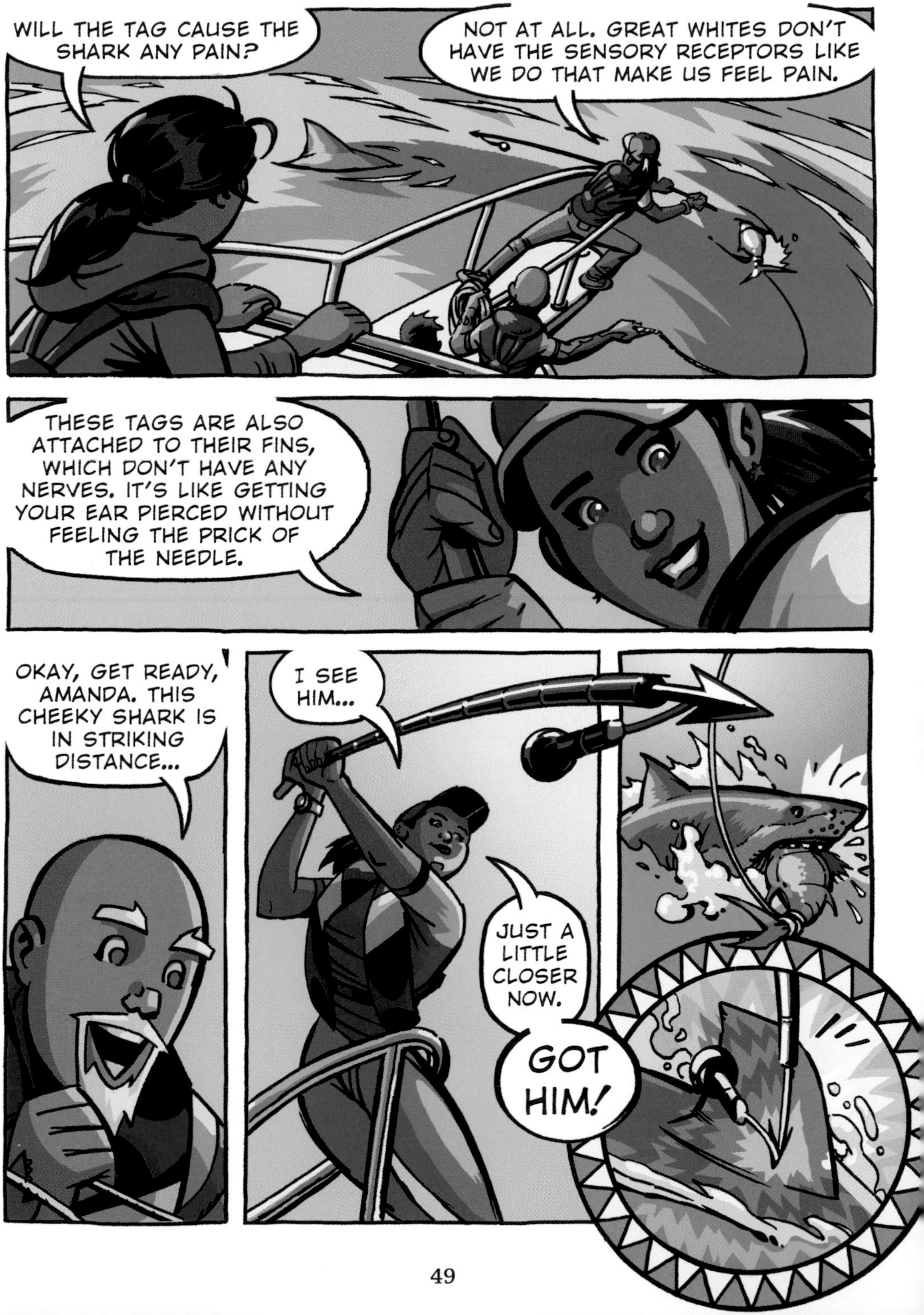
WILL THE TAG CAUSE THE SHARK ANY PAIN?
NOT AT ALL. GREAT WHITES DON'T HAVE THE SENSORY RECEPTORS LIKE WE DO THAT MAKE US FEEL PAIN.
THESE TAGS ARE ALSO ATTACHED TO THEIR FINS, WHICH DON'T HAVE ANY NERVES. IT'S LIKE GETTING YOUR EAR PIERCED WITHOUT FEELING THE PRICK OF THE NEEDLE.
OKAY, GET READY, AMANDA. THIS CHEEKY SHARK IS IN STRIKING DISTANCE...
I SEE HIM...
JUST A LITTLE CLOSER NOW.
GOT HIM!

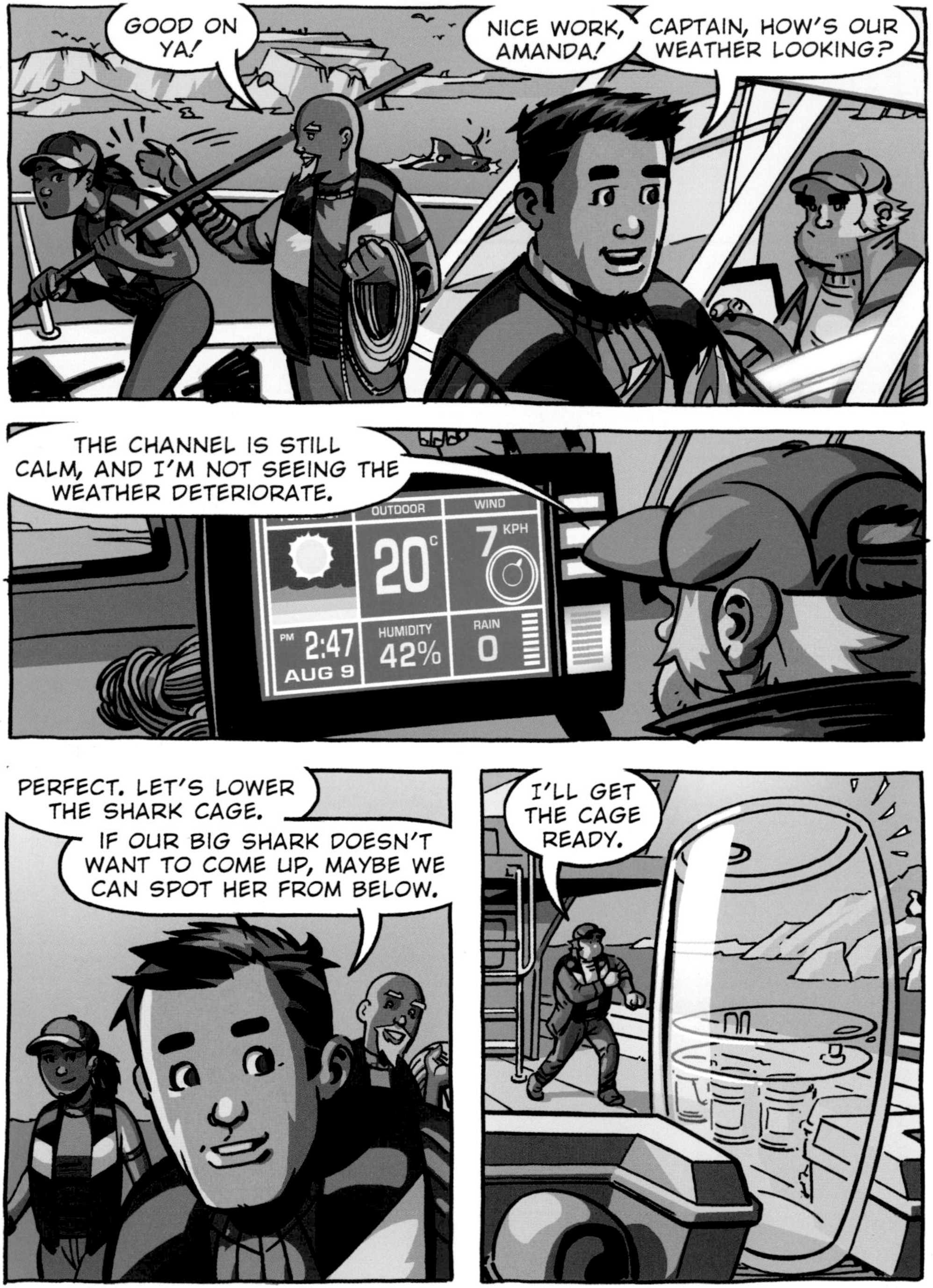
GOOD ON YA!
NICE WORK, AMANDA!
CAPTAIN, HOW'S OUR WEATHER LOOKING?
THE CHANNEL IS STILL CALM, AND I'M NOT SEEING THE WEATHER DETERIORATE.
OUTDOOR
WIND
20°C
7 KPH
PM 2:47
AUG 9
HUMIDITY
42%
RAIN
0
PERFECT. LET'S LOWER THE SHARK CAGE.
IF OUR BIG SHARK DOESN'T WANT TO COME UP, MAYBE WE CAN SPOT HER FROM BELOW.
I'LL GET THE CAGE READY.

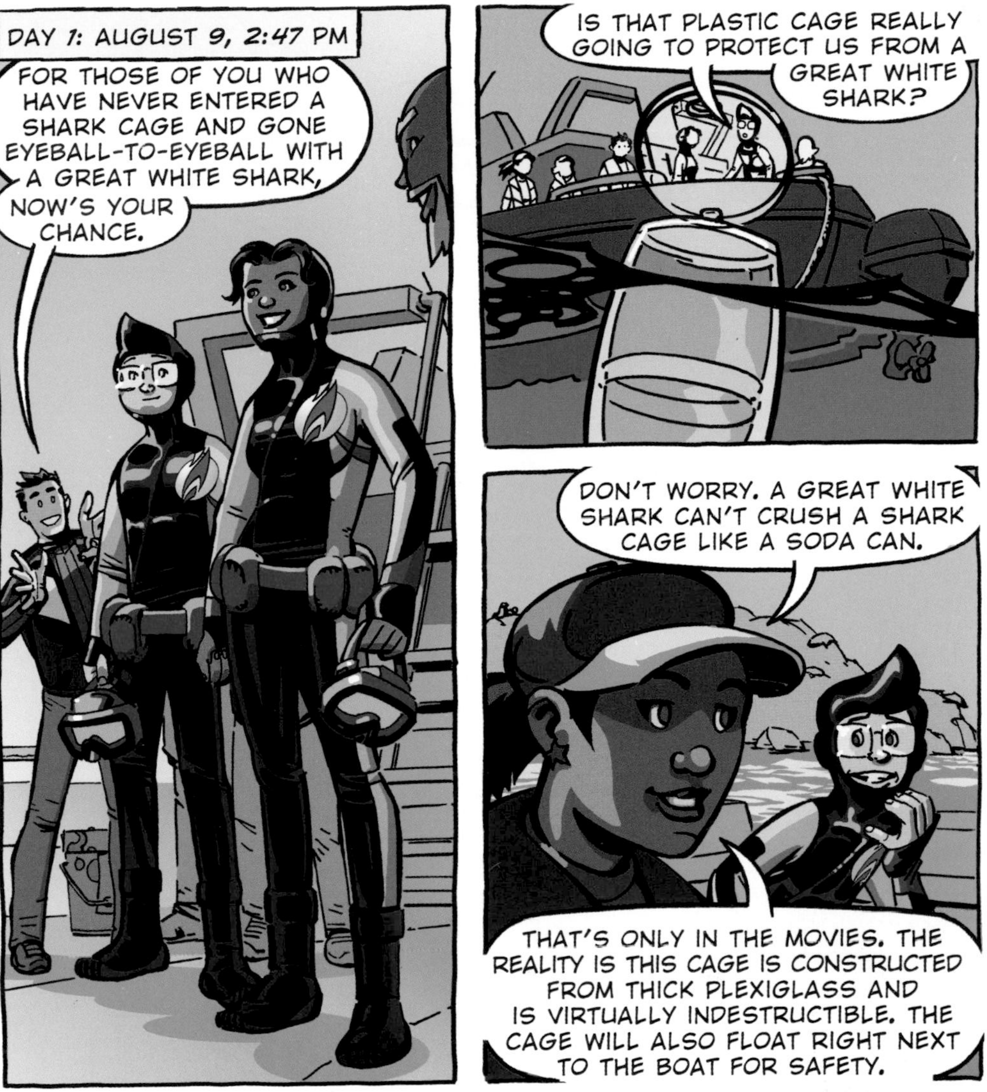
DAY 1: AUGUST 9, 2:47 PM
FOR THOSE OF YOU WHO HAVE NEVER ENTERED A SHARK CAGE AND GONE EYEBALL-TO-EYEBALL WITH A GREAT WHITE SHARK, NOW'S YOUR CHANCE.
IS THAT PLASTIC CAGE REALLY GOING TO PROTECT US FROM A GREAT WHITE SHARK?
DON'T WORRY. A GREAT WHITE SHARK CAN'T CRUSH A SHARK CAGE LIKE A SODA CAN.
THAT'S ONLY IN THE MOVIES. THE REALITY IS THIS CAGE IS CONSTRUCTED FROM THICK PLEXIGLASS AND IS VIRTUALLY INDESTRUCTIBLE. THE CAGE WILL ALSO FLOAT RIGHT NEXT TO THE BOAT FOR SAFETY.

A SHARK CAGE IS GENERALLY MADE FROM ALUMINUM AND STEEL MESH THAT'S MELDED TOGETHER. HOWEVER, NEW TECHNOLOGY IS NOW ALLOWING FOR OTHER MATERIALS TO BE USED, SUCH AS PLEXIGLASS. WITH A PLEXIGLASS CAGE, THERE AREN'T ANY METAL BARS TO OBSTRUCT ONE'S VIEW AND THERE AREN'T ANY SHARP EDGES ON WHICH A SHARK CAN INJURE ITSELF. MOST COUNTRIES HAVE REGULATIONS ON CAGE STRENGTH AND WHERE AND WHEN YOU CAN USE THEM. TYPICALLY, A SHARK CAGE WILL FIT TWO TO FOUR DIVERS AT A TIME.

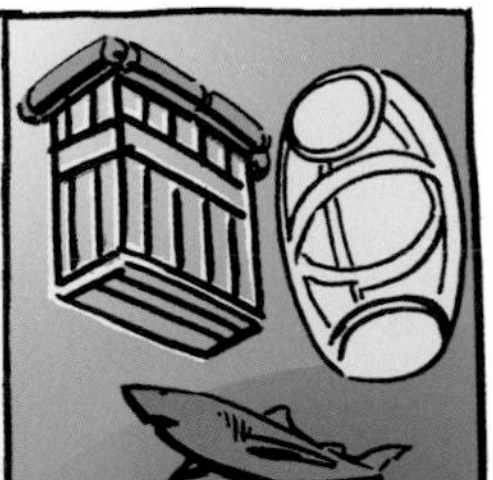

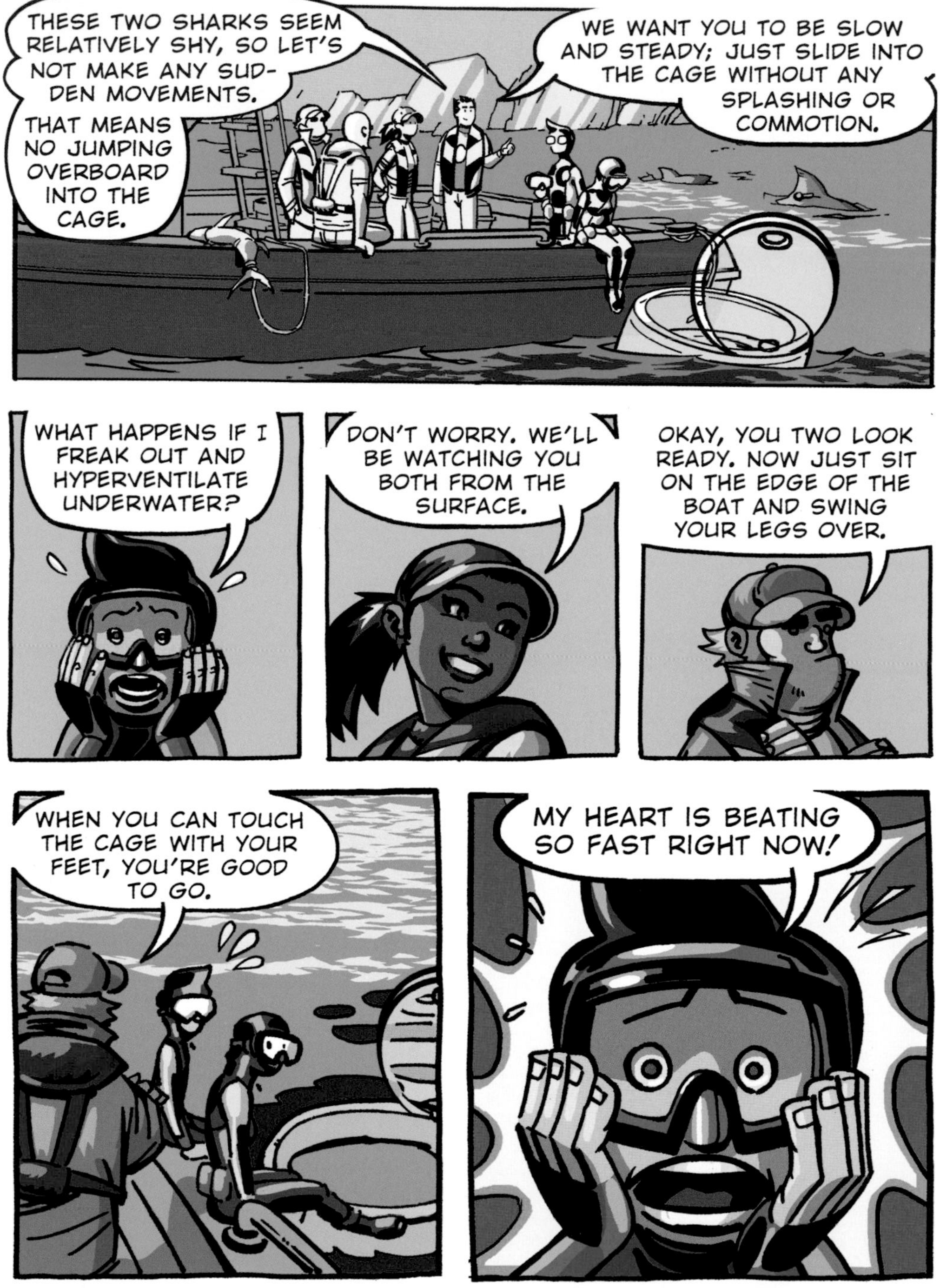
THESE TWO SHARKS SEEM RELATIVELY SHY, SO LET'S NOT MAKE ANY SUD-DEN MOVEMENTS.
THAT MEANS NO JUMPING OVERBOARD INTO THE CAGE.
WE WANT YOU TO BE SLOW AND STEADY; JUST SLIDE INTO THE CAGE WITHOUT ANY SPLASHING OR COMMOTION.
WHAT HAPPENS IF I FREAK OUT AND HYPERVENTILATE UNDERWATER?
DON'T WORRY. WE'LL BE WATCHING YOU BOTH FROM THE SURFACE.
OKAY, YOU TWO LOOK READY. NOW JUST SIT ON THE EDGE OF THE BOAT AND SWING YOUR LEGS OVER.
WHEN YOU CAN TOUCH THE CAGE WITH YOUR FEET, YOU'RE GOOD TO GO.
MY HEART IS BEATING SO FAST RIGHT NOW!

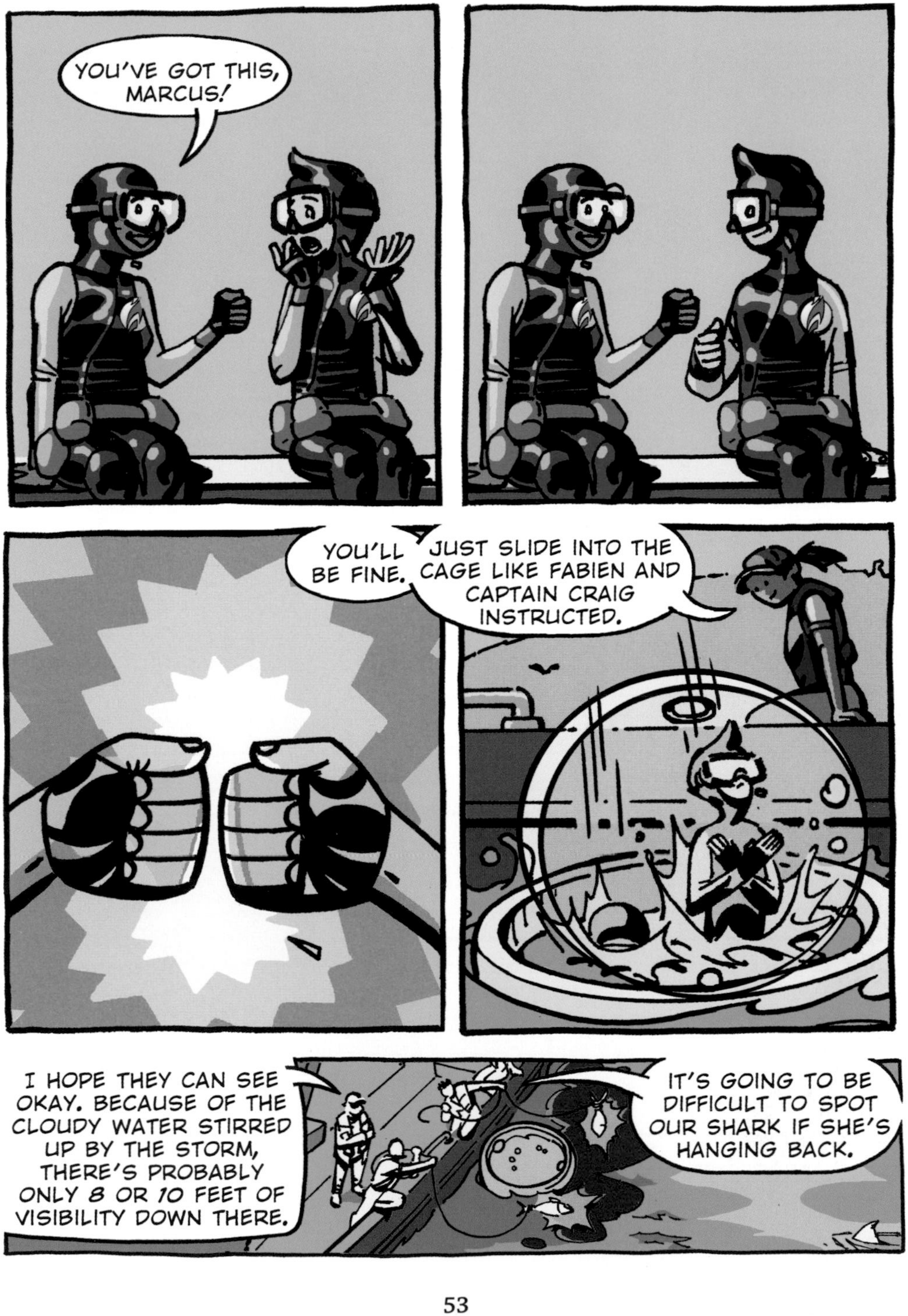
YOU'VE GOT THIS, MARCUS!
YOU'LL BE FINE.
JUST SLIDE INTO THE CAGE LIKE FABIEN AND CAPTAIN CRAIG INSTRUCTED.
I HOPE THEY CAN SEE OKAY. BECAUSE OF THE CLOUDY WATER STIRRED UP BY THE STORM, THERE'S PROBABLY ONLY 8 OR 10 FEET OF VISIBILITY DOWN THERE.
IT'S GOING TO BE DIFFICULT TO SPOT OUR SHARK IF SHE'S HANGING BACK.

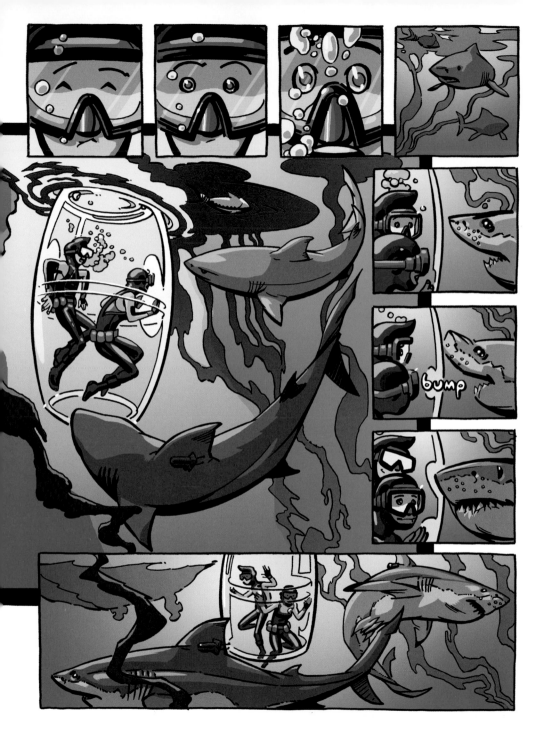

bump

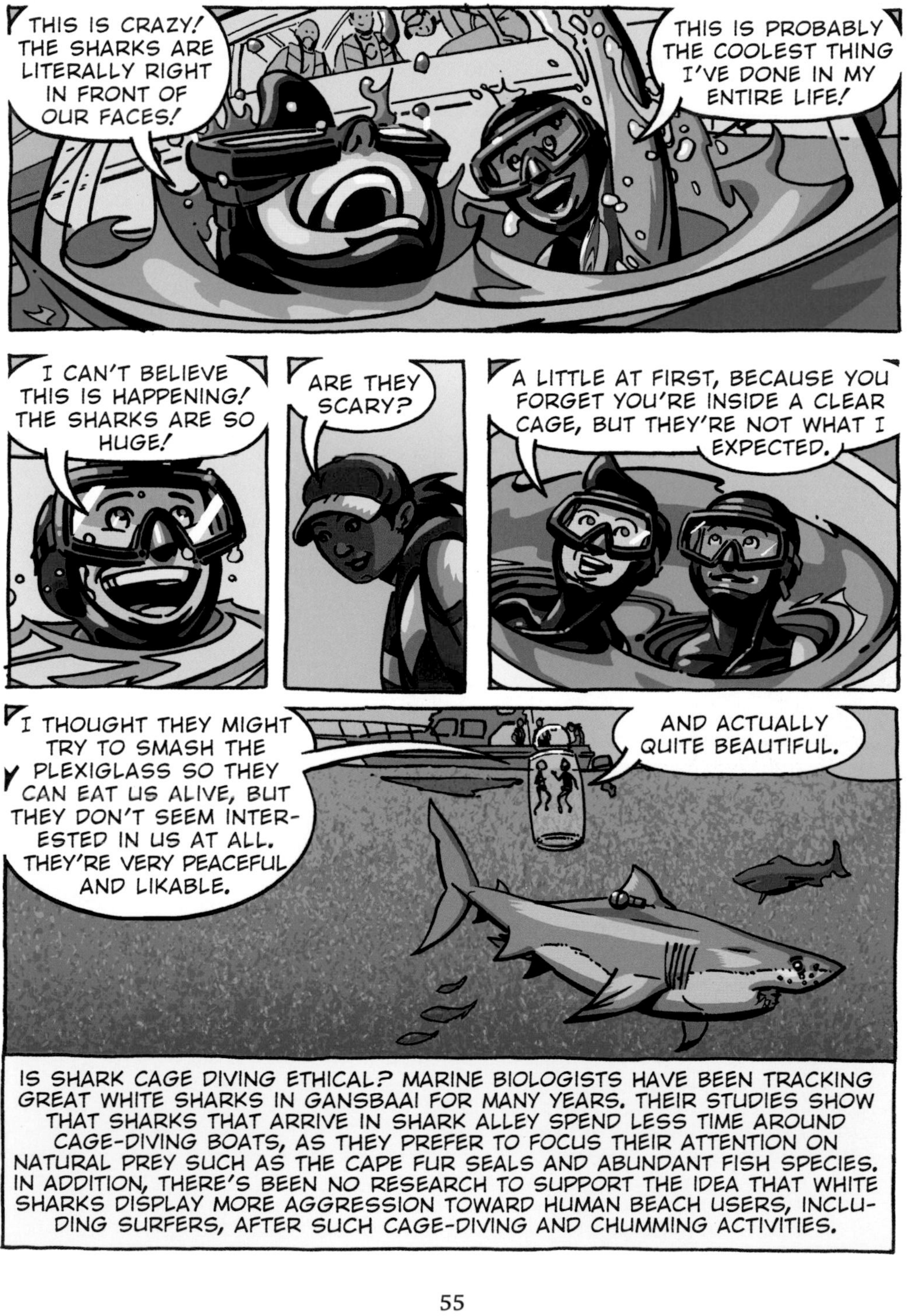
THIS IS CRAZY! THE SHARKS ARE LITERALLY RIGHT IN FRONT OF OUR FACES!
THIS IS PROBABLY THE COOLEST THING I'VE DONE IN MY ENTIRE LIFE!
I CAN'T BELIEVE THIS IS HAPPENING! THE SHARKS ARE SO HUGE!
ARE THEY SCARY?
A LITTLE AT FIRST, BECAUSE YOU FORGET YOU'RE INSIDE A CLEAR CAGE, BUT THEY'RE NOT WHAT I EXPECTED.
I THOUGHT THEY MIGHT TRY TO SMASH THE PLEXIGLASS SO THEY CAN EAT US ALIVE, BUT THEY DON'T SEEM INTERESTED IN US AT ALL. THEY'RE VERY PEACEFUL AND LIKABLE.
AND ACTUALLY QUITE BEAUTIFUL.
IS SHARK CAGE DIVING ETHICAL? MARINE BIOLOGISTS HAVE BEEN TRACKING GREAT WHITE SHARKS IN GANSBAAI FOR MANY YEARS. THEIR STUDIES SHOW THAT SHARKS THAT ARRIVE IN SHARK ALLEY SPEND LESS TIME AROUND CAGE-DIVING BOATS, AS THEY PREFER TO FOCUS THEIR ATTENTION ON NATURAL PREY SUCH AS THE CAPE FUR SEALS AND ABUNDANT FISH SPECIES. IN ADDITION, THERE'S BEEN NO RESEARCH TO SUPPORT THE IDEA THAT WHITE SHARKS DISPLAY MORE AGGRESSION TOWARD HUMAN BEACH USERS, INCLUDING SURFERS, AFTER SUCH CAGE-DIVING AND CHUMMING ACTIVITIES.

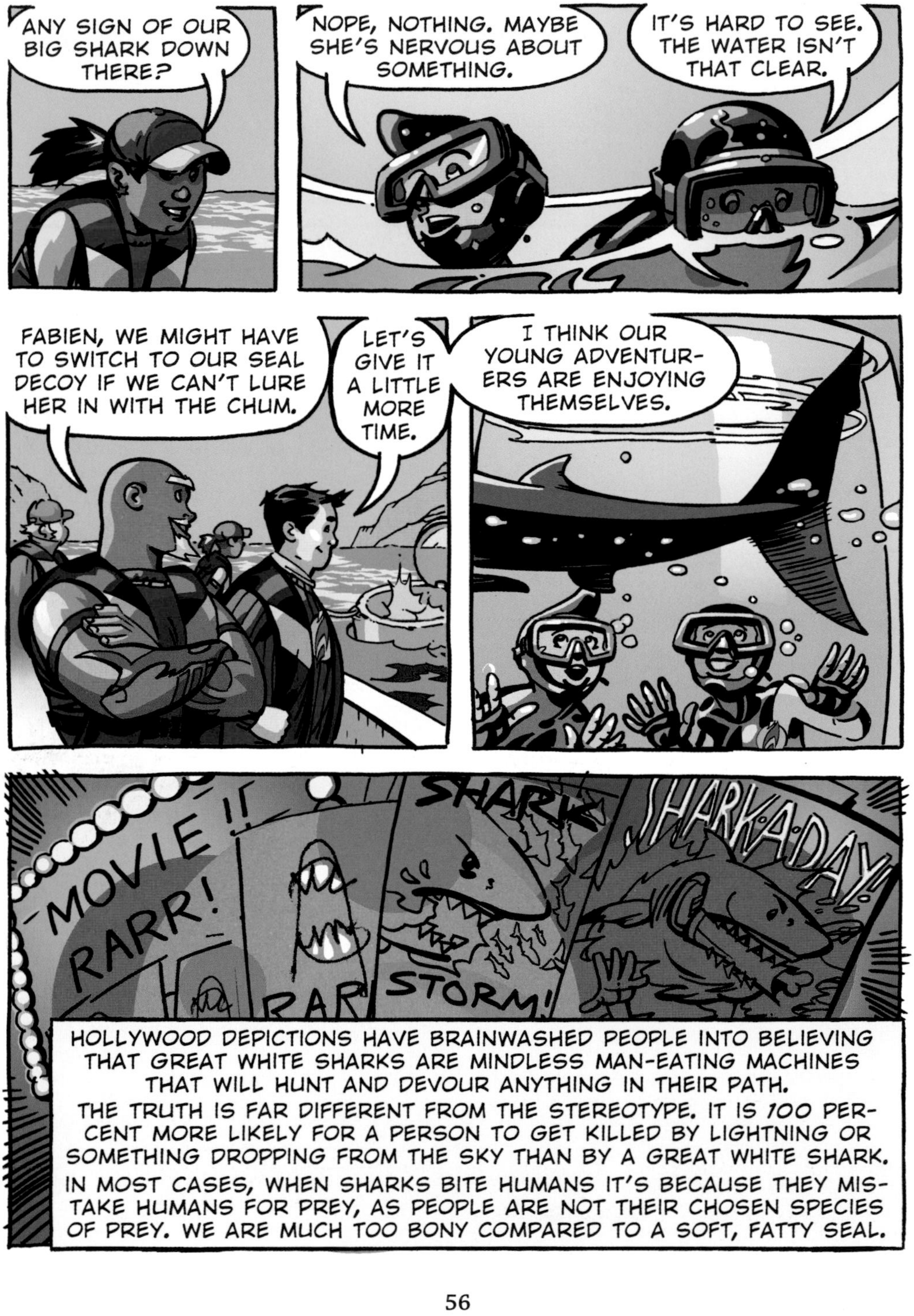
ANY SIGN OF OUR BIG SHARK DOWN THERE?
NOPE, NOTHING. MAYBE SHE'S NERVOUS ABOUT SOMETHING.
IT'S HARD TO SEE. THE WATER ISN'T THAT CLEAR.
FABIEN, WE MIGHT HAVE TO SWITCH TO OUR SEAL DECOY IF WE CAN'T LURE HER IN WITH THE CHUM.
LET'S GIVE IT A LITTLE MORE TIME.
I THINK OUR YOUNG ADVENTURERS ARE ENJOYING THEMSELVES.
MOVIE!!
RARR!
RAR
SHARK
STORM!
SHARKADAY!
HOLLYWOOD DEPICTIONS HAVE BRAINWASHED PEOPLE INTO BELIEVING THAT GREAT WHITE SHARKS ARE MINDLESS MAN-EATING MACHINES THAT WILL HUNT AND DEVOUR ANYTHING IN THEIR PATH.
THE TRUTH IS FAR DIFFERENT FROM THE STEREOTYPE. IT IS 100 PERCENT MORE LIKELY FOR A PERSON TO GET KILLED BY LIGHTNING OR SOMETHING DROPPING FROM THE SKY THAN BY A GREAT WHITE SHARK.
IN MOST CASES, WHEN SHARKS BITE HUMANS IT'S BECAUSE THEY MISTAKE HUMANS FOR PREY, AS PEOPLE ARE NOT THEIR CHOSEN SPECIES OF PREY. WE ARE MUCH TOO BONY COMPARED TO A SOFT, FATTY SEAL.

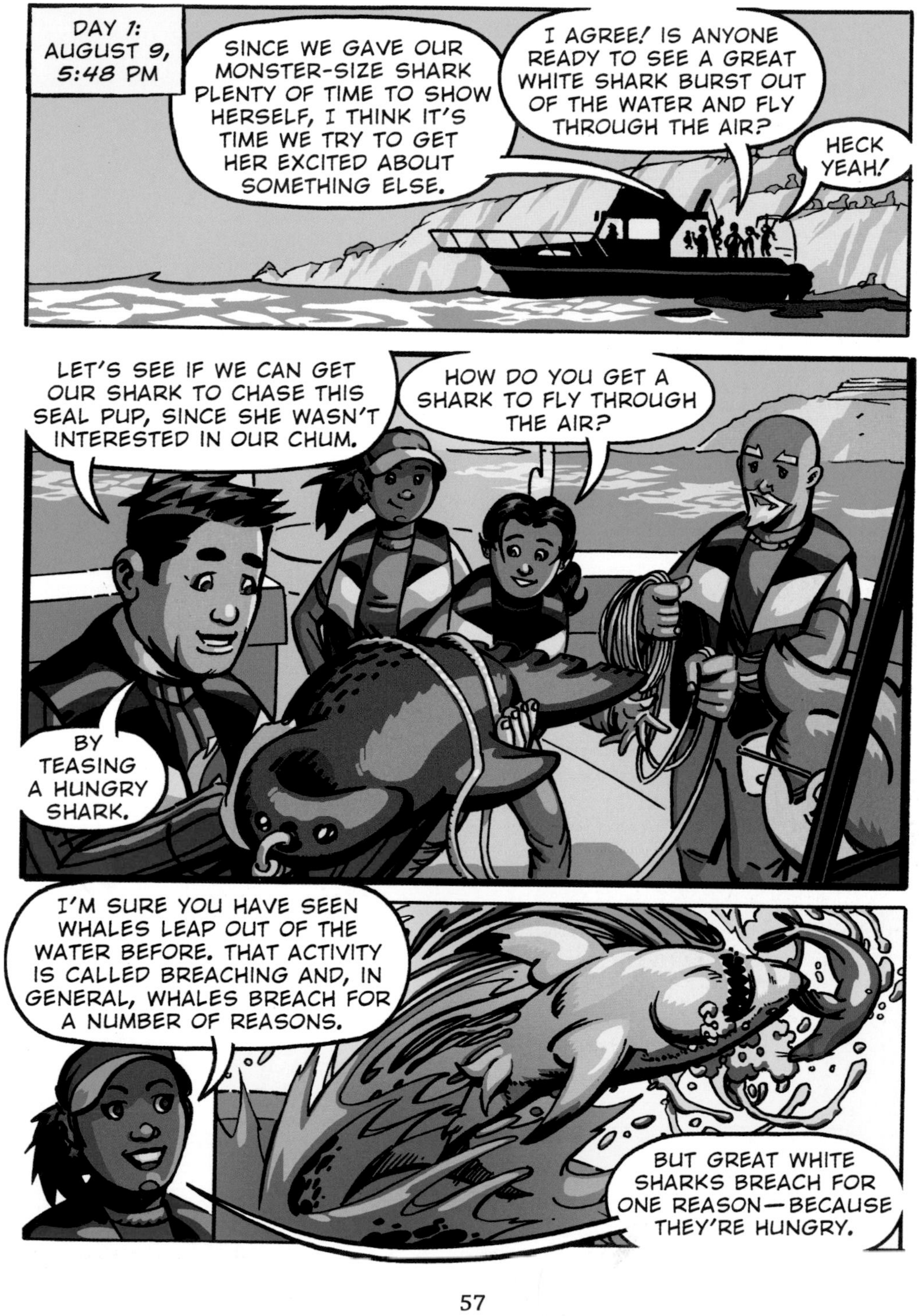
DAY 1: AUGUST 9, 5:48 PM
SINCE WE GAVE OUR MONSTER-SIZE SHARK PLENTY OF TIME TO SHOW HERSELF, I THINK IT'S TIME WE TRY TO GET HER EXCITED ABOUT SOMETHING ELSE.
I AGREE! IS ANYONE READY TO SEE A GREAT WHITE SHARK BURST OUT OF THE WATER AND FLY THROUGH THE AIR?
HECK YEAH!
LET'S SEE IF WE CAN GET OUR SHARK TO CHASE THIS SEAL PUP, SINCE SHE WASN'T INTERESTED IN OUR CHUM.
HOW DO YOU GET A SHARK TO FLY THROUGH THE AIR?
BY TEASING A HUNGRY SHARK.
I'M SURE YOU HAVE SEEN WHALES LEAP OUT OF THE WATER BEFORE. THAT ACTIVITY IS CALLED BREACHING AND, IN GENERAL, WHALES BREACH FOR A NUMBER OF REASONS.
BUT GREAT WHITE SHARKS BREACH FOR ONE REASON—BECAUSE THEY'RE HUNGRY.

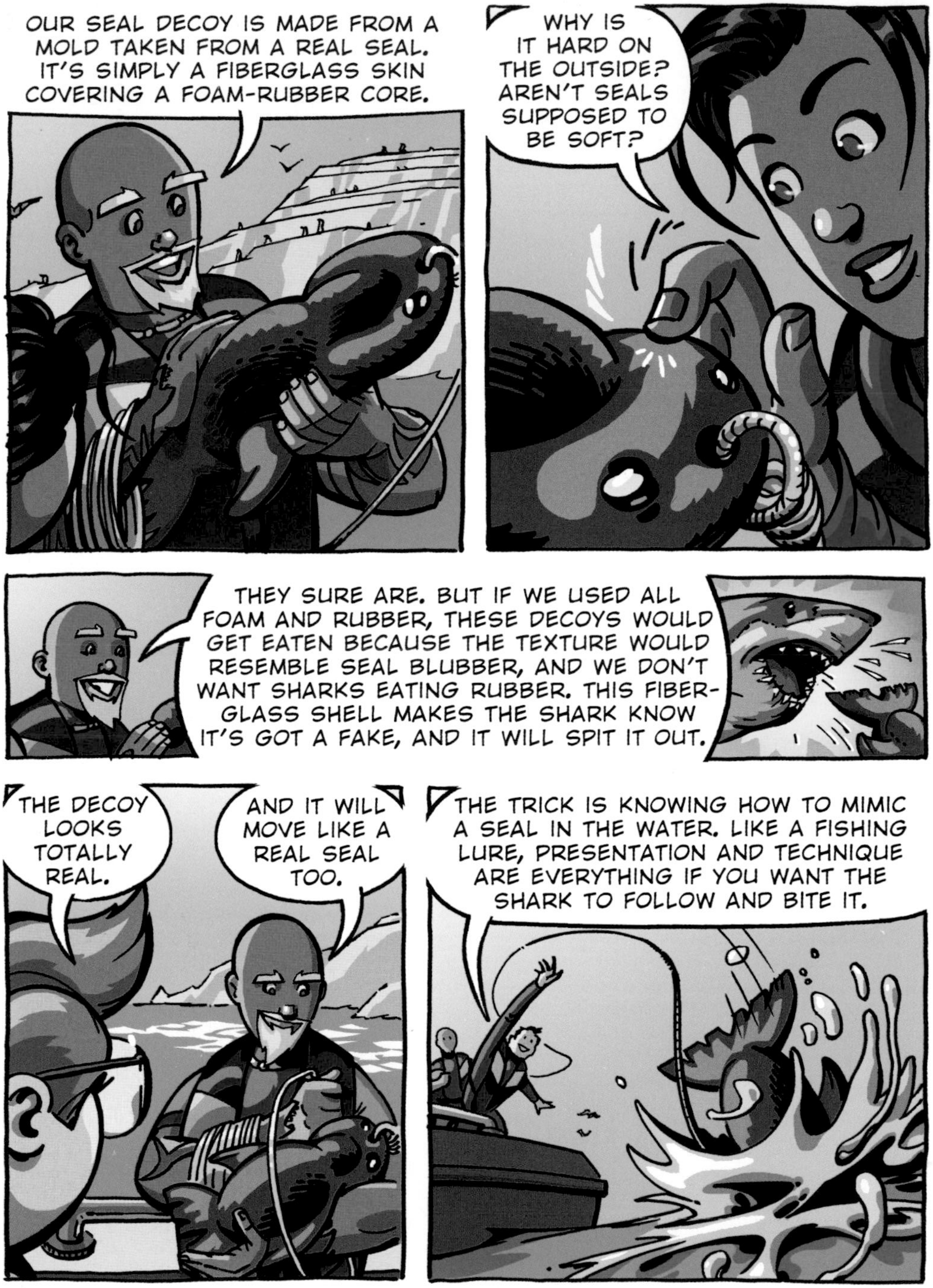
OUR SEAL DECOY IS MADE FROM A MOLD TAKEN FROM A REAL SEAL. IT'S SIMPLY A FIBERGLASS SKIN COVERING A FOAM-RUBBER CORE.
WHY IS IT HARD ON THE OUTSIDE? AREN'T SEALS SUPPOSED TO BE SOFT?
THEY SURE ARE. BUT IF WE USED ALL FOAM AND RUBBER, THESE DECOYS WOULD GET EATEN BECAUSE THE TEXTURE WOULD RESEMBLE SEAL BLUBBER, AND WE DON'T WANT SHARKS EATING RUBBER. THIS FIBER-GLASS SHELL MAKES THE SHARK KNOW IT'S GOT A FAKE, AND IT WILL SPIT IT OUT.
THE DECOY LOOKS TOTALLY REAL.
AND IT WILL MOVE LIKE A REAL SEAL TOO.
THE TRICK IS KNOWING HOW TO MIMIC A SEAL IN THE WATER. LIKE A FISHING LURE, PRESENTATION AND TECHNIQUE ARE EVERYTHING IF YOU WANT THE SHARK TO FOLLOW AND BITE IT.

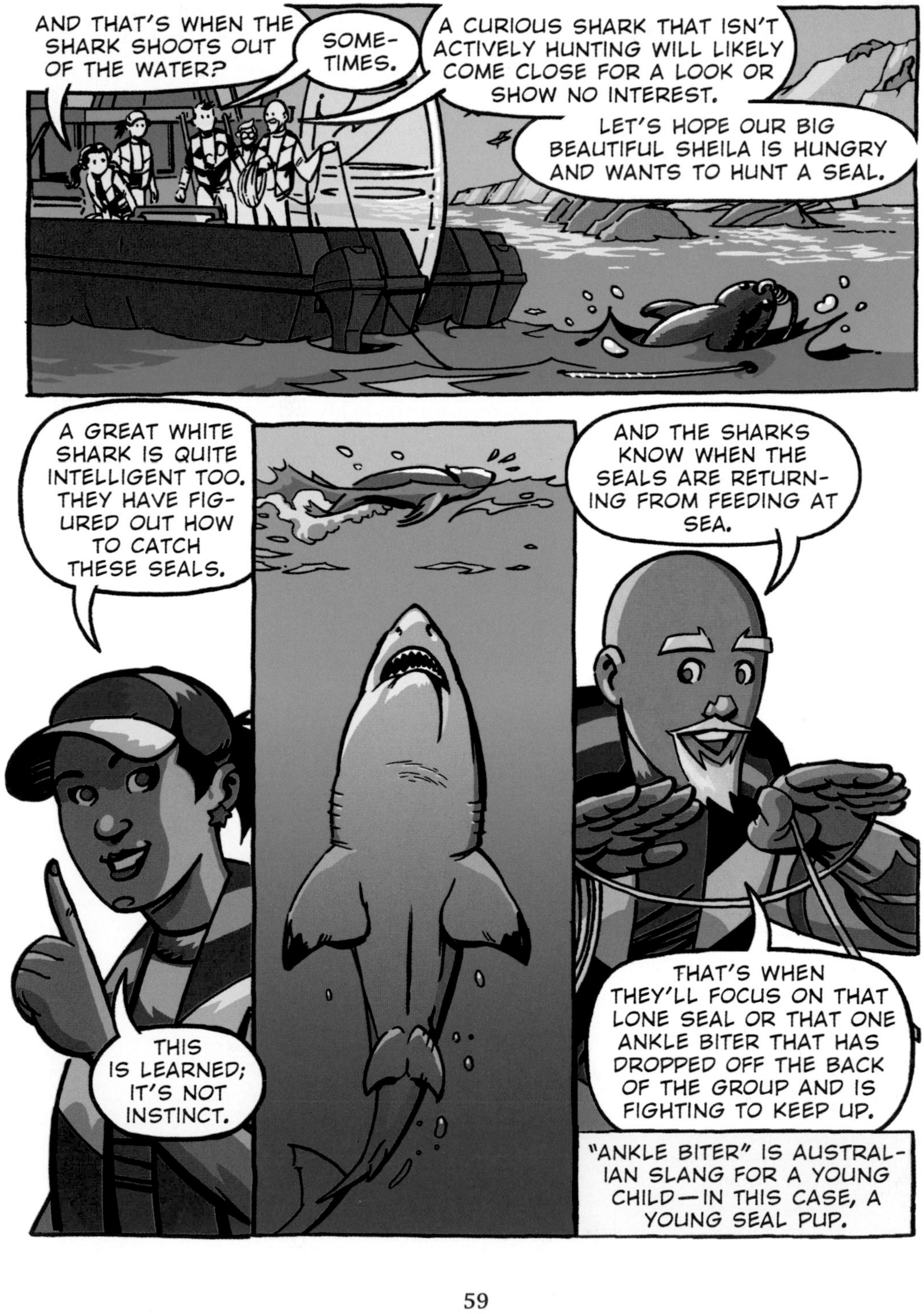
AND THAT'S WHEN THE SHARK SHOOTS OUT OF THE WATER?
SOME-TIMES.
A CURIOUS SHARK THAT ISN'T ACTIVELY HUNTING WILL LIKELY COME CLOSE FOR A LOOK OR SHOW NO INTEREST.
LET'S HOPE OUR BIG BEAUTIFUL SHEILA IS HUNGRY AND WANTS TO HUNT A SEAL.
A GREAT WHITE SHARK IS QUITE INTELLIGENT TOO. THEY HAVE FIG-URED OUT HOW TO CATCH THESE SEALS.
THIS IS LEARNED; IT'S NOT INSTINCT.
AND THE SHARKS KNOW WHEN THE SEALS ARE RETURN-ING FROM FEEDING AT SEA.
THAT'S WHEN THEY'LL FOCUS ON THAT LONE SEAL OR THAT ONE ANKLE BITER THAT HAS DROPPED OFF THE BACK OF THE GROUP AND IS FIGHTING TO KEEP UP.
"ANKLE BITER" IS AUSTRAL-IAN SLANG FOR A YOUNG CHILD—IN THIS CASE, A YOUNG SEAL PUP.

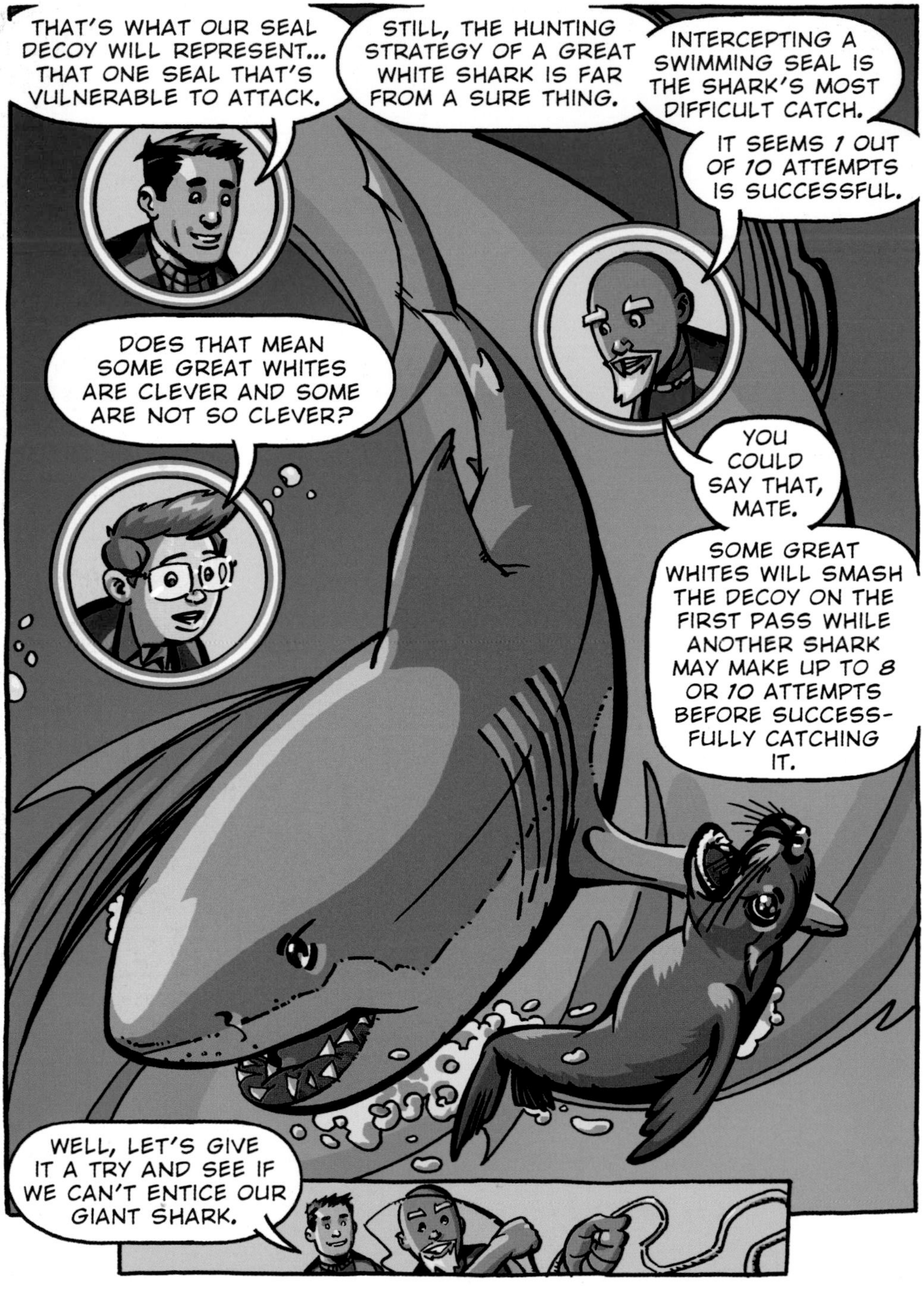
THAT'S WHAT OUR SEAL DECOY WILL REPRESENT... THAT ONE SEAL THAT'S VULNERABLE TO ATTACK.
STILL, THE HUNTING STRATEGY OF A GREAT WHITE SHARK IS FAR FROM A SURE THING.
INTERCEPTING A SWIMMING SEAL IS THE SHARK'S MOST DIFFICULT CATCH.
IT SEEMS 1 OUT OF 10 ATTEMPTS IS SUCCESSFUL.
DOES THAT MEAN SOME GREAT WHITES ARE CLEVER AND SOME ARE NOT SO CLEVER?
YOU COULD SAY THAT, MATE.
SOME GREAT WHITES WILL SMASH THE DECOY ON THE FIRST PASS WHILE ANOTHER SHARK MAY MAKE UP TO 8 OR 10 ATTEMPTS BEFORE SUCCESS-FULLY CATCHING IT.
WELL, LET'S GIVE IT A TRY AND SEE IF WE CAN'T ENTICE OUR GIANT SHARK.

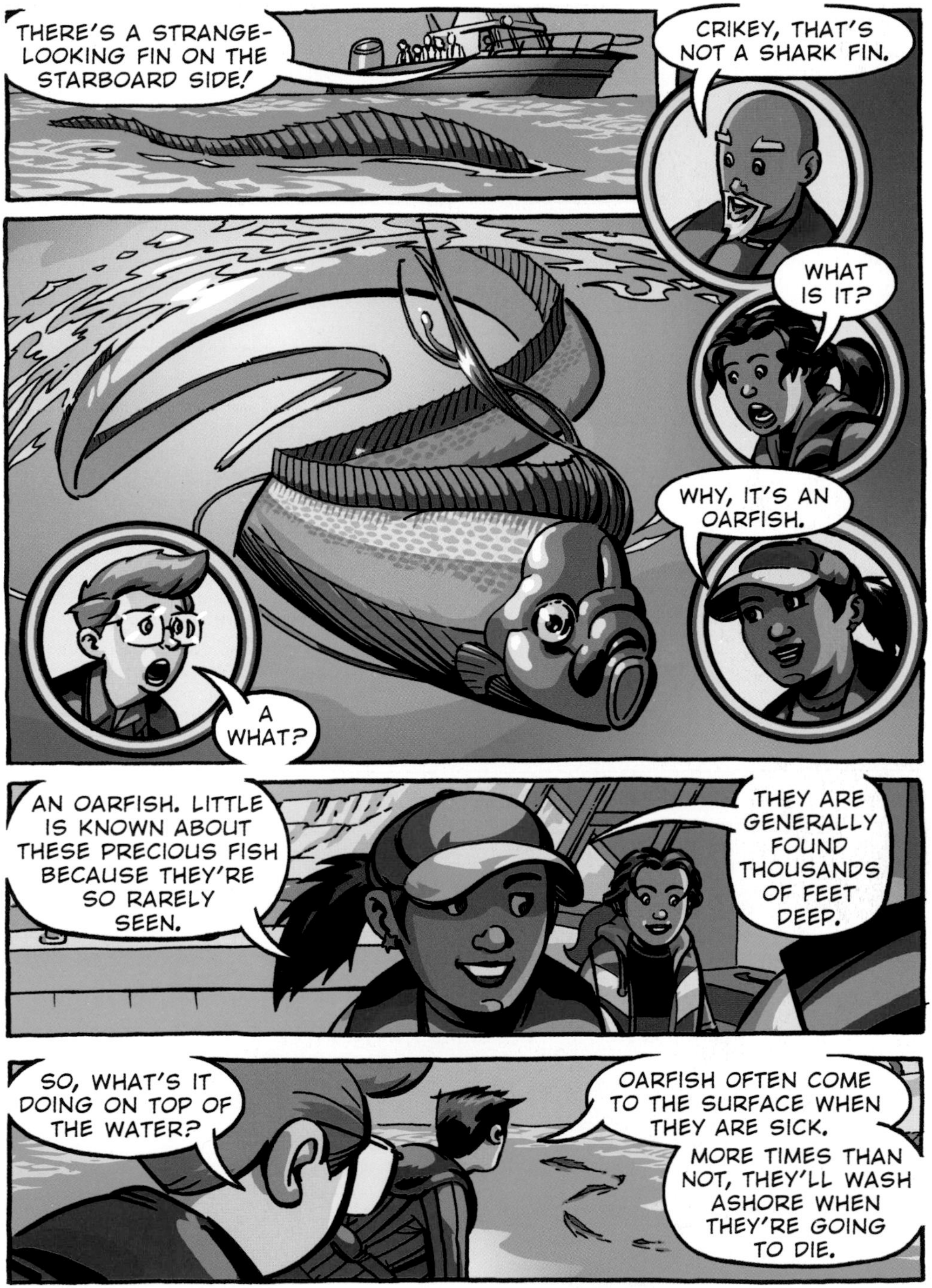
THERE'S A STRANGE-LOOKING FIN ON THE STARBOARD SIDE!
CRIKEY, THAT'S NOT A SHARK FIN.
WHAT IS IT?
WHY, IT'S AN OARFISH.
A WHAT?
AN OARFISH. LITTLE IS KNOWN ABOUT THESE PRECIOUS FISH BECAUSE THEY'RE SO RARELY SEEN.
THEY ARE GENERALLY FOUND THOUSANDS OF FEET DEEP.
SO, WHAT'S IT DOING ON TOP OF THE WATER?
OARFISH OFTEN COME TO THE SURFACE WHEN THEY ARE SICK.
MORE TIMES THAN NOT, THEY'LL WASH ASHORE WHEN THEY'RE GOING TO DIE.

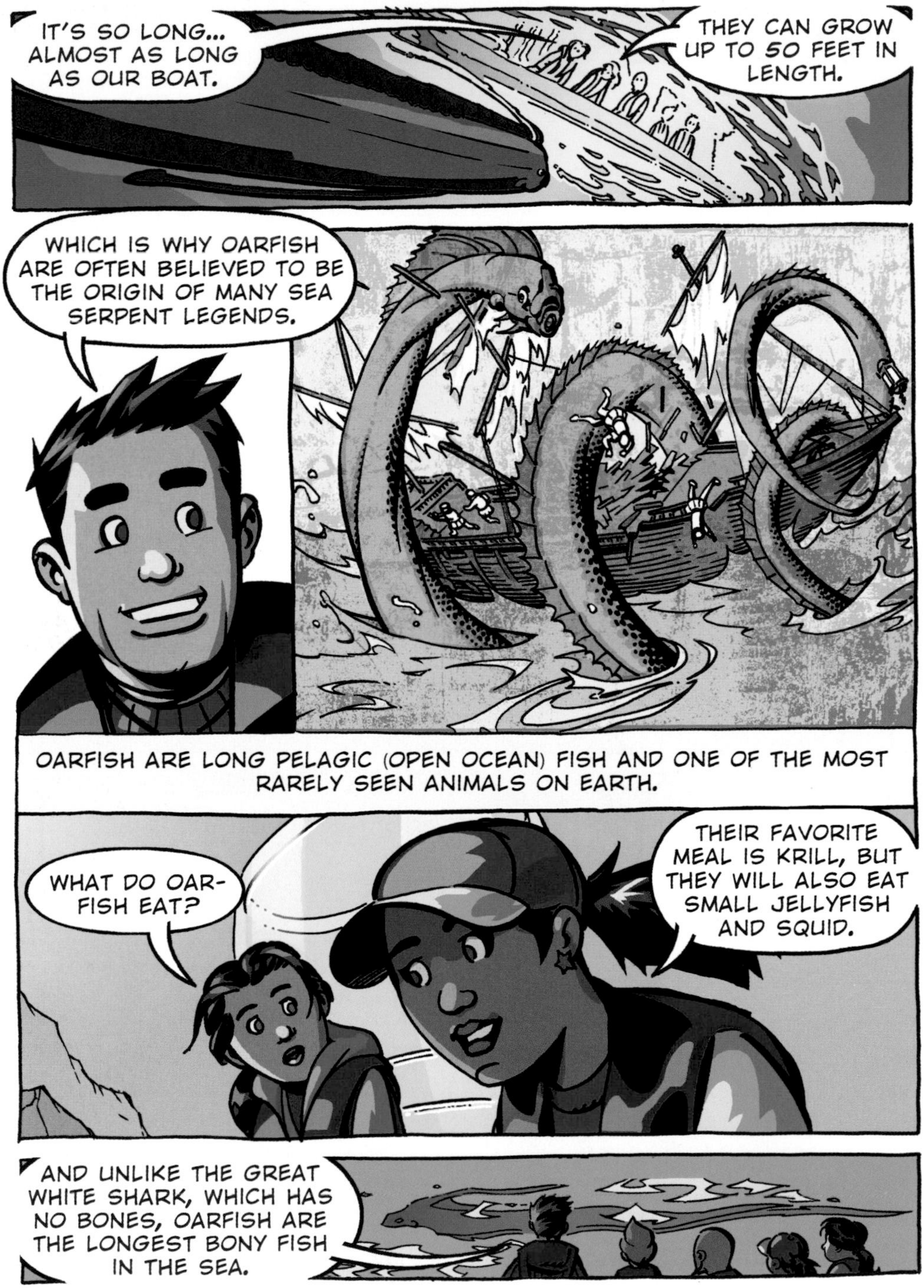
IT'S SO LONG... ALMOST AS LONG AS OUR BOAT.
THEY CAN GROW UP TO 50 FEET IN LENGTH.
WHICH IS WHY OARFISH ARE OFTEN BELIEVED TO BE THE ORIGIN OF MANY SEA SERPENT LEGENDS.
OARFISH ARE LONG PELAGIC (OPEN OCEAN) FISH AND ONE OF THE MOST RARELY SEEN ANIMALS ON EARTH.
WHAT DO OAR-FISH EAT?
THEIR FAVORITE MEAL IS KRILL, BUT THEY WILL ALSO EAT SMALL JELLYFISH AND SQUID.
AND UNLIKE THE GREAT WHITE SHARK, WHICH HAS NO BONES, OARFISH ARE THE LONGEST BONY FISH IN THE SEA.

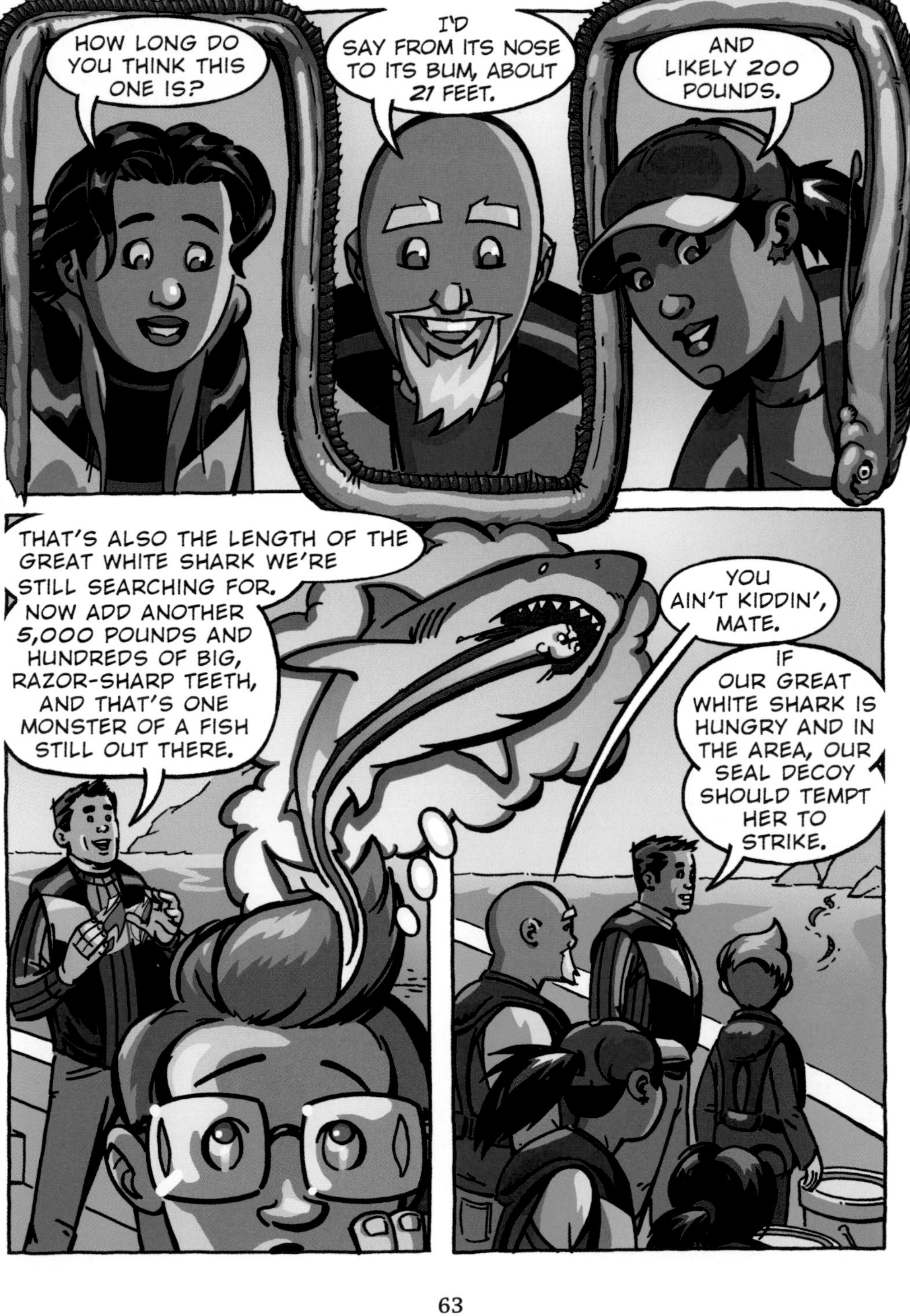
HOW LONG DO YOU THINK THIS ONE IS?
I'D SAY FROM ITS NOSE TO ITS BUM, ABOUT 21 FEET.
AND LIKELY 200 POUNDS.
THAT'S ALSO THE LENGTH OF THE GREAT WHITE SHARK WE'RE STILL SEARCHING FOR.
NOW ADD ANOTHER 5,000 POUNDS AND HUNDREDS OF BIG, RAZOR-SHARP TEETH, AND THAT'S ONE MONSTER OF A FISH STILL OUT THERE.
YOU AIN'T KIDDIN', MATE.
IF OUR GREAT WHITE SHARK IS HUNGRY AND IN THE AREA, OUR SEAL DECOY SHOULD TEMPT HER TO STRIKE.

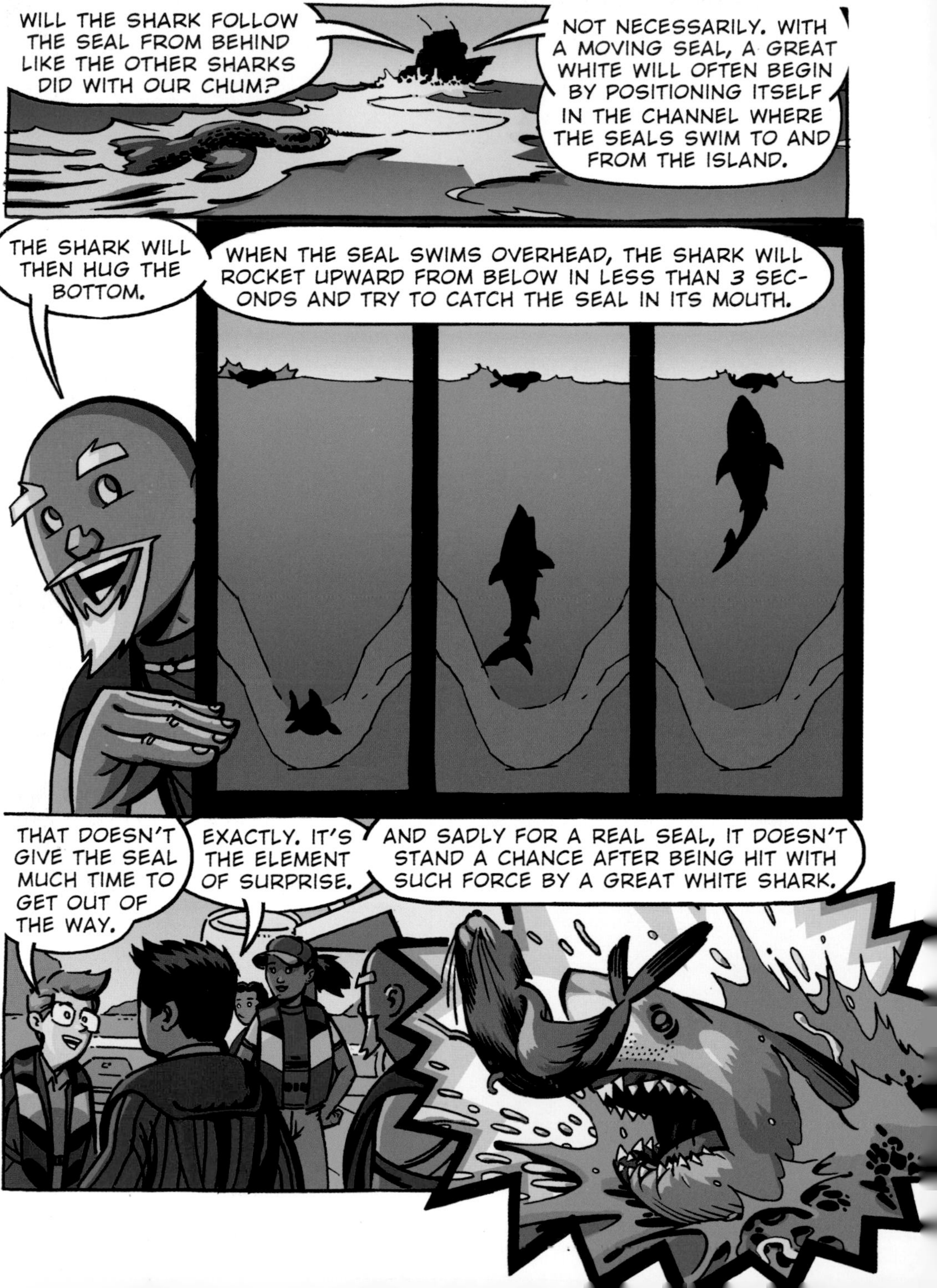
WILL THE SHARK FOLLOW THE SEAL FROM BEHIND LIKE THE OTHER SHARKS DID WITH OUR CHUM?
NOT NECESSARILY. WITH A MOVING SEAL, A GREAT WHITE WILL OFTEN BEGIN BY POSITIONING ITSELF IN THE CHANNEL WHERE THE SEALS SWIM TO AND FROM THE ISLAND.
THE SHARK WILL THEN HUG THE BOTTOM.
WHEN THE SEAL SWIMS OVERHEAD, THE SHARK WILL ROCKET UPWARD FROM BELOW IN LESS THAN 3 SEC-ONDS AND TRY TO CATCH THE SEAL IN ITS MOUTH.
THAT DOESN'T GIVE THE SEAL MUCH TIME TO GET OUT OF THE WAY.
EXACTLY. IT'S THE ELEMENT OF SURPRISE.
AND SADLY FOR A REAL SEAL, IT DOESN'T STAND A CHANCE AFTER BEING HIT WITH SUCH FORCE BY A GREAT WHITE SHARK.

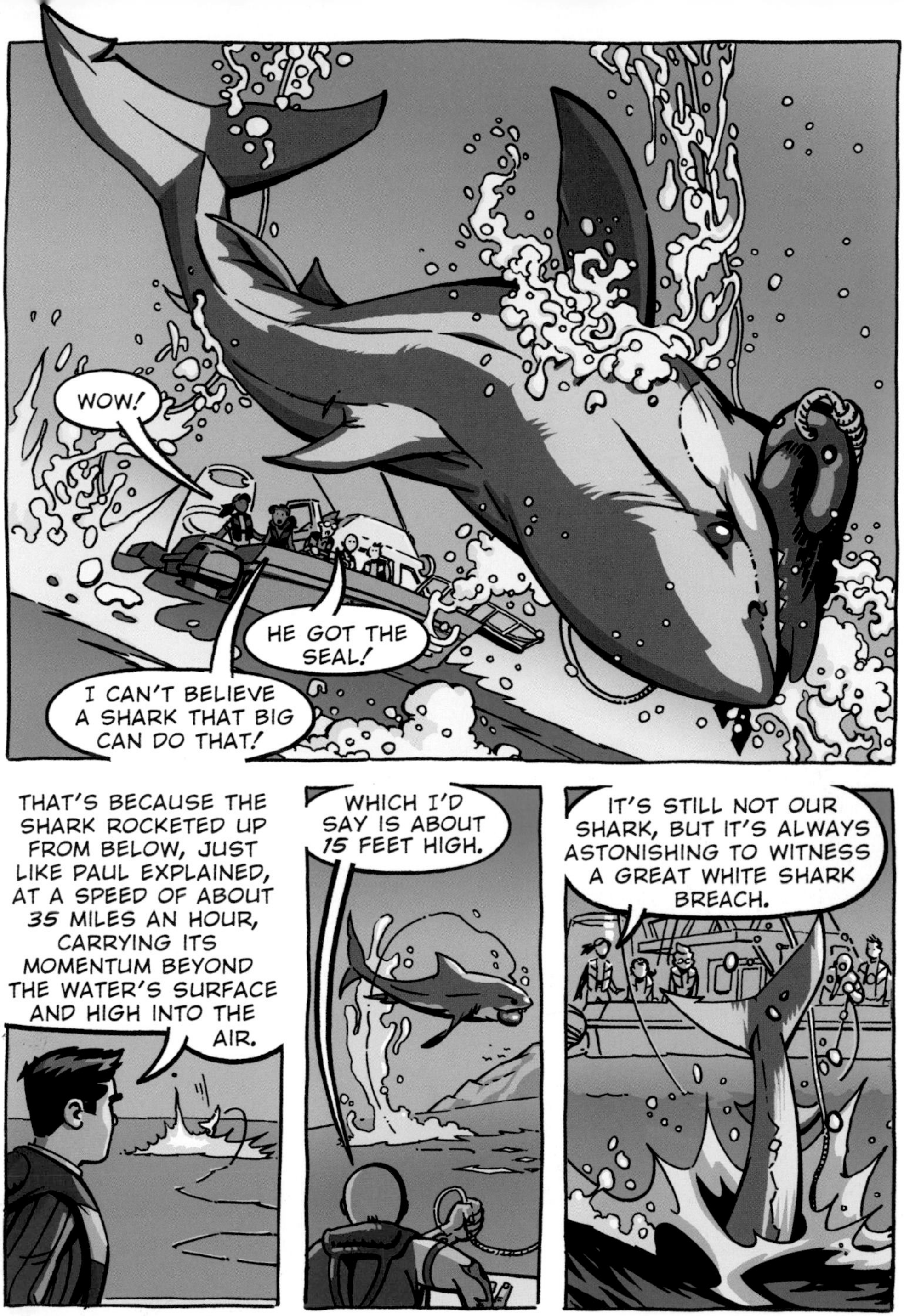
WOW!
HE GOT THE SEAL!
I CAN'T BELIEVE A SHARK THAT BIG CAN DO THAT!
THAT'S BECAUSE THE SHARK ROCKETED UP FROM BELOW, JUST LIKE PAUL EXPLAINED, AT A SPEED OF ABOUT 35 MILES AN HOUR, CARRYING ITS MOMENTUM BEYOND THE WATER'S SURFACE AND HIGH INTO THE AIR.
WHICH I'D SAY IS ABOUT 15 FEET HIGH.
IT'S STILL NOT OUR SHARK, BUT IT'S ALWAYS ASTONISHING TO WITNESS A GREAT WHITE SHARK BREACH.

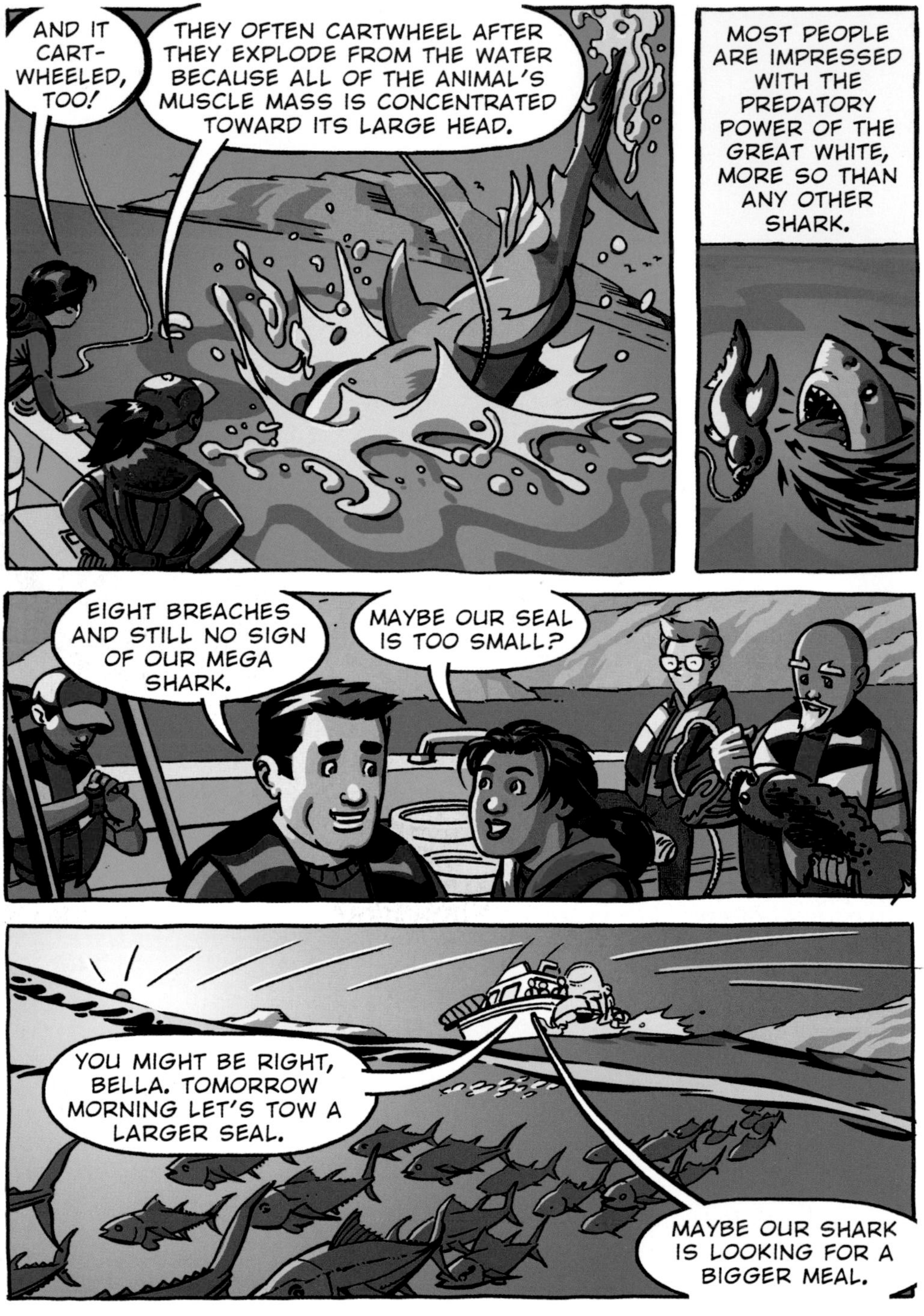
AND IT CART-WHEELED, TOO!
THEY OFTEN CARTWHEEL AFTER THEY EXPLODE FROM THE WATER BECAUSE ALL OF THE ANIMAL'S MUSCLE MASS IS CONCENTRATED TOWARD ITS LARGE HEAD.
MOST PEOPLE ARE IMPRESSED WITH THE PREDATORY POWER OF THE GREAT WHITE, MORE SO THAN ANY OTHER SHARK.
EIGHT BREACHES AND STILL NO SIGN OF OUR MEGA SHARK.
MAYBE OUR SEAL IS TOO SMALL?
YOU MIGHT BE RIGHT, BELLA. TOMORROW MORNING LET'S TOW A LARGER SEAL.
MAYBE OUR SHARK IS LOOKING FOR A BIGGER MEAL.

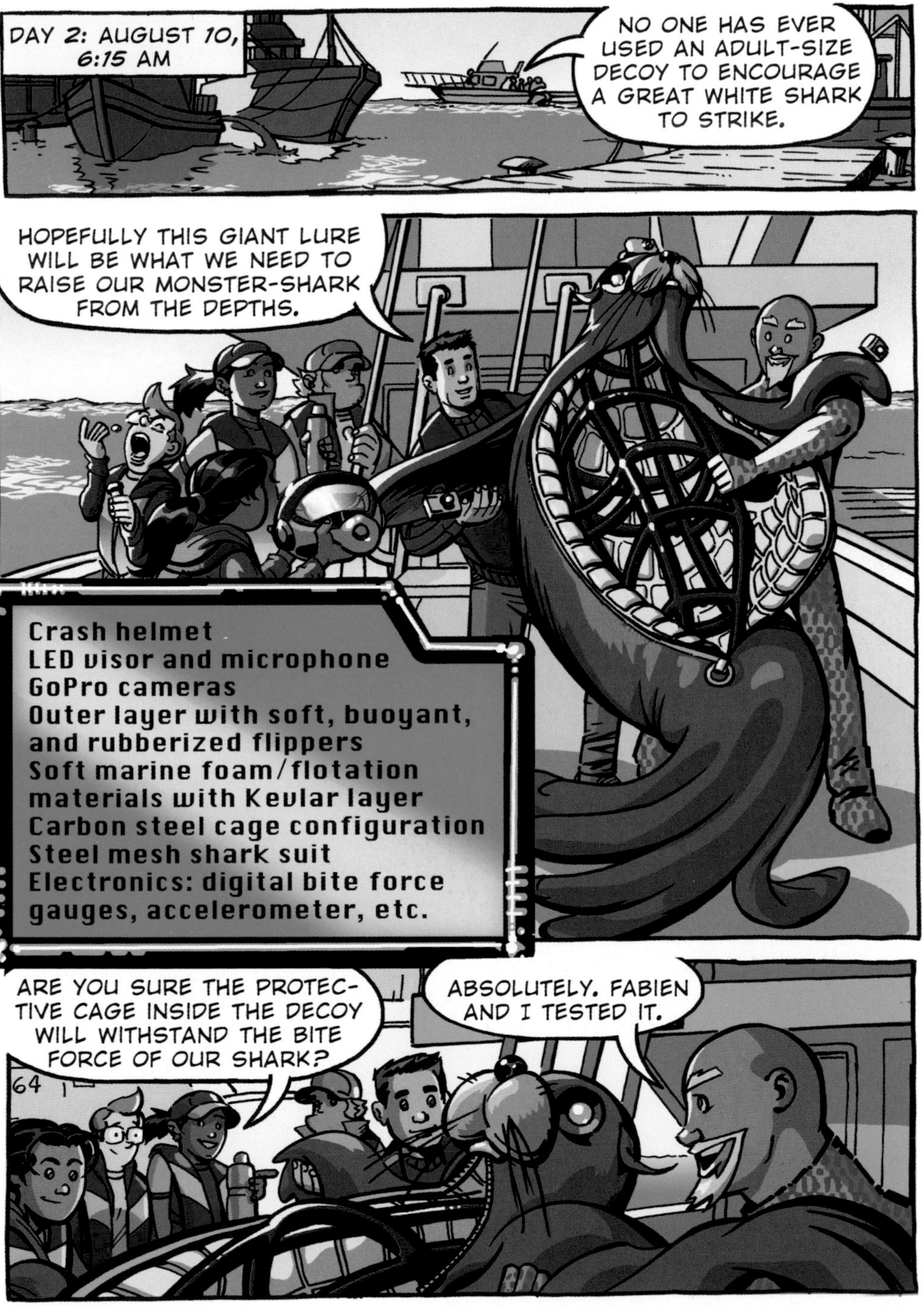
DAY 2: AUGUST 10, 6:15 AM
NO ONE HAS EVER USED AN ADULT-SIZE DECOY TO ENCOURAGE A GREAT WHITE SHARK TO STRIKE.
HOPEFULLY THIS GIANT LURE WILL BE WHAT WE NEED TO RAISE OUR MONSTER-SHARK FROM THE DEPTHS.
Crash helmet
LED visor and microphone
GoPro cameras
Outer layer with soft, buoyant, and rubberized flippers
Soft marine foam/flotation materials with Kevlar layer
Carbon steel cage configuration
Steel mesh shark suit
Electronics: digital bite force gauges, accelerometer, etc.
ARE YOU SURE THE PROTECTIVE CAGE INSIDE THE DECOY WILL WITHSTAND THE BITE FORCE OF OUR SHARK?
ABSOLUTELY. FABIEN AND I TESTED IT.

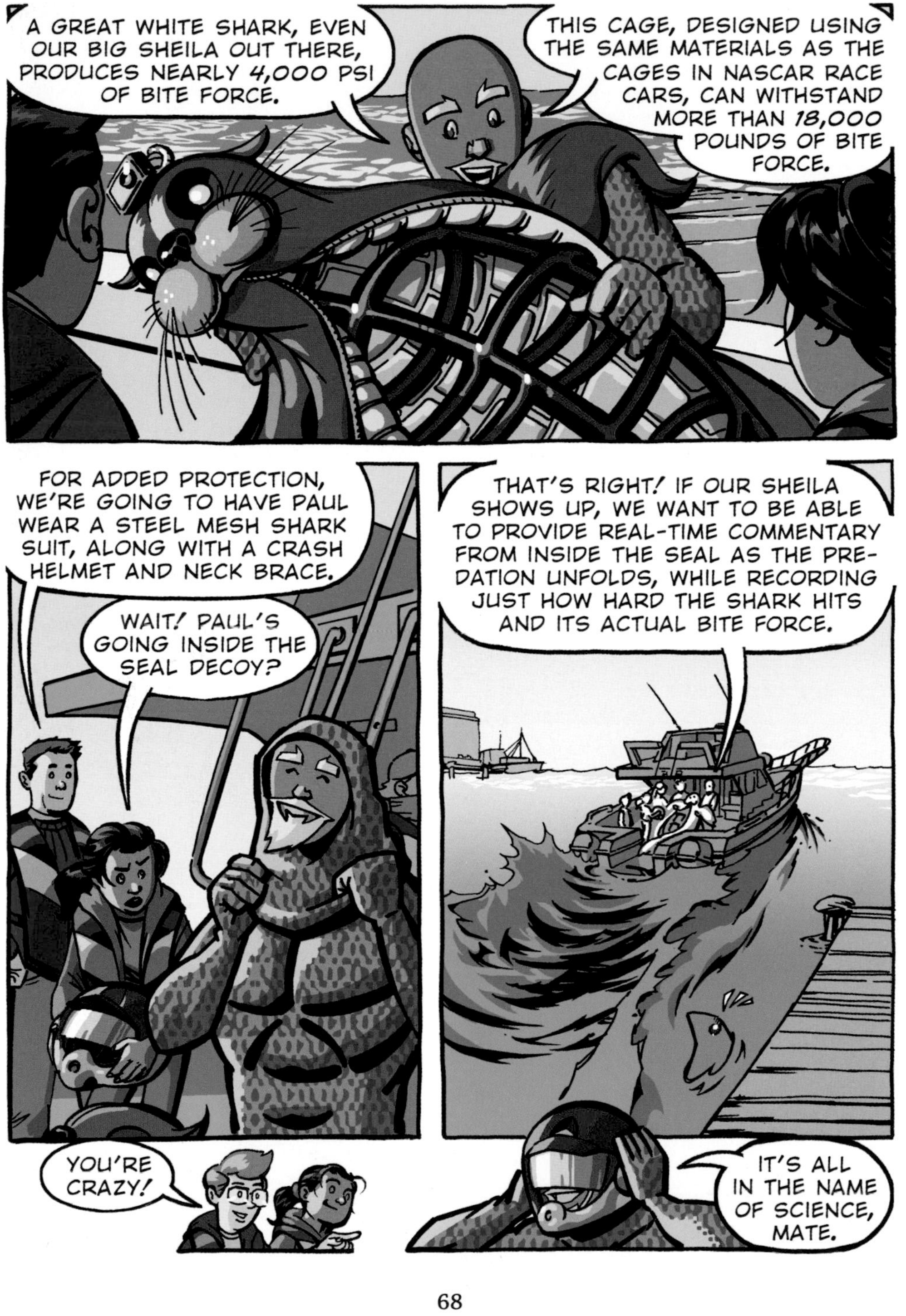
A GREAT WHITE SHARK, EVEN OUR BIG SHEILA OUT THERE, PRODUCES NEARLY 4,000 PSI OF BITE FORCE.
THIS CAGE, DESIGNED USING THE SAME MATERIALS AS THE CAGES IN NASCAR RACE CARS, CAN WITHSTAND MORE THAN 18,000 POUNDS OF BITE FORCE.
FOR ADDED PROTECTION, WE'RE GOING TO HAVE PAUL WEAR A STEEL MESH SHARK SUIT, ALONG WITH A CRASH HELMET AND NECK BRACE.
WAIT! PAUL'S GOING INSIDE THE SEAL DECOY?
THAT'S RIGHT! IF OUR SHEILA SHOWS UP, WE WANT TO BE ABLE TO PROVIDE REAL-TIME COMMENTARY FROM INSIDE THE SEAL AS THE PRE-DATION UNFOLDS, WHILE RECORDING JUST HOW HARD THE SHARK HITS AND ITS ACTUAL BITE FORCE.
YOU'RE CRAZY!
IT'S ALL IN THE NAME OF SCIENCE, MATE.

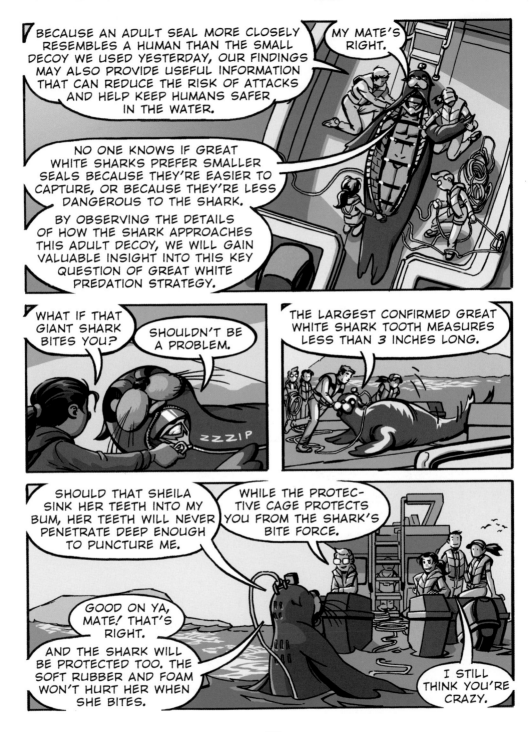

BECAUSE AN ADULT SEAL MORE CLOSELY RESEMBLES A HUMAN THAN THE SMALL DECOY WE USED YESTERDAY, OUR FINDINGS MAY ALSO PROVIDE USEFUL INFORMATION THAT CAN REDUCE THE RISK OF ATTACKS AND HELP KEEP HUMANS SAFER IN THE WATER.

MY MATE'S RIGHT.

NO ONE KNOWS IF GREAT WHITE SHARKS PREFER SMALLER SEALS BECAUSE THEY'RE EASIER TO CAPTURE, OR BECAUSE THEY'RE LESS DANGEROUS TO THE SHARK.

BY OBSERVING THE DETAILS OF HOW THE SHARK APPROACHES THIS ADULT DECOY, WE WILL GAIN VALUABLE INSIGHT INTO THIS KEY QUESTION OF GREAT WHITE PREDATION STRATEGY.

WHAT IF THAT GIANT SHARK BITES YOU?

SHOULDN'T BE A PROBLEM.

ZZZIP

THE LARGEST CONFIRMED GREAT WHITE SHARK TOOTH MEASURES LESS THAN 3 INCHES LONG.

SHOULD THAT SHEILA SINK HER TEETH INTO MY BUM, HER TEETH WILL NEVER PENETRATE DEEP ENOUGH TO PUNCTURE ME.

WHILE THE PROTECTIVE CAGE PROTECTS YOU FROM THE SHARK'S BITE FORCE.

GOOD ON YA, MATE! THAT'S RIGHT.

AND THE SHARK WILL BE PROTECTED TOO. THE SOFT RUBBER AND FOAM WON'T HURT HER WHEN SHE BITES.

I STILL THINK YOU'RE CRAZY.

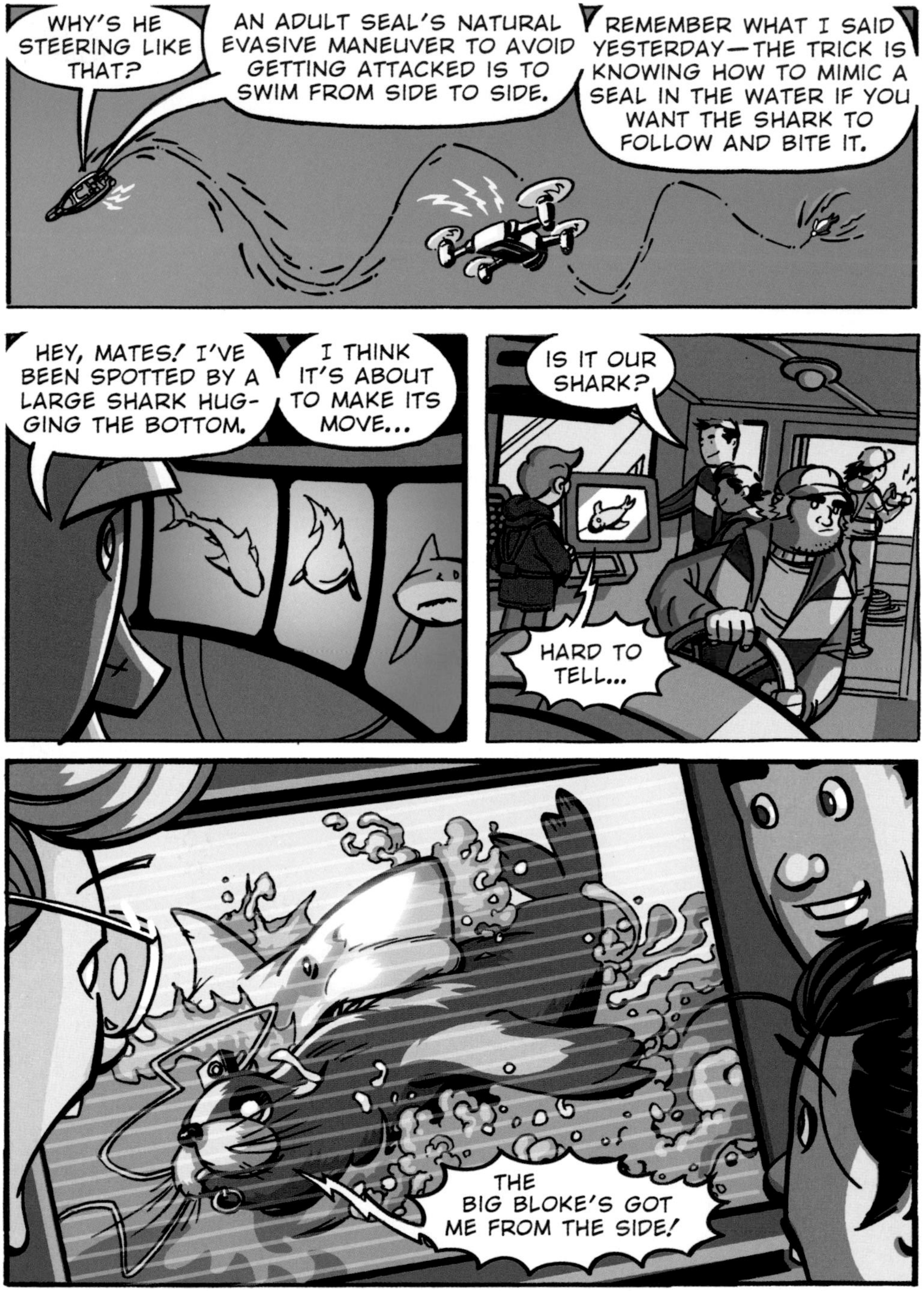
WHY'S HE STEERING LIKE THAT?
AN ADULT SEAL'S NATURAL EVASIVE MANEUVER TO AVOID GETTING ATTACKED IS TO SWIM FROM SIDE TO SIDE.
REMEMBER WHAT I SAID YESTERDAY—THE TRICK IS KNOWING HOW TO MIMIC A SEAL IN THE WATER IF YOU WANT THE SHARK TO FOLLOW AND BITE IT.
HEY, MATES! I'VE BEEN SPOTTED BY A LARGE SHARK HUG-GING THE BOTTOM.
I THINK IT'S ABOUT TO MAKE ITS MOVE...
IS IT OUR SHARK?
HARD TO TELL...
THE BIG BLOKE'S GOT ME FROM THE SIDE!

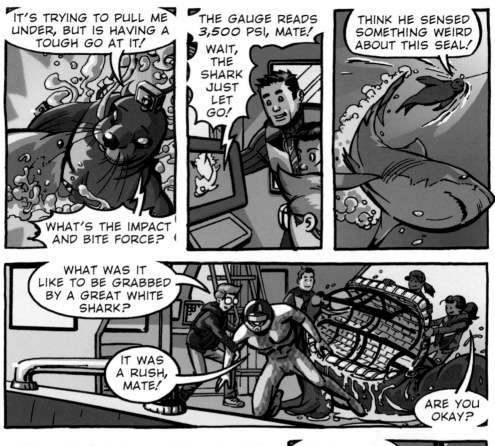

IT'S TRYING TO PULL ME UNDER, BUT IS HAVING A TOUGH GO AT IT!

WHAT'S THE IMPACT AND BITE FORCE?

THE GAUGE READS 3,500 PSI, MATE!

WAIT, THE SHARK JUST LET GO!

THINK HE SENSED SOMETHING WEIRD ABOUT THIS SEAL!

WHAT WAS IT LIKE TO BE GRABBED BY A GREAT WHITE SHARK?

IT WAS A RUSH, MATE!

ARE YOU OKAY?

NOT A NICK! HE WAS A STRONG ONE! I COULD FEEL HIS AWESOME STRENGTH, BUT AFTER A MOMENT HE REALIZED HE WASN'T BITING INTO A REAL SEAL.

OFF THE STAR-BOARD SIDE!

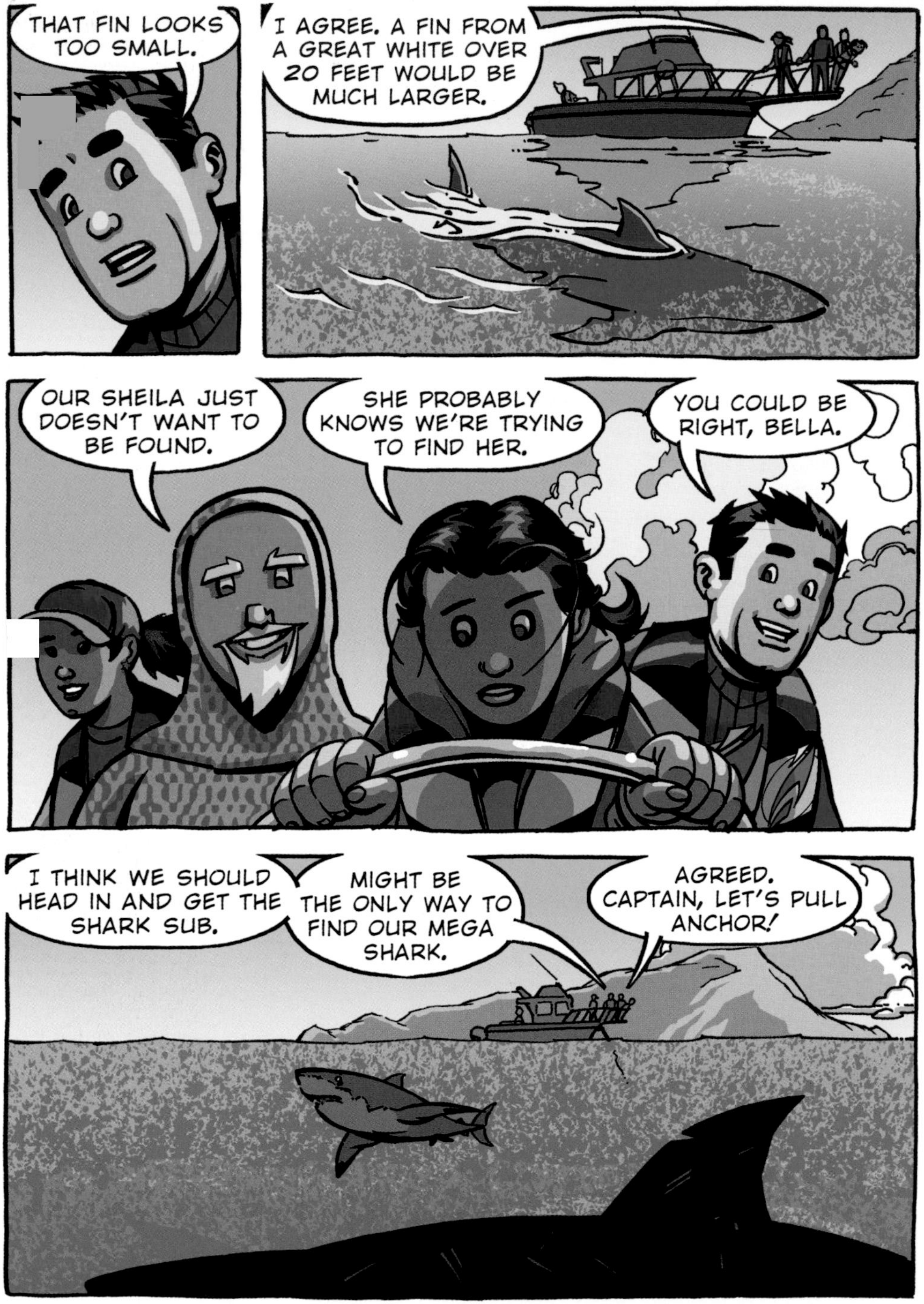
THAT FIN LOOKS TOO SMALL.
I AGREE. A FIN FROM A GREAT WHITE OVER 20 FEET WOULD BE MUCH LARGER.
OUR SHEILA JUST DOESN'T WANT TO BE FOUND.
SHE PROBABLY KNOWS WE'RE TRYING TO FIND HER.
YOU COULD BE RIGHT, BELLA.
I THINK WE SHOULD HEAD IN AND GET THE SHARK SUB.
MIGHT BE THE ONLY WAY TO FIND OUR MEGA SHARK.
AGREED. CAPTAIN, LET'S PULL ANCHOR!

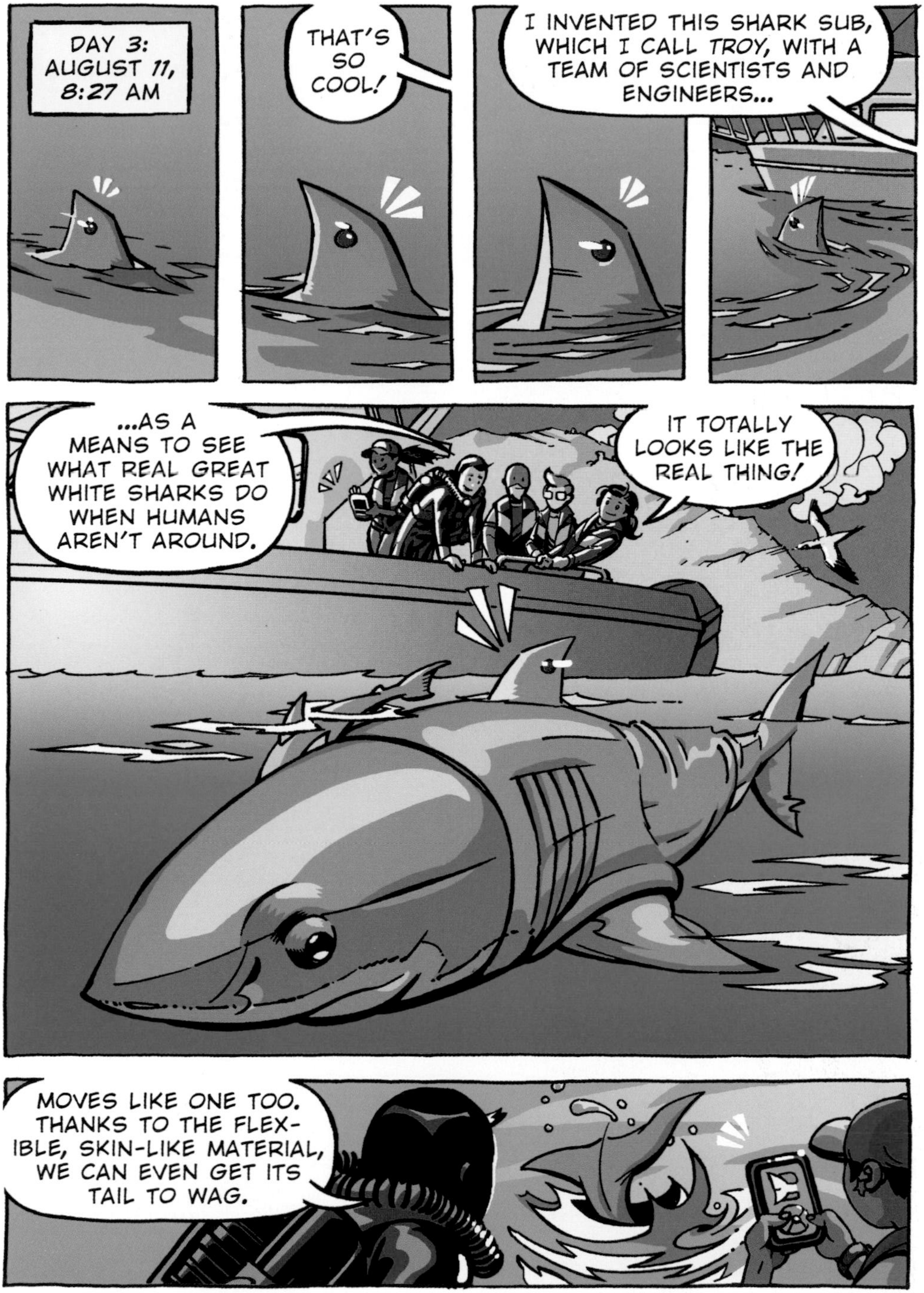
DAY 3: AUGUST 11, 8:27 AM
THAT'S SO COOL!
I INVENTED THIS SHARK SUB, WHICH I CALL *TROY*, WITH A TEAM OF SCIENTISTS AND ENGINEERS...
...AS A MEANS TO SEE WHAT REAL GREAT WHITE SHARKS DO WHEN HUMANS AREN'T AROUND.
IT TOTALLY LOOKS LIKE THE REAL THING!
MOVES LIKE ONE TOO. THANKS TO THE FLEX-IBLE, SKIN-LIKE MATERIAL, WE CAN EVEN GET ITS TAIL TO WAG.

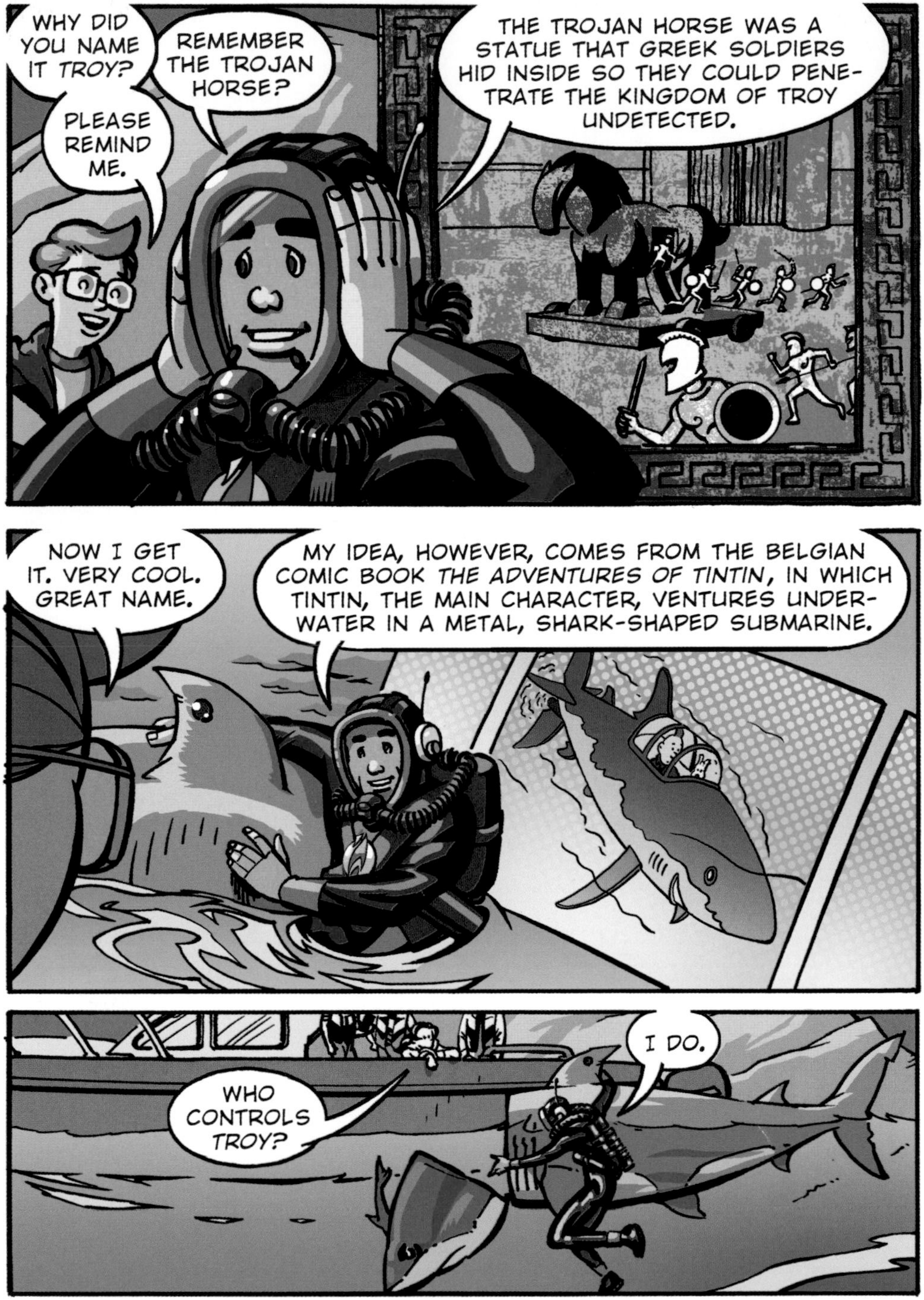
WHY DID YOU NAME IT *TROY?*
REMEMBER THE TROJAN HORSE?
PLEASE REMIND ME.
THE TROJAN HORSE WAS A STATUE THAT GREEK SOLDIERS HID INSIDE SO THEY COULD PENETRATE THE KINGDOM OF TROY UNDETECTED.
NOW I GET IT. VERY COOL. GREAT NAME.
MY IDEA, HOWEVER, COMES FROM THE BELGIAN COMIC BOOK *THE ADVENTURES OF TINTIN*, IN WHICH TINTIN, THE MAIN CHARACTER, VENTURES UNDERWATER IN A METAL, SHARK-SHAPED SUBMARINE.
WHO CONTROLS *TROY?*
I DO.

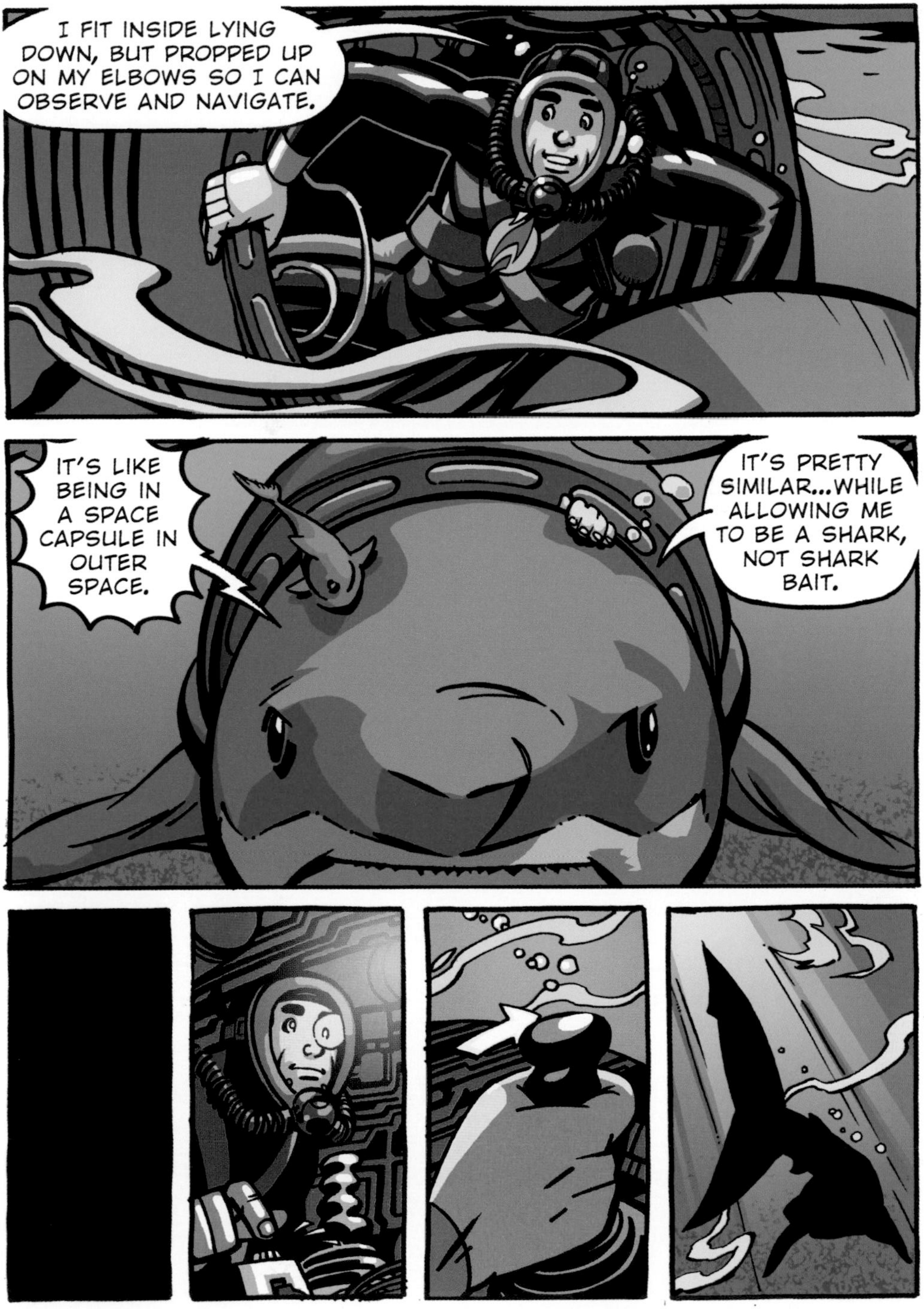
I FIT INSIDE LYING DOWN, BUT PROPPED UP ON MY ELBOWS SO I CAN OBSERVE AND NAVIGATE.
IT'S LIKE BEING IN A SPACE CAPSULE IN OUTER SPACE.
IT'S PRETTY SIMILAR...WHILE ALLOWING ME TO BE A SHARK, NOT SHARK BAIT.

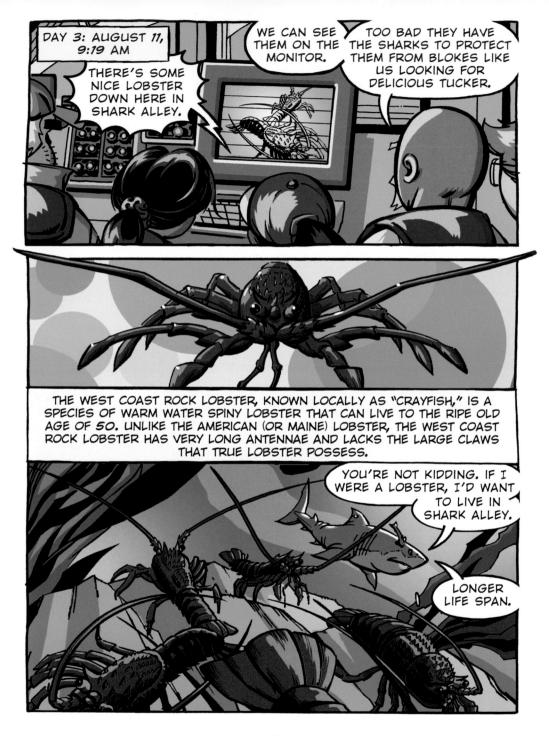

DAY 3: AUGUST 11, 9:19 AM

THERE'S SOME NICE LOBSTER DOWN HERE IN SHARK ALLEY.

WE CAN SEE THEM ON THE MONITOR.

TOO BAD THEY HAVE THE SHARKS TO PROTECT THEM FROM BLOKES LIKE US LOOKING FOR DELICIOUS TUCKER.

THE WEST COAST ROCK LOBSTER, KNOWN LOCALLY AS "CRAYFISH," IS A SPECIES OF WARM WATER SPINY LOBSTER THAT CAN LIVE TO THE RIPE OLD AGE OF 50. UNLIKE THE AMERICAN (OR MAINE) LOBSTER, THE WEST COAST ROCK LOBSTER HAS VERY LONG ANTENNAE AND LACKS THE LARGE CLAWS THAT TRUE LOBSTER POSSESS.

YOU'RE NOT KIDDING. IF I WERE A LOBSTER, I'D WANT TO LIVE IN SHARK ALLEY.

LONGER LIFE SPAN.

76

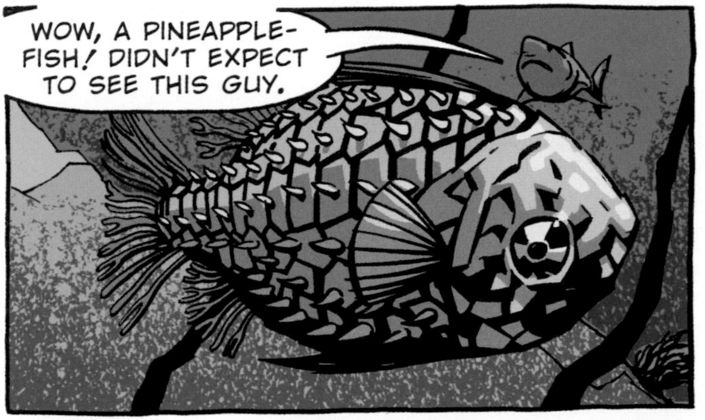
WOW, A PINEAPPLE-FISH! DIDN'T EXPECT TO SEE THIS GUY.

A PINEAPPLEFISH OR PINECONE FISH IS AN UNUSUAL VISITOR IN THE CAPE, AS IT NATURALLY PREFERS CORAL REEFS IN WARMER WATERS, LIKE THE RED SEA. PINEAPPLEFISH ARE SOLITARY ANIMALS THAT OFTEN ONLY COME OUT FROM THEIR HIDING PLACES AT NIGHT TO FEED.

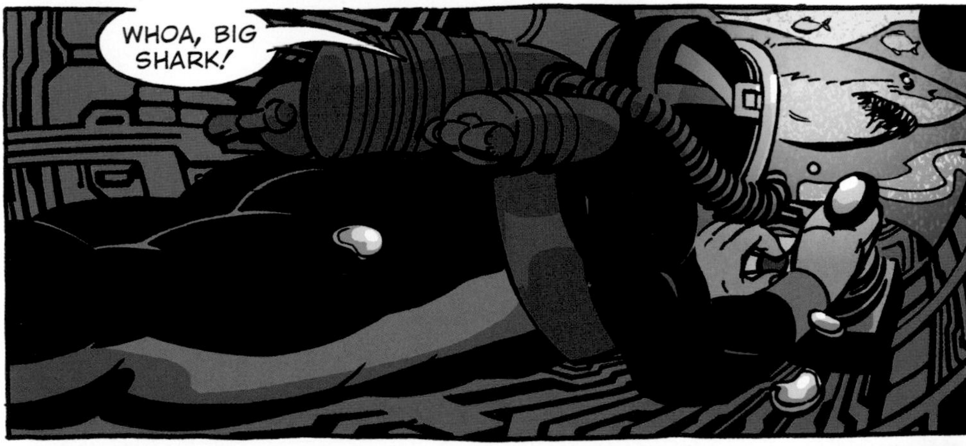
WHOA, BIG SHARK!

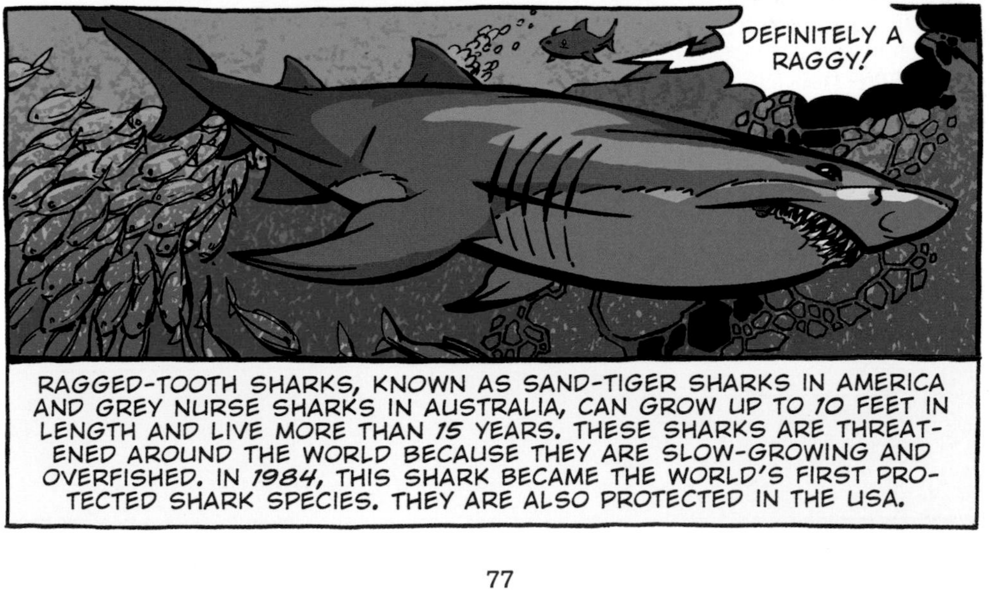
DEFINITELY A RAGGY!

RAGGED-TOOTH SHARKS, KNOWN AS SAND-TIGER SHARKS IN AMERICA AND GREY NURSE SHARKS IN AUSTRALIA, CAN GROW UP TO *10* FEET IN LENGTH AND LIVE MORE THAN *15* YEARS. THESE SHARKS ARE THREATENED AROUND THE WORLD BECAUSE THEY ARE SLOW-GROWING AND OVERFISHED. IN *1984*, THIS SHARK BECAME THE WORLD'S FIRST PROTECTED SHARK SPECIES. THEY ARE ALSO PROTECTED IN THE USA.

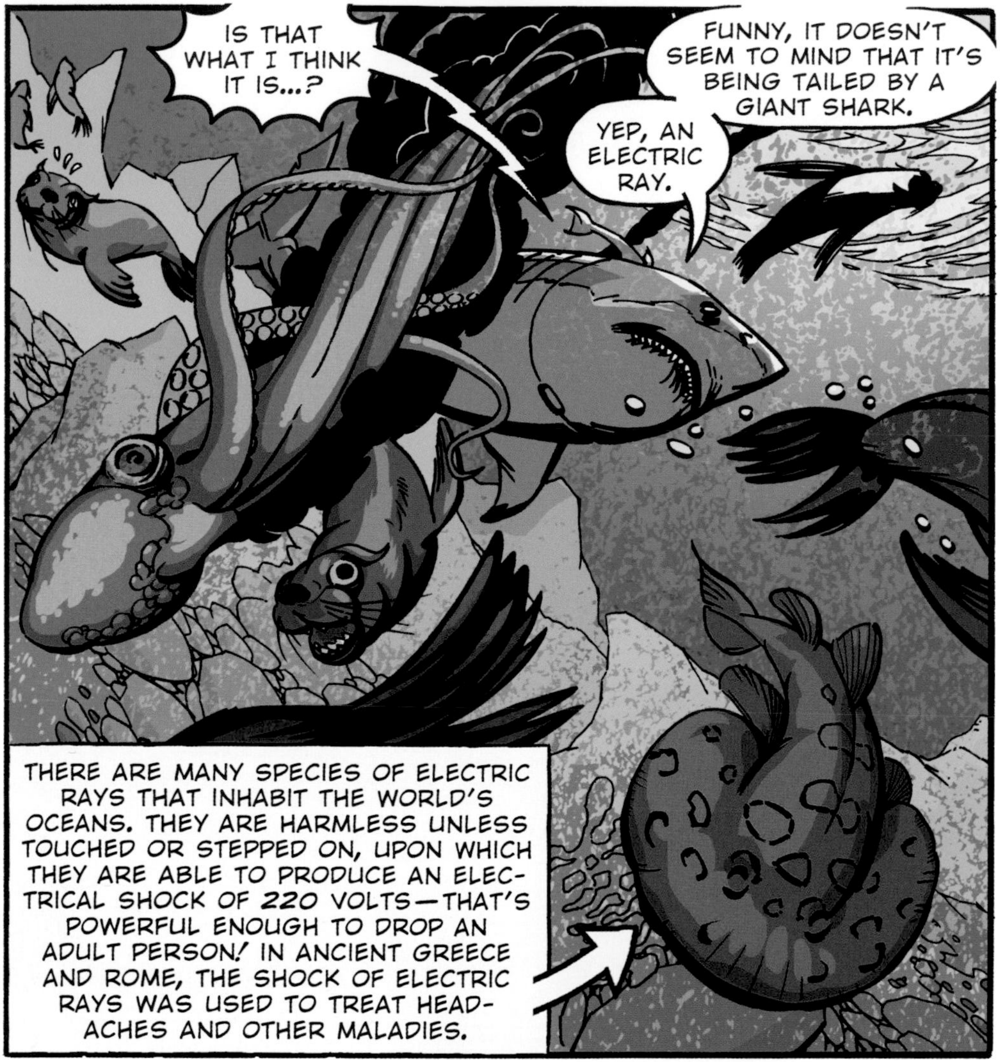

IS THAT WHAT I THINK IT IS...?
FUNNY, IT DOESN'T SEEM TO MIND THAT IT'S BEING TAILED BY A GIANT SHARK.
YEP, AN ELECTRIC RAY.
THERE ARE MANY SPECIES OF ELECTRIC RAYS THAT INHABIT THE WORLD'S OCEANS. THEY ARE HARMLESS UNLESS TOUCHED OR STEPPED ON, UPON WHICH THEY ARE ABLE TO PRODUCE AN ELECTRICAL SHOCK OF 220 VOLTS—THAT'S POWERFUL ENOUGH TO DROP AN ADULT PERSON! IN ANCIENT GREECE AND ROME, THE SHOCK OF ELECTRIC RAYS WAS USED TO TREAT HEADACHES AND OTHER MALADIES.

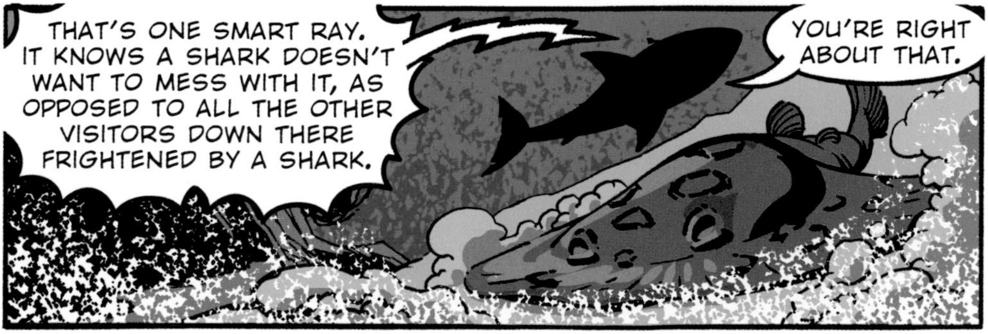

THAT'S ONE SMART RAY. IT KNOWS A SHARK DOESN'T WANT TO MESS WITH IT, AS OPPOSED TO ALL THE OTHER VISITORS DOWN THERE FRIGHTENED BY A SHARK.
YOU'RE RIGHT ABOUT THAT.

GUITARFISH, NAMED AFTER THEIR SHAPE, WHICH RESEMBLES A GUITAR, ARE CLOSELY RELATED TO RAYS AND HAVE A SHARK-LIKE TAIL. THERE ARE ABOUT 50 DIFFERENT SPECIES OF GUITARFISH WORLDWIDE. THEY CAN REACH A LENGTH OF 5 OR 6 FEET, ALTHOUGH THE GUITARFISH FOUND IN THE INDO-PACIFIC CAN REACH 10 FEET.

CUTTLEFISH, MEANWHILE, ARE RELATED TO THE SQUID AND OCTOPUS. A CUTTLEFISH HAS AN ELONGATED BODY AND TENTACLES AROUND ITS MOUTH. THERE ARE ABOUT 120 SPECIES OF CUTTLE-FISH, WHICH ARE A FAVORITE MEAL FOR SHARKS.

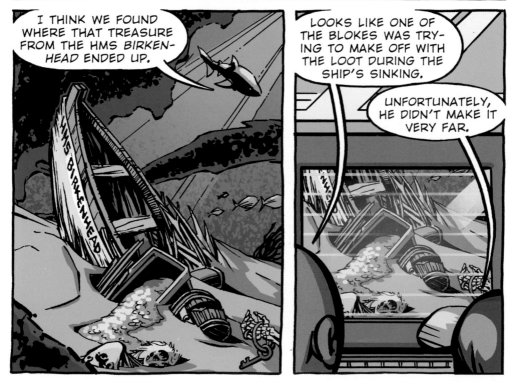

I THINK WE FOUND WHERE THAT TREASURE FROM THE HMS BIRKEN-HEAD ENDED UP.

LOOKS LIKE ONE OF THE BLOKES WAS TRY-ING TO MAKE OFF WITH THE LOOT DURING THE SHIP'S SINKING.

UNFORTUNATELY, HE DIDN'T MAKE IT VERY FAR.

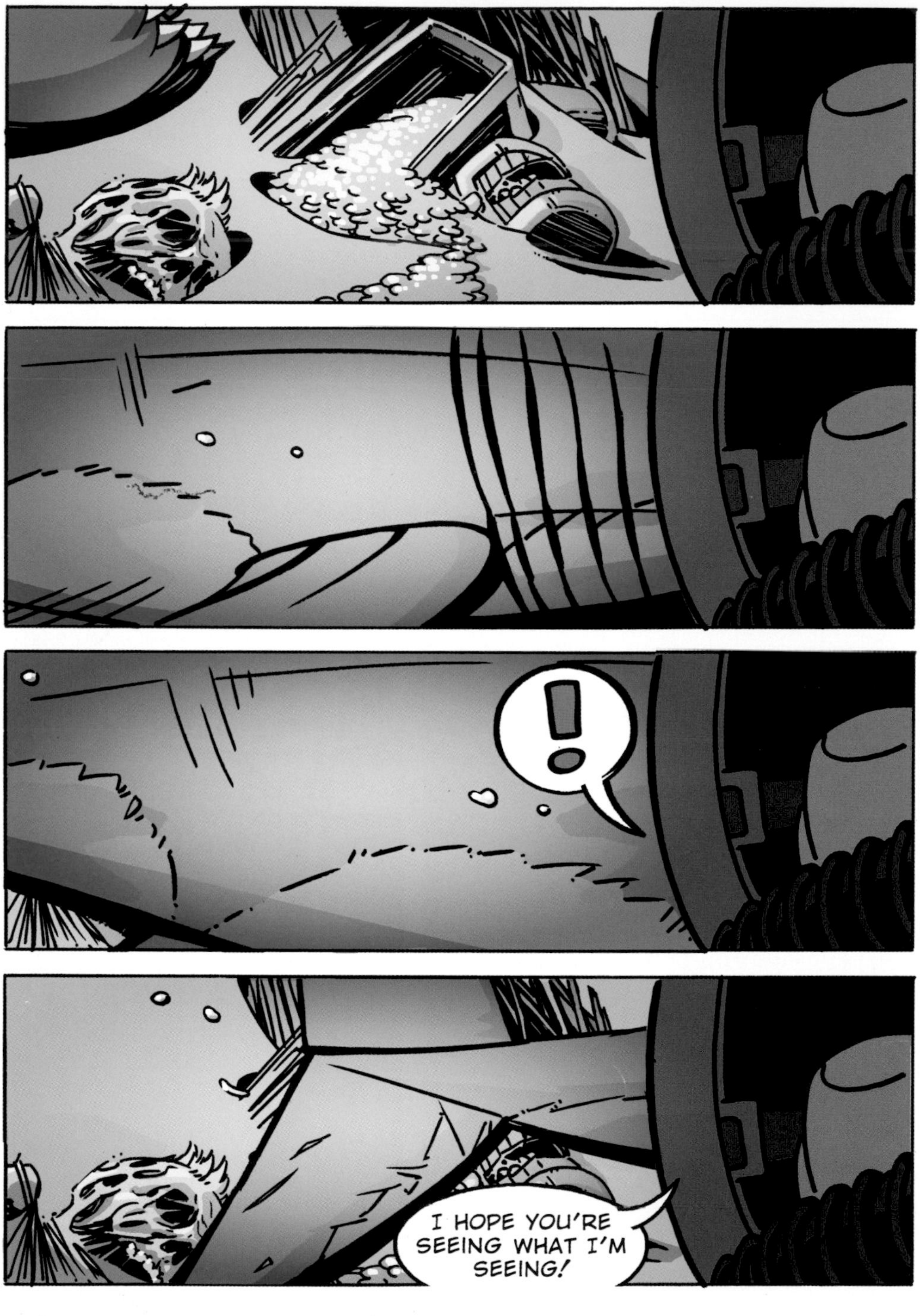
!
I HOPE YOU'RE SEEING WHAT I'M SEEING!

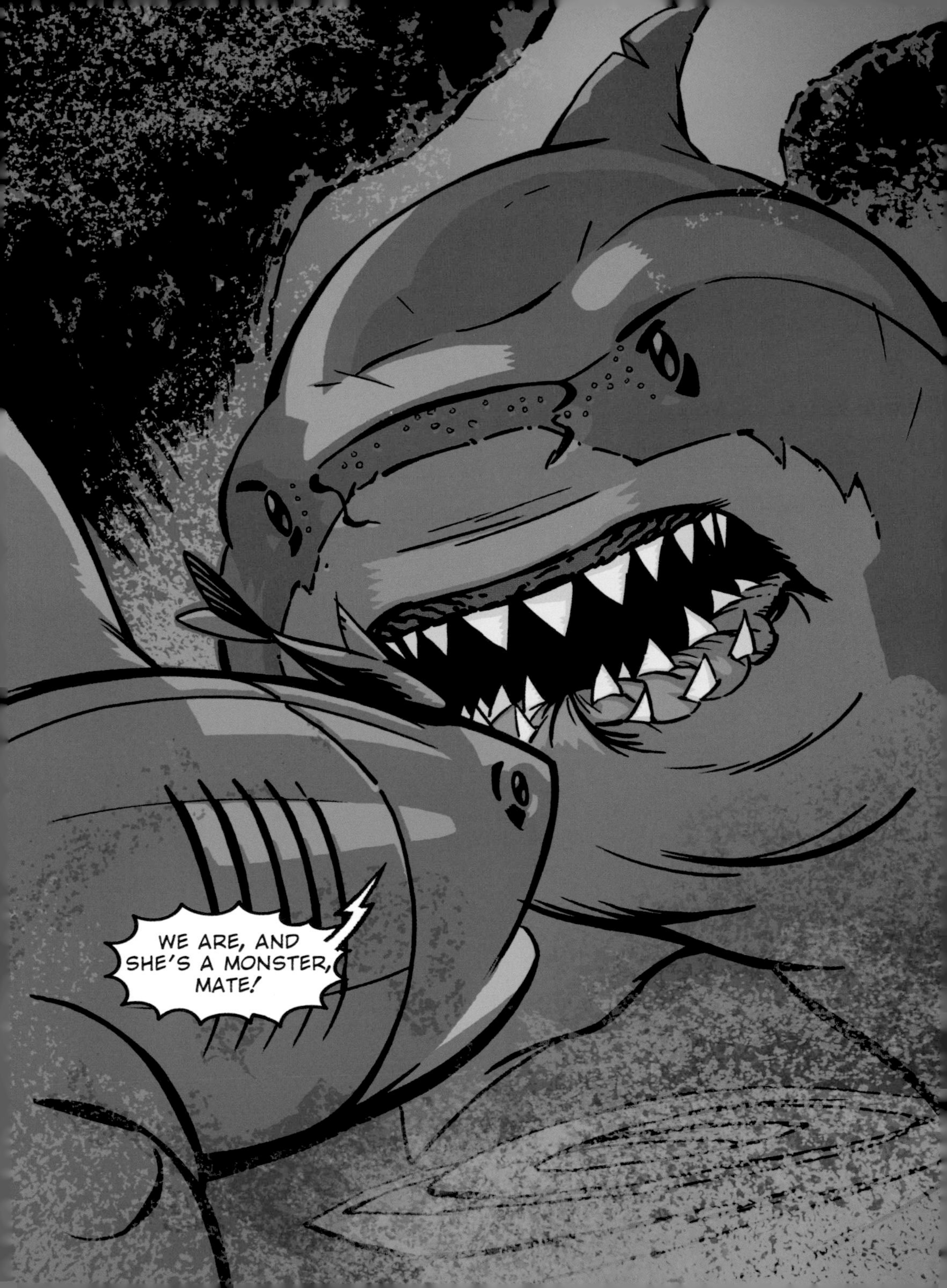
WE ARE, AND SHE'S A MONSTER, MATE!

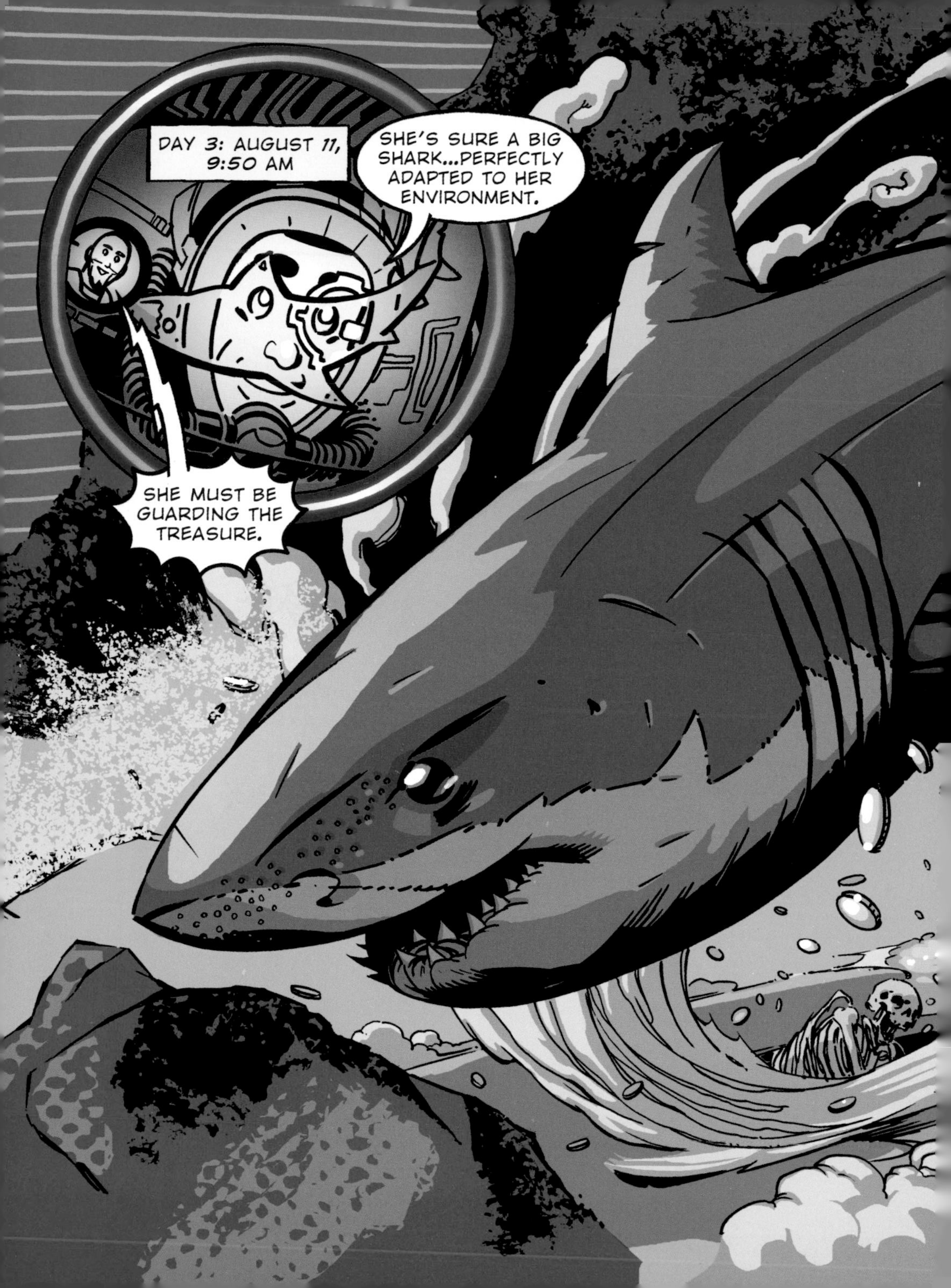
DAY 3: AUGUST 11, 9:50 AM
SHE'S SURE A BIG SHARK...PERFECTLY ADAPTED TO HER ENVIRONMENT.
SHE MUST BE GUARDING THE TREASURE.

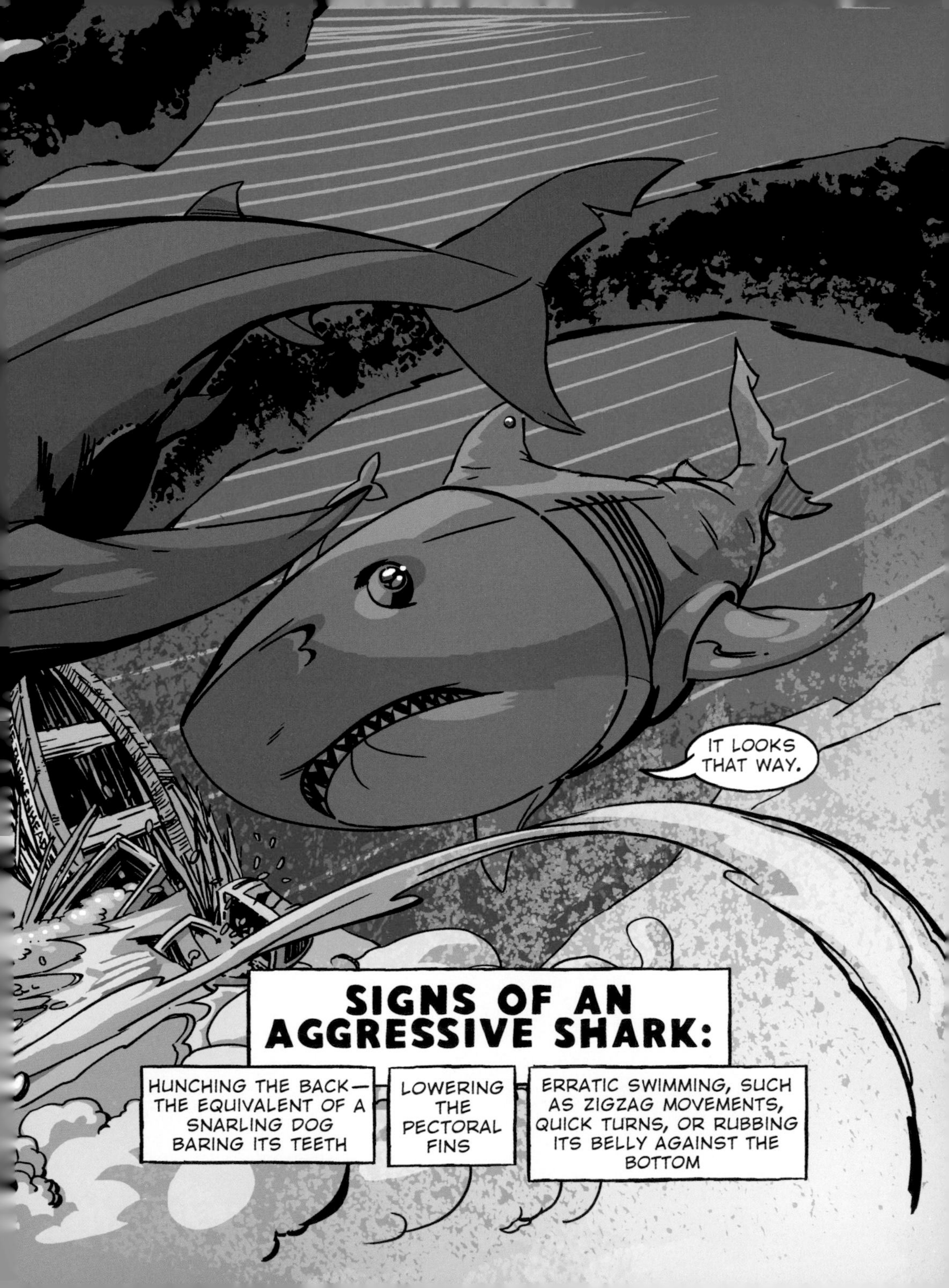
IT LOOKS THAT WAY.
SIGNS OF AN AGGRESSIVE SHARK:
HUNCHING THE BACK—THE EQUIVALENT OF A SNARLING DOG BARING ITS TEETH
LOWERING THE PECTORAL FINS
ERRATIC SWIMMING, SUCH AS ZIGZAG MOVEMENTS, QUICK TURNS, OR RUBBING ITS BELLY AGAINST THE BOTTOM

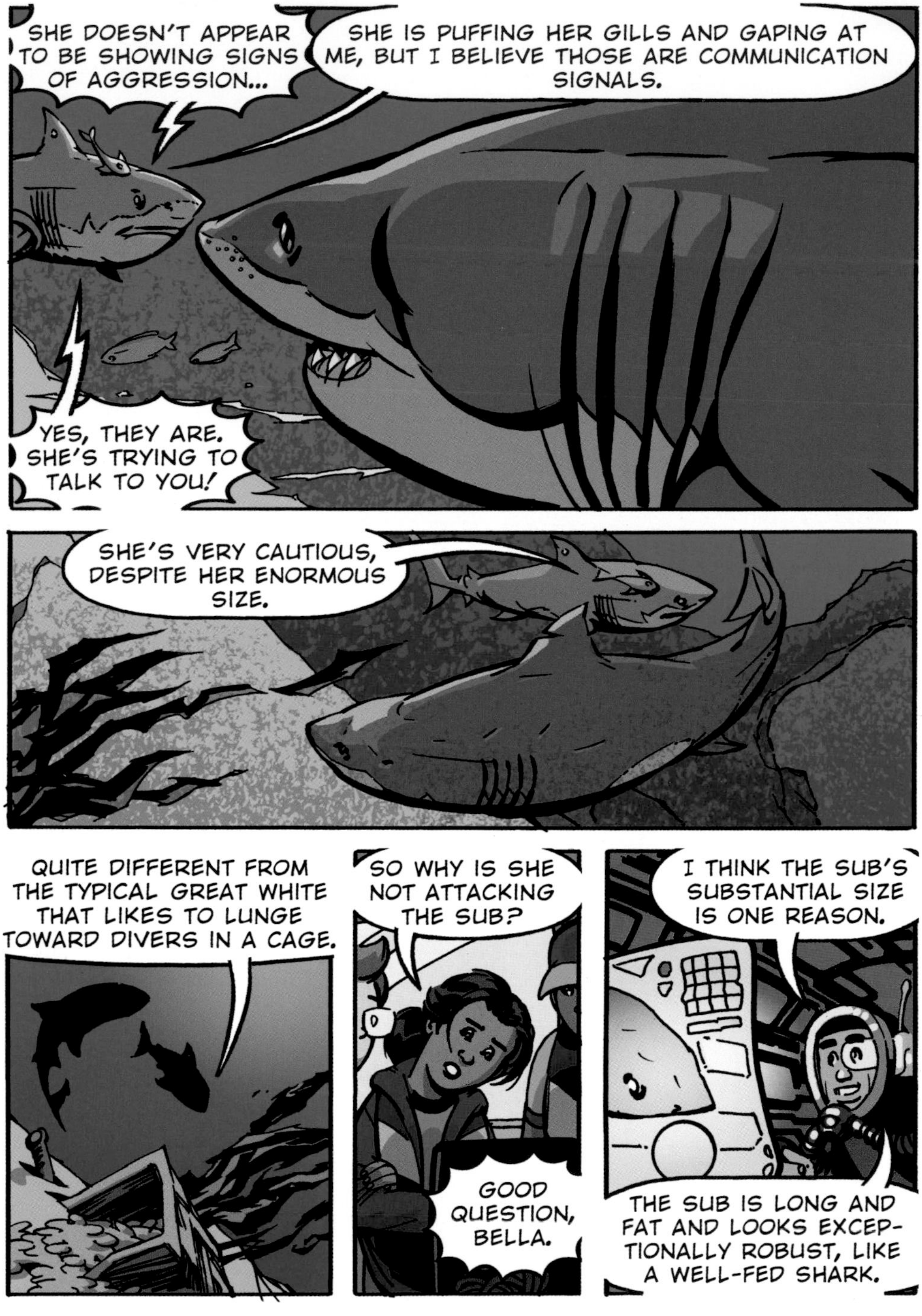

SHE DOESN'T APPEAR TO BE SHOWING SIGNS OF AGGRESSION...
SHE IS PUFFING HER GILLS AND GAPING AT ME, BUT I BELIEVE THOSE ARE COMMUNICATION SIGNALS.
YES, THEY ARE. SHE'S TRYING TO TALK TO YOU!
SHE'S VERY CAUTIOUS, DESPITE HER ENORMOUS SIZE.
QUITE DIFFERENT FROM THE TYPICAL GREAT WHITE THAT LIKES TO LUNGE TOWARD DIVERS IN A CAGE.
SO WHY IS SHE NOT ATTACKING THE SUB?
GOOD QUESTION, BELLA.
I THINK THE SUB'S SUBSTANTIAL SIZE IS ONE REASON.
THE SUB IS LONG AND FAT AND LOOKS EXCEPTIONALLY ROBUST, LIKE A WELL-FED SHARK.

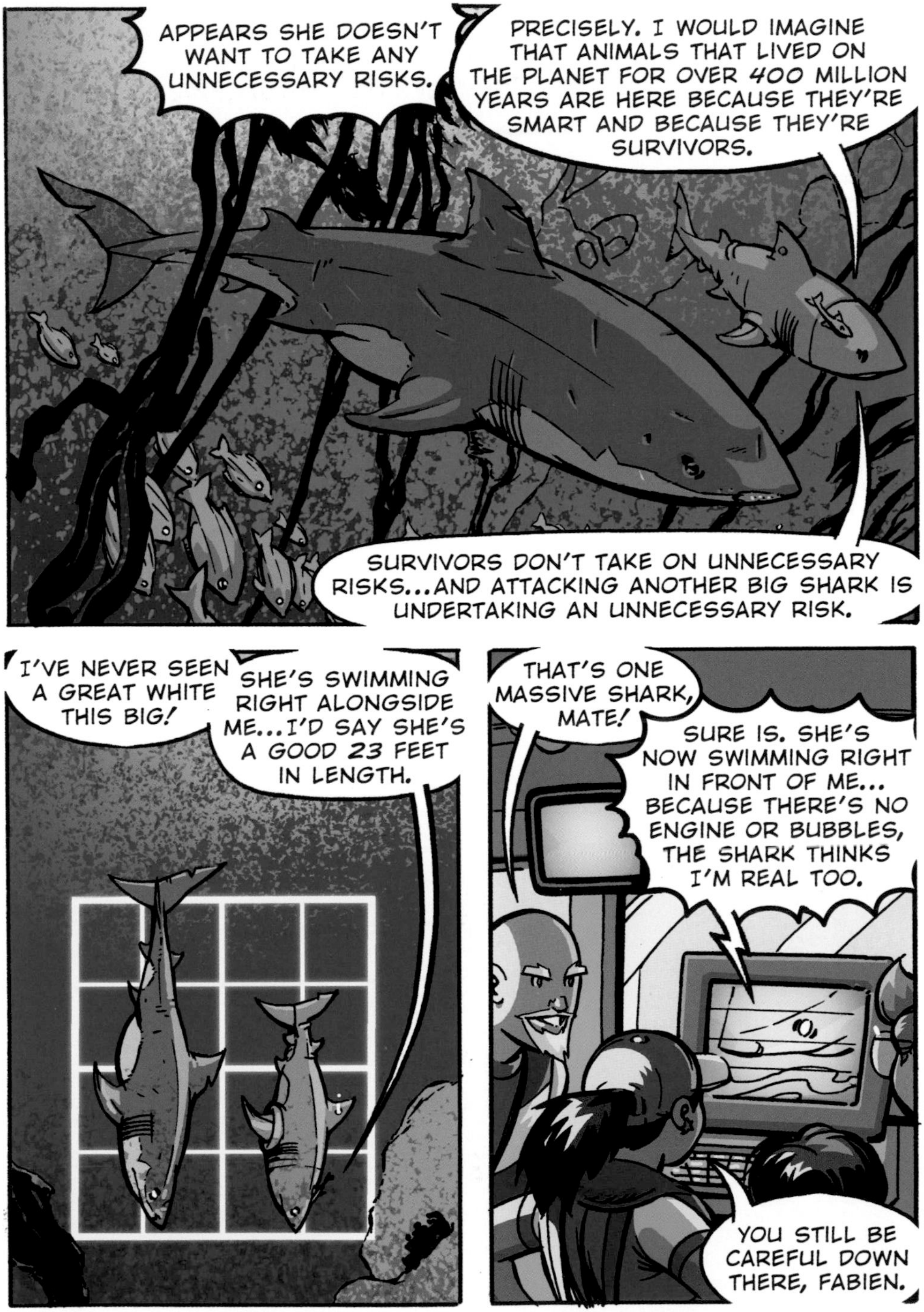

APPEARS SHE DOESN'T WANT TO TAKE ANY UNNECESSARY RISKS.
PRECISELY. I WOULD IMAGINE THAT ANIMALS THAT LIVED ON THE PLANET FOR OVER 400 MILLION YEARS ARE HERE BECAUSE THEY'RE SMART AND BECAUSE THEY'RE SURVIVORS.
SURVIVORS DON'T TAKE ON UNNECESSARY RISKS...AND ATTACKING ANOTHER BIG SHARK IS UNDERTAKING AN UNNECESSARY RISK.
I'VE NEVER SEEN A GREAT WHITE THIS BIG!
SHE'S SWIMMING RIGHT ALONGSIDE ME...I'D SAY SHE'S A GOOD 23 FEET IN LENGTH.
THAT'S ONE MASSIVE SHARK, MATE!
SURE IS. SHE'S NOW SWIMMING RIGHT IN FRONT OF ME... BECAUSE THERE'S NO ENGINE OR BUBBLES, THE SHARK THINKS I'M REAL TOO.
YOU STILL BE CAREFUL DOWN THERE, FABIEN.

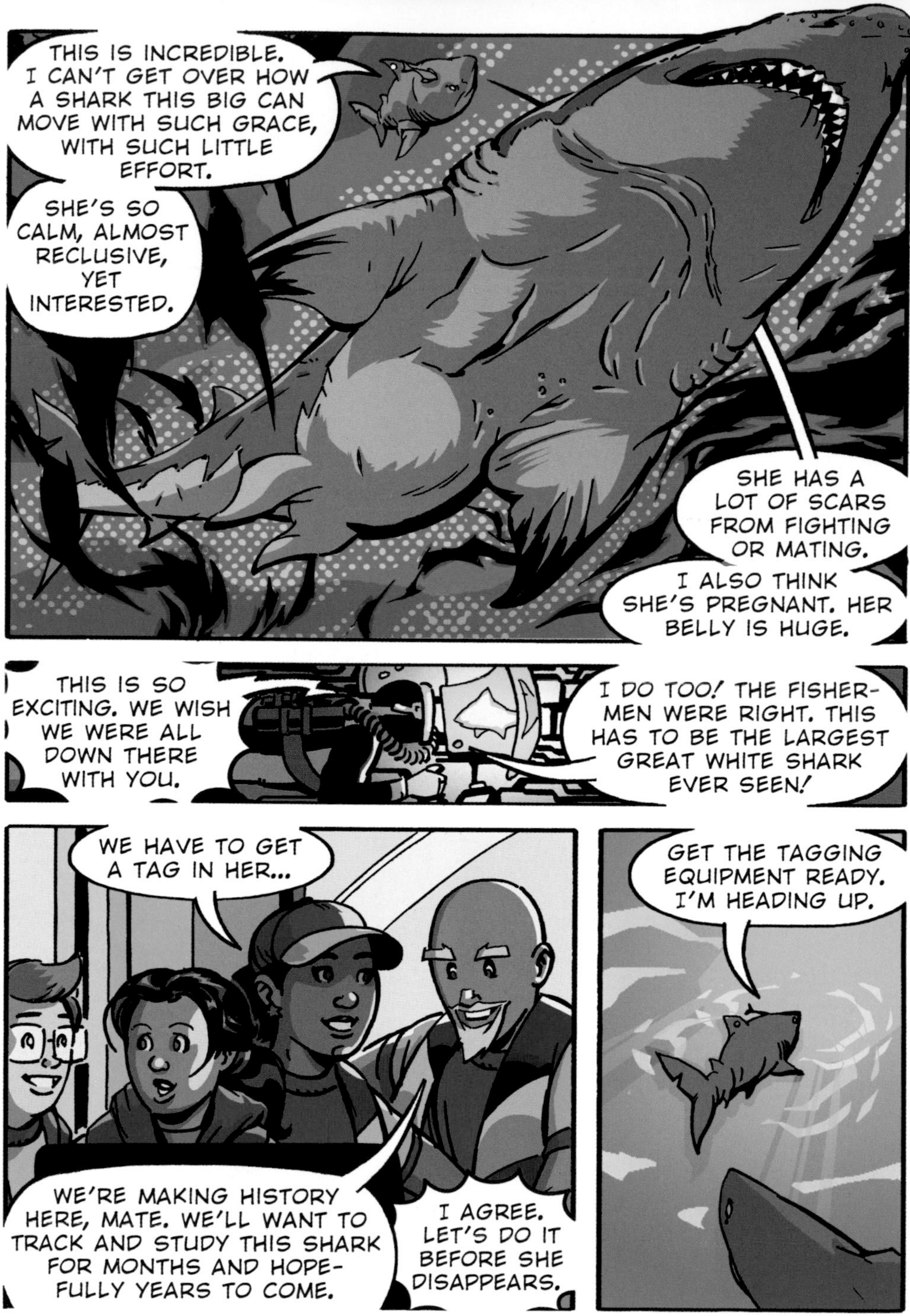
THIS IS INCREDIBLE. I CAN'T GET OVER HOW A SHARK THIS BIG CAN MOVE WITH SUCH GRACE, WITH SUCH LITTLE EFFORT.
SHE'S SO CALM, ALMOST RECLUSIVE, YET INTERESTED.
SHE HAS A LOT OF SCARS FROM FIGHTING OR MATING.
I ALSO THINK SHE'S PREGNANT. HER BELLY IS HUGE.
THIS IS SO EXCITING. WE WISH WE WERE ALL DOWN THERE WITH YOU.
I DO TOO! THE FISHERMEN WERE RIGHT. THIS HAS TO BE THE LARGEST GREAT WHITE SHARK EVER SEEN!
WE HAVE TO GET A TAG IN HER...
WE'RE MAKING HISTORY HERE, MATE. WE'LL WANT TO TRACK AND STUDY THIS SHARK FOR MONTHS AND HOPEFULLY YEARS TO COME.
I AGREE. LET'S DO IT BEFORE SHE DISAPPEARS.
GET THE TAGGING EQUIPMENT READY. I'M HEADING UP.

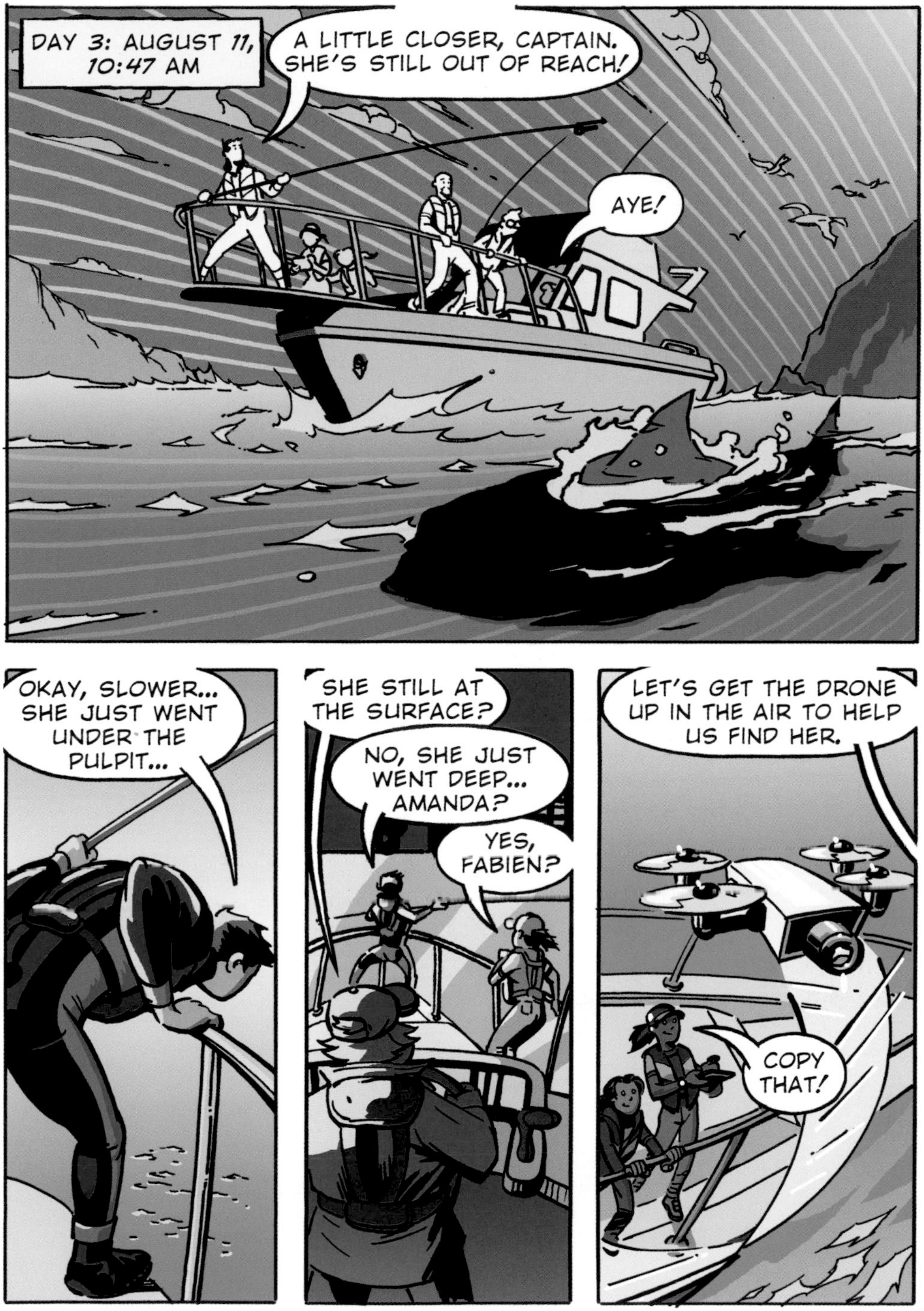
DAY 3: AUGUST 11, 10:47 AM
A LITTLE CLOSER, CAPTAIN. SHE'S STILL OUT OF REACH!
AYE!
OKAY, SLOWER... SHE JUST WENT UNDER THE PULPIT...
SHE STILL AT THE SURFACE?
NO, SHE JUST WENT DEEP... AMANDA?
YES, FABIEN?
LET'S GET THE DRONE UP IN THE AIR TO HELP US FIND HER.
COPY THAT!

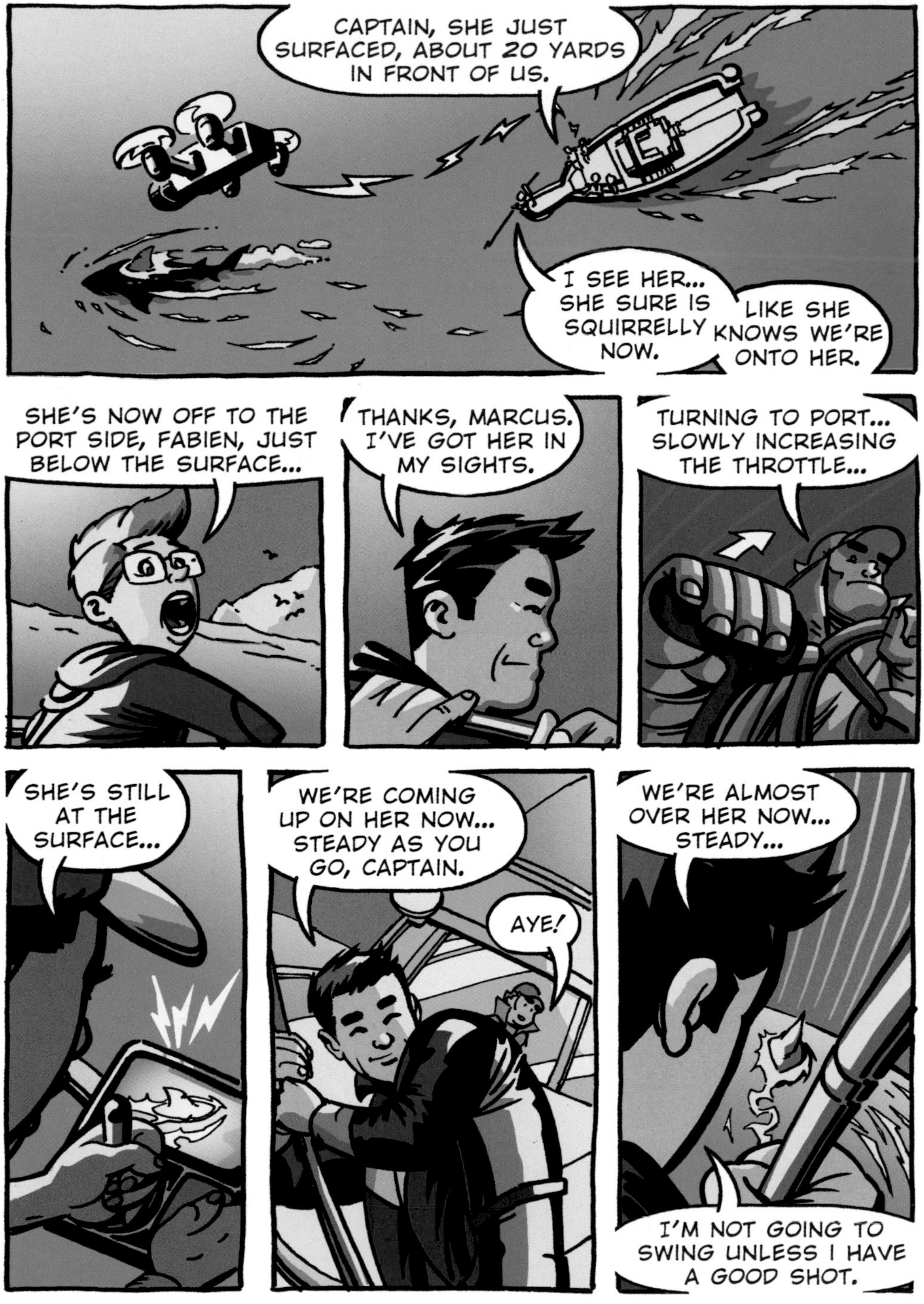
CAPTAIN, SHE JUST SURFACED, ABOUT 20 YARDS IN FRONT OF US.
I SEE HER... SHE SURE IS SQUIRRELLY NOW.
LIKE SHE KNOWS WE'RE ONTO HER.
SHE'S NOW OFF TO THE PORT SIDE, FABIEN, JUST BELOW THE SURFACE...
THANKS, MARCUS. I'VE GOT HER IN MY SIGHTS.
TURNING TO PORT... SLOWLY INCREASING THE THROTTLE...
SHE'S STILL AT THE SURFACE...
WE'RE COMING UP ON HER NOW... STEADY AS YOU GO, CAPTAIN.
AYE!
WE'RE ALMOST OVER HER NOW... STEADY...
I'M NOT GOING TO SWING UNLESS I HAVE A GOOD SHOT.

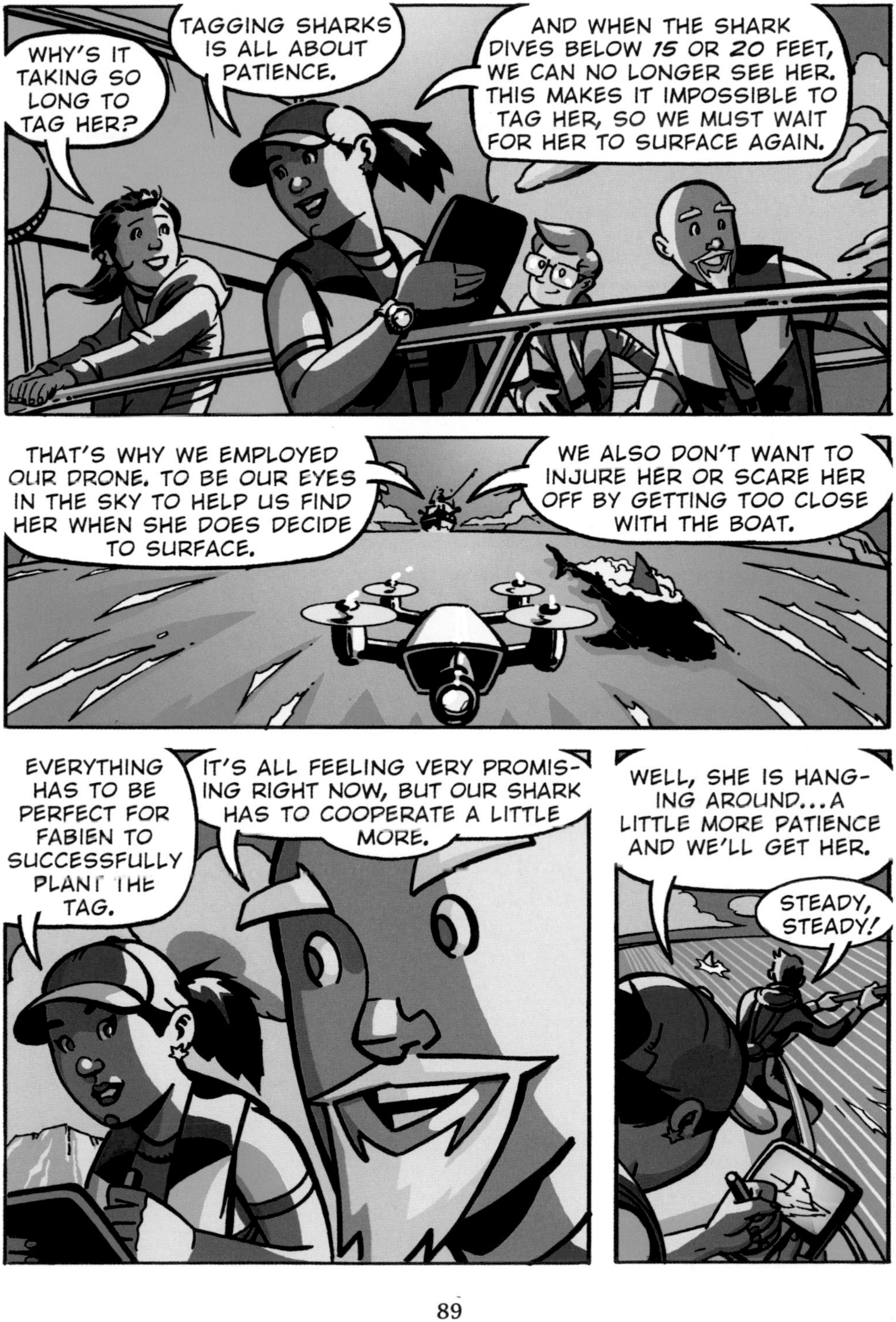
WHY'S IT TAKING SO LONG TO TAG HER?
TAGGING SHARKS IS ALL ABOUT PATIENCE.
AND WHEN THE SHARK DIVES BELOW 15 OR 20 FEET, WE CAN NO LONGER SEE HER. THIS MAKES IT IMPOSSIBLE TO TAG HER, SO WE MUST WAIT FOR HER TO SURFACE AGAIN.
THAT'S WHY WE EMPLOYED OUR DRONE. TO BE OUR EYES IN THE SKY TO HELP US FIND HER WHEN SHE DOES DECIDE TO SURFACE.
WE ALSO DON'T WANT TO INJURE HER OR SCARE HER OFF BY GETTING TOO CLOSE WITH THE BOAT.
EVERYTHING HAS TO BE PERFECT FOR FABIEN TO SUCCESSFULLY PLANT THE TAG.
IT'S ALL FEELING VERY PROMISING RIGHT NOW, BUT OUR SHARK HAS TO COOPERATE A LITTLE MORE.
WELL, SHE IS HANGING AROUND...A LITTLE MORE PATIENCE AND WE'LL GET HER.
STEADY, STEADY!

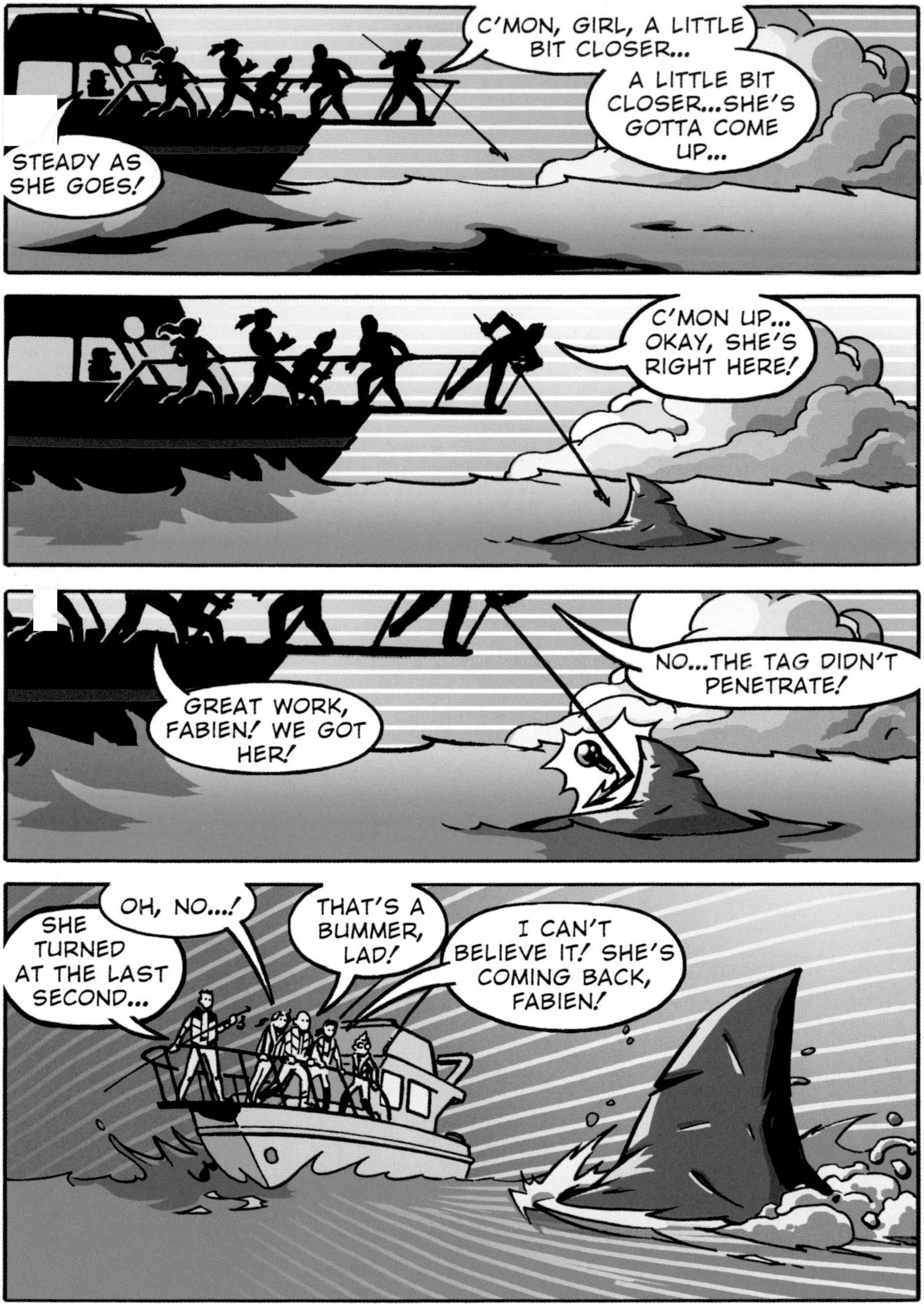
C'MON, GIRL, A LITTLE BIT CLOSER...
A LITTLE BIT CLOSER...SHE'S GOTTA COME UP...
STEADY AS SHE GOES!
C'MON UP... OKAY, SHE'S RIGHT HERE!
GREAT WORK, FABIEN! WE GOT HER!
NO...THE TAG DIDN'T PENETRATE!
SHE TURNED AT THE LAST SECOND...
OH, NO...!
THAT'S A BUMMER, LAD!
I CAN'T BELIEVE IT! SHE'S COMING BACK, FABIEN!

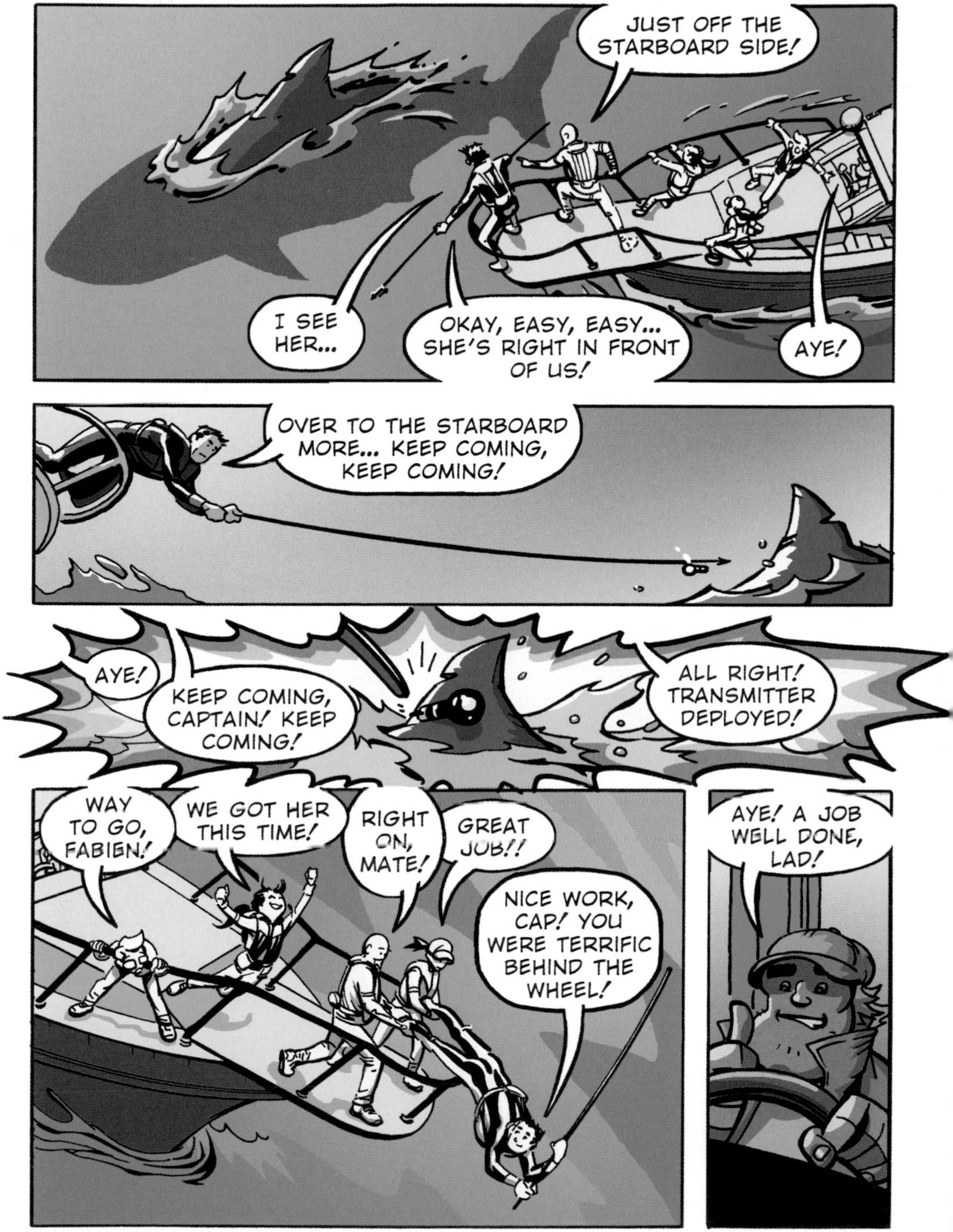
JUST OFF THE STARBOARD SIDE!
I SEE HER...
OKAY, EASY, EASY... SHE'S RIGHT IN FRONT OF US!
AYE!
OVER TO THE STARBOARD MORE... KEEP COMING, KEEP COMING!
AYE!
KEEP COMING, CAPTAIN! KEEP COMING!
ALL RIGHT! TRANSMITTER DEPLOYED!
WAY TO GO, FABIEN!
WE GOT HER THIS TIME!
RIGHT ON, MATE!
GREAT JOB!!
NICE WORK, CAP! YOU WERE TERRIFIC BEHIND THE WHEEL!
AYE! A JOB WELL DONE, LAD!

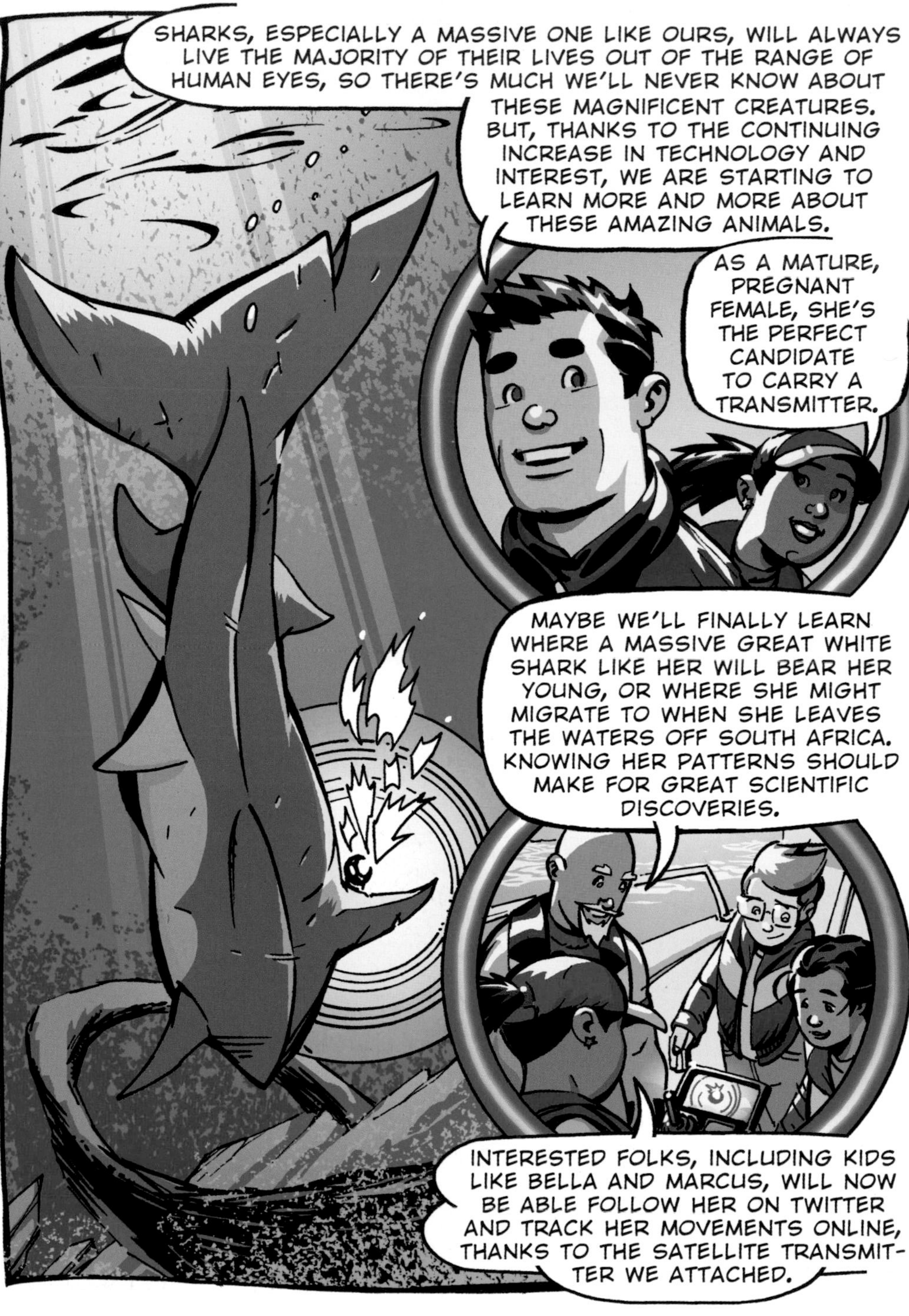
SHARKS, ESPECIALLY A MASSIVE ONE LIKE OURS, WILL ALWAYS LIVE THE MAJORITY OF THEIR LIVES OUT OF THE RANGE OF HUMAN EYES, SO THERE'S MUCH WE'LL NEVER KNOW ABOUT THESE MAGNIFICENT CREATURES. BUT, THANKS TO THE CONTINUING INCREASE IN TECHNOLOGY AND INTEREST, WE ARE STARTING TO LEARN MORE AND MORE ABOUT THESE AMAZING ANIMALS.
AS A MATURE, PREGNANT FEMALE, SHE'S THE PERFECT CANDIDATE TO CARRY A TRANSMITTER.
MAYBE WE'LL FINALLY LEARN WHERE A MASSIVE GREAT WHITE SHARK LIKE HER WILL BEAR HER YOUNG, OR WHERE SHE MIGHT MIGRATE TO WHEN SHE LEAVES THE WATERS OFF SOUTH AFRICA. KNOWING HER PATTERNS SHOULD MAKE FOR GREAT SCIENTIFIC DISCOVERIES.
INTERESTED FOLKS, INCLUDING KIDS LIKE BELLA AND MARCUS, WILL NOW BE ABLE FOLLOW HER ON TWITTER AND TRACK HER MOVEMENTS ONLINE, THANKS TO THE SATELLITE TRANSMITTER WE ATTACHED.

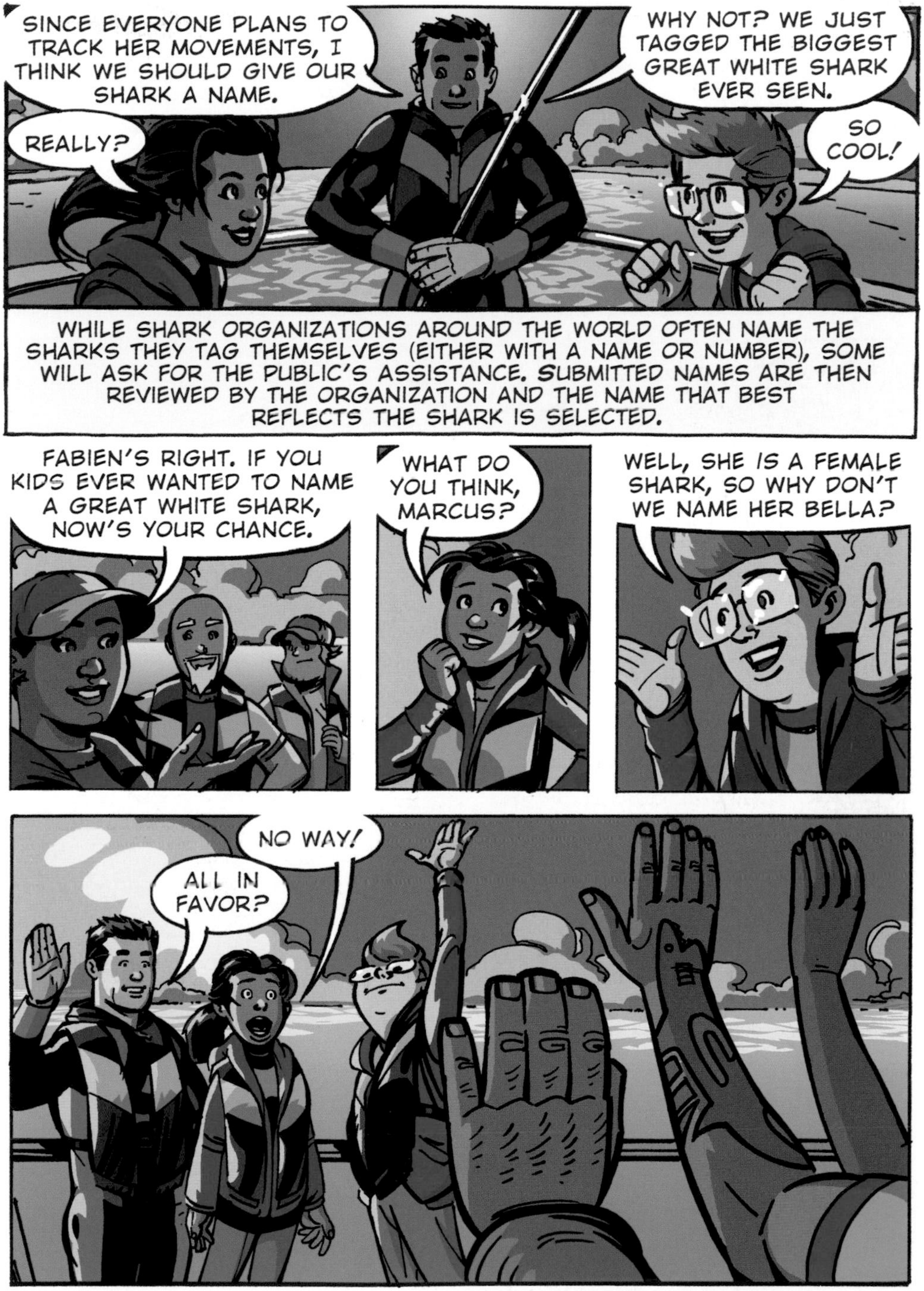
SINCE EVERYONE PLANS TO TRACK HER MOVEMENTS, I THINK WE SHOULD GIVE OUR SHARK A NAME.
REALLY?
WHY NOT? WE JUST TAGGED THE BIGGEST GREAT WHITE SHARK EVER SEEN.
SO COOL!
WHILE SHARK ORGANIZATIONS AROUND THE WORLD OFTEN NAME THE SHARKS THEY TAG THEMSELVES (EITHER WITH A NAME OR NUMBER), SOME WILL ASK FOR THE PUBLIC'S ASSISTANCE. SUBMITTED NAMES ARE THEN REVIEWED BY THE ORGANIZATION AND THE NAME THAT BEST REFLECTS THE SHARK IS SELECTED.
FABIEN'S RIGHT. IF YOU KIDS EVER WANTED TO NAME A GREAT WHITE SHARK, NOW'S YOUR CHANCE.
WHAT DO YOU THINK, MARCUS?
WELL, SHE *IS* A FEMALE SHARK, SO WHY DON'T WE NAME HER BELLA?
ALL IN FAVOR?
NO WAY!

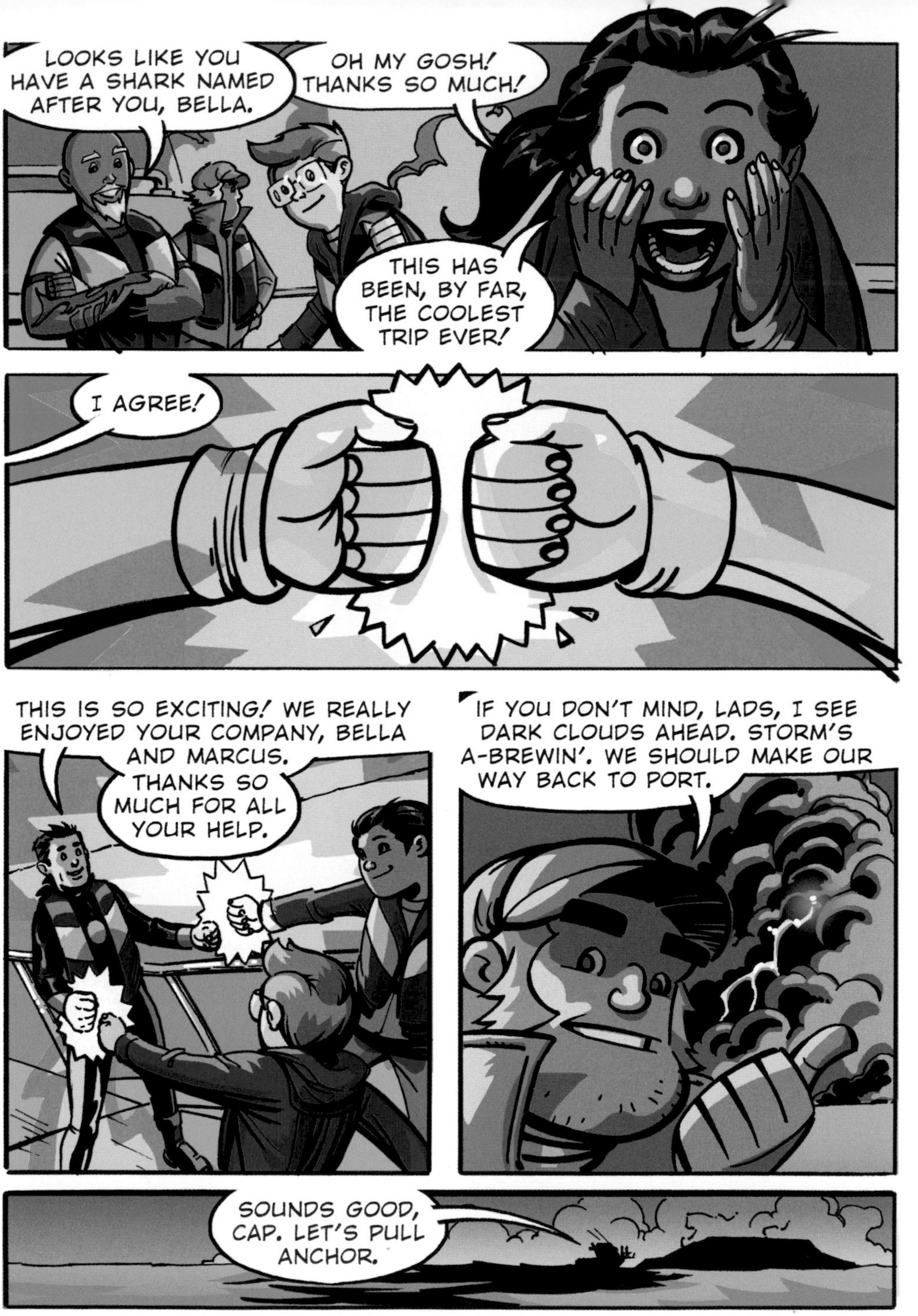
LOOKS LIKE YOU HAVE A SHARK NAMED AFTER YOU, BELLA.
OH MY GOSH! THANKS SO MUCH!
THIS HAS BEEN, BY FAR, THE COOLEST TRIP EVER!
I AGREE!
THIS IS SO EXCITING! WE REALLY ENJOYED YOUR COMPANY, BELLA AND MARCUS.
THANKS SO MUCH FOR ALL YOUR HELP.
IF YOU DON'T MIND, LADS, I SEE DARK CLOUDS AHEAD. STORM'S A-BREWIN'. WE SHOULD MAKE OUR WAY BACK TO PORT.
SOUNDS GOOD, CAP. LET'S PULL ANCHOR.

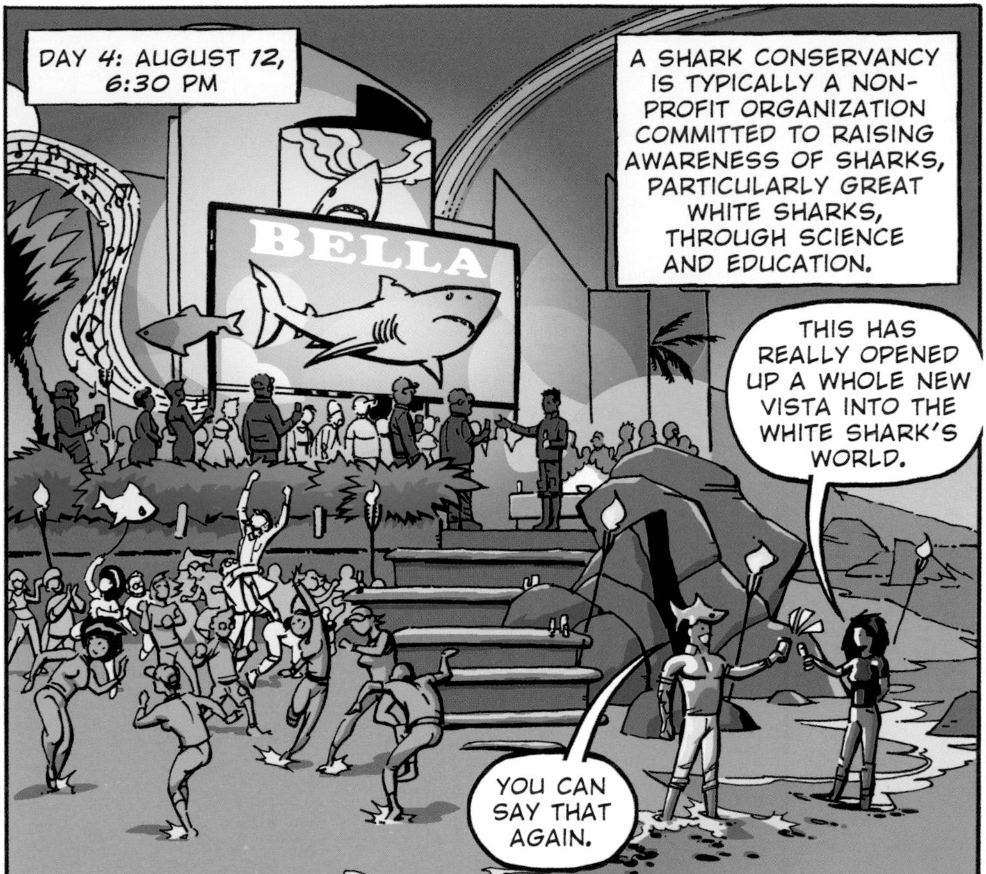
DAY 4: AUGUST 12, 6:30 PM
A SHARK CONSERVANCY IS TYPICALLY A NON-PROFIT ORGANIZATION COMMITTED TO RAISING AWARENESS OF SHARKS, PARTICULARLY GREAT WHITE SHARKS, THROUGH SCIENCE AND EDUCATION.
BELLA
THIS HAS REALLY OPENED UP A WHOLE NEW VISTA INTO THE WHITE SHARK'S WORLD.
YOU CAN SAY THAT AGAIN.

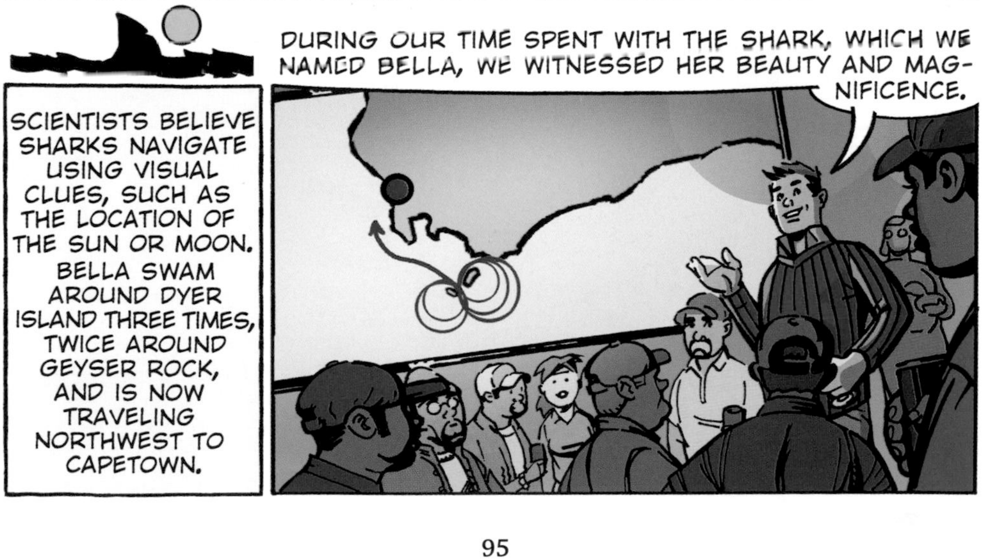
DURING OUR TIME SPENT WITH THE SHARK, WHICH WE NAMED BELLA, WE WITNESSED HER BEAUTY AND MAG-NIFICENCE.
SCIENTISTS BELIEVE SHARKS NAVIGATE USING VISUAL CLUES, SUCH AS THE LOCATION OF THE SUN OR MOON. BELLA SWAM AROUND DYER ISLAND THREE TIMES, TWICE AROUND GEYSER ROCK, AND IS NOW TRAVELING NORTHWEST TO CAPETOWN.

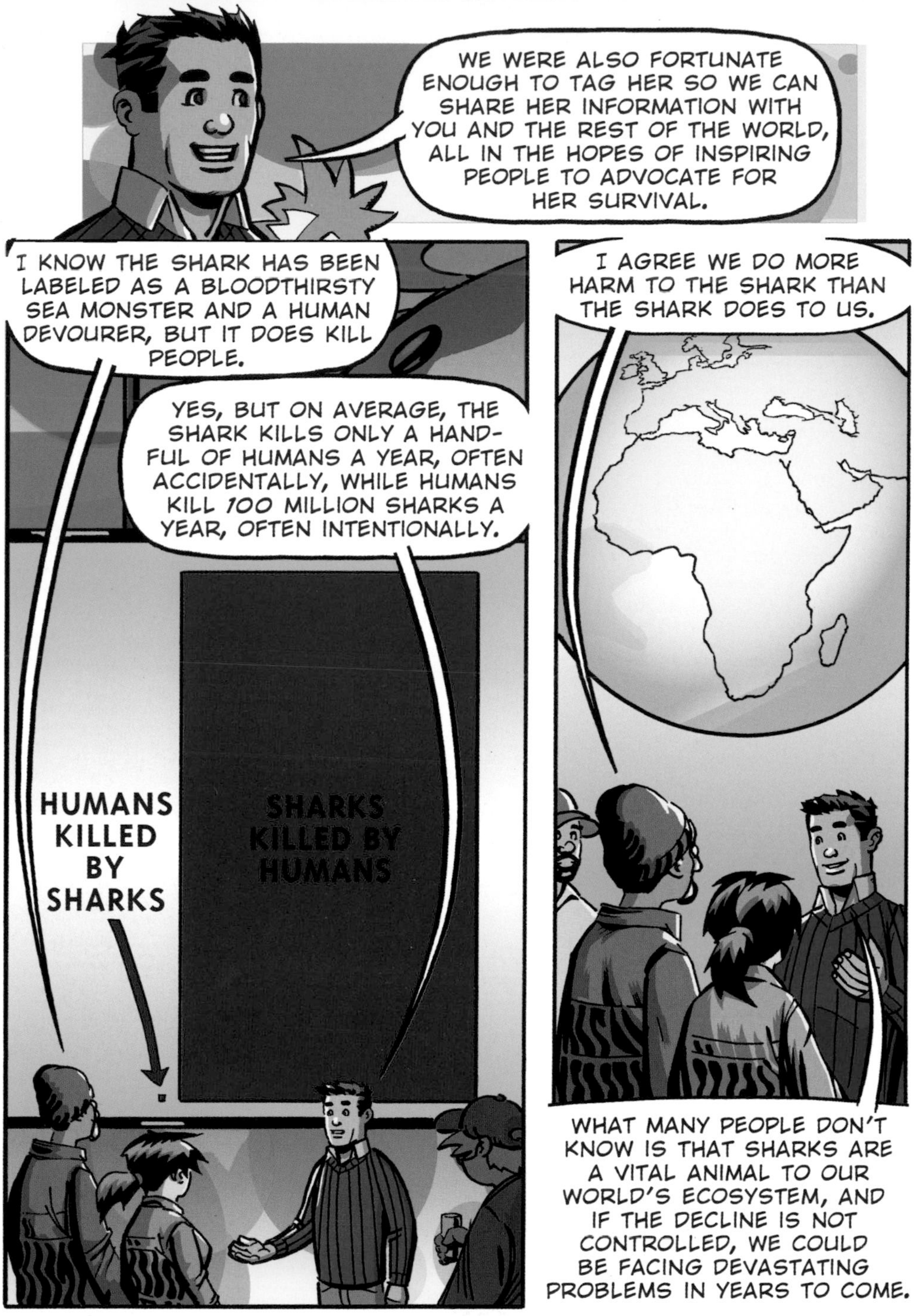
WE WERE ALSO FORTUNATE ENOUGH TO TAG HER SO WE CAN SHARE HER INFORMATION WITH YOU AND THE REST OF THE WORLD, ALL IN THE HOPES OF INSPIRING PEOPLE TO ADVOCATE FOR HER SURVIVAL.
I KNOW THE SHARK HAS BEEN LABELED AS A BLOODTHIRSTY SEA MONSTER AND A HUMAN DEVOURER, BUT IT DOES KILL PEOPLE.
YES, BUT ON AVERAGE, THE SHARK KILLS ONLY A HANDFUL OF HUMANS A YEAR, OFTEN ACCIDENTALLY, WHILE HUMANS KILL *100* MILLION SHARKS A YEAR, OFTEN INTENTIONALLY.
HUMANS KILLED BY SHARKS
SHARKS KILLED BY HUMANS
I AGREE WE DO MORE HARM TO THE SHARK THAN THE SHARK DOES TO US.
WHAT MANY PEOPLE DON'T KNOW IS THAT SHARKS ARE A VITAL ANIMAL TO OUR WORLD'S ECOSYSTEM, AND IF THE DECLINE IS NOT CONTROLLED, WE COULD BE FACING DEVASTATING PROBLEMS IN YEARS TO COME.

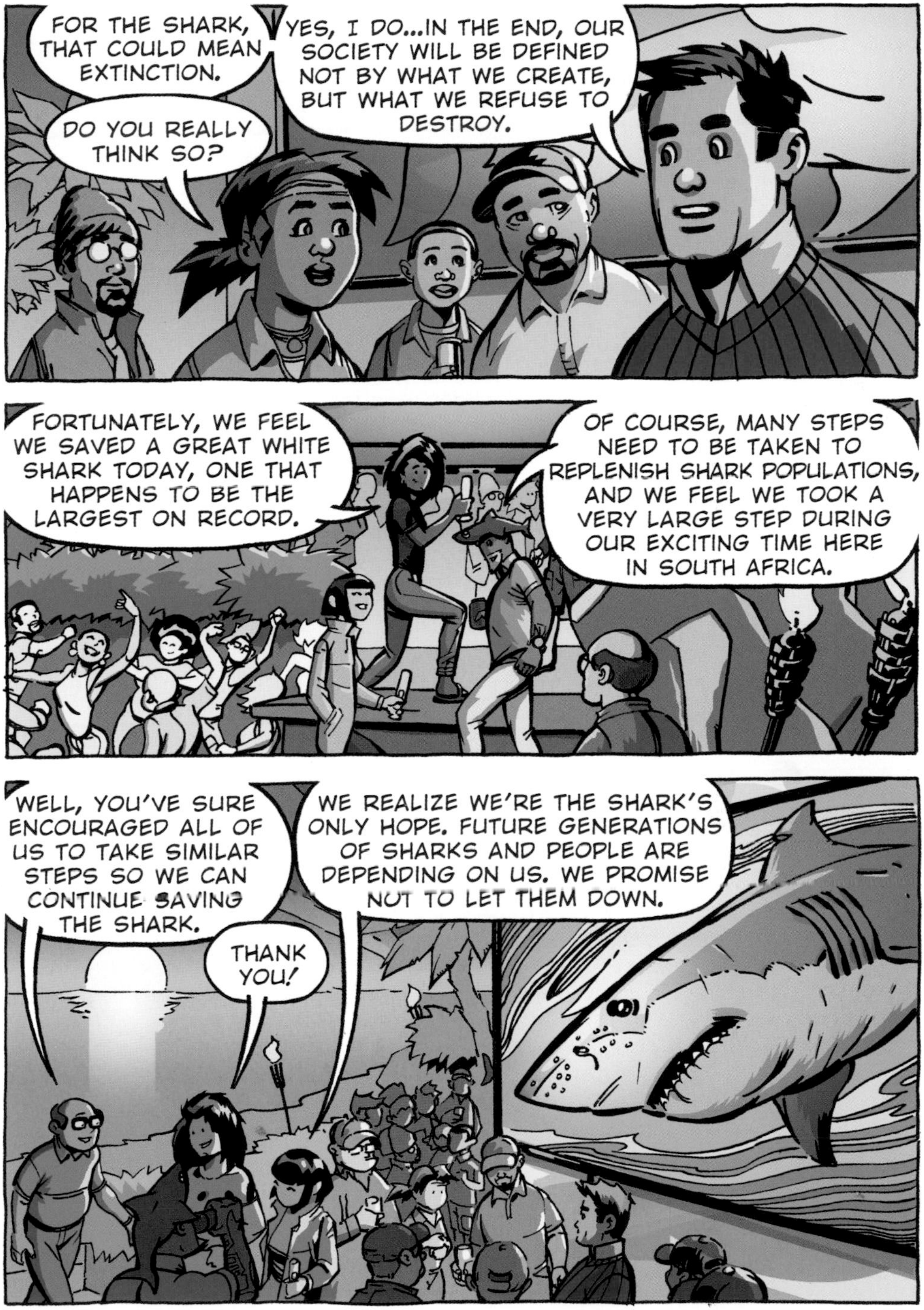
FOR THE SHARK, THAT COULD MEAN EXTINCTION.
DO YOU REALLY THINK SO?
YES, I DO...IN THE END, OUR SOCIETY WILL BE DEFINED NOT BY WHAT WE CREATE, BUT WHAT WE REFUSE TO DESTROY.
FORTUNATELY, WE FEEL WE SAVED A GREAT WHITE SHARK TODAY, ONE THAT HAPPENS TO BE THE LARGEST ON RECORD.
OF COURSE, MANY STEPS NEED TO BE TAKEN TO REPLENISH SHARK POPULATIONS, AND WE FEEL WE TOOK A VERY LARGE STEP DURING OUR EXCITING TIME HERE IN SOUTH AFRICA.
WELL, YOU'VE SURE ENCOURAGED ALL OF US TO TAKE SIMILAR STEPS SO WE CAN CONTINUE SAVING THE SHARK.
THANK YOU!
WE REALIZE WE'RE THE SHARK'S ONLY HOPE. FUTURE GENERATIONS OF SHARKS AND PEOPLE ARE DEPENDING ON US. WE PROMISE NOT TO LET THEM DOWN.

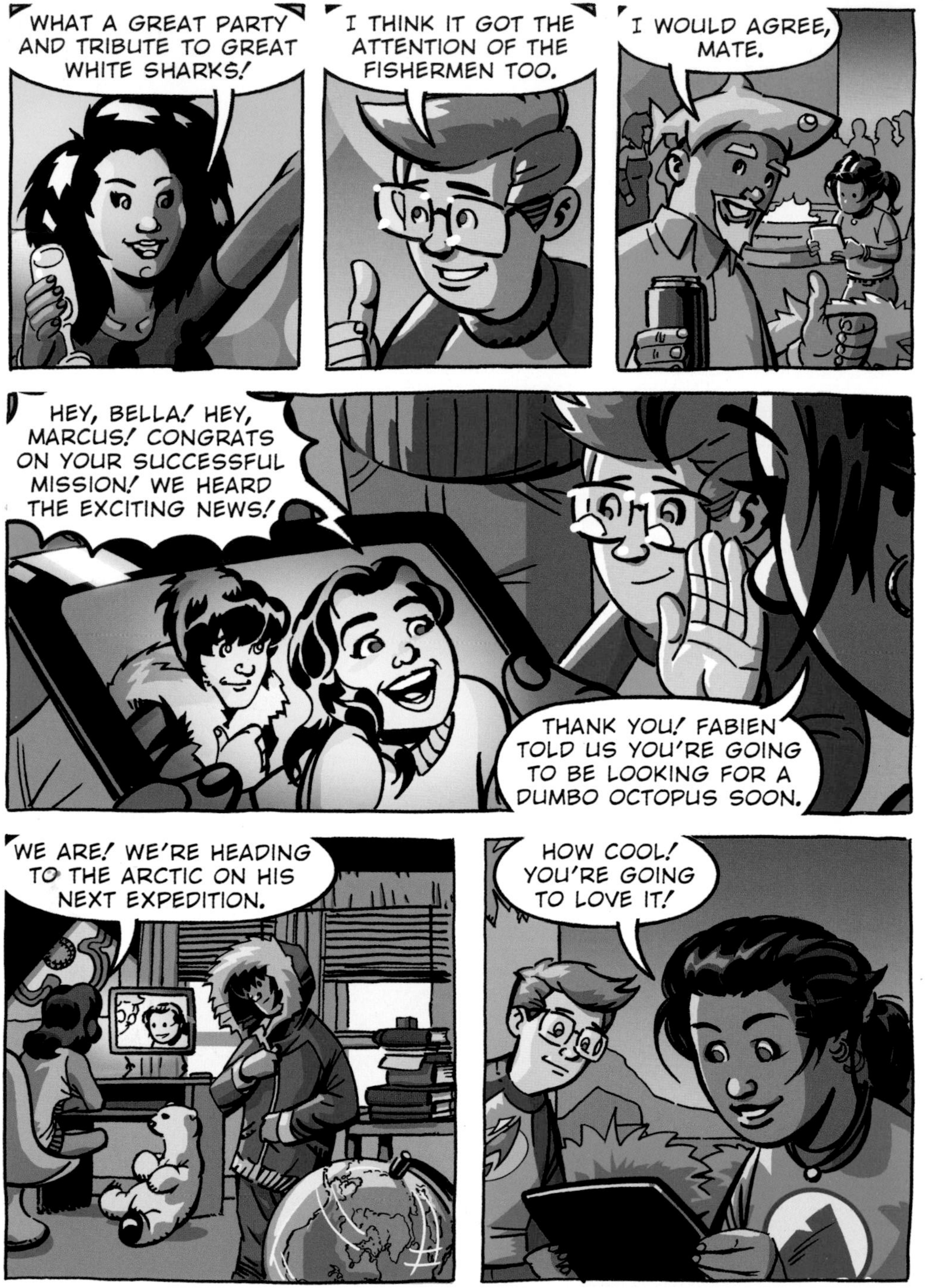
WHAT A GREAT PARTY AND TRIBUTE TO GREAT WHITE SHARKS!
I THINK IT GOT THE ATTENTION OF THE FISHERMEN TOO.
I WOULD AGREE, MATE.
HEY, BELLA! HEY, MARCUS! CONGRATS ON YOUR SUCCESSFUL MISSION! WE HEARD THE EXCITING NEWS!
THANK YOU! FABIEN TOLD US YOU'RE GOING TO BE LOOKING FOR A DUMBO OCTOPUS SOON.
WE ARE! WE'RE HEADING TO THE ARCTIC ON HIS NEXT EXPEDITION.
HOW COOL! YOU'RE GOING TO LOVE IT!

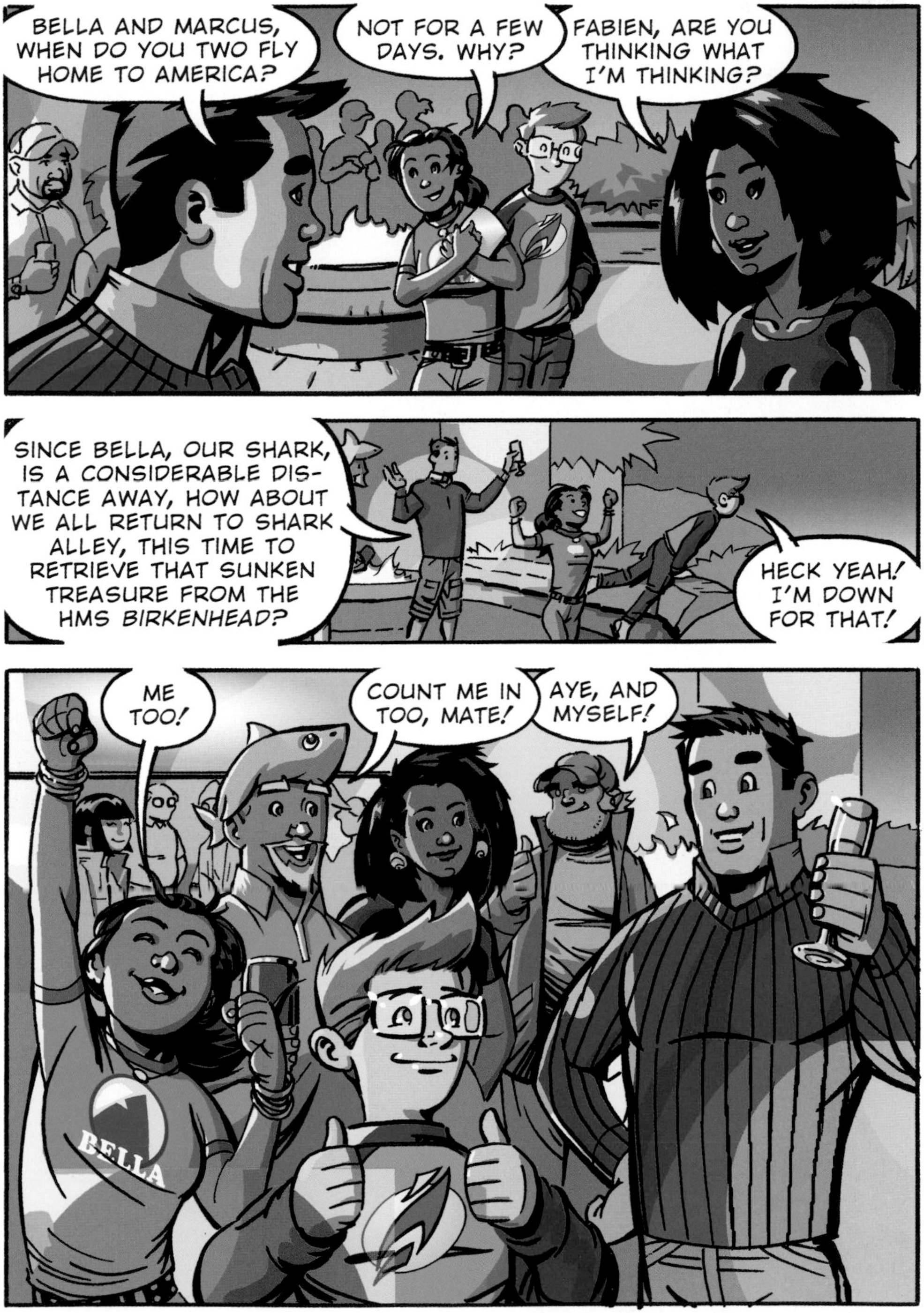
BELLA AND MARCUS, WHEN DO YOU TWO FLY HOME TO AMERICA?
NOT FOR A FEW DAYS. WHY?
FABIEN, ARE YOU THINKING WHAT I'M THINKING?
SINCE BELLA, OUR SHARK, IS A CONSIDERABLE DISTANCE AWAY, HOW ABOUT WE ALL RETURN TO SHARK ALLEY, THIS TIME TO RETRIEVE THAT SUNKEN TREASURE FROM THE HMS *BIRKENHEAD*?
HECK YEAH! I'M DOWN FOR THAT!
ME TOO!
COUNT ME IN TOO, MATE!
AYE, AND MYSELF!
BELLA

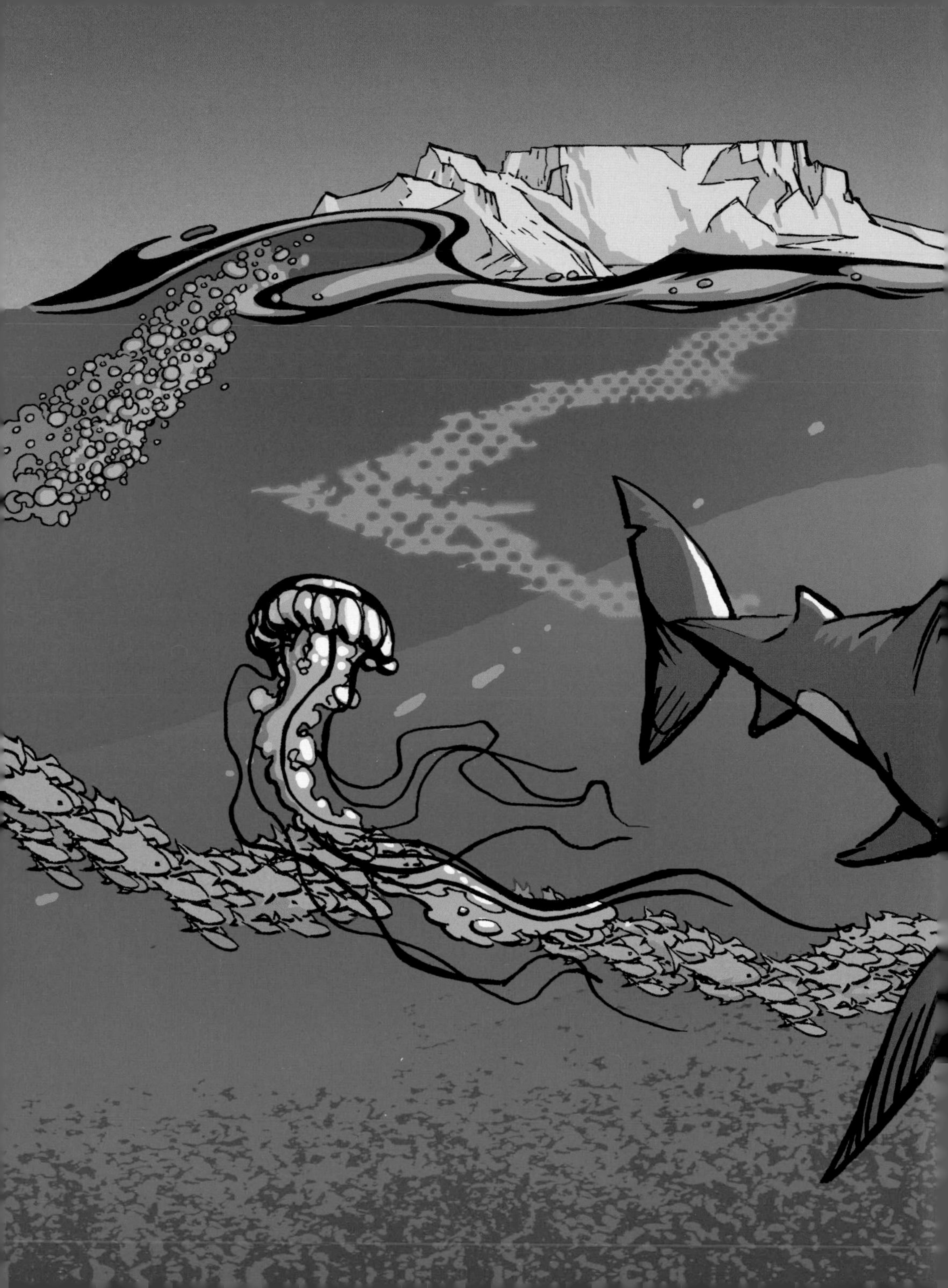

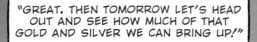

"GREAT. THEN TOMORROW LET'S HEAD OUT AND SEE HOW MUCH OF THAT GOLD AND SILVER WE CAN BRING UP!"

THE END

The authors would like to personally thank:

Illustrator Joe St.Pierre and agent Gail Thurm

Paul Zemitzsch and Explore Green

Craig Ferreira, white-shark-expeditioner
and researcher extraordinaire

Literary agents Sharlene Martin and Clelia Gore
of Martin Literary Management

Karen Wojtyla of Margaret K. McElderry Books

Marcus Kloss and Isabella Osseiran

Joe St.Pierre wishes to thank
Sonya Pelletier and Kael Arbon
for their coloring assistance.

FABIEN COUSTEAU is the grandson of famed sea explorer Jacques Cousteau and a third generation ocean explorer and filmmaker. He has worked with National Geographic, Discovery, PBS, and CBS to produce ocean exploration documentaries and continues to produce environmentally oriented content for schools, books, magazines, and newspapers. Learn more about his work at fabiencousteauolc.org.

JAMES O. FRAIOLI is a published author of twenty-five books and an award-winning filmmaker. He has traveled the globe alongside experienced guides, naturalists, and scientists, and has spent considerable time exploring and writing about the outdoors. He has served on the board of directors for the Seattle Aquarium and works with many environmental organizations. Learn more about his work at vesperentertainment.com.

JOE ST.PIERRE has illustrated for Marvel and DC Comics, and has the distinction of penciling the most #1 issues featuring Spider-Man and the Spider-Man family. Joe also works in the fields of intellectual property design, commercial illustration, and storyboards for animation and video games. Joe's publishing company, Astronaut Ink, highlights his creator-owned properties: the award-winning Megahurtz, Bold Blood, and New Zodiax. See his work at astronautink.com.